The Profession

ISBN: 9798639313271

Cover by Christopher Civale

www.HarrisLKligman.com

*Dedicated to my son **Rob**, whose relentless urging motivated me to start writing.*
And
*To my wife **Nancy**, whose strength and fortitude kept our family intact over the many lengthy absences.*

Chapter 1

As she mingled with the people exiting the theater, Nancy Gault curled her gloved fingers around her purse. Once through the doorway she turned left on west 45th Street.

When she reached 43rd Street, she turned left again, and then stopped in front of a store selling cheap New York City trinkets and souvenirs. Moving closer to the store's front, Gault studied the window reflections. The cascade of bodies passing behind her appeared normal. As she let her eyes roll over the floating figures, nothing she observed triggered concern.

She turned slowly as she canvassed left, then right, before continuing to walk west on 43rd Street. Midway, she stopped by a trash receptacle, took off her calfskin gloves and dropped them into the can.

For several seconds she stared at the receptacle and watched the images of what transpired earlier float across her mind. Then she felt the chill again. It wasn't because of the early autumn air – it was something else, but she couldn't nail it down. There was always the after action high and then the onset of lows – the alternating effects from the adrenaline rush, but her body always normalized. That wasn't happening now.

She let her mind freewheel. This wasn't anything special, just another assignment that sent her target on a long vacation. She'd always been devoid of feelings – they liked that when they recruited her, and it was something that continually worked in her favor.

At the sound of the voice, she turned around quickly and looked over at the rag-clad man crouched against the wall.

"I was watching you Missy. I like watching you. Your ass....it's nice and curvy," and then he started to laugh before it was cut short by a coughing spell. After a few seconds he wheezed out the words, "What did-ja drop in there, Missy?" Then he started coughing again.

Nancy gave him a look of disgust, then took a couple of steps before she stopped and turned back, so that she partially faced the man.

"I hope you fucking choke."

The sound of her heels clicking against the sidewalk were intermingled with thoughts of what she would have done to the foul-mouthed bum if circumstances were different, but all she wanted to do now was distance herself from 45th Street.

As she picked up the pace, her thoughts shifted again to herself....nothing was traceable....nothing. The ticket was purchased in cash months ago. Even if there was a camera, her brunette wig, heavy make-up and tortoise rimmed glasses, would show only a middle-aged woman.....a far cry from the twenty-six year old petite blonde that resided underneath.

She felt the hands around her neck before she could react.

Lost in mind chatter, she neglected to stay focused – violating a cardinal rule. As the pressure increased, the flow of oxygen to her brain slowed. Moments later she felt herself falling, then she impacted with the concrete sidewalk. The pain from the fall reverberated up and down her left side.

She felt herself being dragged away from the street. Instinctively, she tried to fight back. Unable to gain any leverage, she went into a defensive mode using her arms and hands in an attempt to ward off the blows that now rained down, unrelentingly, against her head and chest.

Then, as it had happened many times before, her inner self, her Chi as the practitioners of the Martial Arts call it, momentarily over-rode the pain. She curled her right hand into a tight fist, and using the forearm of her left arm she pushed up, while simultaneously smashing her fist into the side of his head.

She felt the bone shatter on contact, probably his eye socket, and then she felt the full weight of his body as it dropped on top of her.

Nancy lifted the inert body just enough to manage some wiggle room, then she crawled out, and away from the motionless form.

Gasping for breath, and struggling with the inertia that overwhelmed her, she remained on her hands and knees for seconds. Finally moving into a standing position, Nancy waited as her body slowly normalized.

As she let her eyes scan her immediate area, she realized just how far she'd been dragged. The shadows, and the distance from the street, gave her attacker the seclusion he sought.

As her eyes focused on the unconscious man, she tasted the bile that flowed upward from her stomach. She went back to where her attacker was lying and then went slowly to her knees. She made a fist with her right hand, and then smashed it into his face until she lost all sense of what she was doing.

The wail of sirens in the distance brought her back to the moment. She looked at her bloody knuckles, then down at the pulp-like face of her attacker, and then began to dry-heave until her lungs hurt. She wiped her bloody hand against his filthy jacket, and then realizing what she did, wiped it against her dress. After still more seconds, she slowly made her way into a standing position and then started walking toward the street.

When Gault reached the intersection she crossed quickly, then continued walking along 43rd street until she saw an alcove. Moving into the shadows, she discarded the wig, the damaged eyeglasses, then brushed at her dress.

Nancy canvassed the street, calculating she had a minute here – no more. She took out a mirror from her purse and maneuvering it in the minimal light, caught a glimpse of her face. He did more damage than she thought as her left eye was starting to turn blackish. The skin above the eye was swollen and bruised, both lips were cracked and caked with dry blood, and her make-up was streaked and blotched.

She ran her fingers through her hair, and then looked back at the mirror.

She spit on the back of her hand, and moved it gently across her face and lips. The only thing she accomplished was reopening the cuts. She dabbed at the open wounds and then moved away from the alcove.

Glancing right, she saw the couple slowly moving in her direction. She crossed to the opposite side of the street, then continued walking toward 7th Avenue. She heard the sound first, then glancing back, she saw the cab turn onto 43rd street.

Stepping into the street, Nancy waived her arm. From where she stood, she couldn't tell whether the roof light signaled the taxi was occupied or vacant.

When the cab pulled to a stop, Nancy inched closer and watched as the driver leaned toward the open passenger side window, and called out, "Where to Missy?"

The words the hack used to address her brought back all the bad memories of what transpired just minutes ago. The bum used the same word. Despite the urge to lash out, she simply replied, "Hilton."

The cab pulled away from the curb, and made a right turn at the corner of 43rd and 7th Avenue. She stared out the window briefly and then turned her head toward the front of the taxi. The driver was staring at her in the rear view mirror.

"Is something wrong?"

"I'm not sure, Missy. You don't look too good. Do you need help?"

"No....I don't need any help, and don't call me Missy....okay?"

"Sure Missy....sorry....sure Miss."

The remainder of the short ride was made in silence.

The doorman opened the taxi door, and stared at the woman as she left the cab. After she entered the hotel, he eyed the driver who gave him an I don't know look, and then pulled away.

Once inside, Gault walked toward the elevator bank, fully cognizant of the questionable stares. Part way, an assistant manager stepped in-between her and the elevators, and asked if she needed help.

Gault tried to smile back, but her face wouldn't cooperate.

"I'll be okay. The police have already taken a report, and....I'm okay....I just need to clean up a bit."

This time she forced a half smile despite the difficulty.

The man nodded and was about to turn away, but instead continued to stare at the disheveled and bruised woman, whose streaked make-up gave her a macabre look.

"What room are you in Miss....?"

"Four Four Six, and it's "Benson....Patricia Benson."

Nancy held the half smile as she moved around the man and continued toward the elevators.

Once she reached her floor she walked quickly toward her room, then gingerly leaned her head against the door before inserting the key card into the slot. When the light turned green, she opened the door.

Gault kicked the door closed. After flicking the bathroom light on she leaned on the sink as the reflection in the mirror stared back. Not good, she thought, and then took off her clothes and stepped into the shower.

As soon as the water touched her skin, Nancy let out a prolonged moan, then clenched her teeth as she moved her face closer to the shower head.

She scrubbed her body several times hoping to rid herself of his stench.

Toweling herself dry, she moved into the bedroom and dressed quickly. After one last look around, Gault picked up her purse and then walked out.

As she passed the elevators, she glanced at her watch noting that it took her twenty-four minutes exactly from the time she entered the room.

Using the stairwell, Nancy continued past the lobby, exiting at the parking garage level. As she pushed the door open, she placed the palm of her right hand around her mouth and nose, lowered her head, and walked quickly toward the ticket booth. Whatever surveillance cameras were operating wouldn't get much of a descriptive image.

She walked through the exit door and onto 7th Avenue. Pausing briefly, she considered several options, then began walking toward 57th Street.

*

The assistant manager knocked several times and then at the insistence of the two police officers, inserted his key card and opened the door to room four four six.

The taller of the two officers motioned with his hand, and then said, "You….stay here."

Several minutes later, the two policemen came out.

"There's no one there, some clothes scattered on the floor, some with blood stains. Lock this up, and no one gets in until the detectives arrive….do you understand?"

He shook his head in a way that conveyed he did.

"Good. Now let's go back down, and you'll show me what you have when she registered."

*

When the connection was made, the voice simply acknowledged with a yes.

At that moment, for some inexplicable reason, Nancy lost her train of thought. Only when the voice said yes again did she collect herself and respond.

"I had some after action difficulty."

When the voice didn't respond, Gault continued, "I'm okay."

"Is there anything you need?"

As she moved her head sideways in disgust, she answered, "Negative.…wait for my email." Then she pushed down hard on the end button, and watched as the cell phone screen changed from sky blue to black.

*

The discreet brass plate on the left side of the doorway read "Il Gatto Nero," The Black Cat. After sending a picture, Nancy walked inside.

The maitre d' lost his smile as he stared at Gault's face, then recovered quickly. In heavily accented English he asked, "Will there be only one, Signora?"

"No....two. I'll wait at the bar."

"Molto Buono, Signora," (Very good, Madam) and then he walked away.

In-between the moments when her mind propelled her back to the incident on 45th Street, Nancy occupied her time by staring at her watch, and stirring her second drink with her index finger. She wondered what was keeping him, and then she turned toward the muted conversation behind her.

She watched the man separate from the maître d'.

He smiled the same way he did in the theater, and held it until he was a step away.

"Hello."

"Hello Janco."

His facial expression revealed nothing, as his eyes scanned her face.

"Do you want a drink?"

"No....I'll pass."

"Sure you do. I hate drinking alone."

She motioned to the bartender, then looked back.

"Okay....I'll have what she's having."

"It's an Absolute on the rocks with a twist."

Arias Janco nodded then asked, "Didn't you like it the way it was?"

"The way what was?"

"Your face."

Despite herself, she smiled and felt her lip crack open again. She moved her hand up, touched her mouth, then looked at her fingers and saw minute traces of blood.

Janco lifted his glass, and pushed the cocktail napkin toward her. "Try this."

"Thanks."

Nancy touched the paper napkin to her lips, and then brought it down to eye level.

"No more jokes Janco. I can't smile, and you're a funny guy."

"Sure I am....a real funny guy."

Then he laughed and Gault was caught up in the moment.

"Wanna tell me about it?"

Nancy shook her head yes. "It happened on 43rd street. A bum started wisecracking about my rear end, and the next thing I knew he had his hands around my neck. It was all him until I managed to free my arm."

Nancy stopped and dropped her head slightly.

Janco broke the silence. “And the bum?”

“Not sure. Broken eye socket….cheekbone maybe, and probably more.”

“And you? Do you want to see a doctor?”

“I’m alright. I left the hotel with what you see.”

“Okay. If you’re leveling with me about how you feel, the rest can be handled. Your credit card, driver’s license, passport, and your legend (bogus biography) are shuttered. Here’s a new set of clothes.”

Janco reached into his jacket pocket and handed her a small manila envelope, which she placed in her purse unopened.

“You can buy what you need once you get there.”

“Where is there?”

Janco ignored the question. “You don’t have a lot of time. The plane leaves at eleven-thirty, and that’s p.m. tonight.”

“Then I guess I should be going.”

Janco nodded.

“I understand the food here is pretty good.”

"We'll try it next time you're in town."

"Yeah….next time I'm in town."

Gault slid off the bar stool, and looked over at the bartender. She pointed at Janco.

"He'll take care of the tab."

Arias Janco watched her as she walked through the doorway. As he turned back, he thought, she does have a nice ass.

Janco finished the drink, then peeled off two bills from a roll and placed them on the bar. As he was about to get up, he noticed that one was a ten denomination note from the National Bank of Boka Ami. He picked it up, tossed a second U.S. ten dollar bill across the first one, and then re-banded the roll with the Boka Ami bill on top.

When he had the bartender's attention, he motioned toward the money, then waived a thank you.

Moments later Arias Janco walked into the night.

Chapter 2

The ninety-four mile flight to Philadelphia from JFK New York, took forty minutes.

As Nancy Gault walked through the nearly deserted terminal and through the exit reading Taxis, she was keenly aware of every detail of her surroundings. No more 43rd Street – never.

She walked up to the lone taxi and waited. When nothing happened, she sidestepped to the passenger side window and tapped. When the dozing driver came back to life, she opened the rear door and got in.

"Sorry about that Lady….long day, if you know what I mean."

"Fifteen hundred block of Pine."

"Fifteen hundred Pine it is."

Nancy leaned her head back and closed her eyes. She thought about Janco. The omission of the theater incident during their brief meeting, told her everything she needed to know. Rashid al Samir was now with the Virgins in paradise. She smiled at the thought, and then quickly moved her hand to her mouth. She cursed silently as she waited for the pain in her lips to subside.

She felt the car slow, and then heard the driver's voice. Caught up in a half sleep Nancy had to ask him to repeat what he said.

"This is Pine, Lady....the fifteen hundred block of Pine. What address?"

"Just pull over."

Once the vehicle was curbside the driver looked up, and studied his passenger from the rear-view mirror.

Nancy avoided eye contact, and glanced at the meter. She was about to hand the driver the money when he said, "There's an additional night charge, lady."

Gault wondered whether he was shitting her, but quickly decided to let it go.

"How much?"

"Three dollars....makes it thirty even."

She was about to place thirty-five dollars in the plexiglass slot when the driver said, "We can take it out in trade."

"Nancy heard him clearly, but she still asked, "What did you say?"

"We can cover the fare another way."

She shook her head, and placed five singles back in her purse. Then she crumpled up the three ten dollar bills, shoved them into the plexiglass slot, and opened the door.

Purposely leaving the cab's door open, she could hear his curses as she walked in the opposite direction from where she wanted to be.

Gault smiled inwardly, then slowed down as the screeching sound of tires faded.

The address was a three story townhouse adjacent to another townhouse whose street floor was a Mexican restaurant. Both the restaurant, and its red and yellow awning, seemed out of place for the neighborhood.

As she started up the steps, Nancy felt the mild rumbling in her stomach, and realized she was hungry. Reversing herself, she walked back to the restaurant and saw the closed sign.

"Figures."

Nancy reached into her purse, spread open the manila envelope with her index finger and thumb, and then took out the brass colored key. She opened the door and instinctively glanced back at the street before going inside.

Leaving the door partially open, Gault searched for a wall switch.

When the light came on she closed the door and locked it, then looked toward the room to her immediate right. It appeared to be a library of sorts. She took several steps toward the room before changing her mind and turning back toward the staircase.

When she reached the second floor landing, she stopped and scanned the floor's layout. In the dim light she could make out three doors.

She walked to the closest one, turned the handle, and then pushed. The door swung open, ricocheted off the wall, and then started back. Nancy held out her left hand until the door made contact.

Keeping her left hand on the partially closed door, she reached for the light switch with her right. Before she could locate it, she heard the movement.

Turning quickly so she faced the doorway, Nancy took several steps back until she was enveloped in darkness.

"We've been expecting you."

Silhouetted just beyond the door frame was a man about six feet tall. The dim hallway light combined with the way he stood, insured that his facial features were masked.

Gault's eyes moved quickly over the outline, noting that his hands were held at his side….there was no hostile inference.

Nancy answered, "Who are we?"

"Maybe I should have said, "I." The "We" is accurate, but I'm the only one here now."

The man stopped speaking and waited. After several moments, and a lack of a response, he started again.

"I didn't mean to frighten you. Sleep seems evasive for me right now, so I was about to make some coffee when I heard the door open, and....well, the rest you know. Would you care for a cup of coffee?"

Gault shook her head, and then realized he wouldn't see the movement.

"No. What I need is sleep."

"Okay. If you change your mind I'll be in the kitchen....downstairs through the library."

The silhouette moved away. When it was out of her line of sight, she heard him say, "My name is Monday, Robert Monday. I'll see you in the morning, Nancy."

*

She went into a comatose sleep as soon as her head touched the pillow, then inexplicably, she jolted awake, fully cognizant of where she was. Her eyes searched the darkness as she listened for anything that would convey danger.

Suddenly aware of the droplets of perspiration that beaded her forehead, Nancy lifted her shirt and dabbed. Then she began swallowing mouthfuls of air, as she tried to bring her racing heart under control. It's over, she told herself....this is just the after action jitters – the come-down from the adrenaline rush.

Then her hand went to her stomach....the dull ache, low blood sugar balance....who knows.

She got up and went to the bathroom. After she flushed the toilet, she looked at herself in the mirror as she leaned on the sink. Gault watched the reflection nod, and heard the voice somewhere inside her head. 'Your own fault.'

She answered back, "Yeah....I've got to live with it a while longer – don't I? But everything heals in time, doesn't it?"

Nancy continued to stare at the reflection, but this time the face staring back remained without emotion.

Well screw you. I know you better than you think I do.

She left the light on as she walked out of the room, down the staircase, and through the library. There was a sliver of light shining through the partially opened doorway. Nancy pushed on the door, and squinted as the brightness momentarily blinded her.

"Couldn't sleep, or didn't want to?"

As her eyes adjusted, she saw him sitting at a small table, the coffee mug held with both hands, elbows propped up on the table.

"Does it matter?"

"Not really."

"Would you like a cup?"

"I think I need some food."

"We have some of that too," and the man pointed to a refrigerator to her left.

Nancy went to the small stainless-steel frig. Her eyes scanned the contents, and then she looked over at the man.

"Is any of this edible….I mean how long has it been here?"

"Just arrived myself, but it hasn't killed me yet, so I'm guessing it's still good to go."

The answer was a turn-off of sorts. She reached for the egg carton, thinking, probably the safest play.

Using her shoulder, she pushed the refrigerator door closed. Then holding the carton with both hands, Gault walked to the stove, put the eggs down, and went back to the fridge This time she closed the door with her hand, as she held the butter and bacon with the other.

A few minutes later she was seated at the table.

He watched her eat in silence.

His stare bothered her, and she spoke up. "Do you have to do that?"

He knew what she was referring to. “I’m sorry. Yeah, sorry.”

Then Nancy shook her head. “Forget it. I’m just edgy….it’s been a long day, and even longer night.”

He didn’t say anything as he stood up and reached for her cup. She watched him walk to the sink, pour out what remained in the cup, and then refill it. When he returned to the table, he placed the cup in front of her plate.

“It’s always better hot.”

Nancy, forgetting about her damaged lips, smiled. She let the smile fade as the pain escalated.

When she finished eating, she pushed the plate aside, and looked at him over the rim of her cup.

“How did you know my name?”

“A mutual friend told me you were coming.”

“Janco?”

The man confirmed with a head motion.

“And why are you here Mr. Monday?”

“That’s better explained by Arias.” He paused, then continued, “He’ll be here tonight.”

She studied his face, unsure of what she was looking for. His jet black hair, brown eyes and complexion, didn’t type fit him….he could be from anywhere – Greece, Turkey, the Middle East….Italy.

Monday, or whatever his name actually was, seemed too young to be sitting here….here as one like herself. Yet there was something that belied his youthfulness….something that shouted, 'Caution.'

Her mind raced with questions, but she held back, deciding to leave the matter where it was.

"Tonight, that gives me some time to buy what I need, and what I need is some make-up and a change of clothes."

"There are some up-scale shops near Rittenhouse Square….that's about a ten minute walk from here, but they won't open until 10 a.m. You've got eight and a half hours of waiting time. What I really think you need, Nancy, is some sleep. I'll clean up here."

She leaned back in her chair, nodded, then stood up. "You're right Mr. Monday. Sleep….that's what I need right now."

As she disappeared through the doorway, she called out, "Thanks for the coffee."

*

Janco leaned back and looked up at the library's ceiling.

"You know something....I've never noticed the ornate woodworking before." Then he paused, and placed both hands on his chest, interlocking his fingers before continuing.

"Well, maybe I did....but if I did, I never took the time to marvel at its intricacy....obviously old school craftsmen."

Then Janco paused once more. When he started speaking again, he separated his hands and leaned forward.

"One should always make time to reflect, wouldn't you agree Nancy?"

"At every opportunity."

Arias Janco nodded, then looked over at the man.

"And you Mr. Monday....what do you say?"

"Reflections....they're negative or positive....sometimes both simultaneously, but I've learned along the way, that some things are best left compartmentalized."

Janco's eyes shifted back to the woman.

When she didn't respond, Janco started looking away, then reversed direction as she began to speak.

"If what's compartmentalized is forgotten, and it usually is, the difficult lessons learned, are of little value. As such, the individual is prone to repeat the mistakes, and from mistakes comes failure, and failure has only one reward. That reward is final. That's all the motivation anyone needs to ensure that it never happens. Look at me. A simple lapse, and look at what happened. If I had stayed focused, this," and she pointed to her face, "this….," and she left the sentence hanging. "Yeah I know….it could have been worse, but this is bad enough. I have no intention of compartmentalizing this or any other experience….ever. Okay….now that we're past whatever all that was, why am I here, and who is this?"

Her tone had an edge to it, as she pointed to Robert Monday.

"That man, Nancy, is your new partner. We have another assignment for you."

"Who says I want another assignment. Maybe Janco, this," and again she pointed to her face, "….was a wake-up call. I never approached you….you approached me. I already had a career. In case you've forgotten, I'm a concert pianist, and not a bad one at that."

Gault smiled, and then grimaced as the gesture re-opened cuts on her damaged lips.

"Damn it," and then she moved the back of her hand over her mouth.

In almost a whisper, Janco replied. "Yes. I've heard you play. Outstanding indeed, and…."

Nancy's hand cut through the air. "Okay Janco, I'm listening. Tell me what you have and I'll say yes or no....okay?"

Arias Janco held the smile as he looked over at the man. He continued to hold his gaze as he spoke.

"It doesn't matter whether the Executive Order was signed by Ford, Carter, Reagan or Bush....no American Intelligence agency or person acting on behalf of the United States is authorized to engage in assassinations. That's why organizations like ours exist. We are the conduit between what "they" want and from whom "they" want it. Does that mean that these executive orders are infallible?" Janco tilted his head, and then moved it slightly side to side.

"Hardly the case, but most of the wet work gets farmed out, and both of you have been the beneficiaries of that work. That townhouse on Egerton Crescent, is notably located on one of the most expensive streets in London. And that home in Greenwich, Connecticut, Nancy, where you live among the titans of the hedge fund industry. Honestly, do either of you think that lifestyle can be maintained as a university language and history professor, or as a concert pianist?"

Nancy spoke up. "Yes....you bet I do. Most of those who come, come to be seen....others come for the mistakes they hope I make, and a few others come for the pure love of the music I make happen. But whatever their reason, they come, and they will continue to come whenever I play. The remuneration is sufficient to support my lifestyle, or close to the way I'm living now....so whatever you are trying to spin, Janco, it isn't going to stick."

"On the other hand, if Monday is actually a language professor, the hundred grand or so he might make a year at some left leaning, liberal-arts factory, assuming he was tenured, certainly wouldn't support a townhouse on Egerton Crescent. I've been there – nice white stucco-fronted facades with black doors and neatly manicured box trees. They refer to it as Billionaires row, so the professor just doesn't fit in too well on that hundred thou. Even as part of this....what we are, I don't see him there; twelve million pounds for a four bedroom with a small garden....grandiose by any measure, so he probably couldn't sustain it. But he's not me, Janco. The million plus, I spent for a place to crash, doesn't impede me one iota, if all of this comes to a screeching halt. I still can afford the place on what I make as a concert pianist."

Nancy leaned back, rubbed her eyes, and looked over at Arias Janco as the silence enveloped the room.

Her words reverberated inside his mind as he locked eyes with the woman. He liked her....admired her individuality, her toughness, and her confidence. Despite the lapse of the other night, he felt she's better for it. There were no outward signs of anything psychological that he could detect....she seemed in every way, herself.

Janco's mind framed the words at the end of her retort....the word picture of how someone like Monday could afford a home on Egerton Crescent.

The thought faded as the sound of clapping shattered the silence.

"Very good, Miss Gault. Assumptions and conclusions all at the same time. Maybe I'm just frugal with my money, or maybe I'm one hell of a stock-market player, or maybe I've got some rich, over the top woman, keeping me in….how do you say it….oh yes, a grandiose style for services rendered."

Monday stopped, and let the hostility in his voice ebb. As he formed a half smile, he asked in a tone of civility, "It's simple….I live there because I can."

Janco looked away from the man, and directed his attention toward the woman. After several seconds, he looked back.

"All things have an ending Mr. Monday. Each day brings us one day closer to the grave. Life is fluid….subject to constant change. What 'is' today, doesn't necessarily mean that it will be the same tomorrow. That applies to life as well as material things, such as your home," and then he moved his head so he faced the woman, "…. or yours Miss Gault."

Janco continued to keep his eyes on the woman as he spoke.

"What 'is,' is only the moment that we're presently experiencing….nothing more, and that brings us back to this moment."

“Before you state the obvious, Miss Gault, I do understand exactly how you feel.” Arias Janco’s voice inflected when he mentioned the words, “feel.”

“But that is a temporary sensation. Your face will heal, and you will again become confident in your skin. I have an assignment for you and Mr. Monday. The remuneration,” and Janco nodded as his mouth opened slightly, “….will be ample…. as always.”

“We have arranged, through diplomatic channels, for a concert recital to be held in Paramarmico, capital of the Democratic People’s Republic of Boka Ami….at the wedding of the Head of State. In case, neither of you are familiar with this gem of a country, a sliver of land sandwiched between Lakopta, and the storied French Guyana.”

Janco paused as he looked up at the ceiling again. Keeping his eyes focused on some distant point, he said, “French Guyana – Devil’s Island…..you’ve heard of it….the Ile du Diable – the largest of the Islands in the Iles du Salut group, and the infamous Alfred Dreyfus affair; the French Army Officer falsely accused of treason, and sentenced to a life of servitude on Devil’s Island….he along with many other lost souls.”

Arias Janco looked back at each of them for the confirmation that wasn’t necessary. He was only trying to ascertain if they were listening.

Monday nodded, and so did the woman, so he continued.

"On 11 March 2017, a Sergeant named Muguanasi led a coup that ousted the Dutch from Boka Ami, He declared the place, "Independent," formed a Socialist Republic, and promoted himself to Lieutenant Colonel."

Janco locked eyes for a few seconds with each of them before he picked up where he left off.

"I always thought these types promoted themselves to General. Idi Amin....the sergeant from Uganda, comes to mind."

He smiled as he pictured the be-medaled Ugandan dictator standing in the hot African sun, wearing the ornate uniform, custom made from Seville Row in London. Then he let the smile fade and continued.

"Boka Ami has been riddled with on-going insurrections of one form or another, emanating primarily from the Maroons; the run-away slaves under the command of Ronnie Dajan who inhabit, and control the interior, and from the Bush Commandos who are freelancers and roam just about everywhere. The Dutch have so-so relations with Muguanasi, and are content with that. Muguanasi, on the other hand, has drifted closer to the Communist....notably The Cicoms (Chinese Communist) and to a lesser extent, the North Koreans, both of who have embassies in Paramarmico."

"Boka Ami exports about $1.4 billion worth of aluminum, gold, crude oil, lumber etc. The Cicoms want the Alumina and the oil....in fact they want it all, so they've been doing whatever is necessary to secure closer ties with Muguanasi....namely loans and military assistance. The Cicoms, in a show of solidarity, are sending the head of the ILD there for the festivities."

"That's your target....Min Qua Fu. The ILD, the harmless sounding International Liaison Department, is an organization engaged in a wide range of covert activities. The Cicoms want Boka Ami as a launching pad for their activities in South America, and it seems Muguanasi's off-shore bank accounts reflect a growing closeness. Certain interests have stated that they want Min Qua Fu terminated (assassinated). This is a rare chance to do just that."

Arias Janco scratched an imaginary itch as he looked at both their faces, and then continued.

"Fu is not to be underestimated – he's not a soft target" (someone who is not properly trained in intelligence). While schooled and grounded in tradecraft, (intelligence work) there is another layer to his persona. As a child, he was a protégé of sorts. Fu was trained as a classical pianist into his early adult years. His associations and his rise through the ranks of the ILD, are clouded, but obviously intertwines with the Cicom power structure. To have maintained his position and power for a longer time than most of his successors, demonstrates that he knows how to play political politics in one of the most challenging arenas in the world. Perhaps this knowledge may prove of some value."

Janco stopped, and waited, anticipating questions that never came. "The methodology, I leave to your own devices. Additional background data is in the envelope, there."

Arias Janco pointed to a manila envelope on a nearby table. "You'll read it....no notes....no copies. You leave the envelope where you found it. You know the drill."

"You're free to leave whenever you like. You have three weeks to prepare....for your concert. You'll pick up your tickets at the airport on Monday the 17th."

Janco studied each of them for several moments as he pinched his lips together with his thumb and index finger.

"I suggest you get to know each other. Much will depend on your ability to anticipate, and compliment one another. Are there any questions?"

Before either of them could respond, Janco held up his hand. "I mentioned this previously, but I'll restate it. The remuneration for the successful conclusion of this assignment, will be ample....in fact it will be double the usual amount. If there is nothing further, Bon Voyage."

Arias Janco stood up, and walked quickly out of the room. Gault stared after him and when he disappeared, she looked back at Robert Monday.

*

She handed the four, double spaced pages along with the envelope to Monday, and then sat quietly watching him as he began reading.

The memorandum was simple….a flight to Miami, then Delta to Paramarmico…. reservations at the Paramarmico Tori Hotel, then a meeting at the Embassy. After that, a connection with a Lebanese named Hayek.

She had three weeks of practice ahead of her….grueling six to eight hour days. Besides the personal pride she felt in being a concert pianist, Gault felt she owed something to the dead composers. It was their music….they composed it, but it was her interpretation of that music that brought their notes to life centuries later.

As she watched Monday, her mind began to formulate the selections she'd play. She toyed with the idea of making it an all Chopin concert, and the more she thought about the idea, the more she liked it. She would start off with Chopin's Polonaise in A-major opus.40, no.1, and then play his Second Sonata in B-flat major. Those would be followed by Chopin's most beloved Nocturne in E-flat major, opus 9, no.2, and then his Raindrop Prelude in D-flat major, opus 28, no.15. She'd end the concert with two of his waltzes, in A-minor, and C-sharp minor.

Gault saw her fingers floating across the black and white ivory keys, and then she turned toward the sound of his voice.

"Pretty clear cut....wouldn't you say?" Monday waived the papers, but he didn't wait for a reply. "We need a plan. Since you need to practice, my suggestion is we use your home to formulate one. That's means you'll have a house guest for the next three weeks....me. I assume that's okay with you?"

"You assume incorrectly, Mr. Monday. There are a number of hotels in the area which cater to transit guests, such as you."

She stopped speaking....she made her point.

As she looked at Robert Monday, Nancy sensed it wasn't the response he expected, but despite the blow to his ego, he maintained his composure.

Recovering quickly, Monday held the slight smile as he moved his head in a way that Nancy assumed meant, "Touché," the French word that acknowledged a verbal hit. If it wasn't that exactly, it was certainly close.

"That'll work Nancy. This will be my first time in Greenwich....perhaps you'll have time to show me around."

She bristled at the smart-aleck remark. Seems Mr. Robert Monday had a thing about him, something that was becoming more irritable over time.

Nancy ignored the remark, and pointed to the papers Monday still held in his hand. "I'm going upstairs....when you're finished, leave the papers on the table. If you're here when I come down, I'll give you my telephone number and address. Otherwise I'll leave it on the table next to the envelope. Call me after you're settled, and no surprise visits. Don't come without contacting me first."

Despite her attempt at normalcy, the tinge of hostility was evident in her voice.

As she left the room, she felt uneasy, and she knew it had nothing to do with the previous night. The feeling was a premonition…a warning – her senses telling her that this assignment was fraught with yet undefined problems, and Mr. Robert Monday would be the catalyst for those problems.

Chapter 3

Nancy Gault picked up her small suitcase, and then using her free hand to steady herself, edged into the aisle, and then toward the exit doors.

Once the doors opened, she followed the Metro-North Conductor onto the platform. After a cursory glance around she made her way to the line of taxis. As she waited her turn, she shifted from leg to leg impatiently, and then caught one of the drivers' eyes moving from her breast to her legs, and back again.

Men are all alike! The thought amused her and she held the smile until she heard the thick accented voice of the driver.

"North Street. I'll show you where to turn."

The driver nodded.

Once Nancy closed the rear door, the driver, looking at her in the rear view mirror, said, "North Street," in barely understandable English.

This time, Nancy nodded as she wondered, where do they come from….how do they get here? Then the thought quickly dissipated as she became aware of the unpleasant odor inside the cab.

Her right hand reached for the automatic window button, and depressed it, but the window remained closed. She tried it again with the same result.

"Please unlock the rear windows."

“Sorry Lady, broken.”

“Then open the other one.”

“Hot.”

“I don’t give a damn how hot it is. Open the window or take me back to the station.” Then after a moment’s hesitation, “forget the window, take me back to the station.… Now!”

As the driver began fumbling with the console buttons, he pleaded. “Please lady, no back, please.”

As he pressed two buttons simultaneously the two front windows opened, while the back window closed. Then, as if the windows had a mind of their own, they began opening and closing at will.

Despite her dour mood, Nancy started laughing.

In seconds, the driver was caught up in the moment and began laughing as well. When he managed to stop, he turned and said in a serious voice, “Voodoo.”

“Yeah....sure.”

Nancy, still laughing, motioned him on with a wave of her hand.

Who’d believe this? Maybe I’m ready for a loony bin.

She rubbed her eyes, and then refocused on the driver. As she stared at the blackness of his neck, she saw herself again in the alley off 43rd Street, the alley where that wretched excuse for a human being tried his best to rape her, or worse. Is there anything worse than rape? Yeah....maybe, but that's as scarring as it gets....the physical, and the psychological aspects that becomes an ingrained part of the mindset – forever.

"North Street, Lady."

The driver had to repeat it twice before Nancy reacted.

"Turn right at Saint Mary's Church. Then it's the second street on your right."

*

When she closed the front door she went to one side of the piano. Standing at an oblique angle, she watched the Lincoln town car pull away.

She thought how accommodating he always was, and why not? He was expensive. The retainer came with certain benefits. James Fallan, Esq., had been her attorney since she moved to Greenwich, and came highly recommended by Janco. He was old school Yale, old money, and his roots went back to Revolutionary times, but did she really need that resume, when all that was required was a periodic update on her growing holdings.

Her eyes drifted toward the ebony Steinway medium grand piano. Then she brushed at her skirt as she sat down on the bench.

She stared at the piano while her mind lapsed into the events of the past several days. Then she shook off the feeling and started playing. In moments she became one with the piano.

Her improvised rendition of Scott Joplin's, "Maple Leaf Rag," filled the room, and drowned out the sound of the telephone.

When she stopped, she felt invigorated. Well it wasn't Chopin, but it was damn good. Nancy smiled, Variation – the spice of life, and then she heard the phone.

Her intuition told her who was on the other end before she lifted the receiver. The male voice confirmed it.

He said her name twice, and then she answered.

"Did you just get home? I've been trying to reach you."

"Yeah....I just got home."

Monday didn't like the tone of her voice, the agitation was evident. He usually didn't let things like that bother him and he wondered why he was letting it bother him now.

"I'm at the Le Grande Harbor Hotel in Greenwich."

She let the silence build before she answered, and when she did, their voices came across simultaneously.

"Okay Mr. Monday, you first."

"I'm at the Le Grande…." Nancy interrupted. "You said that."

"I did, didn't I? I'd like to come over. Is it convenient?"

She thought, No time is convenient, then after a deep breath, she said, "…. in forty-five minutes. You have the address, and don't show up early."

Nancy heard the click terminating the connection, and then lowered the phone slowly, thinking, either I find a way to overcome whatever it is that's bothering me about him, or I tell Janco to cancel the op. No other choices.

She looked at the piano, and then walked back. Standing at one corner she let her fingers move along the keys until they reached the ebony frame. After a deep breath, she walked toward the staircase.

*

After she dried herself, she stood naked in front of the mirror. Her face looked better, or was that just something she wanted to believe. She leaned closer until her body contacted the ceramic sink. Then she tilted her head toward the mirror and slowly scanned her face.

Yes….some definite improvement.

Then she became aware of the pressure against her vagina. She lowered her hand and touched the pubic area as she moved back. She tried to remember how long it had been....the relationship with the newspaper guy. She had doubts from the beginning, and her instincts proved right once again, but she wanted this one to be the one. He seemed to have enough of what she thought important....the things that first attracted her to him, and maybe that was the problem....good looks, easy conversation, a pleasant smile, position, but there was emptiness....a shallowness....a hollowness, that was evident from the start. That emptiness overrode everything else.

Maybe it was her....not him. Maybe what she did for Janco, prevented her from giving what she had to offer, and maybe that doomed the relationship. Maybe her work prevented other relationships from ever happening....maybe.

She closed her eyes as her index and middle fingers stroked her clitoris. As her passion escalated, she increased the rhythm until she felt the heightened arousal. When she felt the onset of her first orgasm, she threw her head back, and let the sound escape as she shuddered from the waves of pleasure.

Nancy was half way down the stairs when the doorbell rang. She stopped and remained in place listening as the soft notes of the bell sounded a second time.

When she finally reached the door and opened it, Robert Monday's hand was suspended in mid-air, his fingers poised to press the bell again.

"My, My, what a surprise Mr. Monday."

A thin smile formed on his face. "Yeah, I'm known to do that from time to time."

"Do what Mr. Monday?"

"Surprise people....sometimes they form an initial impression of me that's inaccurate."

"First impressions are usually telling."

"In some cases, yes, but not all. An astute person realizes that quickly, and if not, there is always the possibility for consequences."

Nancy let the words replay, trying to discern if they amounted to a subtle threat, or was he jockeying for some initial advantage.

"Do you want me to stand here until I've passed inspection?"

Nancy refocused as she heard, ".....passed inspection," but said nothing.

"Well, have I passed inspection?"

When she didn't reply, he said, "May I come in, or will we conduct business in-between the front door frame?"

Nancy smiled as she shook her head. "Of course Mr. Monday, please come in."

She moved sideways and closed the door as he walked past her, and then stopped.

"To your right, Mr. Monday….the living room."

Robert Monday hesitated, as he quickly scanned the room noting the exit routes and the upscale furnishings. His eyes settled on the piano, and then he looked back at her.

"Is that my competition?"

Nancy wasn't expecting the question. The way her mind processed the four words, he was way out of line, and she suddenly felt uneasiness about having him here.

She waited several seconds before answering. "As far as anything here, me or that object called a piano, you have no competition because you don't exist in my real world. You exist in the other for only one purpose, and that purpose is to help me accomplish a mission.

"You continually seem to misinterpret the words I say. I'm not a funny guy, and maybe my attempt at levity isn't going over so well. I just thought that since we obviously have gotten off to a bad start, I'll try another approach….a lighter approach. Obviously, that's not working either. I just wanted to get beyond whatever it was about me that was bothering you. If you would care to tell me specifically, maybe we can clear the air."

Robert Monday paused, and then began again. "Maybe an apology is in order. I'm not entirely sure why, but please accept my sincere apology for anything that I've done or intimated, that may have offended you in any way. I am truly sorry."

Nancy let her eyes drift down for a moment.

"Maybe I'm becoming too sensitive....too judgmental, but it's part of the territory. I don't know you Mr. Monday. I'm cautious by nature....more so because of what I do. We come together because of Janco. Obviously there's a reason he wants us to work this mission together, but we've never crossed paths before, and I don't know you. That's as it should be."

Nancy paused longer than necessary before continuing.

"Because of all the unknowns, coupled with what I've seen of you, I've formed an opinion and that opinion screams, "Run." Do I have to run, Mr. Monday? After all, my life is important to me, and I can't afford to place it in the hands of someone who is not competent enough....professional enough, to warrant that trust. I've survived because I'm cautious. I don't intend to change that for anyone, or for any mission. I'd rather tell Janco to get someone else – me or you. From what I've seen of you so far, you don't measure up as someone I can confide in. Maybe I should contact Janco....do I have to do that Mr. Monday?"

Monday stared back, his chest rising with the intake of air. He let it out slowly, and then in a modulated voice slightly below normal said, "That won't be necessary. Janco placed us together because we have similar qualities that might not be apparent to you at this moment. I am a competent professional, tested in some of the most difficult places on earth....tested, and survived. I've never worked with a woman before. Perhaps that's why we got off to a bad start....my fault....completely my fault. If you'll accept my apology, perhaps we can move on. However, if whatever I've done has damaged my credibility, and my professional character to such an extent where you feel you cannot trust me, then by all means contact Janco."

Gault locked eyes with Monday for several seconds, then walked to the piano, and sat down. As the music flooded the room, he recognized the song, and then the lyrics began dancing across his mind-screen.

"I see trees of green, red roses too. I see them bloom, for me and you, and I think to myself, what a wonderful world....I see skies of blue, and clouds of white. The bright blessed day, and dark sacred night, and I say to myself, what a wonderful world...."

When Nancy glanced sideways, she saw him mouth a silent, thank you, and then she smiled as her fingers flew across the keys.

Chapter 4

"We're down to two weeks and a few days Mr. Monday. I need to practice, so that cuts into our time to formulate a working plan. I envision several serious unknowns. First, we don't know the country. What we can get from an area assessment is a vague word picture. Without an actual feel regarding the pulse of the country, the people....the players and all that, we're not going to get close enough to Min Qua Fu to terminate him without endangering ourselves. He needs to be taken out by remote."

"Partly correct, whatever we do involves an element of risk for both of us. What we have to do is minimize that risk. I haven't forgotten that piece of information Janco provided....the bit about Fu being a pianist. I think we can use that to our advantage."

As Monday paused, Gault waited for him to continue. When the time lapse exceeded what she thought was reasonable, she spoke up.

"I've thought about that too, but how can we use it to our advantage?"

Monday moved his head to clear away the mind fog, and then looked at the seated woman.

"Okay, let me lay my idea out in rough form. You're going to give a recital. The place....a theater will be crowded....foreign dignitaries from the Embassies in Paramarmico, local government officials, business types, and some of the locals. Security will be heavy – both local, and from the respective Embassy staffs. I'm thinking that after you finish playing your last song, you announce that you have an added surprise for the evening. Then you invite Fu up to the stage to play. He may be hesitant, but you continue to insist. The more you insist, the louder the applause will get. Applause is contagious and others will pick up on it. Min Qua Fu will eventually concede and come on stage."

"Once he's there, you will clap along with the audience. When the clapping stops use the mike, assuming there is one, or speak loud enough incorporating the following....you know of an ancient Chinese song that is an enduring classic, and perhaps he'll honor us by playing it. The song is entitled, "Ambush from all Sides," or "Shimian Maifu" in Chinese. While very old, this is still a very popular piece....he'll know it. Every classical pianist in China does. It depicts a famous battle between the Chu and Han groups at Gaixia, during the waning years of the Qin Dynasty. During that critical battle, the Han Army strategically used ambushes, virtually from all directions, to defeat the Chu Army. The loss by the Chu established the famous Han Dynasty. The tempo of high and lows, as the music is played, presents a vivid picture of the fierce fighting between the two groups."

Nancy sat quietly until he paused, her eyes never moving from Monday's.

"My, My, Mr. Monday. You are full of surprises. Please tell me how do you know this?"

"You've evidently forgotten, Miss Gault. As Janco stated, I'm a language and history professor. I know about the Chu and Han people, and China in general. That's one of the reasons why we're paired together."

Nancy shook her head in a way that acknowledged what he just said, and to give her time to process the words. She heard her inner voice repeat….that's why we're paired together. Okay, another piece of the puzzle that makes up Robert Monday has just been revealed.

"Please go on, Mr. Monday."

"Fu sits down at the piano….on a cushion you'll use during your recital. Inside the cushion will be a cell phone packed with C-4 composite explosive. You'll walk off to one side of the stage as Fu begins to play. Once you're away from the stage, you'll get behind some type of partition….a wall, stairwell, or whatever. We'll start the sequence off with a diversionary explosion - car bomb, or the like. We'll get more specific once we're on site and make a visual. Once the initial explosion occurs, I'll trigger the cell phone through a remote frequency, and send our friend on a long vacation."

"Whoa…. you want me to sit on a cushion wired with explosives? Are you serious?"

"The C-4….composition 4, is less sensitive to shock and heat than most explosives….that's why I'm thinking of using it. Sitting on the cushion won't trigger the explosion….I will."

When she didn't comment, he continued. "Miss Gault….Nancy, C-4 is a relative stable explosive with a consistency similar to molded clay. There's nothing to worry about....you're safe. Our problems will come afterwards."

"Somehow Mr. Monday, I'm not getting those positive vibes you're throwing my way. I'm supposed to play a recital, sitting on an explosive cushion, and not be concerned. Are you serious?"

"I think you've asked that before."

"What did I ask before?"

"Whether I'm serious."

"Well, are you?"

"Yes....as I've stated, you're not in harm's way."

Nancy remained quiet with her eyes revealing the doubts she held onto.

Before she could say anything, Monday moved his head in a way that conveyed he understood her concerns, and then he held up his hand.

"Okay, maybe if I was in your place, partnered with a stranger you've never worked with before, and with a less than positive start, yeah, maybe I'd have concerns too. But to allay your fears, Miss Gault, I know about explosives. I was part of the British Army's 11th EOD – the Explosive Ordinance Disposal Regiment in Afghanistan...I am somewhat of an explosives expert."

Nancy simply stared as her mind processed the additional information. After a few seconds, she nodded. "Okay, that helps, but I'm still not comfortable. I need time to think about what you've suggested....the methodology....and I need time to practice. Let's meet here tomorrow. Come early, but not too early....say a little after ten. Does that work for you Mr. Monday?"

*

At twenty minutes after ten, Robert Monday and Nancy Gault were huddled around a kitchen table. The coffee cups were pushed off to one side, and the area in front of each of them was occupied by a legal sized, yellow lined pad, and crumpled papers.

Nancy looked at her notes. "You say you can't send the stuff you need through a diplomatic pouch....why?"

"As I stated, Janco wants the Embassy left out of the loop – they're to remain cold, and secluded regarding our mission. The smaller the circle of who knows what, the better for us. There are too many unknowns to begin with, and we don't have to add to the equation by involving others without a need to know. As far as the stuff goes, we'll take along what we can. What we can't take, we'll buy on the local market or improvise."

"You're going to improvise on a bomb?"

"Yes, if there's no alternative."

Nancy sat still, eyes locked with his.

Monday knew what she was thinking and wanted to get the confidence level, as little as there was, back to reasonable. He took a deep breath and began.

"Look Nancy, eh, Miss Gault, I need some things to make what I have in mind work. There's nothing I need that will tax either of us or, as I see it, cause a problem once we're in country. For example, I'm going to need petroleum jelly, rubbing alcohol, candle wax, several packages of pipe cleaners, clear gelatin, canola oil, a battery hydrometer, and a heat source like a hot plate or stove....no item that's going to present us with a problem. We'll take what we can with us, placed in cover items like a shaving can, toothpaste tube, perfume atomizer, and the like. We shouldn't have any trouble clearing customs, and I'll need only a day to make what I need once we're in place."

He held his gaze, until she started to speak. Then he broke eye contact and listened.

"What makes you think some of what you mentioned won't be uncovered as we exit here and clear customs there?"

"While there's always a concern, much of what I indicated should not arouse any suspicion.... petroleum jelly, pipe cleaners for a pipe along with a small pouch of tobacco. The clear gelatin will be placed in a small tube and marked hair pomade. The canola oil goes into a perfume atomizer....other items like the rubbing alcohol, candle wax and the flour or cornstarch will be....can be purchased from the local market. I'll wear the battery hydrometer on my wrist like a watch."

As Monday finished, he re-established eye contact and waited. This time Nancy looked away, and began staring at some distant spot on the wall. "What happens if Paramarmico customs raises a red flag over any one, or a combination of articles either of us are carrying?"

"It could happen, but I'm not concerned."

As Nancy moved her mouth formulating a reply, Monday held up his hand. "Remember we are….you, are the honored guests about to give a recital for Muguanasi. There will be an official delegation there to meet us. You'll be ushered through customs quickly. This is big....really big. How often does a renowned classical pianist come to Paramarmico, and with a companion – her manager carrying a jigsaw puzzle worth of explosive components, with the intention of blowing up an important Chinese operative."

Nancy let the words roll around her mind, and then the smile slowly took shape. In seconds she was laughing, and so was Monday.

When she stopped laughing, she tilted her head toward Robert Monday and then started laughing again. When she stopped moments later, Nancy held up her hand.

"This is serious. Why are we laughing?" and then it started again.

After a few moments of quiet, Nancy asked, "Why can't we mold the C-4 into several stems placed among a bouquet of flowers we'll hand to Fu?"

"Several reasons. First, what happens if Fu hands the flowers back to you to hold? I can't detonate the device unless you're out of harm's way. Janco doesn't want you to become a sacrificial lamb as far as I know."

"Okay, what's the other reason?"

"I can't pack enough C-4 into enough flower stems, and camouflage them to make the effort worthwhile….I can't be certain the target will be neutralized, like I can with the cushion."

Monday knew her suggestion was amateurish, but he treated it as if it were an actual possibility. It was frustrating, but necessary to explain the salient points of why something couldn't work, so that at some point, she'd stop questioning him. He had always adhered to a strict modus-operandi, his method of handling a kill. The characteristics of which were well established over a lengthy time frame, both in the military, and as part of the tradecraft that he was now part of.

"As I've stated, I need time to think and practice, so let's start again tomorrow. Same time okay with you?"

Monday was about to ask whether she wanted to have dinner with him, but held himself in check.

"Sure, tomorrow is fine. See you at the same time."

"I'll call a taxi."

"No need for that. I've rented a car. Thanks for the coffee and I'll see myself out. Until tomorrow."

Monday was opening the door before Nancy replied. As the door closed, she called out, "See you tomorrow."

He waved his hand.

Nancy waited until she heard the car engine, then she went to the piano, sat down, and let her fingers ripple along the keys until she began a slow, melodic rendition of "What a Wonderful World."

Chapter 5

"How's the practicing coming?"

"I seem to be playing better at night and I'm wondering if that's an omen of sorts?"

"The mind is an interesting mechanism. It's never at rest even when we're sleeping, and some of what it conjures up is stimulating, frightening, worrisome, and probably a few things more. Why concern yourself about it?"

"You're not giving the concert." Then Nancy paused as she stared across the table at Monday. "I always go with my seventh sense....the one I've developed along the highways and bi-ways that Janco sent me on. Until I'm sure, I'm apprehensive and cautious. By the way, you sounded like a professor. I guess that's because you are," then Nancy smiled.

"That, and a few things more," then Monday smiled back.

Nancy picked up her yellow legal pad and let her eyes scan the word she had circled. When she looked up, she asked, "The phone....a cell phone is traceable....the parts, even a fragment of plastic can be traced back to the point of manufacture. If the forensic types go over the blast scene, and they will, that phone, and the type of explosive, could result in a blowback. That could involve our Embassy and ...."

Before Nancy could finish, Monday interrupted. "No reason for concern. I'm going to use a burner, one that was manufactured and purchased in Egypt. The North Koreans introduced a mobile phone service in 2008 through a joint venture with the Egyptian company Orascom. The phones can't dial out of the country, but that doesn't matter. It has the markings we need and I'll rewire it, to make sure it does what it's supposed to do. As far as the C-4 is concerned, it's universal....obtainable anywhere, and everywhere."

Nancy Gault knew what Monday was referring to when he used the word burner; a disposable phone, whose terminology was commonly used by law enforcement, and those on the other side of the law.

"Why that phone?"

"I plan to leave the phone behind....the one I use to trigger the explosion. Let Muguanasi's people find it. Let them wonder why the North Koreans would kill a senior Chinese Intelligence operative," then Robert Monday smiled.

"Interesting, Mr. Monday....interesting."

Monday nodded his head slightly, and waited for the next question which came quickly.

"What about exiting the country?"

"We can't leave the country too quickly. We need to hang around for appearance sake."

"Obviously, all that changes if the situation dictates otherwise."

"How will that determination be made?"

"If either of us, or both of us, are considered suspects, then we exit Paramarmico. I'll get back to that in a moment. Now let me walk through how I see it. Immediately after the blast, pandemonium sets in....first the screaming, and then the herd mentality comes into play. People will claw, and fight, in order to distance themselves from the perceived danger. It's a natural phenomenon called survival....then some semblance of order will be restored. Initially everyone will be considered suspect, some more so than others based on how the Paramarmico authorities view it. We hook up with the American delegation if we can, otherwise we tag along with some other diplomatic group as they scramble out of the theater. If we can't do either and we can't connect with each other, we make our way out as best we can. If we're sealed off, we just play it by ear and wait it out until we are cleared. If I make it out before you I'll wait. Where I'll wait can be determined once we're in country. If we separate, and you make it out first, don't wait for me...is that understood? You make your way to your Embassy and hold up there. I'll get there as soon as I can."

Monday waited a moment, then continued. "If we're considered prime suspects, we use the services of the Lebanese to exit the country. "How," will be discussed with Hayek once we connect with him. If Muguanasi's security personnel, or military, form a cordon around you, for protection, just go along with it until you have an opportunity to break free."

Nancy nodded. She remained silent, her mind churning, then she asked, "How are they going to connect us?"

"You are the closest to Fu....they could and probably will start with you."

"Then we're on their radar from the start."

Monday slowly nodded. "They'll put into place what they can regarding safeguards....doing what they can to prevent an international incident. With crowds, there's always a possibility for something disruptive to happen. Usually it's a minor skirmish from dissidents or the like, which can be put down easily. This time, however, it will be a more telling blow."

Nancy locked eyes with Robert Monday. "Let me tell you how I see it. I've got to play a recital sitting on a cushion loaded with explosives, then after the detonation, I'm going to become a prime suspect. That sounds like two strikes against Nancy Gault, and that's not the kind of odds I'm accustomed to. Sure, there's always a significant risk element involved in what we do....that's why we're remunerated the way we are, but this has a different feel....something surreal, and too many loose ends."

Monday rubbed his palm against his forehead. "I think I need a drink."

Nancy looked at her watch, then back at Monday. "It's only eleven o'clock."

"Like everyone seems to say nowadays, it's five o'clock somewhere in the world."

Gault moved her shoulders up slightly as she thought, what difference does it make? This entire mission is fraught with maybes, could be, and other bullshit words that didn't seem to coagulate the way it should. Then she wondered why she used the term, "coagulate"....something she equated with blood. Another omen perhaps?

"Sure Mr. Monday, why not? In fact I'll join you. What are you drinking?"

"Stolichnaya on the rocks, with a twist of lemon."

"I'll see what I have. This isn't the local bar."

Nancy called out from the kitchen, "No vodka....have some Crème de Menthe or Kahlua liqueur."

Monday called out, "No thanks," as he made a gagging motion with his hand at his throat.

As Nancy walked back to the living room, Monday was removing his hand from his throat, but somehow let it remain suspended in mid-air.

"I take it you don't like my alcoholic stock."

"I'd rather use them for mouth wash."

Nancy laughed despite herself.

"Let me take you to lunch….someplace crowded where you'll be safe from me."

"Would I be safe in a crowd Mr. Monday? Are you concerned that I can't take care of myself?"

"I'm sure you're quite capable Miss Gault. You've survived to this point, obviously because you have the ingrained qualities that insure longevity in our profession. My reference to a crowded place was simply word play, to ally any apprehensions you might have by accepting my invitation."

*

The table at "Don Juan Nabisco's" Spanish restaurant was positioned next to two tables of children chaperoned by young blonde mothers, who populated the town of Greenwich, Connecticut, like so many flowers.

The waitress apologized profusely, but indicated no other tables were available. She said the food was good and worth the minor inconvenience, nodding toward the two tables of annoying children.

Monday looked over at Nancy, and waited, then spoke up. "Like the lady says, the food is good….wanna give it a try despite what's next to us?"

Nancy nodded yes.

Monday looked up at the waitress. "You've convinced us to stay. If the food isn't good…." and then he let his voice trail off.

"It's better than good, Sir. Would either of you care for something to drink?"

"For me, a "Stolie" on the rocks….twist of lemon," then he looked over at Nancy.

"Iced tea, unsweetened."

The waitress nodded and left two menus by Monday's right arm.

Monday shook his head as his eyes stayed focused on the table. Nancy caught the slight movement and asked, "Re-thinking why we're still sitting here?"

"Nope. Just wondering how I keep giving you the impression…. conveying to you, something that I'm not."

"And what would that something be, Mr. Monday?"

"Less than professional."

"Why would I think that? I've worked for Janco for a long time. He wouldn't pair me with someone who is any less professional than I am. He knows all too well, the shadow world in which we operate, and what it requires to be effective there. We all have our quirks….can't be helped….like you for instance….your eleven o'clock drink. Personally I don't care….really I don't, about anything you do, as long as your first priority is the mission. Secondly, those quirks….your quirks, whatever they are, will in no way negatively impact the mission, or place me in more danger than we'll come by naturally….that's so, isn't it Mr. Monday?"

Monday, waited a few moments before he replied. When he spoke, it was in a low, modulated voice. "Okay, clear and understood. For starters, I'm a social drinker. This is a bit unusual for me, but I've had drinks with lunch before. There's nothing you have to read into it, it's simply what it appears to be….a drink at lunch. As you've stated to me earlier, you never worked with me before. That's a two way street. I have apprehensions about you as well. You're a pianist, but will you have my back covered if the need arises? Can I count on you to follow through once we've determined the plan? Can I assume you'll stand up under adverse circumstances that may necessitate deviating from the plan? You get what I'm saying, don't you, Miss Gault?"

"I've had the reoccurring thought, Mr. Monday, that maybe I should call Janco. But as quickly as that thought comes, it dissipates. We're paired for a reason, and maybe Janco is the only one who knows that reason, but I know Janco as well as anyone in the organization. I know he's a professional, like we are. He's placed us together because he knows our backgrounds compliment each other. While I have mostly worked alone, I have had partners. All of them have come back in one piece despite…." and then Nancy paused as she searched for the words, “despite the necessity to deviate from the plan.”

Before Monday could reply, the waitress placed the drinks down. Nancy moved the iced tea glass to her left and pointed to Monday’s drink. “Leave the iced tea, and please bring me what he’s drinking.”

Chapter 6

The Boeing B737-8, carrying 173 passengers, banked slowly to its left, in its final approach to Paramarmico's International Airport. Nancy Gault turned to her seat companion, and then pointed out her window.

"It looks serene from here, doesn't it? Almost picture perfect."

"Yes....always does, no matter what third world shit hole it is. At twelve hundred and fifty feet, everything down there looks beautiful. However, that doesn't last long. Once you're on the ground, it becomes something entirely different....a hot and dirty place, with the teeming masses all fighting for survival, except for those at the top....those who control the guns, and who rule the mob like a herd of sheep. Eventually that top dog is overthrown in some coup, and the mob gets a new dictator. He enriches himself, his friends and family, always making sure to keep the mob in check by throwing them a bone or two now and then. The cycle continues from dictator to dictator, ad infinitum. Amazing isn't it.... it never changes."

Nancy shook her head in agreement. "Seems that way, and for the life of me, I can't understand why generation after generation is satisfied with the status quo."

"Not much they can do about it. They've been beaten down so much, and over such a long period of time, they think it's a natural progression of their miserable lives. Look at the North Koreans under the Kim dynasty, the top echelon dines on steak and champagne, while the masses eat grass and tree bark soup. The military controls the mob and Kim Jung Un controls the military….same here with Muguanasi, and the same in most shit holes like Boka Ami."

"Once we've exited the plane, Nancy….Miss Gault...."

"Enough with the names. Call me Nancy, or Miss Gault, or anything else you want, but let's keep it uniformed from now on....only one name, and I don't have any problem with Nancy, okay Mr. Monday?"

Monday grinned. "Okay, Nancy, it's a deal, and from now on you call me Monday or Robert, and leave out the "Mr."....okay?"

"Deal. Now what were you saying about disembarking?"

"Most likely, we're going to be met by a delegation….photographs, etc. Once we've cleared customs, and done the "hello bit," we'll be driven to our hotel. Could be more photos there. We'll play it by ear. Again, not to worry…..nothing we're carrying with us will seem out of place. Just play the role of a concert pianist, smile a lot, wave, and don't let the people, or the hot as Hell temperature, get to you. Just let nature take its course."

Nancy was about to reply when she felt the aircraft's tires make contact with the tarmac. Instinctively, she grabbed her armrests, and then as quickly, let go, as the announcement in Dutch and English came over the intercom.

"Ladies and Gentlemen....we have arrived at the Paramarmico International Airport. The temperature is thirty-two degrees Celsius, or ninety degrees Fahrenheit. It's hot....welcome to the tropics. Please stay seated until the seat belt sign is turned off. The Captain and I would hate to have any of our passengers arrive at the gate before the plane does. First class, and the business sections will exit through the front....economy section, through the rear portal. For those of you continuing on to other destinations, flight information is available at the transit lounge. For those of you who are ending your flight in Paramarmico, enjoy your stay, and thank you all for flying Delta Airlines."

"That was cute, wasn't it, Monday....the bit about arriving at the gate before the plane does. A little laugh, kind of eases the tension a bit."

"Yep....and as I've stated, there's nothing to worry yourself about."

"Not just yet....right? I know, just let nature take its course."

"Exactly," and Monday smiled.

As the stewardess secured the open first class door, both Gault and Monday watched as several tropical attired men, and a woman entered through the portal. After several moments of dialogue, the stewardess pointed in their direction.

Monday held the smile as he whispered with the corner of his mouth, "The welcoming committee, or our jailers."

'That's not funny Monday," and she unbuckled her seat belt just as the first man reached her seat,

"Miss Gault," and then he glanced momentarily at Monday…."I am Rafi Derma, Minister of Arts and Culture. These are my associates, Mr. Rio Bundi, and Miss Eka Bulan. I bid you welcome to Boka Ami. You do us honor, and we are looking forward, with anticipation, your concert here."

Nancy smiled, and extended her hand, as she thought how his English somehow grated on her nerves. Then she let it fade as she thought, I'm just tired….it wasn't really all that bad.

"It is I who is honored, Minister…." and then she wondered whether Rafi or Derma was his last name. She decided to leave it at Minister, "I am overjoyed at being in your beautiful country. I look forward to playing here….by the way, this gentleman is my manager, Mr. Robert Monday."

Monday stood, awkwardly, hunched over as he extended his hand.

Derma looked back at the stewardess, and nodded. She picked up the plane's intercom and announced that there would be a momentary delay, and that all passengers should remain seated.

"If you'll kindly follow me," and he stepped back allowing both Nancy and Monday to enter the aisle "We have a welcoming party on the tarmac….just a few pictures, and a short interview for the local press, and TV stations. I hope you don't mind."

Nancy smiled. "I look forward to it."

Rafi Derma made a forward motion with his hand. "Then, shall we?"

As Nancy stepped through the cabin door, and onto the stairway, the dense, tropical air immediately enveloped her. She suddenly felt as if her lungs were contracting and stopped in place as she tried to adjust to the intense heat.

Once she reached the tarmac, several reporters and photographers approached. Maintaining her composure, despite the stifling heat, Nancy waved and smiled.

The slight pressure on her left elbow caught Nancy by surprise, and she turned quickly. Minister Derma smiled back, as he urged her toward several men, one holding a microphone, and the other a camera, who were standing several meters away from the others.

When they stopped, the Minister whispered, "From the local TV." Nancy nodded, then smiled at both men as they moved their microphone and camera closer.

The one holding the microphone asked, "Is this your first trip to Boka Ami, Miss Gault?"

"Yes, it is, but I hope it won't be my last."

"Any initial impressions, Miss Gault?"

"It's very hot here."

The reporter laughed. "Yes, but that makes us a tropical paradise. Everyone gets used to the heat, and I'm sure you will as well."

"Anything is better than the snow….and there's a lot of that where I come from. I'm happy to be here."

"Your concert will be broadcast on live TV, so many of our citizens will be able to enjoy your music. What selections are you planning?"

"It will be an entire Chopin concert. He's always been one of my favorites, and I hope to do him justice."

"I'm sure you will Miss Gault."

Then the reporter moved toward the Minister, followed closely by the cameraman.

"Excellency, we would like to thank you, and President Muguanasi, for arranging this most auspicious event. It brings honor to you and our beloved President, and credit to our great country, The Democratic People's Republic of Boka Ami."

The Minister bowed slightly and nodded. "Now if you'll excuse us, we must get Miss Gault to her hotel, and then the concert hall for some practice."

He looked over at Nancy, and smiled as he said, "There's never enough time for practice and other things," and then he turned back and faced the reporter. "I'm sure Miss Gault will have time to speak with you later."

Derma, again, placed his hand on Nancy's elbow, and urged her forward.

Monday held back until they were several meters away, then started walking. He watched as the Minister and his two associates waved at the local crowd, which was cordoned off behind a chain link fence that secured the airport perimeter. Monday smiled as he thought that the locals were probably here to see the planes take off and land, and their arrival, was simply a coincidence that brought some excitement into their otherwise, mundane lives. Wasn't it the same in all these third world cesspools, and then he shook his head in a reflective gesture to confirm the truism that just flashed across his mind screen.

The two black Cadillac Escalade SUVs were parked just to the right of the customs portal. Monday watched as Nancy handed the Minister's assistant something, and then pointed back in his direction. He started walking faster, and then heard Nancy say, "Do you have your luggage tags Monday. Mr. Bundi will get our bags."

After Monday reached into his suit pocket, the baggage tags fell to the tarmac.

"It's a good thing you're not playing the concert Mr. Monday."

Monday looked back at the smiling Minister and shook his head in confirmation. "My fingers always seem to have a mind of their own," and then he smiled back.

Once the bags were loaded, the Minister pointed at Monday and then to the second SUV. "Mr. Bundi will ride with you in that vehicle Mr. Monday, and Miss Gault and I, along with Miss Bulan, will ride in the first one. Enjoy the scenery along the way, and we'll reconnect at the hotel."

*

After several minutes of non-essential chatter, Bundi and Robert Monday fell into a welcomed silence.

As Monday stared out his window, his mind blotted out the dilapidated huts, the disheveled people, and the ever-present military checkpoints. He focused instead on the mission, the preparation, the execution, and the exit. As he let his mind freewheel, he felt the sudden chill. As quickly as it came, it faded. There were always those moments - moments of uncertainty….moments of apprehension. It went with the territory, and he knew that he had to compartmentalize these quickly, so that the advantage always remained with him.

"Beautiful, isn't it Mr. Monday?"

Monday wasn't sure what the man was referring to, but decided to answer yes, rather than ask.

"Our country is a paradise that is unique. We have a very safe, homogenous country, and in the world today, that is a remarkable statement, wouldn't you agree Mr. Monday?"

"The world is an okay place, Mr. Bundi. It's just the people in it that make it a chaotic place. You are fortunate that your country is relatively safe."

Bundi shook his head as he replied, "No, not relatively safe, as you put it. It's safe because we make sure to control those elements of outside agitation that would seek to alter the tranquility of Boka Ami."

Monday moved his head in agreement, feeling he said enough, and then settled back into an uncomfortable silence as he watched the first vehicle pull curbside, and Nancy, Derma and the woman exit.

In less than a minute, the group made its way across the lobby and through the milling Press Corps and guests, and toward the bank of elevators. In another four or five torturous minutes, they were situated in their respective rooms.

"Please use the afternoon, Miss Gault, at your leisure. We have arranged a cocktail reception tonight at the hotel's roof garden, which will be attended by many from the diplomatic, business and foreign community. They will be in attendance there."

Nancy couldn't help but smile again at the man's awkward English. Derma interpreted the smile as something entirely different.

She held the smile as she said, "Thank you for everything. I'm looking forward to tonight."

As Rafi Derma started to leave, Nancy asked, "Will I be able to see the place where the concert is to be held, and is there a piano there I can practice on?"

"I'm glad you asked me about that, since my mind has skipped it. Yes, we will visit there tomorrow. I will pick you up at 9 a.m. and by the way, there is a piano at the roof garden, and if I may presume to be presumptuous, perhaps we can induce you to play something for the guests….a song or two."

"I'd be delighted. Now if you'll excuse me, I think I'll get some sleep."

Derma bowed slightly. "Until tonight....that's at six sharp. Goodbye until then Miss Gault."

Nancy locked the door, then leaned back against it. She brought her hands up to her mouth to cover the on sought of laughter as she thought that if the mission didn't kill her, Derma's English would. After a few moments, she dropped her hands away and headed for the bathroom.

*

The ring of the telephone jarred Monday from his momentary mind fog. Anticipating that the call was from Nancy, he was surprised by the male voice.

"I'm a friend from your past, can you hear me old friend, and don't say my name."

"Yes, I know the voice. I didn't see you in the lobby."

"You must be slipping. I am one of the reporters," and then he laughed…."and would some interesting parties like to know what I could report."

"I bet they would. Are you coming up?"

"No. I don't have any time right now for tap dancing. There's a small garden just outside of the dining room, known as Sapphire. Easy to find….just follow the signs," and then he chuckled. "I don't think you'll have any trouble. Come alone."

"Okay, see you in five."

Monday focused on the word immediately – "tap," a catch-all for tapped, tracked, or monitored….the voice was telling him that the room telephone was probably bugged….an easy possibility for analogue networks like the one used in this hotel.

*

Nancy placed the telephone receiver back, wondering why he didn't pick up. She hesitated, and then picked up the telephone again, pressed the O button and waited for the operator's voice.

"Yes, Miss Gault. How can I help you?"

"Please try Mr. Monday's room again. Thank you."

After six rings she hung up. Her mind shifted through the possibilities, and then she let it go. She felt hungry and thought about room service and then realized that after being cooped up in a silver tube for four and a half hours, the last thing she needed now, was staying in a claustrophobic hotel room.

Nancy went to the bathroom, stared at herself in the mirror, and pronounced herself ready.

As she walked into the restaurant, the young woman attired in a colorful orange and green tropical skirt and blouse greeted her. "Welcome to the Sapphire Restaurant Miss Gault. Please follow me."

Nancy was surprised that the woman knew her name, and as soon as she was seated, she let her curiosity spill out. "You know who I am?"

"But of course. I saw your picture on TV and the Manager here had told us to expect you."

Nancy smiled back as she thought, probably so....after all I'm the distraction, and then she wondered why she used that word.

The young woman held her smile as she walked away. In moments she was replaced by a waitress in a similar style dress. The waitress also greeted her by name as she handed her a menu.

Nancy handed the menu back as she said, "I'd like an iced tea, unsweetened with lemon, and a fruit platter."

The waitress nodded as she turned and walked away.

Nancy rubbed her eyes with her fingers, and then slowly looked around the restaurant, noting primarily the exit routes. That simple movement was ingrained; it was the first thing she did when entering a room, a building, or other enclosure.

She noted the business types engaged in conversation, and several young couples. None of them seemed interested in her, and she was relieved that she could garner a few moments alone.

She leaned back in her chair, stretched, then turned her head to the left and saw the two figures sitting in rattan chairs, at one corner of the garden. As she watched them through the floor to ceiling window, their conversation became animated. Whatever it was that was being discussed, it was with an intensity that consumed Monday and the man he was interacting with.

She ate her salad methodically, without tasting the food….her eyes riveted on the two men. When she finished, she signed the check, and then returned to her room. Her training taught her that if she was not invited to participate, there was always a reason, whether that reason was logical to her, or not. Monday, obviously, wasn't in his room because he was in the garden with someone else. Her mind locked onto the name, "Hayek"….the Lebanese. She'd ask when the time was appropriate.

Chapter 7

"Why is it always about money Hayek?"

"Because of the chances I take. What else would be my motivation….love of country? I have no country. I gave that up when I first crossed over to your side, and against them. We have a relationship because it is beneficial to both of us. I do things for you, in places whose names most people can't pronounce. You make sure I'm taken care of, but lately, my dear Mr. Monday, I've gotten that sinking feeling that you don't love me anymore. The amount is not commensurate with the risks I'm taking. For instance, take this shit hole that the tourists refer to as a paradise, with its white sand, and sun....they don't mind getting ripped off by the locals, because they think they're having a good time. Me, I'm not having a good time. I'm here to service you, but this is no-man's land, and problematic in more ways than I care to cover at this point. I'm not interested in spending the next decade or two, inside a Boka Ami prison. Have you ever seen the wretches that come out of there, and not many do. Do you get my drift, Mr. Monday?"

"You knew what the risks were when you agreed long ago. Only two things ever change….the targets, and their location. The danger is always there….the risk of getting caught is always there….the chance of never getting back in one piece is always there. This is just another mission, like the others….nothing more."

Monday smiled. "You've seen the world… places people only dream of. Take Boka Ami, a tropical paradise, where you'll spend some time on the dole, enjoying what this shit hole has to offer," and then he laughed. "You're well paid. You know that I have never held back….that I always believed that the money should be commensurate with the risks, and the risks are ample….ample for both of us. We live lifestyles that most people can't even imagine....the houses, cars, the bespoken suits, the women, the bank accounts….do you want me to go on?"

When Hayek didn't answer, Monday continued. "You like the Bennies….all those benefits that money buys, just like I do. When we're enjoying them, the risks are distant memories….aren't they, my Lebbo friend? (Slang for Lebanese – considered to be a lesser class of Arab)."

"Eire fik, (Fuck you - Lebanese) my English Limey, who teaches little shits with short skirts about Chinese philosophy and languages they'll never master. Sure, you pay me well, but I feel under-compensated."

"Janco indicated that we'll be well compensated for this mission. His exact words were, "The remuneration for the successful conclusion of this assignment will be ample….in fact double the usual amount."

"You remembered his exact words?"

"When it comes to money, I always remember what's stated. While Janco didn't specifically mention you by name, he did mention you during our briefing. You're included. We all get paid by him, but, okay, let's assume that for some inexplicable reason, Janco doesn't include you. Then I'll make sure that you're taken care of from anything I get beyond the normal....say thirty-five percent. Will that work?"

"Thirty-five percent of what?"

"I don't know how much more, but thirty-five percent of something, is better than one-hundred percent of nothing."

Hayek just stared back.

Monday waited, and then began again. "You know me, Hayek. I've never given you cause to doubt me. I'll speak to Janco when this is over....in fact we both can speak to him, and we'll get the matter resolved. If it isn't resolved to your satisfaction, I'll come across with the thirty-five percent....on my word, and you've never had cause to doubt me."

Hayek shook his head. "Okay, now let's put the matter behind us. What do you need from me?"

Monday removed a folded paper from his shirt pocket and handed it to Hayek.

Hayek took a moment to scan the paper. "These should be obtainable locally. I don't think I'll have a problem. If I do, you'll be the first to know."

Monday, smiled. "But of course I will. I need that stuff pronto. What I have to do requires some prep time, so the faster you come up with those items, the sooner I can begin work, and the sooner we can all get out of here. By the way we need, as always, an alternative exit route. Do you have one established?"

"Working on several. I'll let you know before the operation begins."

It wasn't what Monday wanted to hear, but he let the matter slide. "Okay, if we're done here, I'll check in with my other partner."

Hayek stood up, and extended his hand. "You know how it is Monday. It's strictly business, nothing personal. You understand that, don't you?"

Monday nodded, and forced a smile. "Sure I do. Now get me that stuff. Don't contact me until you have it, and remember I need it like yesterday."

"Consider it done."

Robert Monday watched Hayek as he walked through the restaurant door, and then disappeared inside. He waited for several additional minutes while slowly scanning his surroundings, then he followed Hayek's route inside

*

Monday stared out of his hotel window, and toward the tropical rainforest that stretched across the distant horizon. He tried to gauge the distance from the edge of Paramarmico to the beginning of the jungle. His thoughts were interrupted by the ringing of the telephone. He picked up on the fourth ring and answered, yes.

"This is Nancy Gault." She paused for a moment as she contemplated whether to bring up what she saw. Deciding why not, she formulated her initial probe by saying, "I thought we could have lunch together, but I couldn't reach you."

"I had a meeting. I'll bring you up to date if you come over."

"Okay....give me a minute or two," and then the connection was terminated before Monday had a chance to change what he said.

When the knock sounded on his door, Monday opened it slowly and held out the note. As Nancy took the paper from him, she watched as he made a "stay quiet" gesture with his index finger pressed against his lips.

Nancy read the note, then looked back at Monday who shook his head in the affirmative, and then said, "Come in, or if you prefer, stay here and I'll join you in a second."

"I'll wait here."

Six minutes later Monday and Nancy Gault were seated in the same two rattan chairs in the garden.

"How do you know?"

"Hayek mentioned it during our initial contact."

Nancy was relieved that Monday opened up so quickly. It alleviated some of her gnawing doubts.

"You have to figure it's the norm in a place like this. Everyone in power is paranoid that someone is out to get them – locals or foreigners, or both. It goes with the territory. Being a dictator is hard work….dangerous too," and then Monday laughed.

Nancy smiled back…."I guess my room is bugged too."

"Most likely, and the room phones as well. I was surprised that Hayek used it to communicate with me, but then rethinking it, it was his way of warning me not to say anything that would cause the listening party to become suspicious. Just play it natural…. keep in mind what's out there, and exercise caution when we're together in any room."

"Noted. Anything interesting discussed?"

Monday thought about the dominant part of the conversation with Hayek and whether he should bring her into it. He decided in the affirmative based on his policy of ensuring that his partner was included in every facet of what was happening. If, or when things went haywire, his partner had the same information and facts he had to react with.

"Could be a problem although I don't anticipate one. It's about money. Hayek thinks he's worth more, and that he's under compensated."

"Doesn't everyone?"

Monday smiled. “Yes, most do.”

“Does that present a problem?”

“It could, but I think I’ve got it under control. I offered him thirty-five percent of whatever Janco pays me, above the normal for this mission.”

“Is he okay with that?”

“Wouldn’t you be….that is unless you’re offering an additional thirty-five percent from your share.”

“No, I wasn’t offering, but if you think it’s necessary….” and Nancy let the words trail off.

“I think it’s okay.”

“One more thing to worry about.”

“I’m not a worrier Nancy, and you shouldn’t be either. It’s just business....one party thinks he’s worth more than he is. Nothing is going to be compromised. Hayek knows what a sweet business arrangement he has.”

“Business is it? It’s a Hell of a lot more than business.”

“Just a tad more,” and then Monday smiled.

“Okay Monday, I’m tabling this discussion for a while. I’ll expect you’ll keep tabs on Hayek.”

“We’ll both keep tabs on Hayek. You’ll meet him shortly.”

Nancy glanced at her watch. "We don't have much time. In case you don't know it.....there is a cocktail reception tonight at the hotel's roof garden at 6 p.m. I need some time to make pretty. Knock on my door about a quarter of, and we'll go up together. You can finish anything you didn't cover later....okay?"

*

Rafi Derma smiled as he approached Nancy Gault. He bowed slightly and took her hand, acknowledging Monday with a slight nod.

"If you'll follow me Miss Gault, I'll introduce you to President Muguanasi and his wife."

The man standing near the piano, and surrounded by several well attired men and women, was an imposing figure. He was over six feet tall, with a contoured body, accented by the military uniform he wore.

The woman to his left, and obviously his wife, was exceptionally attractive. Her classic facial features defined her ancestry as Eastern or Western Europe.

"Excellency, may I introduce Miss Nancy Gault."

Derma moved slightly to his rear, and into Robert Monday. Slightly perturbed, Derma quickly recovered without looking back.

Nancy extended her hand and smiled.

"It is a sincere pleasure to meet you Miss Gault. This is my wife, Jeni."

Nancy turned, and again extended her hand. "It is a pleasure to meet you both."

"The pleasure is ours Miss Gault." Muguanasi turned toward several uniformed men, several business types, and their accompanying women, and made the introductions. At first Nancy tried to remember the names using the first initial as a reference point, but quickly let what few she had mastered, fade.

"Would you care for a cocktail, Miss Gault?"

"Very definitely, but since I plan to play several songs for you tonight, I don't want to reach the point where I'm playing one song and thinking about another. Perhaps afterwards."

"I understand, so may I suggest you play something now, and then once that's over you can enjoy the party without reservation….perhaps play later as well. I'm sure by that time it won't matter what you play for our guests," and then Muguanasi laughed."

"Perfect."

Muguanasi tapped his finger nails several times against the crystal glass he was holding. The room became quiet, and he pointed to Nancy.

"Ladies and Gentlemen, this is our honored guest, Miss Nancy Gault, who will be giving the concert in two days. She says that she cannot begin to participate in our festivities tonight, until she has played for us….sort of a preview. Since we want our honored guest to begin enjoying herself, I've asked her to play for us now, rather than later."

The room broke out in applause. Nancy smiled and seated herself at the piano. She looked at the faces of those who had moved closer, and said to no one in particular, "I'd like to start with a Chopin favorite of mine….opus 28, no.7 Prelude."

Nancy pressed down on the ivory keys as she closed her eyes and moved her mind into the music. It was slow and beautiful, and when she finished, she thought Chopin himself would be pleased with her.

The room erupted into thunderous applause and shouts for more. Muguanasi leaned over and whispered that he never heard such beautiful music before, and could she please play another Chopin composition.

"But of course."

She looked over at Monday who was still standing behind Rafi Derma, and nodded. Then she looked at the crowd who had moved even closer, and said, "His Excellency has asked for another Chopin. It's one I'll play at the concert….I hope you'll enjoy it. "

Then Nancy began playing, perhaps Chopin's most famous, and recognizable composition, his Heroic Polonaise, opus 53.

When she finished the applause went on for several minutes before Muguanasi motioned to the crowd. Before he could say anything, Nancy announced that she would like to play one more song, one of her favorite, non-Chopin songs. The applause started again.

The room hushed as she began, and the music of "What a Wonderful World," filled the room. She played it first in a Latin style, then played it again in a more contemporary rendition. As she neared the end, Jeni Muguanasi moved beside the piano and asked, "Can you start from the top in the key of "C," I'd like to sing along."

Nancy complied, wondering what to expect, and was pleasantly surprised as the melodic voice of Jeni Muguanasi captivated the room.

"I see trees of green, red roses too
I see them bloom, for me and you,
And I say to myself, what a wonderful world.

I see skies of blue, and clouds of white,
The bright blessed day, and the dark of night,
And I think to myself, what a wonderful world.

The colors of the rainbow, so pretty in the sky,
And also the faces of the people going by,
I see friends shaking hands sayin' "How do you do?"
They're really sayin' "I love you."

I hear babies cryin' I watch them grow.
They'll learn much more, than I'll ever know,
And I think to myself, what a wonderful world."

When Jeni Muguanasi finished, Nancy stood up and hugged her. The shouts and applause continued as they waved and smiled, each pointing to the other.

Nancy whispered, "That was truly amazing. I've never heard it sung better, and I mean that."

Jeni Muguanasi smiled back. "And I've never heard it played better. You are truly a wonderful musician, and I can't wait until the concert. Let's have a drink, shall we, and get this party started."

Chapter 8

Nancy slouched in her chair as she looked over at Monday. “Now that’s what I call a party. I never thought they could drink like that.”

Monday laughed. “When it’s free, people seem to find the will.”

“Guess so….I was apprehensive when Muguanasi’s wife asked to sing, but I didn’t have a choice, did I? It didn’t really matter whether she was a songbird, or came across like Satchmo…sing she would.”

When Nancy saw the quizzical look on Monday’s face, she followed up with, “Louis Armstrong”…. they called him Satchmo, or Pops. Certainly, even you English types have heard of Louis Armstrong.”

“But of course….even us Neanderthal types from that rainy island called England, have heard of him. It’s the nick-names, and clichés which you Colonials use so frequently, that threw me for a moment.”

After a momentary pause, Monday continued. “That little happening between you and Muguanasi’s wife, cemented things for us. You’re to be congratulated on how you interacted with her afterwards….simply bloody marvelous, as we Limeys like to say.”

Nancy smiled, and moved her head from side to side in a girlish way.

They turned, simultaneously, when they heard the footsteps.

"Hayek."

The tall man with the olive complexion smiled.

"The hotel operator told me you were here in the garden," and before Monday could make the introduction, Hayek said "You must be Miss Nancy Gault, the pianist."

Nancy nodded as Hayek sat down. He placed the medium size satchel next to the right leg of his chair.

"May I have a cup of coffee?"

"Sure....although it's been sitting for awhile." Monday glanced at his watch. Eight-thirty already. Seems like we've been here for a while."

"We have....we haven't been to bed yet. Why don't you two have a cup of coffee? I need to leave. Rafi Derma is picking me up at nine and driving me to the concert hall. I'll practice there for a few hours and then come back here."

Nancy looked over at Hayek. "Nice to meet you," and then she turned and walked away.

"I have what you need....everything on the list, and before you ask, yes, the hotplate too. I needed to rewire it and depending on how long you're going to keep it on, will depend how long it works."

"Like that–huh?"

Hayek nodded yes.

"Not a bad looking woman, my dear Monday, and obviously talented being a pianist and all."

"Too early in the morning to think about that stuff....besides I need to get to work, and I'm beat....not much sleep since Miami, and well, you know how it goes."

"Yes, been there myself."

"Let's get together tonight....go over a few things."

"Will the woman be there?"

"Yes. Let's make it for six....here, for a drink and then maybe dinner, depending on how far I get with what I need to do."

"Okay....here at six....see you later, and by the way, the coffee is cold."

Hayek waived without turning around.

Monday walked into the restaurant, and motioned the waiter over. "Charge the coffee to my room, and add twenty percent for yourself. If you're on duty here tonight, I need a reservation for three....out there," and Monday pointed back toward the garden. "Drinks and dinner there....same chairs....same table....okay?"

The waiter nodded. “Understood, Mr. Monday.”

*

Robert Monday sat in a darkened corner of the hotel lobby, the satchel resting on his legs, As he pictured his hotel room, his mind-screen silhouetted the phone on the table between the twin beds. If the phone was tapped, then maybe the room had cameras as well. Then again, that might be too sophisticated for this regime, and why would his room have cameras? After all, his role-play was as a manager of a concert pianist, and as far as he could surmise, he projected nothing more. Then the element of doubt started to creep into his psyche, and he re-thought the conversation with Hayek.

Monday decided to err on the side of caution….a floor to ceiling search, and then some. Okay Professor….you’ve been there before….slow and methodical.

Monday let his eyes move slowly around the lobby before he pushed up and walked toward the elevator bank.

When the chime sounded and the door opened, Monday instinctively looked up at the floor signal light, then stepped out. Hall might be monitored too. Play it natural….no quick eye movements….no looking around.

After the key card was inserted, the green light flashed twice. Monday opened the door and went inside. He walked directly to the bathroom, placed the satchel in the sink, and after twenty or so seconds, flushed the toilet for effect.

Monday turned on the TV, and pushed on the volume button until the sound was louder than normal. Then he moved methodically around the room, starting clockwise, and then reversing direction. Every item of room furniture, including the lights, air conditioner and mirrors were checked. Concluding that while the room may be bugged for sound, there was no camera overlap.

He went back to the bathroom, and carefully placed the items from the satchel on a cloth towel.

Monday plugged the hotplate into the wall receptacle, and turned the knob to medium. He poured two cups of tap water into a metal container, and then placed the container on the burner. When the water started to boil, he unscrewed the bottom of his shaving cream can and with a spoon he borrowed from the restaurant, maneuvered some of the encased gelatin into the boiling water. He stirred the contents thoroughly and then removed the metal container allowing the mixture to cool.

After testing the water with his finger tip, Monday added three ounces of cooking oil from Nancy's perfume atomizer, and stirred until a thin layer of solids began to form near the top of the container. Using the spoon, Monday removed the solids, and placed them in a smaller cup. Then he walked to the mini-bar refrigerator located below the TV and placed the cup inside.

As Monday was straightening back up, he noticed the images of Nancy on the TV screen, scenes of their arrival at Paramarmico International Airport. His concentration shifted when the tapping sound grew louder.

Standing several steps away from the door, Monday called out, “Yes.”

“It’s Nancy.”

Monday opened the door and shook his head. “Over so soon….the practice?”

“It’s not so soon. It’s been three and a half hours since I’ve seen you. It’s time for lunch, interested?”

Monday moved his index finger to his lips as he leaned toward her. Then he whispered, “I’m presently cooking some soup, and I can’t leave until it’s finished.”

In just above an audible tone, Nancy said, “Soup….what are you talking about?”

Monday motioned, with his hand, toward the bathroom.

After he shut the bathroom door, he again moved his index finger to his lips, and then pointed toward the floor. He tilted his head and whispered, “Stay here….I’ll be back in a moment.

Monday opened the door of the small refrigerator, and removed the cup, then retraced his steps back to the bathroom. He placed the cup on the rim of the sink, and held it there with one hand. "Soup.....partially cooked."

Nancy moved her head up and down. "Looks like I'm lunching alone."

Monday moved his head up and down, and then spoke in his normal tone. "I've made a reservation for 6 p.m. tonight....usual table in the garden area. See you then."

That was Nancy's signal to depart. She knew what he was doing, and that was stressful enough without her occupying either his space, or time now.

"See you at six. If you get there a little earlier, I'll fill you in on my day," and then Monday heard the room door close.

*

Carefully, Monday mixed in some petroleum jelly, cooking oil, silly putty, and cornstarch, until the contents of the bowl had the consistency of ice cream.

Knowing that the mixture was highly unstable at this point, Monday continued to stir with a deliberate slowness. After several minutes, he took off the hydrometer from his wrist and tested the mixture. He breathed a sigh of relief when the reading indicated seventeen.

His eyes quickly cascaded over the contents from the satchel. Finally realizing that he overlooked the matches, he turned the hotplate onto high, then lit several small candles, and placed them in a glass.

As he waited for the candles to melt, Monday formed three, wafer thin, rectangular shapes from the cooled mixture. He continued to form each of the compounds, until they had a thickness of approximately one-eighth of an inch. Using the spoon, Monday removed the melted wax, and gently spread it over the C-4. The wax would seal the compound from moisture that was excessive in a climate such as Boka Ami.

Monday removed one of two cell-phones from his pocket, and placed it on the sink. With the back off, he molded the three forms so that they overlapped forming a tiered formation. This would cause a cascading detonation effect that would be devastating to anyone in close proximity.

Two wires running from the blasting cap which was inserted in the C-4, were connected to the phone battery, and then the vibrator. The phone battery would act as the power source and supply the electricity to the vibrator, which in turn would trigger the detonation.

Both cell-phones were calibrated to a GSM (Global System for Mobile) frequency of 335 Megahertz. Once the C-4's phone number was dialed, the electromagnetic wave would initiate the sequences.

After Monday secured the phone's back, he looked down at his hands, and then smiled. Not a movement….not a tremor. Then he looked at his reflection in the mirror and smiled.

*

He rose as Nancy Gault approached the table.

"Hi there."

"Hi, yourself. Did you manage to get any sleep?"

"A little….after I finished the soup."

Nancy just stared, her unstated question bouncing around his head. Monday answered, "Yes, it's finished."

"How did you know I was thinking about that?"

"I'm a Professor with extrasensory perception."

"Of course you are," and they both laughed.

The voice asked, "What am I missing?"

Nancy and Monday turned toward Hayek.

"Well, what am I missing?"

"Nothing much....Monday here was telling me about his extrasensory perception abilities."

Hayek smiled. "They are extraordinary, aren't they?"

"By any measure," and they all laughed.

"Sit down Hayek, we're about to order a drink."

After the waiter served the drinks, and disappeared, Nancy began the conversation.

"Before we hear about your day," and she looked over at Monday, "Let me tell you about mine."

"The concert hall is smaller than those in the states." Nancy quickly added, "Or the UK. There are two main entrance/exit doors at the front of the theater. There's a small balcony situated above, and slightly to the rear of the orchestra section. The stage, where the piano is located, is small....it doesn't seem to inhibit movement on or off. There are two stairwells on either side of the stage, and two exit doors that lead to an alley, or more like a half street, which runs the length of the building at the back. From what Rafi Derma tells me, when I inquired about security, is that all exit routes from the theater....meaning the adjacent streets, will have roving patrols. Several armored vehicles will be stationed at major intersections. All streets/roads leading away from the theater area will have manned checkpoints. Seems like they're paranoid about something happening."

Nancy looked at Hayek, and maintained her gaze for longer than necessary, before looking back at Monday.

"I used the pillow, the duplicate, and in fact made mention of my never performing without it to Derma, and the woman, Bulan. The acoustics are fair-to-middling....not good, not bad, but this isn't Carnegie Hall or Prince Albert Hall....is it?"

Monday nodded, then asked, "How did the practice go?"

"Fine....just fine. I decided to change my repertoire a bit....stay with the Chopin songs I particularly like. Makes it easier to concentrate on what I must do, considering what I'm sitting on." Nancy smiled, and both men smiled back.

"After the first few minutes I was acclimated to the piano....surprisingly a 1984 Baldwin SD10, Concert Grand. In this tropical paradise, there's just one surprise after another." Nancy took a sip of her drink, then lowered her hand part way as if contemplating the movement. She placed the drink on the table, and then looked at Monday. "I've pictured the after-action. It's going to be one hell of a confusing state, and once the pandemonium sets in, getting out isn't going to be easy. I can maneuver myself to either end of the stage after Fu seats himself, and get out one of the doors, but you're going to be caught in the mêlée."

Monday just kept staring, and then he spoke. "Yeah....it's going to be hairy, as you Colonials say, but manageable. The way I see it playing out...." and then Monday paused again.

Gault and Hayek remained silent, each knowing that Monday was re-thinking the sequences of anticipated events. When he spoke again, his voice was modulated just above a whisper, drawing them into him.

"During your concert, I'm standing at the rear....at back of the theatre. Once you conclude your program, and once Min Qua Fu is sitting at the piano, I'll signal Hayek, who will leave the diversionary vehicle as close to the theater as feasible. Once Hayek receives the phone signal, he triggers the relay, and sets off the car bomb."

"Nancy exits one of the two doors into the alley. I'll try to get out through one of the two front entrance ways…. get caught up with the crowd surging in that direction….makes it easier to maneuver out, and away from the security forces, or whatever is trying to get into the theater. Hayek will have a car waiting at the American Embassy located at 156 Lindonstraat. Whether we use the car, or go inside the Embassy, and wait it out, will be determined then....if there is a then."

Reaching into his shirt pocket, Monday removed a small piece of paper. As he opened the paper, Monday hunched over the table, using his body mass to block what he was doing. He placed his finger on a circle with the number one in the center. "This is where we are, and here is where we need to be after the concert." Monday moved his finger to another circle with a two at the center. "This is the Embassy…Lindonstraat…..three long New York type blocks from the theater. Study the paper Nancy….memorize the route I've traced in red, and an alternative one, in green.

"Hayek will be here waiting….right Hayek?"

Hayek acknowledged with a slight nod.

Monday looked over at Nancy Gault. "As I've stated before, once we're on location – the

Embassy, we decide whether to go inside, or use Hayek. I've reconsidered what I mentioned earlier. Once you're outside the theater, you don't wait to hook up with me. Instead, you go straight to the Embassy. If I don't get there....to the Embassy timely, then you go inside. Make sure you carry your passport the night of the concert, understood?"

Nancy shook her head to confirm.

"The two cars Hayek....the usual way?"

Hayek nodded. Nancy didn't need to ask about the usual way. She knew the vehicles would be stolen.

Gault studied the paper, and then pushed it back toward Monday.

They locked eyes with each other, confirming that both understood what had transpired so far. Then Monday motioned to the satchel near his right foot, and looked back at Hayek. "It's the stuff you supplied me with, or what's left of it. Make sure you get rid of it."

Hayek nodded, then leaned down and moved the bag in-between his legs.

"I'll visit the theater tomorrow during your practice session. I want to see everything for myself. If we have to, we can modify whatever we've covered here over dinner tomorrow night. If there's nothing else," and Monday looked at each of them, "then we can have another drink and eat."

Chapter 9

Nancy Gault continued playing with her left hand as she acknowledged Monday with a wave of the other.

After saying hello to Rafi Derma, Monday took a seat near the rear of the theater. His eyes scanned the exit routes, as his mind pictured the crowded theater and the ensuing pandemonium after the detonation.

After ten or so minutes, Monday started walking toward the stage, but veered off toward Rafi Derma. "The acoustics are not very clear," and then he pointed back toward the rear of the theater. "I want to check the connection to the piano's microphones."

Derma moved his head in a way conveying he understood, then moved his hand back and forth until several men dressed in overalls and standing to the left of the stage, looked his way.

As Monday made his way onto the stage, the two men moved in his direction. He knew Derma was watching his movements as he pointed toward the microphones, amplifiers and speakers, then looked toward Nancy briefly.

"It seems to be a loose connection….difficult to hear back there," and then Monday turned toward the rear, and pointed. When the two men didn't react, Monday looked over at Derma, raised his arms, palms up, in a gesture meaning they didn't understand.

When Derma reached him, Monday pointed to the microphones and equipment again. "There's probably a loose connection between the microphone, the amplifiers or the speakers. As I mentioned, it's not clear at the rear."

Derma nodded, then spoke rapidly to the two men. They shook their heads and started checking the wiring.

As they worked, Derma looked back at Monday. "These are electromagnetic induction microphones, and like the ones used in your country, they produce an electrical signal from air pressure variations. Those microphones are connected to the state of the artist amplifiers and speakers. I'm surprised that you are not hearing what Miss Gault was playing, but it is better to have the problem now rather than a problem or more, during the concert. We will, of course, check everything for its workability."

Monday smiled, more at the man's use of English, than to convey he understood. As far as he was concerned, the sound was perfectly okay in the rear.

"While they're checking, do you want to get some fresh air?"

Nancy nodded, and as they both walked off the right side of the stage, Derma called out, "Don't be too long....we'll find the problem quickly so you don't lose more of your practice timing."

"Nancy whispered, "It's hard not to break out in laughter, isn't it?"

“Comic relief when we least expect it,” and he smiled.

Monday pushed open the door and braced it with his shoulder until Nancy was standing outside. A quick scan of the street confirmed what she had stated the night before.

Monday looked back before he spoke, to make sure that Derma hadn’t followed.

“This is your way out.”

Nancy moved her head down twice. “Yes, seems so. I’ll use the stairwell, and then brace myself against the wall until I hear the detonation. I’ll wait about five seconds, and then I’m through the door.”

“Sounds right. Just make sure you’re running toward the Embassy. The quicker you get there, the better.”

“In high heels?” and then their conversation was interrupted by Derma’s voice.

Monday called back, “Thank you Mr. Minister, we’ll be back in a moment.”

“I thought you women were born in high heels, so what’s the problem?”

“Yeah sure….we better get back.”

*

Nancy leaned against the piano as Derma spoke with Monday.

"If you say that nothing is wrong Mr. Minister, then that's a relief. Maybe it was me," and Monday smiled.

"Well....if you gentlemen are finished, I need to get back to that," and Nancy pointed to the piano. "Tomorrow is show-time."

"Goodbye Mr. Minister," then Monday looked at Nancy, who was now seated at the piano. "See you later. Call my room when you get back."

Nancy moved her head slightly as she shifted her position on the cushion. Moments later her fingers moved across the keyboard, and the opening notes of Chopin's "Marche Funebre," filled the theater. The melody followed Robert Monday as he walked, but he was oblivious, his mind-screen replayed the sequences of events that would take place in less than twenty-four hours.

*

Monday's eyes slowly scanned, and then re-scanned the rectangular shaped C-4, the blasting cap, and then the wires connecting the battery to the vibrator. Satisfied, he re-attached the back, and then carefully placed the cell phone inside the foam cushion. Using the nails on his index finger and thumb, Monday zipped closed the small side opening, and then brushed the fringes back into place.

As he stared down at the cushion, his mind again played out the anticipated sequences of events, this time in colorful, slow-motion. Feeling the increasing pressure at his temples, Monday sought to dispel the images as they floated in front of his eyes. In moments, the images and color dissipated into a grey nothingness. As Monday slowly returned to normal, he felt the perspiration beading on his face, and the dampness under his armpits.

He wondered, why is it always like this? I'm supposed to be the consummate professional. Maybe that's the reason….we're always anticipating. That's why we experience these adrenaline rushes at the beginning, the lows after it's over, and in between, where there's just the numbness.

He placed the cushion on the bed, and the cell phone he would use as the trigger on top. Then he walked to the bathroom, stopping so that he was framed in the doorway. His eyes moved methodically….first to the sink, then the floor, and finally, the bathtub. It looked clean, but he wondered. He shrugged his shoulders and thought, it's because I know what's been done here. They don't. I'm just anticipating, but it's clean....I know it's clean. Yet as he continued to stare, he then wondered.

Uncharacteristically, he looked down at his hands, and was relieved when he saw his fingers and thumbs, steady….without any movement. He stayed that way, prolonging the exercise, just to make sure they didn't begin to shake.

Monday let his hands drop, and then he turned and walked to the bed. He sat down next to the cushion, and after a few moments, leaned backwards until his head rested on the bed pillow. "It's just another mission....just another mission." The words were just above audible, as the heaviness behind his eyes, forced his eye-lids closed.

Monday drifted into a sleep-mode, called hypnagogia, where he oscillated between being fully awake, and sleep. After several minutes, his body began experiencing a myoclonic twitch, where the muscles move suddenly, and without any rhythm, or pattern.

He was jolted awake by a ringing sound, which at first, seemed distant, and then excessive.

As his mind began clearing, he semi-rolled his body across the bed. When he extended his arm toward the phone, his lower body shifted, and his feet knocked the pillow and cell-phone off. He let out a string of curses, then placed the receiver against his ear.

"Was that for me?"

"What," was all Monday could say, and then as he quickly reprocessed it all, and said, "Sorry Nancy....nothing was directed toward you. I knocked over something when I reached for the phone....sorry."

"I'm back from practice. It's a little early for dinner, but do you want to meet to go over anything?"

"Sure....give me about five minutes, and I'll come to you."

"I'll need a few more minutes than five. Let's meet in a half-hour...okay?"

"That'll work. I'll knock on your door."

Monday kept the receiver to his ear after the click that indicated Gault had hung-up. He closed his eyes, and remained motionless, and then he heard it....a faint, high pitched humming of a probable phone tap.

*

As Nancy watched the three poolside couples from her bedroom window, she tried to guess their nationality. Their animated conversation, and semi-loud voices said Italy, but before she could decide, the knocking sound distracted her.

"Coming."

When she opened the door, Monday handed her a small piece of paper, and then pointed to the pillow under his left arm.

Her eyes scanned the paper quickly, and then she turned and walked back to the small living room area. She picked up the duplicate pillow and went back to where Monday was standing. Once the pillows were exchanged, Monday said, "See you downstairs in a few minutes."

Nancy nodded, and then parroted his words, "See you downstairs in a few minutes."

*

"How did the practice go?"

"Good….in fact better than good. I was one with the music, and that's the way I like it. Some TV types were there, but they were respectful when I was playing. All in all, like I said, it was good."

"Then you're ready for tomorrow night?"

"Not exactly….that pillow….upstairs….kind of unnerving. It sent chills through my body when I realized I was holding a bomb."

Then after several moments of silence, Nancy started to laugh.

"What's so funny?"

"I was thinking that I'll be sitting on a bomb, and how many people get to do that while they're giving a concert for a dictator in a tropical paradise?" And then she giggled in a girlish way.

Monday joined in, and soon they were caught up in the moment.

"Crazy isn't it, Mr. Monday?"

"It's the occupational hazards we face in our chosen profession. One day, when things are back to normal, you'll have to tell me how you became part of all this."

"Sure, why not? But you'll tell me your story as well."

"Deal," then Monday extended his hand.

She took his hand, and then locked eyes with him. "It's going to be alright, isn't it Robert?"

He stared back, trying to read something that wasn't apparent, but sensing that something wasn't a hundred percent as it should be.

Monday held her hand as he spoke. "There will be that time Nancy, when all of this is a distant memory. But right now, it's a reality. We're paid to take chances. As professionals, we're not impetuous. We think through our decisions, and reckon the consequences, both positive and negative. I've checked, and rechecked what's inside that pillow. It's functional, but not operable until I trigger it. You'll be off-stage when that happens. If I see that you're in the slightest danger, we abort the mission."

Nancy pulled her hand away from his and looked down. "I hope I can concentrate tomorrow on the music instead of thinking about"….and her voice became a murmur.

"You'll be able to do what you have to do. Nothing will trigger that…." and Monday paused as he searched for a word. He finally said, "phone."…. "only I can do that. I've set the megahertz at a frequency that isn't used here....meaning the frequency band used by tourists from the US, Europe or other South American countries, even Africa, won't accidentally trigger the phone."

Monday paused again, then said, "Look at me Nancy....look at me."

When their eyes met, he continued. "I would never place you in danger. Of course, there's always an element of uncertainty....the unexpected, when something can go wrong, but that's not going to happen in this case. We'll complete the mission, and then we're out of here....right?"

"I trust you Robert. I'm nervous, but I'll be okay when the time comes.....pre action jitters combined with too much adrenaline."

"Then I suggest we have a drink to calm ourselves"

"Okay, but my limit is one. I have a concert to play tomorrow, and some fireworks to watch."

Monday smiled, and motioned to the waiter.

Chapter 10

Nancy stood behind the black velvet curtain, peering out toward the audience. She saw Robert Monday seated, as he had been during several of her practices, in an aisle seat in the last row of the theater.

Then her eyes moved to the orchestra section where President Muguanasi and his wife were seated, along with members of the diplomatic and business communities.

The theater was filled to capacity, with many locals standing in a roped off area at the theater's rear.

She breathed deeply, when she looked at the piano bench. As she stood transfixed, an image of a fireball began forming behind her eyes. Nancy suddenly felt cold, and then, as if coming from some distant place, she heard her name, and then it was repeated several more times, followed by applause. Ignoring the chill that riveted her body, she forced herself to take the first of several steps away from the curtain. As she moved toward the piano, the image of the fireball dissipated.

Minister Rafi Derma held a microphone with one hand, as he reached out with the other. When they joined hands, they faced the audience and Derma began speaking.

"President and Lady Muguanasi, Honored Guests, Ladies and Gentlemen, tonight, one of the world's most celebrated concert pianists will honor us with a repertoire of beautiful Chopin music. You have seen her being interviewed on television, and I know you are eagerly awaiting with anticipation her performance tonight."

As she listened to Derma, Nancy thought, this is just what I need to relax me….nothing like Derma's English to bring on a smile or a laugh

"There is a paper program that you can refer to, and following along as Miss Nancy Gault, pianist extraordinary, is performing for us tonight."

Nancy laughed, and smiled at Derma, and then shook her head ever so slightly, rethinking the words he used in the introduction. She bowed to the audience, and then seated herself on the cushion. For a fleeting moment she thought about the bomb, and then her mind filled with the musical notes of her opening piece, Chopin's opus 28, no 7 (Prelude).

As she played, Nancy and the piano seemed to fuse into one entity. Her fingers danced across the ivory keys, the music beautiful, and mesmerizing. She moved effortlessly into other Chopin selections, and ended the concert with her favorite piece, Chopin's Polonaise, opus 53 – Heroic.

When she finished, the theater erupted into ecstatic applause that continued for five full minutes. Shouts of "one more" filled the theater, and finally, Nancy acquiesced.

Smiling and waving at the audience, Nancy took the microphone from Derma, who had re-appeared on stage and was standing near the piano.

"Your enthusiastic applause is what every pianist hopes for. I am honored to have been given this privilege to play for you tonight. Since you have been such an appreciative audience, I would like to play one more selection, and this won't take long." Nancy smiled and then continued. "It's Chopin's Waltz, number 6 in D flat major, opus number 64 – the Minute Waltz."

At the conclusion of the encore, the audience rose in unison as thunderous applause cascaded throughout the theater. Rafi Derma, again, came on stage, and motioned to Nancy, and then to the audience, and then back again at Nancy. Several young girls approached carrying bouquets of flowers, as the applause continued unabated.

Nancy held up her hand repeatedly, trying to quiet the audience, but to no avail. Finally, she took hold of Derma's microphone, and speaking slightly above her normal voice, said, "I have a surprise for you….a surprise that I think you will enjoy."

Anticipating that they would get to hear another Chopin classic, the applause became intermittent, and then stopped.

"We have a very distinguished gentleman with us this evening, who is also a classic pianist. We, who live in this rarified world of classic music, know each other, either through personal association, or by reputation. Music knows no bounds. It is part of a country's heritage, and culture, and music is what transcends everything that separates us, and in the end, binds us together. With your applause, let us ask Mr. Min Qua Fu from the Chinese Delegation, to join me on stage."

As the applause started, a tall Chinese man sitting in the seventh row rose slightly, and waved his hand in a negative way. Seeing the hesitation, Nancy spoke into the microphone again.

"Please Mr. Fu," and using her hand, motioned toward the now seated man. When he still hesitated, she turned and faced the audience. "You do want to hear Mr. Fu play don't you?"

The sustained applause, and shouts continued until Mr. Min Qua Fu began edging his way to the center aisle. Nancy met Fu once he reached the stage, and escorted him to a place in front of the piano before turning again toward the audience.

"I know of several Classical Chinese pieces that perhaps our guest would agree to play. These are "Wild Geese Landing on Sandy Beach," and a personal favorite of mine, "Ambush from All Sides."

Nancy lowered the microphone as she faced Fu. "I know this was a surprise, but I have heard about you, and if you'll excuse the liberty I've taken, would you kindly play, "Ambush from all Sides?"

Nancy held the smile until Fu nodded yes, and whispered "not much choice at this point, correct?"

"Sometimes we are motivated by unknown forces that propel us to a place where we must be. Perhaps tonight is one such place for you and me."

"I will have to return the honor someday."

She let the words resonate in her mind as she turned to the audience and said, "Ladies and Gentlemen, Mr. Fu will honor us by playing the Chinese Classic, "Ambush from all Sides."

The applause continued as Nancy moved off stage. When she looked back, she saw Fu removing the pillow, and placing it underneath the piano bench.

As she stood frozen in place, watching the seated figure, her breathing became erratic, and her mind-screen cluttered with negativity.

When she heard the first resounding notes of "Ambush from all Sides," Nancy's mind slowly returned to the moment. She realized that she couldn't change what Fu did, and then became acutely aware that Monday was about to set the sequence of events in motion.

She turned quickly, pushed on the exit door, and was in the street moments later. A guard with an automatic rifle slung diagonally across his chest, stood off to her right. Unsure whether he understood English, Nancy used a series of hand motions to augment her brief conversation. She moved her fingers like she was playing the piano, and then pointed back at herself. She moved her hands in a circle, and then touched her nostrils, trying to convey she was getting some air.

It didn't seem to be working, as the guard motioned with his hands to return the way she came.

She nodded, and as she turned, she heard the muted detonation inside the theater. This was followed, almost simultaneously, by a series of loud explosions that tore gaping holes in the building exterior. Confused and somewhat dazed, Nancy remained transfixed just as the shock waves struck, propelling her off her feet, and driving her into the road surface.

She felt the numbing pain to her left elbow, as it came in contact with the street's surface. Rolling onto her side, Nancy closed her eyes, willing the torment to subside, when suddenly she felt the excruciating pain impact her left shoulder. Unable to contain, or understand, what radiated up and down her arm, she screamed until the only sound was a mixture of sobs, and guttural noises.

Unaware of the uniformed men that rushed past her, and through the now open doorway and wall breaches to the theater's interior, Nancy closed her eyes and drifted into a dark space, somewhere deep within her subconscious.

*

Monday watched as Nancy moved off stage. He cursed silently when he saw Fu remove the cushion, and place it under the bench.

When he began playing, Robert Monday started a slow, silent count. At ten, he reached into his pocket, brought out the remote phone and signaled Hayek. After another fifteen seconds he pressed the pre-dial, which activated the electrical source, triggering the detonator and initiated the explosive sequence.

Several seconds later, a series of explosions tore through the interior of the theater, trapping Monday in the ensuing pandemonium.

*

As she felt the pain subside, her mind focused on what should have happened inside the theater. She pictured the explosion from the cushion underneath the piano bench, and wondered if the Chinese had been killed. The explosion would have two phases, with the initial explosion causing most of the damage. The second phase would be a pressure shock, or small blast wave, and then she thought about Monday….is he out, or still in there? What about those secondary explosions?

Then she focused on her own situation. She knew she was hurt, but to what degree? As she shifted her body position, she felt the pain transverse her left side. Willing herself to get up, she fought through the pain until she was standing.

Despite the time of night, the fire from the theater lit up her immediate area. Debris was scattered everywhere, and then she became aware of the fleeting figures rushing past her.

And then, as if someone pushed an “on-button,” Nancy Gault became aware of the noise, the screaming that seemed to continue without end.

She closed her eyes, and then moved her right hand up and massaged her forehead. When she opened her eyes, the word, “Lindonstraat,” seemed suspended in mid-air.

The word immediately registered, and then motivated her to take the first slow, painful step. The second and third steps were equally as slow and painful as the first one, but she willed herself forward. After a few more steps, Nancy was walking at a quickened pace and then she broke into a run.

Ignoring the searing pain that vibrated up and down her left arm, she pictured the route….the route that would take her to the American Embassy three long blocks away. Ignoring everything….the confusion that surrounded her, Nancy kept running with only one objective in mind – self-preservation.

*

Ronnie Dajan, Commander of the runaway slaves known as Maroons, was positioned with a reinforced platoon of thirty plus men. They were approximately 80 meters from the theater’s rear.

Earlier, Boka Ami military, police and security personnel, guarding that area, were dispatched silently and efficiently, and replaced by Dajan’s men.

To Dajan's right, and far left, were two additional platoons of men. Each platoon had several Russian manufactured, PPG-7V2 shoulder launched missiles, capable of firing both high explosive and fragmentation warheads.

Dajan tapped the kneeling soldier's shoulder and watched as the 93mm HEAT warhead with a muzzle velocity of 115 meters per second, impacted the theater's wall. The detonation tore away pieces of concrete and reinforcing bars, leaving a large, jagged breach. This explosion was followed by several others, both at the rear, and front of the theater.

Once the missiles were released, the intermittent small arm's fire escalated from the Maroons, who were now moving in unison toward the damaged building.

Those inside, who managed to reach the exits at the front, or rear of the theater, were cut down by withering gun fire. Screams, from both the wounded, and those caught up in the frenzied kaleidoscope of horror, seemed to rise above the sound of exploding ordnances.

Monday turned quickly, climbed over the row of seats, and maneuvered himself into the small space between the rear row, and a half wall, which separated the orchestra section from the theater's lobby.

He stayed in that position until the gunfire resonating inside the theater stopped. Monday calculated it had been about twenty, maybe twenty-five minutes since he triggered the cell....it was time to move. Blotting out the screaming, and cries of the injured, which continued unabated, Monday started crawling toward the center aisle. As he advanced, his hands felt the sinew, and bone matter that covered the floor. His mind screen formulated a picture of carnage, which daylight would soon reveal in all its grotesque forms.

When his fingers touched the carpeted center aisle, Monday stopped. His eyes locked onto the torn bodies, and body parts scattered across what remained of the orchestra section. He crawled over several bodies with missing limbs, as he edged his way toward the lobby.

As his knee brushed against something, it made a dull metallic sound. Monday froze in place.

Moving his eyes slowly to the left, and then back to the right, Monday tried to detect any hostile movement. While continuing to scan his immediate area, he gingerly reached down with his right hand. Seconds later, he was on his knees and holding the Kalashnikov, AK-47 assault rifle.

He wondered how many rounds were still left in the thirty round magazine, and then moved his head slightly, hoping he wouldn't need to find out. Pushing up into a standing position, Monday waited several seconds before he stepped over the dead and dying, and toward the nearest wall breach.

*

Her lungs screamed for oxygen she couldn't provide. Finally, giving into the dictates of her body, Nancy stopped, dropped to her knees, and then crawled behind a damaged vehicle.

She slowly moved onto her right side, and briefly closed her eyes. As the rapid automatic gun fire shattered the momentary stillness, Nancy forced her eyes open. She watched, as small fires silhouetted people, as they tried to escape the theater through the numerous wall breaches, only to be cut down by unknown assailants.

Turning away, she placed her chin on the road surface, and looked to her immediate front. From her prone position, the vehicle's undercarriage gave her an unobstructed view, and she quickly zeroed in on the staggered line of advancing figures. Whether it was fear, apprehension, or a combination of the two, her body involuntarily shivered in the tropical heat.

She forced herself to move….to crawl under the vehicle. Ignoring the throbbing pain, resonating from her left side, she inched her way until she was concealed underneath.

From her vantage point, she watched as the boots and legs ran passed. Then she placed her face into the crux of her right arm, and willed everything into silence.

*

Robert Monday stopped in place, realizing that he couldn't exit the theater. The gunfire outside had escalated, which meant a firefight was in progress. His only choice was to remain inside, until whatever was happening, ended or he was killed.

He went back to his knees and began crawling in the reverse direction. When he was again situated in the small space between the last row of seats and the half wall, Monday let loose a low modulated string of curses. Moving his hand along the barrel of the AK-47, he thought that at least he'd take a few with him. Then he shook his head….the thought wasn't comforting…..it wasn't an option he wanted.

*

Nancy stirred, when her mind registered to the ominous sound. Forgetting, for an instant, where she was, she moved too quickly, and struck her head against the vehicle's undercarriage. Emitting something between a sob and a whimper, she registered on the slow, grinding sound. Suddenly she felt the ground move, or she thought she did. Looking toward the sound, she saw the outline….an outline of a tracked vehicle coming directly toward her. Several seconds later, her brain shouted, APC, an Armored Personnel Carrier.

Ignoring the pain, Nancy rolled out from beneath the vehicle. As she lay still, the gunfire seemed distant. Then she realized the APC's movement was drowning out everything else as it continued directly toward her.

She moved painfully to her knees, ignoring the jagged pieces of concrete and stone that cut into her skin. Scanning a one hundred and eighty degree arc, she saw the armed men in various groups. "Hostiles or Friendlies," she kept repeating over and over again. Then concluding that she had no choice, she went back to a prone position, and started crawling toward the nearest vehicle, which she estimated was fifteen meters away.

Using her right forearm, and what she could of her left, Nancy slowly transversed the distance until she was again underneath the vehicle. Seconds later, she felt the heat and shock waves of an explosion that rocked, and shifted the vehicle so that the tire on the rear quarter panel came to rest only inches away from her body. Gasping for breath, and unable to normalize her breathing as she thought about what could have been, Nancy was seized with a panic attack. During the few lucid moments, she thought, this isn't how it's supposed to be....then her senses fogged over, and her mind drifted away from the moment.

Chapter 11

From the time Nancy Gault left the theater, Hayek watched her movements through night vision glasses. The seventh story balcony of his room at the Tropicana Hotel, gave him an unobstructed view of the theater, and what was transpiring below.

As he stared through the glasses he wondered, what are the odds of the woman surviving under the vehicle that he was supposed to detonate as part of Monday's plan.

Shaking his head, as if it was all too surreal, he remembered clearly how the attack began. First the series of explosions impacted the theater, then sustained small-arms fire, followed by the ensuing pandemonium, both inside and outside the theater. Quickly concluding, that it made no sense to detonate the car bomb at that point, he pocketed the cell…. nothing to be gained then, but now it was different. The APC was moving in a way….a route, which would crush the first vehicle, and tear away part of the second one, where the woman was now hidden.

Would the stolen C-4 he secured from the Army Colonel be enough to blow off a tread? Only moments now before he would find out.

*

The earth seemed to move as the ominous sound grew louder. Instinctively, Nancy used her forearms and legs to change her position, and then realized that the feeble act would make no difference in altering the finality of what was approaching.

Deducing quickly, she realized her alternative, which by definition meant two. One was to remain where she was. If she chanced crawling out, she would most likely be cut down by the advancing fire from the Friendlies. She doubted the Hostiles had armored equipment, so what she saw coming at her, was Boka Ami Military or Paramilitary units. The second option was to stay where she was… chance it, that the APC wouldn't crush her to death.

She let her head fall on her forearm as she thought, not much of a choice.

*

Hayek watched through the glasses as the left track of the APC impacted with the original vehicle Nancy hid under. When the track reached the vehicle's center mass, Hayek pushed on the remote button.

The ensuing explosion blew off one of the APC's steel sprockets, causing the tread to dislodge from the guide system, and stopping all forward movement.

*

Nancy opened her eyes, and stared at the APC as it rested at a twenty-five degree angle-a-top of what was left of the car.

She watched the soldiers' fire in various directions at perceived or real targets. Then the firing became sporadic, before finally stopping. The wounded and dying from the blast, were left in place, as the others re-assembled and began moving toward the theater area.

Counting off a slow twenty, Nancy started edging out from underneath the vehicle. She continued to crawl away from the vehicle, until she reached a grassy knoll. Despite the pain, she forced herself into a half crouch and began running

Running blindly, her thoughts were only to distance herself from impending doom. Everything back there represented death, and she wouldn't....couldn't fathom the possibility.

She had no idea of where she was, although she reckoned she was in close proximity to the American Embassy. She stopped in place, and moved her hand to her head. What was the street?

Yeah....yes, that was it.... Lindonstraat. Before she could move, a hand covered her mouth, and an arm locked around her neck

*

Monday listened to the unintelligible language, then the broken English stating that the theater was secure. From his position between the last row of seats, and the half wall, he watched as several people hesitantly stood up. Staying put, he watched more rise, and then he became attuned to the cries for help.

He pushed the AK-47 under the nearest seat, and slowly moved into a standing position. He stood quietly waiting as the armed men moved further into the theater. When one of them pointed his rifle at his midsection, and then moved it quickly toward the center aisle, Monday slowly started side-stepping until he was ordered to stop.

He waited in place, as others, both expats and locals, crowded the narrow space. After the command was issued, the group began moving in the direction of the lobby.

Once there, individuals were separated into groups comprising foreigners, and locals. In seconds the din of conversation over-rode the cries for help from the dying and wounded that still remained inside the theater's main area.

Watching the crowd, Monday began formulating a rudimentary plan. He knew he couldn't stay in place, and let it play out as he anticipated it would. He surmised that after a cursory check, certain diplomatic types would be permitted to leave. Others would be interrogated. He wasn't sure which category he would fall into, but he didn't want to wait around to find out.

Locking eyes, for an instant, with a European looking woman in her late forties or early fifties, and assuming she was with a mission or part of an Embassy staff, Monday waved, and started moving in her direction. When he reached her, she had a look of confusion and fear.

"I'm sorry. I thought you were someone from the American delegation. I didn't mean to startle you."

The woman didn't respond, as her eyes moved from his face to his body, and then back.

Monday looked down, and saw what was so obvious to the woman, his torn and filthy clothing covered with sinew, pieces of flesh and bone matter.

The woman was a duplicate of his own appearance, but her mind-set didn't register that. She saw only his condition and that frightened her.

Monday smiled, and moved away from the woman. In her fragile state anything could have happened, and he didn't want to draw any more attention to himself than was necessary. His idea of using the woman somehow to assist in getting out of the theater was useless now. He was on his own.

Thinking, what do I have to lose, Monday straightened up, and then started moving between the clustered bodies, and toward the nearest wall breach. When he reached it, he simply climbed through, and started walking away without looking back. Thinking, it was just that easy....just that easy, gave him a renewed sense of bravado.

He walked past running soldiers who were all but oblivious to the western looking man, whose clothes were torn, and caked with dirt and bone matter.

Ignoring the scene of death and confusion around him, Monday continued walking with his head slightly down, picturing the route to the Embassy with each step. With continued luck, he estimated he'd be there in fifteen maybe twenty minutes.

*

As the hand over her mouth, and the arm around her neck dropped away, Nancy Gault turned too quickly, and stumbled backward as she tried to distance herself from the perceived danger. When she regained her footing, her eyes widened, as she stared at Hayek.

"I'm sorry for the scare. I didn't want to frighten you by appearing suddenly from nowhere."

"And what the Hell did you think you just did? You frightened the Hell out of me, and I've got a good mind to beat you within an inch of your life."

The absurdity of the comment made Hayek smile.

When Nancy realized how idiotic her retort sounded, she laughed as she shook her head. Then she looked up at Hayek, and her eyes locked with his. "Don't be fooled Hayek, I meant what I said, and I'm very capable of making it happen."

Maybe it was the tone she used, but Hayek, for a fleeting moment, believed that she was capable of carrying out the threat.

In an effort to defuse the situation, Hayek said, "I've watched you since you left the theater."

When he saw the quizzical look, he added, "from the balcony over there," and he pointed back toward the Tropicana Hotel. "My room has a balcony, and it gave me an unobstructed view of everything transpiring below. I saw you crawl under the first vehicle and then, when the APC appeared, leave that vehicle, and crawl under the second one. The first car was the one I packed with C-4, and I wondered about the odds of your picking that one to hide under."

He smiled, but Nancy simply stared back without indicating anything.

"I didn't blow the vehicle as planned, since the attack began before I could trigger it. Once the attack was in full mode, I didn't need to."

Hayek stopped again, and when she still didn't reply, he continued. "Once you were under the second vehicle, I waited until the APC made contact with the first car. When it started riding over the car....when it reached mid-way, I detonated the C-4, and it successfully damaged a tread, rendering the APC inoperable. The rest you know," and he let a half smile form. "For the moment, we're safe."

*

Monday turned right onto Lindonstraat, a street running parallel to a small park. He saw the outline of the main Embassy building, some forty or so meters away, rising above the heads of the soldiers whose rifles were pointed at him.

"I'm an American, and I'm trying to reach the Embassy."

There was no reply as the soldiers remained in place, their weapons still menacing.

Using his hand, Monday pointed to himself, and said "American," more times than necessary, and out of sheer frustration, he waived his hand at the building's outline, interjecting the word "Embassy," after every "American."

He suddenly became aware that what he was saying bordered on comical....as if it was an Abbott and Costello TV skit, and then Monday laughed. Realizing what he'd just done, and the gravity of his situation, Robert Monday became quiet.

*

With Hayek leading, they made their way toward the American Embassy. Despite the resonating pain to her left side, the bruises, and cuts that intersected her body, somehow Nancy managed to keep up.

She stopped in place as Hayek waived his hand back and forth, and then motioned toward the ground. Nancy watched him assume a prone position, and although unable to understand why, duplicated his movement.

Hayek pointed forward, and slowly Nancy's eyes focused on the figures.

As they waited, Nancy became more certain that one of the figures was Robert Monday. Maybe it was the outline, or the way he stood, but whatever it was, she knew it was him.

She turned her head slightly, and whispered, "It's Monday....out there. I'm sure it's Monday."

"Stay here....I'm going to slowly walk toward them."

"No. Staying here isn't what I want to do. We'll walk together."

Hayek shook his head, knowing it was useless to argue with the woman.

Hayek rose first, and then helped Nancy up.

Before they covered fifteen meters, several soldiers ran forward, shouting, and moving their weapons in a menacing way.

Hayek stopped, and extended his arms to his sides. From the corner of his mouth, he said, "Do the same."

The three soldiers formed a crude semi-circle. When neither Hayek nor Nancy responded to the rudimentary sounding language, one of the soldiers closed in on the space that separated them, until he was inches away. Nancy could smell the putrid odor emanating from the soldier's unwashed body.

His eyes moved quickly, darting from left to right. His voice was several octaves above normal, and his adrenaline rush high. The temperament of anyone at this point of unknown, is fragile, and Hayek hoped that the woman zeroed in on the soldier's demeanor, and wouldn't do anything to set him off.

The soldier stared, then took a step back, as he motioned the others forward. When they joined him, he pointed to the woman, and said something in a quick, guttural way. Then he moved his head up and down, and pointed at Nancy again. After he cradled his M-16 rifle, in the crux of his left arm, he moved the fingers of his right hand across an imaginary keyboard. He did this several times, until Nancy acknowledged with a shake of her head and a smile.

The soldier continued to point at Nancy, as his head moved up and down. She heard the word "TV" as he spoke with his comrades. Then he bowed slightly, and placed his hands together like he was going to pray.

She knew what he was trying to convey. He recognized her from TV segments, announcing her arrival....she was the American pianist.

Nancy took advantage of the moment, and pointed toward the outline of the Embassy. She said several times, "American Embassy," and Hayek parroted her words. In seconds, they, together with Monday, were being escorted to the front gate of the American Embassy.

*

After a brief exchange with a Marine guard standing inside the front gate, they were given the okay to enter the Embassy compound. They walked across the small courtyard, past a number of armed Marines, and then up the six steps to the Embassy's entrance, where they were again stopped and questioned by a Marine Guard.

Once inside, Nancy, Monday, and Hayek were directed to a desk where a Marine, Staff Sergeant, asked them to state their business.

Nancy spoke first, explaining who she was, who Monday was, and mentioned that they came across Hayek along the way here. Then added simply, "The theater was attacked."

After the Staff-Sergeant examined her passport, he handed it back, then looked at Monday, and Hayek, and made a "give me" motion with his hand.

Both men handed over their passports and waited.

"You two are in the wrong Embassy."

"I'm with her. As she said, I'm her manager. This is the only Embassy we could get to....we're all lucky to be here, and fortunate to be in one piece."

"We know there's been some trouble out there," and the Sergeant pointed. "What exactly happened, and by the way, all of you look like Hell."

Nancy explained her circumstances, then Monday stated his, followed by Hayek who made up a fictitious story that even Monday thought convincing.

"Okay, this is a sanctuary for a while. I'll arrange some food for you, and a place to wash up and crash. You look like you could use a doctor."

The Marine paused, then added, "I'll arrange for you to see her. Can't offer much more than that."

Nancy smiled. "Whatever you can do will be appreciated. Is it possible that I can see the Ambassador?"

"He's at the theater attending your concert. No word on him or his whereabouts."

"I think my manager should see the doctor as well." Then she looked at Hayek, who shook his head no.

"I'm okay too. You're the one that needs the attention." What I need is a shower, then Monday smiled, as he thought, we did it, with a little help from our unknown friends.

*

She felt the hand on her body, and then she tuned into the voice.

"I didn't mean to wake you so soon, but the Ambassador has returned and he would like to see you. There's a pair of jeans and blouse at the end of the bed. Make-up, is in the bathroom. When you're ready, we'll go back to the Embassy."

Nancy, and an Embassy secretary whose quarters she shared walked past numerous people milling about in various size groups. She wondered if these were Americans living and working in Boka Ami, or expatriates who sought refuge here, just as she did. Then she let the thought fade thinking, what difference does it make….we're all on our own.

When the elevator door opened at the sixth floor, Nancy followed the woman along a semi-lit corridor, which had a heavy Marine presence. When they reached the end of the hallway, the woman knocked on the door and waited until it opened.

"This is as far as I go. Good luck."

"Thanks for the loan of the bed. It's appreciated, and if you are ever around wherever I'm playing, look me up. You'll have a center aisle, orchestra section seat for you, and your significant other. Thanks again for the hospitality Alice."

The woman smiled, then turned away.

Nancy walked past the civilian attired man, and stopped just inside, watching him close the door.

"This way Miss Gault."

Although that was her name, she was somewhat surprised at his use of it. Then she thought, Why not? I'm here to meet the Ambassador, and of course my name would be known….even to this man. As she followed, she tried to remember what the Ambassador looked like. Her thoughts drifted back to the reception and how long ago that seemed now.

The Ambassador came around his desk and extended his hand. Nancy took hold and smiled. She shook her head as she said, “You look like I did a few hours ago,” and laughed.

“Haven’t had a chance to change into my Ambassadorial clothes,” then he smiled.

Ambassador Joseph Patrick MacMahon pointed to a sofa at one corner of his office. “Let’s sit down.”

“First of all, I’m glad that you’re okay, despite the bandages.”

“Fortunate, and thankfully the shoulder isn’t as bad as I first thought. A few more stitches than I’d like, and a bruised elbow….could have been worse.”

“Please tell me what you can about what happened at the theater. I’m trying to piece it together.”

Before Nancy could reply, there was a knock on the door and then it opened.

“Come in Roland. We’re just getting started.”

A six foot plus, Black man, who Nancy surmised was in his mid-thirties walked toward them, stopping when he was a few paces away, and nodded to the Ambassador.

“I got word early, JP, that you arrived back in one piece. From the information we’re correlating, the Maroons tried to make a statement.”

"They did more than make a statement."

The man's lips tightened, and then he moved his head down, and then back up several times, conveying he understood.

"Perkins and Turner, along with the Military Attaché formed a protective cordon around my wife and me. We all hunkered down where we were….no place to run or hide….lucky….just plain lucky we weren't hit. Word is, we took some casualties among the staff. I'm trying to get a status report."

"My people are working on that also. I'll get it to you, as soon as I can, and then you can make a comparison with what your guys come up with."

MacMahon looked at Nancy. "Sorry for the late introduction. Nancy Gault, meet Roland Evers, part of the Embassy staff, and a close personal assistant. Roland, Nancy is the concert pianist who played for President Muguanasi."

Her mind thought Central Intelligence Agency, or personal bodyguard….maybe one in the same. She nodded, and he returned the gesture.

"Pull up a chair, Roland."

Then the Ambassador looked back at Nancy, "You were saying."

"After I finished the recital, I encouraged a member of the Chinese delegation to come on stage, and play for the audience….an extra bonus of sorts. I knew that the individual was a trained classical pianist….it's a small world, and in this classical music world of ours, we know each other, personally, or by reputation. When he began to play the first notes of his piece, I walked off stage, and thought it would be a good time to get a breath of fresh air. I was in the theater's alleyway, the door ajar so I could listen to his music, when the attack came…..and after a stressful back and forth with several Boka Ami troops, we, my manager along with the straggler we picked up, made our way to the Embassy."

Ambassador MacMahon looked over at Evers and then asked, "What was his name….the Chinese?"

Roland Evers and Nancy Gault answered almost simultaneously, "Min Qua Fu."

The Ambassador locked eyes with Evers for several seconds, and then looked back at the woman.

Chapter 12

The unexpected, for those first few seconds, can be numbing. That was the case for Min Qua Fu, until his mind was capable of processing what he had just heard.

When his name was mentioned, by the woman on stage, his brain made a conscious analysis of the linkage she used, ...fellow concert pianist....well known in his home country....and with some encouragement, perhaps he will honor us by playing one of China's most famous classical pieces.

Bao Chen, Fu's principal assistant turned in his seat and smiled.

Fu spoke just above a whisper, "Wo Cao." (Holy Shit)

"Do you want me to translate anything she said, Comrade Director?"

"Wo Wan Quan Ming Bai." (I understand perfectly)

Min Qua Fu rose slowly, and then turned and faced toward the audience, waving his hand in a "no-no" fashion.

The applause followed him on stage. Bowing slightly and waving, Fu moved toward the piano with Nancy Gault at his side. After stating he would play "Ambush From All Sides," he extended his hand. "I have to return the honor some day."

Nancy held her smile until Fu was seated. She watched him remove the pillow and place it under the piano bench. As she stood listening to the first stanza of the music, his words, while innocent enough, seemed to project an ominous connotation. They continued echoing through the caverns of her mind, as she made her way into the street behind the theater.

*

As Min Qua Fu played, the experience became surreal, transporting him back to a time, a time when as a child protégée at the Chinese Conservatory of Music, he was playing for a select group of military and government officials at Jade Spring Hill – the villa area of the Central Military Commission.

He was playing the same piece, and then, as now, he was totally consumed by the majestic and passionate highs and lows of the music, as it depicted the raging battle scenes. He remembered how the leader of the People's Republic of China, Deng Xiaoping, congratulated him at the end of his performance, and presented him with the silver rice bowl and silver chop-sticks.

Then Min Qua Fu returned to the moment as he was engulfed in an orange/red mist.

As the C-4 detonated, stress waves moved upward carrying energy, pieces of debris and a small fireball. As all three impacted Min Qua Fu, he quickly became disoriented, realizing only that he was entrapped in a world of excruciating pain. The explosion caused serious burns to his face and arms. Skin bubbles dotted every exposed surface of his body, and his last thoughts, before the cover of blackness shut everything down, was the animalistic screams that seemed so distant, yet so near.

*

Two pairs of eyes followed the woman and watched the door close softly behind her.

"What's your take, Roland?"

"Not bad looking, and obviously talented in many ways."

A smile formed at the corner of his mouth.

MacMahon shook his head and smiled. "Didn't mean it that way, but I tend to agree. Quite an adventure for someone not used to the happenings in a Third World shit hole like Boka Ami."

"Yeah, she's fortunate to be in one piece. I don't see any reason why we can't accommodate her request, and fly her, and her manager, out with the rest of the injured. No need to wait for Muguanasi replacement, or whoever is in charge to say we can."

"Did Ronnie Dajan and his Maroons damage the airport?"

"No....no report that anything happened there. On second thought, JP, if the airport is operational, and I'll check it out, why not let her fly out on commercial?"

"No, I want her on one of our planes. I need to know a little bit more about Nancy Gault."

Evers gave MacMahon a curious look, then said, "I think I've lost you."

"Doesn't it scratch your curiosity, Roland, that she would…." and he paused as he searched for the words, "…. ask someone to share her stage, and that someone just happens to be Min Qua Fu, Director of ILD….an intelligence organ of the PRC?"

"Okay, Mr. Ambassador, I'll play devil's advocate for you. Isn't he a trained classical pianist? Don't answer….I'll answer for you. Yes, she stated as much, so what's the big deal….just another treat for the locals."

"There's something more. You weren't there Roland….I was. Just before the Maroons hit the theater, something happened on stage. As soon as Min Qua Fu left his seat until the moment he started playing, I never diverted my eyes, and I mean not for a nano-second. I could swear that just before the RPGs (rocket propelled grenades) or whatever hit the theater, there was an explosion….the piano."

Ambassador Joseph P. MacMahon held up his hand, as Roland Evers was about to speak.

"The explosion was detonated by a remote controlled device. When the attack started, there were other issues. Those issues are obvious, so what

I witnessed was compartmentalized until I was back here, and had a quiet moment to reconstruct things." The Ambassador paused again. "Could Miss Nancy Gault be something other than she appears to be?"

*

At Boka Ami's General Sabroka Military Hospital, doctors sedated, and then scrubbed the affected skin off Min Qua Fu. The areas were left uncovered exposing raw nerves to the hot, tropical air.

Fu oscillated between a comatose sleep, and a semi-state of wakefulness. During those periods when his pain sensors and his mind registered as one, his animalistic screams shattered the quiet, as the pain resonated through his body.

Bao Chen waved off the doctors as he moved closer to the screaming man. He looked back, the hatred evident in his eyes, and pointed to his immediate superior. No words were exchanged between Bao Chen and the doctors as they re-attached a morphine drip.

After several more moments, the screaming subsided, and Bao Chen returned to his chair.

Except for infrequent bathroom breaks and quick meals, Bao Chen never left his Director's bedside.

It was into the next morning when a semi-sedated Min Qua Fu was conscious enough to recognize his assistant. His few labored words were spoken in an unnatural voice, just above a whisper.

Bao strained to hear what his superior was saying. While the speech pattern was fractured, the meaning was clear, and Bao motioned with his hands and head that he understood.

*

Monday and Nancy Gault completed their second circle around the Embassy's compound. Their pace was purposely slow….nonchalant, and while conveying the appearance of two bored people, among many who were using the Embassy grounds as a sanctuary, they were completely attuned to their surroundings and the people who occupied space there.

"I know Evers is with the Company….probably Chief of Station. (Central Intelligence Agency, Head of Intelligence Operations attached to an Embassy) It was his demeanor. Confident, but not overly so….he was the laid back type. You know the kind."

Monday acknowledged with a head movement. "Yeah, I know the type. So what you're telling me, is they think you're a bit more than a classical pianist?"

"Not necessarily, but I'd rather err on the side of caution. You triggered the remote, and you were in the theater when it detonated. Can you recall what happened precisely at that moment?"

Monday stopped walking, and stared at the woman. "I saw an orange haze for a second or two, debris, and saw Min Qua Fu topple over. Seconds later, the rockets impacted the theater, and all Hell broke loose. Those who could, tried to get out....most with little success. It was pandemonium akin to a scene from Dante's Inferno."

"Let's say, Mr. Robert Monday, that the Ambassador or someone with him, saw the explosion on stage before the rockets hit. Suppose they reached a conclusion that Min Qua Fu was the target of an assassination. Suppose further, that what I did by calling Fu up on the stage and cajoling him into playing, was out of the ordinary, and that I was....that I had to be the conduit which facilitated his assassination."

"In your world, how many classical pianists are there of renown? I mean, well known. A handful, maybe fifteen, twenty....perhaps twenty-five. Then why shouldn't you know of Min Qua Fu, and why shouldn't you ask him to play? He was a child protégé, and that reputation is still relevant. Besides, at this point in time, can anyone be sure how the explosion at the piano occurred? Fu is dead, and all this Evers character has, is a handful of speculation, and that isn't going to convict anyone of anything."

Monday paused, and then started again. "The way things turned out is better for us. Suppose the target was eliminated in the way we planned. You, we, would be under suspicion from the start. With the luck we had, and yes, it was damn good luck, the attack gave us an unexpected cover. Fu's death can be blamed on Ronnie Dajan, and his Maroons. Think for a moment, Nancy, suppose we carried out the assassination as originally planned. We'd be interrogated by the local Five-O, probably harassed to a degree, and then hopefully let go. Now that Muguanasi, his wife, and some other government officials have been murdered by the Maroons, the onus is on the local intelligence and police communities to track down Dajan and his horde, and give them some payback. We're not in that equation."

"I hope you're right, but I have that feeling....the one that tells me that all things are not okay."

*

"Good morning Madeline, is the Ambassador in?"

"He is Mr. Evers, I'll tell him you're here."

"No need....I'll announce myself," and Roland Evers continued past the now standing Secretary, who for a fleeting moment, considered repeating what she just stated, then let the thought lapse.

She watched as Evers knocked once, turned the knob and walked into Joseph P. MacMahon's office.

MacMahon cupped his palm over the bottom portion of the phone, and motioned toward a chair with his head. Once Evers was seated, the Ambassador turned slightly away and said, "I'll call you back in a few minutes. Something just came up that I need to address. Yes, that's understood, five, ten minutes should be enough. Yes, I understand," and then he cradled the phone.

"This better be good, Roland."

"Thought you'd like to know a few things about our celebrity guest and her manager."

"And that couldn't wait?"

"No, it couldn't, considering they already gave notice that they're booked out tomorrow, commercial to Miami."

"Okay, what do you have?"

"The woman comes up squeaky clean. Lives alone in Greenwich, Connecticut - a high rent district, considered by many to be a suburb of New York City. It's well above our pay-grade. Nice home, where everything sells in the millions. Understandable since she commands a good salary for what she does. Not married, no children, and doesn't seem to have anyone on a string. She had a long-term relationship with some newspaper type, but that's dead and buried. She lives a cloistered life, and if I may add, a real waste of some interesting machinery."

"For shits sake Roland, is that all you think about?"

"It occupies a good portion of my waking hours, but between you and me, JP, I think mostly of what I have to do for that oath I took long ago."

"Okay....okay Roland, go ahead."

“Anyway, Gault seems legit….couldn‘t find any skeletons….no overindulgences in anything that shakes the antenna. Now, her manager, on the other hand, comes up with some interesting bio-points. He’s English….British, and there’s no law against that, but an interesting twist is that he’s a teacher….a professor of Linguistics and History, with a fluency in Mandarin Chinese.”

Evers watched the Ambassador’s eyes narrow slightly and his gaze intensify.

“The icing on the cake is that our Mr. Robert Monday was with the British Army’s EOD in Afghanistan….an Explosive Ordnance Disposal group.”

“Okay, Roland, you’ve justified the interruption. Is the information confirmed?”

“Comes from Thames House, London…. (Headquarters of MI5 – British Internal Security Service) ….from Martin, who’s reliable.”

The Ambassador nodded once.

“You know how it goes, JP. We build bridges over troubled waters, to quote the Simon and Garfunkel song, and we need each other at times….and that’s in spite of the screw ups.

The look on the Ambassador’s face forced Evers to continue. “I’m not getting political JP, and I’m not riding any soap box….just an off handed comment because of what we’re facing, and the indifference articulated, and formulated into policy by those who should know better. That's it….just letting off some steam….just stating that my….our job becomes more difficult because they….." and then Evers let his voice trail off.

"Okay Roland….okay. I understand. It's as frustrating for me, as it is for you. Sometimes I wonder what the American people are thinking, or not thinking, when they vote. But that's in the past, and this is now. What I don't understand is the connection with the woman....yeah I know cover and all, but if she's sterile, why or how did anyone convince her to become a part of this?"

"Who says she's sterile?"

Evers watched the Ambassador's head move ever so slightly up and then down, and then repeat the movement several more times.

*

Chen Boa leaned on his elbows as he shifted his upper body closer to the center of the table. The man sitting opposite, inadvertently, pressed back into his chair. He had heard the instructions clearly, and acknowledged as much. There was no reason for any misunderstanding, and the movement by the Deputy Director, unnerved him.

As the seconds ticked away in his brain, Deng Wu Ling, thought that a response was necessary to neutralize the situation.

"I completely understand Comrade Bao. Your instructions will be carried out so the desired results are achieved. I can assure you that…."

Bao's hand cut through the air, and Ling stopped in mid-sentence. The Deputy Director looked down at the papers on the table's surface as he said, "I assume you have preparations to make?"

Ling rose slowly, unsure whether the meeting had ended or an answer was required. Deciding that the meeting had concluded, Deng Wu Ling walked around the table and then out of the room.

*

Hayek listened patiently until Robert Monday and the woman finished.

"I have some thoughts," and then he again waited until both heads were turned in his direction.

"Based on what you've stated, each time either one of you was called to the Ambassador's office, the other was absent. That's one of the basic interrogation techniques, as you well know….used by police forces/security forces throughout the world….separate, then analyze any differences in the information elicited, and then use that to your advantage against the other one, either to collaborate, or extract additional information.'

"Secondly, from what you've stated, this Roland type is definitely a practitioner of Trade Craft. (Intelligence) You're both under suspicion, and I emphasize the word suspicion. So far there's no linkage, but that could change. If they had anything now, you wouldn't be free to go."

Monday interrupted. "Even if they had anything more than suspicion, why would they take it any further? The death of Min Qua Fu is a plus, not a negative. It gets rid of a major Intelligence Operative who's been a thorn in the side of the United States for quite a while. You'd think they'd thank us," and Monday smiled.

"You've encroached into their territory, and you know how temperamental the United States is when confronted with an international incident, and any linkage that they're involved. The "Company" (term for the CIA) may want to ruffle some feathers here, but they want to do it with their personnel, and at their time of choosing. Whoever sent Min Qua Fu on a long vacation, and let's assume they think….maybe they know somehow, that he was assassinated, is rogue, and they want to know who, why and the connections. The compass arrow, right now, points to Miss Nancy, and why she called Fu on stage….maybe someone saw the detonation before the rockets hit. You stated that the Chinese forensic people would probably be investigating the scene….the piano or what's left of it, with the locals."

Monday broke in again. "They're not going to find much. Maybe some minute pieces of a cell phone manufactured in North Korea under Egyptian license….and calling Fu up on stage may seem odd for some, but is it all that strange to ask a fellow classical pianist to play?"

Nancy looked at Hayek and then back at Monday. “Yeah....maybe it was out of character, considering that I was the main attraction....but we agreed it was the way we were going to take him out, and rethinking it....it’s not all that strange for one classical pianist to mention another one sitting in the audience, and even call him up on stage. I’m not on anyone’s radar as a possible threat, whether it’s our Embassy, Chinese Intelligence, or the late Min Qua Fu.”

“The offer of transportation back to the States on a military aircraft was a gesture of convenience, in order to keep an eye on both of you. They....Evers, would most likely have someone on that plane.”

“That’s why we decided to go commercial Hayek....Delta tomorrow. Why chance anything? Besides, the first military transport left yesterday with some of the injured and a few Americans tourists.”

“You know there’s going to be someone on that plane tomorrow as well.”

“Just make sure you get us to the airport. We’ll deal with the rest.”

“You needn’t worry about that old chap....I’ve got a vested interest in you,” and then Hayek paused. “You do remember our conversation, the one in the hotel garden, which now seems so very long ago.”

Chapter 13

Hayek turned, and faced Robert Monday, who was occupying the front passenger seat, then looked back at Nancy Gault in the rear seat, and asked, "Is everyone ready?"

"Let's go Hayek….we've got a plane waiting."

"I'm thinking that it might have been safer for both of you to have taken the Ambassador's offer, and flown back to the states on a military aircraft. You're going to get hassled at customs despite your celebrity status."

"Let's go Hayek….we've got a plane waiting."

"You've already said that."

"Yeah, and I don't want to say it a third time."

Hayek shifted into drive, and moved away from the portico of the Tori Hotel. As he joined the early morning traffic flow, he couldn't help sensing something ominous, but the more he thought about it, the less sure he was. Maybe it's after action jitters….then again, maybe it is something else.

Finally he looked over at Monday. "I've had this feeling for a day or so, and especially since we left the hotel, old chum, and that feeling isn't a good one."

"It's your nerves Hayek….you're stressed."

"Sure....that's possible....was thinking the same thing myself. Could be....after all we went through, but it's more than that."

Hayek maneuvered the car onto the dirt shoulder, then turned and faced Monday.

"I've taken a few liberties....some prior-planning. Under your seat is an Uzi (Israeli submachine gun) with a fifty-round magazine. There's another mag under there somewhere. And for you Miss Nancy, there's a .45 caliber pistol behind the armrest. You need to pull the leather cover away to get to it."

"Are you crazy? If we get caught with any of that, we're up a creek without a paddle....holy fucking mother of shit. So that's the logic behind your ominous feeling, and all that goes with that crapola."

"For your edification, Mr. Monday, I've learned along the way, to project....as a precaution. I make sure my bases are covered. I'm surprised that you haven't thanked me....instead you're all over me."

"We're on the way to the airport, for Christ's sake....nothing more. There's traffic everywhere, and the airport will be secured as tight as where your brain is located....you know the place....where it meets the driver's seat."

"Okay, Mr. Monday....enough said. You have a bad attitude, I'm just alerting you to what I have....nothing more. If we don't need them....then nothing is lost. I'll take care of what needs to be taken care of, once I let you two off."

Hayek pulled back on the road. Nothing more was said until they approached a roadblock. After the soldiers returned their passports, they were directed to follow the detour signs.

Hayek was forced to wait in place until a battered, half-ton, Ford F-150 pickup truck, made its way back to the center of the road.

After an angry wave, and shouts from several of the soldiers, Hayek pulled behind the truck.

His forward progress was slowed to a crawl.

Monday leaned over his seat, and looked at Nancy. "Can't seem to catch a break."

Nancy locked eyes for an instant and then without a word turned her head, and stared out the window.

Hayek watched in the rear view mirror as something unexplained took place at the roadblock. With a shrug of indifference, Hayek directed his attention forward watching as the truck's tires created a cloud of brown dust, obliterating a clear view of the roadway.

A quick glance in the rear view mirror revealed that whatever it was at the roadblock, was significant enough to stop all traffic. Hayek let his curiosity build as he began to question whether the lack of vehicle traffic was something he should be concerned about?"

Then he let it all subside and he focused on the truck. He mumbled, just above a whisper, "That truck....that damn truck....and I had to get behind it....can't...."

Before Hayek finished the last syllable, the car smashed into the rear of the truck.

*

The occupant of the silver, 2007, four door Nissan Maxima, watched as the man and woman entered a black, four door Chevrolet, then his eyes shifted to the man loading the bags. He spoke quickly into the cell phone, and then after a few seconds, pulled away from the Tori Hotel, and stayed approximately thirty meters behind the Chevrolet.

The driver closed the distance between the two vehicles, as the black Chevrolet Impala slowed at the roadblock. Again he spoke rapidly into his cell phone, as he watched the Chevrolet finally clear the roadblock.

On a signal from one of the soldiers, he moved the vehicle forward very slowly, until he reached the horizontal barrier. After handing his passport to the guard, the driver moved the gear shift from drive to park, locking the braking system. He then removed a second cell phone from his shirt pocket, and with his index finger pressed against the single button, triggering an electromagnetic wave that acted as a kill switch, and immediately disabled the car's engine.

After repeated attempts to restart the car, he was motioned out with curses and threats. As he moved out from the vehicle, he raised his hands in an act of frustration, and then using a combination of Chinese and English, he tried to explain.

*

Seconds after the impact, the outline of two figures emerged from under the tarpaulin that covered the truck's bay, and started firing at the Chevrolet. The 7.62 millimeter, steel cored bullets, shattered the windshield, and tore through the upper chest and head of Hayek.

The instant Robert Monday felt the shreds of glass pepper his face and neck, he instinctively fell sideways using the dashboard and firewall as protection. His hand went under his seat, frantically searching for the Uzi. When his fingers touched metal, he pried the weapon free, then with his right hand opened the passenger side door and tumbled out.

Using the door as cover, Monday fired on full automatic. When the magazine was empty, he reached under the seat and then inserted the second magazine. This time he fired on semi-automatic, using short, sustained bursts at the silhouetted figures.

Gault felt the bee-like stings against the side of her neck, and lower jaw as she dropped to the floorboard. The confined space hampered her, as she reached toward the armrest. Cursing as she tried to pull the false backing away, she willed herself to relax. Finally freeing the protective cover, Nancy grabbed the .45 caliber semi-automatic, then opened the door on her left side, and gingerly crawled out. She hovered behind the open door as she waited for targets of opportunity to appear.

Peering between the spaces where the car door attaches to the steel frame, Gault watched as the truck driver pushed open his door with his foot, and then leaped onto the road surface.

Bracing the barrel of her weapon against the middle door hinge, Nancy squeezed off three rounds in quick succession. The figure staggered on rubber legs, as he tried to maintain his vertical position, then toppled forward.

As Gault watched the prostrate figure for any sign of life, she became aware of the sudden silence.

That moment of reality forced her to call out, "Monday....you there?"

"Yeah....are you okay?"

"More or less."

"I think whatever....whoever was in the bay, they're dead. What about your side?"

"One....looks like he's dead too....the driver....are there any more?"

"Don't know. Cover me. I'm going to move on the truck."

"Wait until I get into a better position....I'm moving now."

Nancy dropped into a prone position, then crawled behind the left front quarter panel of the Chevrolet.

"Okay....I'll cover you."

Monday ran in a crouched position until he reached the truck's rear. The shredded, blood soaked tarpaulin, and the twisted torsos, told him, in graphic detail, what he wanted to know. To insure himself that what he saw was everything he needed to see, Monday carefully pulled back what was left of the cover. The bay was empty.

"I'm going to check the cab."

Monday went left, and bracing himself against the bay, looked into the cab through the open door

"Clear....keep me covered..... I'll check the driver."

A few seconds later, they were both staring down at the man, whose eyes revealed the pain he was experiencing.

"He's still alive, and he's Chinese."

“The other two were Chinese also.”

Nancy’s eyes widened as her brain processed what she saw and heard.

“Then....then that means they know....they know about us....me.”

“Unfortunately.....yes. It might have been that way regardless....even if we used the original plan. We’re logically suspect....suspect since we were in close proximity to the now deceased Mr. Min Qua Fu. The overriding question is whether they have anything substantial, or is it all circumstantial? And if it’s circumstantial, is that enough to confirm their suspicions?”

She moved her hand across her mouth, and then started breathing in an erratic manner, as if she couldn’t bring enough air into her lungs.

Nancy looked back at the bullet riddled car, and shouted “Hayek.”

As she began turning toward the car, Monday grabbed her. “Don’t go there. He’s dead.”

“How can you be sure?”

“Part of his skull and brain are splattered all over me.”

Nancy looked at Monday’s face, as if she was seeing him for the first time, then her eyes moved slowly over his blood splattered clothing.

She turned away, bent over, and regurgitated. After the bile, and undigested food were expelled, Nancy dry heaved until her throat became raw.

"There's no water....don't have any water for you. Try to get yourself back to normal while I take care of that," and Monday pointed toward the truck. The gunfire is going to bring them here quickly, and you're going to ....." then Monday stopped in mid-sentence.

He went back to the truck, opened the tailgate, grabbed the shredded tarpaulin, and haphazardly threw it across the hood of the car. He wiped his eyes with the back of his hand, as he returned to the truck, and pulled off what was left of the two men.

Monday dragged both bodies to the edge of the river bank, then did the same with the Chinese driver.

He hoisted the smaller of the three bodies above his head and tossed it as far as he could. As the body made contact with the water, the waves rippled. In seconds, the crocodiles were fighting over the carcass.

Monday then tossed the pistol and Uzi into the water.

Without glancing back, but all too aware of what was happening behind him, Monday motioned to the woman. When she didn't respond, he grabbed her arm, and lifted her into a standing position, then he unceremoniously shoved her toward the truck.

"Get in….we've got a plane to catch."

Chapter 14

Monday opened the car's trunk, took out a pair of pants and a shirt from his suitcase, and a blouse and skirt from Nancy's bag. He removed her purse from the back seat, and tucked it under his arm. After striking a match, and igniting the gasoline soaked rag extruding from into the Chevrolet's fuel tank, he ran like a man possessed toward the idling truck.

Ignoring the still open door, Monday slammed his foot against the accelerator, and felt the truck vibrate, as the spinning tires tried to gain traction. Once he eased up on the gas pedal the vehicle surged forward. At twenty kilometers per hour, Monday again pressed down on the accelerator, and kept it depressed, until the vehicle speedometer indicated sixty-five kilometers.

His concentration was shattered by the sound of the explosion. The orange fireball and grey-black plumed smoke, cascaded upward. Monday continued to stare at the rear view mirror until the visual disappeared.

"That should confuse them for awhile, and the burned vehicle will add to the time we need to distance ourselves from all that." Monday motioned over his shoulder, with his thumb, for effect.

"What about the luggage?"

"Nothing we need," and then Monday paused. "You'll change into this blouse and skirt." As he said the words he didn't like what he saw, as he continued to stare at the woman.

"Are you okay?" Before she could respond, Monday added, "I know it was a bit much back there, but we do what we have to do to survive."

"He was still alive."

"The driver....well not anymore. I served him up as lunch."

Re-thinking the words he just uttered, Monday began to laugh. "Funny....lunch," and the more he thought about what he just said, the more he laughed. Suddenly Nancy joined in, and they laughed until the tears rolled down their cheeks.

Once she brought herself under control, she said in a hesitant voice, "back there....when you told me about Hayek....about his parts covering you....well it was too much for me. It shouldn't have been, the melt-down, and all. I....I didn't think I'd react like that, and....and....maybe I'm not cut out for this after all....I'm sorry, for not holding up my end."

"You did just fine. You took out the driver and covered me, just like the book says. So you needed to throw-up.....could be some bad food you ate. Why beat-up on yourself? We're alive, and the crocs had a good lunch."

They looked at each other, and the laughter started again. After a few moments, Monday said, "we play it normal once we get to the airport. I'll see how close we can get. The truck is chewed up at the rear, but the front is okay, and that's what they see first. With a little luck...." and then he shook his head.

"Our clothes....we're not exactly dressed for first class."

"Yeah....I'm looking for a spot along the river, where we can stop and change....clean up a bit."

"You mean like back there....are you crazy?....with what could be waiting for us ....meaning, as you so aptly put it, their lunch."

Monday smiled. "We're just going to clean up....not take a bath, and we've got to do it quickly, and there's just the spot."

Motioning Nancy out, Monday said, "use your soiled skirt or whatever to clean your face and hands. Change your clothes quickly....I'm going to clean up the truck's bay....wash away as much blood as I can, and then let's get the Hell out of here."

Less than six minutes later, they were back in the vehicle, and speeding along the rut encrusted dirt road at over sixty kilometers per hour.

"What's the rush.....my ovaries are bouncing up and down....are you trying to finish what the Chinese couldn't do back there?"

"As I've said before, we've got a plane to catch."

The dirt road finally ended, and they were back on an asphalt road.

"Is this the way to the airport?"

"Don't have the slightest idea, but what's the alternative....either follow this road or what?"

After another two hundred meters, Nancy called out, "That sign....the one you just flew by....it said Boka Ami International Airport......yippee dew?"

"A new language?"

Nope, I'm just somewhat elated."

Monday was about to say something to the effect of, "Don't get too comfortable just yet," but since she seemed to be normalizing, he just let the words drift away.

*

The main entrance to the airport was heavily guarded, by both troops and armored vehicles.

Monday handed both passports to the officer and then pointed to Nancy.

"She's the pianist," and then Monday motioned with his fingers across an imaginary keyboard, "the concert for President Muguanasi and his wife. Delta to Miami....USA," then he made a flying motion with his hand out the window.

Figuring the Officer didn't understand enough of what he was trying to convey, Monday repeated it again, including the hand motions.

The officer turned and called over another man in civilian clothes. When he came alongside, the officer pointed at Monday, and then leaned down and motioned toward the woman.

The civilian attired man stooped and stared at Nancy for longer than necessary.

"Who are you and who is the woman?"

"I'm the manager....the name is Monday, Robert Monday, and the woman is a guest of your country invited here by your President. She played a concert at the theater. Our wounds are a result of what happened there and so is this damaged truck. The rest you know. We're flying out on Delta to Miami, where we will get treatment for our respective wounds. Your hospitals are overcrowded and my Embassy can't help."

The civilian stared at the cuts and lacerations crisscrossing Monday's face, and then looked at the woman. "Are you returning to Boka Ami after your treatments?"

"Well, not right away but Miss Gault assured our Ambassador, Mr. MacMahon, that once the theater was repaired she would definitely return, and play a follow-up concert."

"Will you be using this truck when you return?"

“Monday gave the man a quizzical look, before saying, “I don’t understand.”

“It’s very simple. Mr….” and then the man opened one of the passports, studied it for several seconds, before continuing, “Mr. Monday.”

“If you’re not returning to Boka Ami in a week or so, what will happen to this truck, and also, Mr. Monday, whose truck is this?”

“The truck belongs to a friend who will pick it up later today.”

“And does this friend have a name?”

“He does. It belongs to Mr. Tony Blair, an expatriate living here off and on.”

The civilian official nodded as the name sounded familiar but couldn’t place it. Monday watched as the man made a slow three-hundred rotation around the vehicle, before coming back to the driver’s side.

“It seems that the rear of the truck has sustained some small arms fire.”

“Yes….lucky I guess that it was only the rear, and not the engine block.”

After returning the two passports to Monday, the man turned away from the truck and said something to the uniformed officer, who nodded in confirmation to whatever was said. The officer moved his hand up once, and the two armored vehicles blocking the entranceway moved back.

Monday maneuvered his way through until he had cleared the checkpoint.

"What was that bit about Tony Blair, the former UK prime Minister?"

"It was all I could think of at the moment. I figured he'd recognize the name from somewhere, but wouldn't be able to nail down what or where that somewhere was. I was right," and Monday smiled like a Cheshire cat.

"That was dumb and that smile of yours is dumber."

Monday drove to the parking area bordering the international section of Boka Ami Airport and parked between two vehicles.

"Let's go Miss Gault. We have a plane to catch."

*

Nancy was shaken from a restless sleep by the voice instructing passengers to fasten seat belts. As the plane made its final approach to Miami-Dade International airport, Nancy looked over at the sleeping Robert Monday.

"Could he be dead?" The thought bounced around her mind like a ball bouncing off the walls of a squash court."

She elbowed Monday whose only response was a grunt. She did the elbow bit twice more until Monday was staring at her.

“I thought you were dead.”

“That’s wishful thinking. I’m very much alive, and now my ribs are sore.”

The pained look on Nancy’s face was quickly replaced by a smile. “I had to know.”

“Know what?”

“Whether you were dead.”

Monday shook his head, and then gave her a half smile. “If I didn’t get killed back there, what makes you think I’d die on a Delta flight to Miami, where we’re being served fairly edible food and champagne?”

“Well, you looked comatose….maybe you’ve lived a good life for too long, and your time was up. It would be a nice, quiet way to go….in first class….on an airplane thirty-six thousand feet above it all.”

“I’m not ready to take a dirt nap just yet,” and Monday smiled.

*

When Nancy was motioned forward, Monday went along. The customs agent looked at the woman first, and then back at Monday, before studying their passports.

After a prolonged silence, he asked, "What's the connection," and then looking again at Monday added, "between you and Miss…. eh…. Gault?"

"Business."

"Where are you coming from?"

They answered, almost simultaneously "Boka Ami."

"What were you doing there?"

"I'm a concert pianist. I was giving a concert there," then Nancy looked quickly at Monday and added, "he's my manager."

"You both look like you were in an accident, faces….arms"

The customs agent locked eyes with the woman who responded first.

"We were caught in an insurrection of sorts. Seems the natives got restless."

"Why….couldn't they get tickets to your concert?"

Nancy smiled and Monday chuckled. The customs agent smiled back.

"Mr. Monday, how long are you planning to stay in the states?"

Only a few days, then I'm flying back to London."

The customs officer stamped both passports, then handed them back. "Welcome home Miss Gault, and enjoy your stay Mr. Monday."

*

Once they reached the terminal area, Monday motioned Nancy to one side.

"Stay here. Watch....see if anything seems out of character, while I look for our contact."

"What contact?"

"The one Hayek set up.....phone call."

"I don't understand."

"I gave Hayek a number....a telephone number so they'd know we're coming home, and how."

"I could have made that call. I still have my cell in my purse....why Hayek?"

"I thought it was a more secure way. Once Hayek connected, and the recorded voice answered, all Hayek would say is, "Boka Ami, one six five six, Miami. Who, how and when, would be answered....meaning whoever monitored the calls would know who was initiating the call, what flight we were taking, and the destination."

"Okay Nancy?"

"Okay Robert."

She watched Monday, as he slowly walked to the right of where the majority of waiting people were congregated, and then stopped in front of a small man, dressed in a black suit and holding a sign that read, "Chopin."

Nancy smiled as she thought about the sign. Her mind immediately formulated the word, "apropos," and she thought, that's perfect....maybe too much so.

As she canvassed the general area in both directions, she paused numerous times, scanning the throng of people as she tried to lock-on to anything out of the ordinary. Satisfied, she looked back at Monday, and saw the slight hand motion. Before she reacted, Monday and the small man began walking toward one of the exit doors.

Gault followed slowly anticipating a situation that never materialized. Then she willed herself to relax.

Once through the exit door Nancy followed Monday to a white Lexus SUV parked in the "Limousine Parking Only," section and entered the vehicle quickly.

Silence prevailed throughout the twenty-four minute ride to a Spanish styled house on Miami's upscale, Pine Tree Drive. The vehicle pulled into a driveway on the left side of the house, and then stopped. Monday exited the passenger side, and then held the rear door open for Nancy Gault.

They walked side by side toward the front door. As it opened, framed in the shadows, several feet in from the doorway, was the outline of an indiscernible figure.

Monday stepped aside allowing the woman to precede him. In an almost inaudible voice, he heard her say, “Arias….Arias Janco.”

Chapter 15

The men waiting in the two parked cars positioned on the east and west sides of the Airport Expressway, listened as the description of the target's vehicle was repeated several times. When the request to confirm was asked, both recipients responded in the affirmative.

As the white Lexus SUV turned onto the Airport Expressway heading toward Miami Beach, the U.S. mail truck followed at a discreet distance. In thirty second intervals, after the Lexus and mail truck passed by, both cars moved in behind, and assumed a leapfrog tracking pattern, until the target's vehicle reached the house on Pine Tree Dive.

The information was relayed to a Miami substation, and then encrypted, and sent under "Eyes Only" classification, to the addressee at the American Embassy in Boka Ami.

*

The only indication that Arias Janco was alive, was the occasional twitch of his right hand during the thirty-eight minute report. Otherwise, he seemed comatose.

Monday related the events as they affected him. First, his observations at the theater, and once they were within the Embassy grounds and then during their meetings with the American Ambassador and Roland Evers.

When Monday finished, Nancy began giving her version of events. Her descriptive narrative left nothing to Janco's imagination, as she related the sequences of events in minute detail.

When she finished, she looked over at Monday, who was silently marveling at how precise and detailed her report was. He thought that it probably stemmed from her classical training as a pianist – from someone who is skilled at remembering the complexities of some of the most difficult music ever composed, and then playing that music flawlessly.

Janco sat quietly as he stared at some distant spot on the wall. The silence and semi-darkness of the room allowed his mind to interpret, and correlate what he heard.

As the silence built, Nancy thought about what she said, and wondered whether she left out anything of importance. Then, as quickly, thought, if I did, Monday would have mentioned it. Then she looked over at Monday who saw the head movement peripherally, and turned slightly before locking eyes. He smiled, as much to reassure her, as to reassure himself that they covered all the salient points.

Finally, Janco spoke. His voice was modulated, and his eyes remained on that distant spot on the wall. As the words resonated inside their minds, the question Janco asked unnerved each of them in almost the same way.

"How do you know that Min Qua Fu is dead?"

When neither of them replied, Janco repeated the question in the same modulated tone.

Each waited for the other, until Janco followed up quickly, "you don't know."

Monday moved his clenched fist lightly against his mouth, then looked at Janco whose position hadn't changed, and said, "he's dead. The C-4 detonated….I triggered the remote, and as I've stated, just before the RPGs, rockets, or whatever, impacted the theater, the pillow under the bench exploded. He couldn't have lived through that."

"You don't know that Mr. Monday. He could have been wounded. Where is your confirmation?"

Before Monday could think of a reply, Janco added, "You….and you, Miss Gault, don't have one iota of proof that Min Qua Fu has been sent on a long vacation….not one iota of proof. Wasn't that basic operating procedure to confirm that the target has been eliminated? Are you such rank amateurs that you didn't confirm…." and Janco stopped abruptly.

"If he was alive, MacMahon or Evers would have said something."

"Why….Why would they share that information with you….to what benefit, Mr. Monday? You already mentioned that you thought Evers was a "Christian in Action," (slang for CIA) and you had the feeling that one or both of them, thought you two were involved....but let's not rehash that again. The fact remains that we have an open ended situation....do you both agree?"

Neither Gault nor Monday replied, forcing Janco to turn his head and look at them.

"Do either of you understand English? And if you do, why don't you answer?" Janco's voice was sarcastic. "That incident at the roadblock....three Chinese. How utterly coincidental."

"We don't know, positively whether he was killed. Our assumption is that he was. Maybe someone in his group saw something before the attack, and decided that he'd err on the side of co-mission, rather than omission. Whether that decision was right or wrong....the decision to eliminate us is immaterial. Eliminating us, would appear to even things up, whether or not we were actually involved. So the American pianist is dead, and the English manager along with her. What would be lost? Nothing, but maybe something was gained, at least for appearance sake. That individual could then tell his superiors, that revenge was extracted on the perpetrators."

"Have you lost your mind Monday....babbling that gibberish....those meaningless words. Is this business too complex for that mind of yours to comprehend? Don't you understand what I'm saying, and don't you realize the concerns I have both for the organization and its members? The last thing we need is a blow back and that's what we have."

"Okay….okay, Arias….enough….please. I understand," and Monday glanced quickly at the woman, before adding, "....and so does Nancy"

Monday took a deep breath and let the air out in a rush. "Maybe Min Qua Fu is alive, and maybe he's not. Either way, it doesn't matter….and I concur….someone connected the dots….it wasn't that hard. Whether they, whoever they might be, saw something at the moment of detonation, or came up with some physical evidence when they examined the scene….the piano, the stage area or whatever….we're suspect, and logically so. Min Qua Fu, and his associates will come for us to extract payment. They already made their first attempt back in Boka Ami….at that roadblock. They know who we are, and tracking us down is juvenile stuff."

Robert Monday looked over at Janco who appeared to be staring at the same spot on the wall.

"We can go to ground….hide, but for how long, and where. Eventually we have to surface. Knowing the Chinese, and I do know them, they'll never stop looking for us, and eventually they'll find us."

After a momentary pause, "Our best defense is an offense…..we go back to Boka Ami and neutralize Mr. Min Qua Fu, or get the confirmation."

*

Monday reached for the coffee cup, then let his hand fall away as he thought, probably cold, besides I've had enough.

Janco reacted to what he saw and offered Monday a refill.

Monday shook his head. "Back to business. As I said, I've slept on it, Arias, and that's the only way....go back to Boka Ami. I haven't spoken with Nancy yet, but as I see it we have an alternative, which by definition....for clarification means two. One, we go together, Nancy & me, and she performs again for the...." and Monday paused for a long moment before continuing, "....the relief effort, to rebuild the theater. Or, I go back, and fly solo, meaning I arrive alone, but have someone in country to take care of the sundry details like Hayek did. Word will get to the parties of interest, that we're there or I'm there. They'll come out from their nest, and do what they have to."

The rancor in Janco's voice was evident. Monday let the thought float through his mind whether he should just tell Janco to fuck off and be done with it. Leave all this shit behind and take his chances on his own. But he knew that wasn't so easy. He'd grown accustomed to the lifestyle that the remunerations provided. Besides, he knew that it was his bruised ego talking, not him. He knew what Janco stated, was all true. He failed to confirm the termination of a target....amateurish, and a reflection that he wasn't all his persona projected. He forced his attention back to Janco's voice, and tried to pick up enough of what he was now saying, to understand what he missed while listening to his mind chatter.

"....and back there, in Boka Ami, is their territory, so to speak. They have the assets stationed at their Embassy....more advantages for the other side. The odds are in their favor, but those odds were increased by your lack of attention to detail, and that goes for you as well, Miss Gault. As I see it, the assignment remains unfinished. There are no rewards for failure or piecemeal accomplishments. In addition, we have the death of an asset. While that's expected in our line of work from time to time, as unfortunate as that might be, I question whether it was preventable."

A silence prevailed as Monday and Gault thought about what Janco said. He cut through the silence by saying, "Failure has its own rewards, but half-finished business has none. I'm reminded of a story about an insurance salesman who was in the process of getting fired for not bringing in any business. His response was, "I tried." In case either of you are interested, there is no reward for trying."

Janco waited a moment, and then left the room.

*

"....and they were three of my best men, Comrade Bao."

The thin smile that formed at the corner of the Deputy Director's mouth, unnerved the man who stood at ram-rod attention.

"You didn't state what you did with the bodies."

Deng Wu Ling let his eyes lock with the seated man, and then quickly looked away.

"There were no bodies, Comrade Deputy Director."

'There were no bodies....how could that be? Do you think they took the flight back to America along with the two assassins?"

"No Comrade Bao....unfortunately I have no explanation. It is illogical to me and I don't.... "

Bao waved his hand back and forth, cutting off Ling in mid-sentence.

"You lost three men, and you failed to carry out your assignment. I view that as a gross failure. What shall I report to our superior, who remains gravely injured because of the two who escaped? What shall I tell him, Ling....what shall I tell him?"

Before Ling could reply, Chen Boa lifted a Chinese manufactured type 64, silenced pistol. (Where the silencer is built into the frame) and fired.

After the 7.65 millimeter round entered Deng Wu Ling's prefrontal cortex (forehead), at two-hundred and forty meters per second, it smashed into one or more, of eight cranial bones engineered to keep the brain safe. Once the bullet impacted with the brain, it caused a massive disruption, ten times the diameter of its size. Deng Wu Ling was dead, before his body reached the floor.

*

"You don't have to look at me that way."

"Wha….Oh….just thinking….didn't mean to stare….didn't realize I was doing that….sorry."

Nancy moved her head in a way that conveyed "okay," then once again the silence prevailed.

Finally Monday spoke up. "He's right….Janco is right."

"So what if he is?"

Monday let the words resonate in his brain, then after a prolonged silence, he answered.

"I understand where you're coming from Nancy, but we should have made the confirmation. It wouldn't have been that difficult. If Min Qua Fu was taken to a local hospital, it would probably be one that serviced the President, high ranking government and military officials, foreigners, and the upper strata of the local business community. I'd bet even money that he couldn't be airlifted home with the injuries he sustained, and I'm willing to bet, further, that those injuries are substantial. He's very lucky if he survived the blast, and if he did, his wounds are anything but superficial."

"I need Janco to do something," and Monday stood up.

"What makes you think Janco is going to do anything for either of us?"

"He has a vested interest. Wait here."

Monday walked to the closed door and opened it. Leaning against the left side of the door frame was the driver who drove them from the airport.

As the man turned, Monday stated, "I need to see Mr. Janco. Please inform him that it will only take a few minutes."

The man turned again, and walked away. A few minutes later, the man opened the door without knocking and waited as Monday made his way toward him.

"Mr. Janco is indisposed. Tell me what it is you want, and I'll convey it to Mr. Janco."

"I need the name and telephone number of the hospital in Paramarmico, Boka Ami that caters to the upper echelon of Boka Ami's elite, government, military etc., and which would include select foreign dignitaries. Also I need the telephone number of the American Embassy. Will you do that?"

The man stared back, a look of indifference on his face. Then without acknowledging, he turned again, and walked away.

*

Monday let his head drop slightly as he tried to refine some rudimentary ideas that were bouncing around his mind. It was better to go back….somewhat neutral territory, and less prohibitive regarding what he had in mind. The woman would be his reason why he was returning, but that entailed exposing her to renewed dangers. The place was hostile, but sometimes, maybe most times, the cat has to go to the prey so that he doesn't become what he is trying to corner.

The sound of the footsteps caused Monday to refocus.

He was surprised to see the smallish man return so quickly.

"I have what you've asked for," and he extended the piece of paper toward the seated Robert Monday.

Monday studied the paper, then looked back at the man, and nodded.

As the man left the room, Monday waived the paper back and forth. When he had Nancy's attention, he said, "We…I'll check this out….the number for a Paramarmico hospital catering to the upper strata….a military hospital. If he's alive, and undergoing treatment, that's where he'll be. Also, the number for the American Embassy is here. I'll need your cell, Nancy."

Nancy Gault processed the words but didn't react.

Monday, seeing the hesitation, added, "There won't be a trace, and if you feel uncomfortable, get yourself a new one."

Gault leaned to her left and opened her purse. Once she had the phone in her hand, she looked over at Monday and tossed the phone.

Monday caught the phone one handed and smiled a thank you back.

He dialed and waited, then shook his head and re-dialed.

Cursing silently, he looked at the phone, then pressed the end button with his thumb. Monday waited another twenty or thirty seconds before trying the number again. This time, the voice answered confirming the connection, and asking how the call should be directed.

"This is Robert Monday, I would like to be connected to Ambassador MacMahon, or Mr. Roland Evers….both parties know me. My name again is Monday, like in the day of the week. Also I have Miss Nancy Gault with me."

"One moment, please"

After a prolonged silence, Monday began wondering whether the connection had been broken, then the female voice returned.

"Mr. Monday, both parties are unavailable at present, but if you'll give me your number, I'll have them return the call when possible."

"Will you please tell either Ambassador MacMahon, or Mr. Evers, that what I need to speak to them about is important, and would they please give me a few minutes now."

There was a momentary silence, then the voice stated, "Please hold."

When a male voice came back on line, Monday wasn't surprised.

"Yes Monday, what is it?"

"This won't take very long. The foreign dignitary we spoke about, prior to our departure, is gravely ill, and sequestered in the General Sabroka Military Hospital, but you already know that."

Monday stopped speaking for several seconds as he waited for a response. When none came, he continued. "Miss Gault, who is here with me, would like to return, and give a benefit concert for the people in, shall we say, their moment of need. Would you kindly convey this to the Ambassador. I'll telephone you back in several hours."

"Let me have your number."

"It's of no use, since we're traveling, and experiencing too many dead zones. It's better if we contact you. Just alert whoever answers these calls that Robert Monday should be processed through."

“You’re a piece of work, Monday. Can’t you find enough things to keep yourself occupied, wherever it is that you hibernate?”

“Sure I can, but it's not as much fun as your sandbox.”

Monday heard the click, and then the low din of static indicating the connection had been severed.

“Nancy.”

When she looked up, he used an underhanded motion, as he tossed the phone. Startled by the sudden move, she made a feeble attempt to catch it, but the cell hit the floor, knocking off the back cover, and sending the battery pack skidding across the floor.

“Sit there….I’ll get it, and put it back together.”

Monday offered up the cell, and when she took it from his hand, he said, “Sorry.”

She looked at him without saying a word, picked up her purse, and then left Robert Monday alone in the room.

*

Monday sat with his elbow resting on the chair arm, and his face buried in the palm of his hand. His mind oscillated between wondering how the target escaped death, and how he was going to rectify the matter.

Min Qua Fu was alive….Evers confirmed as much, by letting his comment about the General Sabroka Military Hospital slide by. The best defense is an offense. I've got to be the attacker….can't go back to England, and can't stay here, so that's settled….I've got to confront them there.

Monday started to get up from his chair, when Arias Janco opened the door and walked in.

"All alone with your thoughts, Mr. Monday?"

Monday's eyes narrowed, as he looked back at Janco.

"Things happen, Mr. Monday. In our profession the unexpected is always a calculated risk, and must be anticipated to the degree they can. When the rudimentary things are overlooked, however, that translates back to a serious problem that may well feed on itself….that may manifest itself into something highly detrimental….something that metastasizes like a cancer, and must be cut out quickly, otherwise the infected person dies. You and she have an infection, Mr. Monday that needs to be eradicated. I am leaving now, and I suggest you do the same. Until such time as we meet again…." and Janco let his voice go quiet as he turned, and walked through the partially open door.

*

Janco walked slowly through the narrow hallway, until he reached the first door on his left. After closing the door, he descended the dimly lit stairwell, stopping when his foot touched the concrete flooring.

The tunnel, joining the Spanish style house with its neighbor was directly in front of him.

Janco walked through the tunnel, and was inside the basement of the neighboring house within minutes of leaving Robert Monday. He went up the steps to the first floor, walked through another doorway leading to the garage, and got into the back seat of the Cadillac Escalade.

The man in the black suit, pressed the garage door opener, and then started the SUV. In minutes, the Escalade passed the dark blue car, parked on the east side of Pine Tree Drive, as it made its way toward Florida State Road 112, and Miami's International Airport.

Chapter 16

Monday sat at the kitchen table staring at the partially eaten sandwich when Nancy walked in. He motioned toward the seat facing him, and watched as she sat down.

"Janco is gone."

"Where to?"

"He didn't say. We're on modified speaking terms."

Nancy tried to smile but couldn't. "That tells me we're on our own."

"Haven't we always been?"

"No....we had him, and the organization behind us. I get the feeling now, that we are alone, and can't count on either of them."

"I don't read it that way. I'm not saying you're wrong....it's just that I'm not sensing it that way."

"Then why did he leave?"

"Why did he have to stay?"

"You're answering my question, Monday, with another question."

"He's already read us the riot act. We have an open ended situation, and there's nothing more he wants to tell us about how we fucked up….so he left."

"Fucked up," her voice elevated several decibels, "Well, Mr. Robert Monday, it's one fucked up world. I went through a world of shit back there….RPGs, bullets, dodging soldiers, plus the anxiety of playing a concert sitting on a pillow loaded with C-4."

Nancy stopped speaking but continued to look at Robert Monday, then burst out laughing.

Monday just sat in place, watching her as she laughed.

When she stopped, she glanced down at the table, then lifted her head up. "It's far from funny, but at this moment, I personally don't give a shit about Janco, Fu, the organization, and just about anything else."

"Does that include me, Nancy?"

She stared at him for several seconds, then said, "No, not you, Monday. I've grown accustomed to having you around. Do you want to call Evers back? The sooner we get this finished the better."

"Yeah….the sooner we get this finished, the better."

"You sound like a parrot," and then she smiled.

"I'll need your cell, and please, just hand it to me this time."

Nancy removed the cell from her purse, and placed it on the table, then using her index and middle fingers, pushed it toward Monday.

Monday brought up the dialed calls screen, then moved the line bar to the Embassy's number, and pressed down. He wasn't able to connect until the fourth try. Once the voice came on line, he identified himself and asked to be put through to Mr. Roland Evers.

This time there was no delay. When Evers answered, Monday asked if arrangements had been made for a second concert.

After a momentary silence, Evers said sarcastically, "Maybe in the world of make believe which you obviously live in Monday, things happen when you want them to. In our world, which is a world of reality, things take time, especially in a shit hole like this."

Monday chuckled, then added, "It's a world of your own making....incompetents running everything with very predictable results."

"What's that supposed to mean? It's people like you who seem to think they're empowered by some non-existent mandate to take matters into their own hands with dire consequences."

"I have no idea what you're talking about, Mr. Evers. Miss Gault and I only want to play another concert in Boka Ami for the reasons previously stated. If you find yourself unable to accommodate us, we will seek others who may be more inclined to do so."

"The situation here is anything but stable. The interim head of government is General Beno Aronow. His first official duty was to declare Marshall Law. Boka Ami is under a curfew from midnight to 4 a.m. and there is a virtual lock down during the day. So with that said, why the Hell do you think Aronow or anyone else would welcome you two back to play a concert," then Evers laughed.

"So that the people have something else to concern themselves with. Irate citizens don't make for a happy country. Do you get my drift, Mr. Evers?"

After letting more than enough time pass by without a response, Monday asked, "Are you still there?"

"Yes. I'm thinking."

Monday looked at Nancy, and moved his shoulders up in an "I don't know," motion. Then he cupped his hand over the cell, and mouthed the words, "He's thinking," and smiled as he brought the phone back to his ear.

"I'll see what I can do."

"You said that...." and then Monday heard the static that indicated the phone connection was cut. He stared at the phone feeling compelled by some unknown force, to finish the sentence with the word, "before."

Monday extended his hand, and Nancy took the phone, and placed it back in her purse. "Let's get out of here, Monday"

"My thoughts exactly. By the way, did you see Janco leave?"

"No but I noticed the SUV is still parked in the driveway."

"Then he's still here."

"No....he's gone, but let me check upstairs. Why don't you do the same down here."

After a few minutes Monday returned to the kitchen, and called her name.

Nancy Gault reappeared after several more minutes and motioned Monday with a follow me movement.

"Look what I've found."

"A door leading to a basement?"

"It's more than that," and she pointed down the stairway. "Be careful, there's not much light....only a pull string bulb in the center of the room."

When they reached the concrete floor, Nancy pointed forward, and in the dim light Monday saw the tunnel opening.

“Where does it lead? Did you check it out?”

“It leads to a house next to this one….the one on the right….as you face the house from the street. Janco used the tunnel, so that he could cover his exit without detection. He’s cautious….something we should be.”

“Let me get my purse, then we’ll use the tunnel, go out the back of that house, walk for several blocks, and see if we can get a cab to the airport.”

“I’m not ready to go to Boka Ami just yet.”

“I’m not either. I’m planning to fly to New York, and then get home to Connecticut.”

“Funny, Nancy, I am planning the same.”

“England?”

“No, Greenwich, Connecticut.”

*

“This is mobile one…. no activity, coming or going. Do you want us to extend the surveillance?”

“Yes, mobile one. Augmenting with FedEx decoy. Arriving shortly.”

“Okay….noted.”

The driver turned his head toward the man in the passenger seat, “You heard it. We wait and see.”

*

Approximately twenty-five minutes later, a FedEx delivery van stopped in front of the Pine Tree Drive house. The driver, carrying a package under his arm, walked slowly to the door, and knocked. When nothing happened, he knocked again and then repeated the sequence several more times.

Walking to his left, he stopped by the white SUV, and felt the hood. The line of sight contact with the surveillance vehicle was broken, momentarily, as the FedEx driver went behind the house. Reappearing after several minutes, he stopped, once he could see the vehicle again. With a quick movement of his head, he signaled, no, and then walked toward the van.

The two men watched as the FedEx van started moving away from the curb and seconds later disappeared.

The surveillance vehicle's driver brought his cell up, and said "The decoy is gone….negative re the house. If they're in there, they're giving no indication of it. The white SUV is still parked in the driveway….hood is cold….hasn't been used for awhile. What do you want us to do?"

"Check the house."

"Okay."

The driver looked at the man seated in the passenger seat. "You or me?"

"I'll go."

The man opened the passenger side door and walked to the back of the house. Maneuvering a credit card between the door, and the door frame, the man slowly bent the card away from the spring-lock, turned the knob and pushed the door open.

He took out his pistol and waited, listening for anything that would alert him to a potential threat. Satisfied, he moved into the kitchen area and then cleared the downstairs, room by room.

The man removed his shoes before starting up the staircase, and cautiously avoided the center of each stair to minimize any unnecessary sound. After clearing the second floor the man went back down, and was about to leave, when he decided to check several doors along the hallway.

The stairwell was dimly lit as he made his way to the basement. When he reached the concrete floor, he stopped, slowly transversing his weapon in a hundred and eighty degree arc. When he saw the opening….the tunnel, he let some air escape from the corner of his mouth, then followed it, until he reached the basement of the neighboring house. After a cursory inspection of the first and second floors, he returned through the tunnel, and left the house through the rear door.

Sliding into the passenger seat, he looked at the driver as he closed the vehicle's door. "Tunnel from the basement of the target's house to the house on the right. That's how they got away. Some spoiled food, dirty dishes, soiled towels, and that's about it.

Nothing indicating who lives there….nothing. Pretty barren place….basics only. It's a safe house, with an easy exit route through the tunnel, and then out through the other house. Clever, and like birds flying the nest, our targets have gone."

*

"I'm tired of wearing these clothes. I'll be happy to get home….familiar surroundings and all that."

"I feel the same way. I'll buy some new rags once we get you home."

"Good thinking, Mr. Monday, and speaking of thinking, it was a good move to purchase our tickets round trip. Less of a hassle since we're traveling without luggage. Did you see the look on the clerk's face at check in, when we both said, no luggage? I'll guarantee she thought, "Terrorist."

"Naw….she bought the two houses in Westchester, New York, and Miami bit, and the clothes we supposedly keep in both locations. People are gullible….their minds always expand from the simplest suggested fact, and then they reason it out, until it becomes plausible for them. It's human nature."

"I'm still thinking about Janco. Do you figure he's written us off?"

"Nope. He's pissed, but he knows we'll finish the assignment one way or the other."

“I don’t like that connotation, Mr. Monday, one way or the other.”

“I only mean he knows we’ll handle it, one way or another, until it’s satisfactorily concluded….not that we’re going to come out of this partially whole, or taking a dirt nap. There’s only one way I see us coming out of this, and you know how that is. The less we dwell on the negatives, or Janco, the better. Things will be rosy again once there’s closure. Now wake me up when the stewardess asks if we want another drink.”

*

As Chen Bao listened to the labored speech, he couldn’t help wondering what the Director’s face and torso looked like under the swath of bandages, some areas stained crimson from the oozing wounds.

“I understand completely Comrade Fu, and for your information, the matter of Deng Wu Ling has been resolved…..he has joined his ancestors.”

*

Chen Bao sat quietly as he waited for the woman’s reply. The fact that she didn’t answer immediately was understandable, since the question was asked with a finality that she knew had no recourse. The ultimate responsibility would be hers alone and the consequences for failure, terminal.

“I understand, and I am honored, Comrade Bao, that you have selected me. I shall not fail.”

"Then I suggest you make all necessary arrangements with your department head at MSS (Ministry of State Security). Anticipating your answer, Miss Feng, I have spoken with Comrade Zi-Heng Wang, and he will provide background information on the two individuals. Also he will arrange for an Embassy courier to meet you at your destination airport in New York, with the necessary materials to complete this assignment....your specific requirements can be discussed with him."

Chao Xing Feng, stood up, bowed, and then left the room.

As she walked toward the elevator, she thought about her family. Did they still think about her after all these years....wondering what happened to her when she didn't return home that summer? Her heart was always with her ancestral home, despite her American upbringing. When she visited the Mainland that summer to attend Tsinghua University in Beijing, she remembered how it all began. First the casual conversations in the tea house with classmates. Then the introduction, by her Professor, to "people of influence." Soon she was recruited by the Ministry of State Security, and trained at the University of International Relations (Guoji Guanxi Xueyuan).

She thought about her first name, Chao Xing, which translated, means "morning star," and wondered how brightly that star would be burning after this assignment.

*.

"I'll drop you off first, and then I'll book myself into Le Grande. We can hook up later....if you want to."

"Yes, I do....call me."

"What was the name of that men's store on Greenwich Avenue?"

"Edwards."

"Yeah....that's the one. Can I walk it, or do I need a taxi?"

"You can walk it. When you come out of the hotel, make a left....go under the bridge and keep walking straight. That's Greenwich Avenue, and Edwards is about three or four long blocks on your right."

*

Nancy looked over the rim of her glass, and stared at Monday.

"You look very nice, Mr. Monday."

"And you do too, Miss Gault."

Nancy smiled, and took a sip of wine. "Nice wine selection Monday, and I really mean it....you look very nice. I like the suit, tie, and the trimmings."

“Thank you again, dear lady. These dandy rags, and a few other things, set me back more than a few thousand. That’s one expensive store. Normally, I wouldn’t mention money….worthless paper, by most accounts, but since we haven’t gotten paid for Boka Ami, I’m funding my own salvation now.”

“I know the feeling Monday,” and then she took another sip of wine. “What’s new from the Embassy?”

“He’s dodging me.”

Nancy moved her head up and down several times. “Why do we have to play a concert? Why don’t we just go back and do what we have to do….formulate a plan and just do it.”

“I’m starting to lean that way.”

“Then the sooner we do it Robert, the better. There’s not going to be any closure for either of us until things are settled, and those things need our attention. We’re spinning wheels here, and that’s not accomplishing anything, except wasting precious time, and….and, I’m not sure we have that luxury…..of wasting time.”

Robert Monday let the words spin around his head, and then he looked at her, and nodded. “You’re right. Let’s plan on leaving here three days from today. That makes it Monday, “and then he smiled at the unintended pun. “Well, at least for tonight, let’s put Boka Ami on the back burner and enjoy the meal.”

*

The woman sat at the petite coffee bar in Edwards and sipped a double espresso as she discreetly watched the man move about the men's department.

She thought about the elegance the store projected, from the high end jewelry display on the first floor, to the fashionable women's department on the second floor. Then her mind pictured the French, Dutch and Italian high end stores that lined Sanlitum Road in Beijing's Chaoyang District, and she smiled. All the same….everywhere, when you have money.

*

Armed with Nancy Gault's address, provided by the Ministry of State Security prior to her departure, Chao Xing Feng began surveillance of the woman's house as soon as she arrived in Greenwich, Connecticut. She watched as the Westchester Taxi dropped the woman off, and then followed the taxi as it drove to the Le Grande Hotel on Boat Road.

She parked her car, and waited for several minutes after the man entered the hotel. Then removing her Chanel duffle bag from the rear seat, Chao Xing Feng walked into the lobby.

"I'm sorry, but I don't have a reservation. Greenwich was an unexpected stop. I hope you can help me. I need a room for several nights and might extend my stay by several days."

Chao Xing Feng smiled and waited.

The reception clerk was surprised at the Chinese woman's articulate English and her coiffed appearance. Money, she thought. One of the many moneyed elite from the Mainland and Hong Kong who were buying up property in Greenwich and other Connecticut towns like Westport and New Canaan.

"Yes, of course we are able to accommodate you, Miss….?"

"Yun," and Chao Xing Feng handed the receptionist her maroon colored passport indicating she was a Beijing resident named Lijuan Yun.

*

She placed her duffel on the bed then went to the bathroom. After a quick once over in the mirror, Feng returned quickly to the lobby, and took a seat where she could observe the lobby's entrance/exit doors, and the elevators. She relaxed slightly as she sipped a complimentary coffee and flipped the pages of a fashion magazine.

When the man returned to the lobby, Feng watched him hand his room key to the receptionist, and then walk out through an open lobby door. When he turned left, and moved away from her line of sight, Chao Xing Feng placed the half-filled coffee cup and magazine on the table and walked out the still open door.

Chapter 17

Chao Xing Feng, carrying a glass of wine in her hand, walked slowly along the promenade that ran parallel to the harbor, the hotel's lobby, and its upscale restaurant, L'Escole. She occasionally looked at the wall of windows that separated the interior of the lobby and the restaurant, from the promenade.

A moment before she was about to reverse her steps, she noticed a red, F-type Jaguar coupe parked in a VIP spot. The vehicle was similar to the one she observed parked at the Greenwich house of the female target.

Feng moved quickly along the promenade until she reached a door which opened into the restaurant. Meeting the maitre d' about half way, Chao Xing asked about a reservation for a non-existent person. After checking his reservation log, the maitre d' indicated that no such reservation was made.

"I'll wait in the lobby," and then Feng smiled. As she walked toward the main door, she saw them seated near the center of the room.

*

Feng walked to the reception desk and held out her empty wine glass.

"Seems I've inadvertently taken this from the restaurant. May I give it to you to return?"

“Of course, Miss Yun.”

“You remembered my name.”

The receptionist smiled. “We try.”

“Well, you’ve succeeded. While it’s still early, I think I’ll take a drive around your lovely town.”

“If you get lost, call us. Here’s the number,” and the receptionist handed Feng her card.

“Thank you.”

After placing the card in her purse, she started walking toward the main entrance.

The doorman opened the door as Chao Xing Feng approached and then moved several fingers up, touching the visor of his cap.

Feng acknowledged the gesture with a “thank you,” and then continued walking to her car. She opened the trunk, took out the leather briefcase, and then entered the driver’s side of the Chrysler 300 sedan.

As she placed the briefcase on the passenger’s seat, she glanced at the side-view mirror, and saw the doorman staring at the car.

She started the ignition, and then slowly drove out of the hotel’s parking lot. About a half a block from the hotel, Feng noticed an entrance to a parking lot bordering the Greenwich train station.

She drove to a secluded corner of the lot, and shut off the engine.

Opening the briefcase, Feng removed the Chinese version of a Liberator Pistol, and placed it in her purse. Originally designed during World War II by the United States, the small, single shot, .45 caliber weapon was supplied to resistance fighters in Europe. The Chinese modified the weapon so that it now held two, twenty-five caliber magnum rounds, while still maintaining the pistol's size at 141 millimeters, or five point five inches. Accuracy was still approximately seven point three meters, eight yards.

Feng reached into the bag and removed the M67 fragmentation grenade. After gently placing it on her lap, she turned the briefcase upside down, and emptied the contents onto the passenger seat. Scanning each item, Chao Xing pictured in her mind exactly what she needed. After determining that everything was there, she returned the items to the briefcase, started the car, and drove toward North Street.

After parking the car approximately fifty meters from the two acre property, Chao Xing Feng walked quickly, briefcase in hand, toward the rear of the house.

Removing the wallet-sized lock pick set, Feng inserted a titanium tension wrench into the bottom part of the keyhole. Then she inserted a titanium pick at the top of the lock. As she applied torque to the wrench, Feng moved the pick back and forth in the keyhole, until all the pins of the "Pin Tumbler" lock were set. Then she removed the wrench and pick, turned the knob, and pushed the door open.

She let her eyes adjust to the semi-darkness, and then moved toward the door which connected the laundry area with the garage. Chao Xing studied the layout, deciding to use a washing machine as the anchor for the M67 grenade.

Chancing a quick look inside the garage, Feng switched on the light. After a momentary scan, she flicked the switch off, and then closed the door about mid-way.

Glancing at her watch, she became cognizant of having failed to note the time span from the hotel until now. She estimated twenty minutes....maybe ten minutes more. Realizing that the target could return at any moment, Feng was suddenly gripped with a twinge of panic.

After hastily cutting strips of packing tape with the small, seamstress-like scissors, Feng taped the M67 grenade five inches below the top of the washing machine.

The grenade, positioned waist high, would upon detonation offer the largest kill fan.

Cutting about thirty-six inches from the spool of fishing line, Feng knotted one end around the laundry room door knob, and the other end through the grenade's safety pin.

She touched the line carefully to make sure it had sufficient slack to allow the target to enter the kill zone, before becoming taut and triggering the rapid sequence to the explosion phase.

Feng then removed the safety clip, which prevented the safety pin on the grenade from being pulled off accidentally. Once the safety pin is pulled, the safety lever, or spoon, releases the spring loaded striker, which in turn initiates the grenade fuze assembly, and detonates the grenade within four to five seconds.

Chao Xing closed the garage door, and watched as the fishing line sagged into almost an "I" shape. Less than a minute later, Feng had locked the rear door and was running toward her car.

*

"More espresso?"

Nancy Gault shook her head no. "Won't be able to sleep tonight."

"Too much sleep isn't good for you."

"Who says?"

"The medical types."

"Is that why they all look so old, so quickly?"

"Could be," then Monday smiled. "Something is bothering me. I don't know if you caught it. Do you remember a rather attractive woman....Chinese woman who passed by earlier in the evening, came in from the promenade, and had a brief conversation with the maitre d'?"

"I'm not sure."

"Well it doesn't matter," and then after a momentary pause said, "…but it does matter. I saw her at Edwards. She was sitting at the coffee bar, and although I didn't make direct eye contact with her, I felt she was following my every move. Now before you say it's my imagination….my nerves or whatever, a Chinese woman, somewhat attractive, stands out in Greenwich, Connecticut."

"She could be here visiting someone, looking at real estate or shopping at Edwards. They have a high end women's department on the second floor….Chanel, Pucci, Lanvin, Valentino, and the like. Maybe she just likes coffee, and knows that Edwards serves it complimentary. As far as "here" goes, maybe she likes good food or was meeting someone. There is such a thing as a coincidence."

"Only in nine to five jobs….not ours. I….we can't afford another screw up. I'd rather err on the side of caution. Let's stay focused. If you see her again, I want to know….okay?"

"Okay. Now Mr. Monday, if you excuse me, I think I will try to get some beauty sleep. I've enjoyed the evening. Call me tomorrow, but not before ten."

"You can sleep until ten in the morning?"

"No....not since I was a teenager. I want to practice....I need to practice. I'm a concert pianist, you know."

"Okay, I'll call you at ten."

Monday stood up, shook her hand gently, and watched her walk through the door and disappear into the lobby. He signaled the waiter, and ordered another double espresso and a glass of Armagnac Castarede Vintage 1979. As he waited for the waiter to return, he thought, Why not....life is to be lived by the living, and no one can guarantee how long that will be.

*

Nancy pressed the button under the rear view mirror, and watched the garage door move upward.

After she drove the Jaguar inside, she sat for a moment, as her mind recalled the evening's events. She smiled, inadvertently, as she thought of Monday. He was an imposing figure – tall, ruggedly handsome, and certainly cultured. Her grin broadened as she thought that those lucky enough to speak with a British accent had an advantage – people assumed they're always cultured.

Nancy opened the car door, and walked toward the laundry room entrance. She stopped before reaching the door, to switch on the overhead garage light.

Bending over, so she could see the bottom of the door where the door edge meets the door frame, her eyes immediately locked onto the torn piece of scotch tape. Nancy removed her cell phone, and dialed the hotel. When the operator answered, she asked to be connected to Monday's room. After several seconds, she was told that there was no answer.

"Please try the restaurant. He may be there."

After a few more moments, Monday's voice came on line.

"Hello."

"It's me. I've got a problem."

"Let me guess. You couldn't sleep."

"Monday….for shit sake….this isn't funny."

"My, my, such language."

Monday waited for the retort. When it didn't come, he asked, "Are you still there Nancy? Sorry….just trying to be playful."

"Is it over Monday? I need to have your serious side take over for a few minutes."

Monday thought of a whimsical reply, but decided to let her state whatever it was that was bothering her.

"I want you to come here, and see something….here meaning my house. I can't leave to pick you up, and I'll discuss everything once you're here....not over the phone. It's urgent."

"I'm on my way in five." Then he hung up.

Monday signed the bill, tipped the maître d', and then walked into the lobby. As he approached the receptionist, he watched peripherally, as the Chinese woman entered the hotel through the revolving doors and walked to the elevator bank.

"Sir....Sir, May I help you, Sir."

"Sorry, my mind was somewhere else." Monday refocused his attention on the receptionist, and asked for a taxi. Watching the woman dial, Monday inquired about the Chinese woman.

"I'm sorry Sir, I'm not allowed to give out that information."

Monday shook his head in an "I understand motion," as he smiled.

"The taxi will be here within five minutes, Sir."

Monday nodded, and walked toward the exit doors.

*

Robert Monday listened attentively as the woman spoke.

"I always tape the doors at the bottom when I go out. An old habit. The home invaders always miss it, and types like we're encountering sometimes do. This was one of those times. After I called you, I checked both the rear and front doors….the tape was intact on the front door but not the rear. I decided to go inside….through the front door. I didn't turn the light on right away….thoughts that it might be rigged crossed my mind. I let my eyes get use to the semi darkness, and then I chanced it. Once the light was on. I did a quick three-sixty, and then went to the laundry room. The grenade is taped to the washing machine."

"Move away from the house….to the street, and walk about fifty meters. I'll call your cell when I've neutralized it."

Gault hesitated, as if she was about to say something, then turned, and walked toward the street.

Monday entered through the front door and crossed the kitchen area to the laundry room.

It was a simple, yet effective placement. Anyone entering from the garage would be hit by shrapnel at mid-waist, where it would do the most damage. Monday recognized the grenade as a spherical, steel body, M67, containing six and a half ounces (180 grams) of composition B, which is used as the main explosive filling in artillery projectiles, rockets and land mines. He remembered this type of fragmentation grenade from his Afghanistan service days.

He thought, “Easy enough,” as he studied the grenade’s placement, noting that the safety clip was missing.

Monday carefully untied the fishing line that was knotted around the door handle, and let it drop. His eyes then moved up to the two wooden cabinets anchored above the washer/dryer machines.

He opened the left cabinet door, scanned the two shelves, and then closed it. He did the same with the other one, saw the gray duct tape, and reached up. Tearing several large pieces with his teeth, Monday stuck the strips to his wrist, and then placed the tape down on the dryer’s surface.

After moving to his knees, he taped over the safety pin. Then he took a small knife from his pocket, cut away the packing tape that secured the grenade to the washing machine, and stood up.

Staring at the grenade, Monday wondered if it was secure enough. His experience told him yes, but he still decided to wrap the fishing line around the grenade. Satisfied, Monday placed the grenade in his pocket with one hand, as he pulled his cell out with the other.

“You can come home now.”

*

He heard the footsteps, and turned. Waiting until she was next to him, he pointed at the washing machine.

“Thanks....where’s the grenade?”

“In my pocket.”

“A souvenir?”

“Of sorts....yes, but I’ll dispose of it when I get back to the hotel. Can you take me?”

“Yes, but don’t you want a drink first? I think I can use one.”

“Remember your depleted liquor stock, how about one at the hotel? It’s still early.”

“I’ll think about it on the way.”

Chapter 18

The bar area was crowded. Weekends, for the young business types, locals, and visitors to this community of wealth and privilege, are meant to be enjoyed, and that enjoyment usually centers around drinks at a place that exudes ambiance.

The maître d' saw Gault and Monday enter, and motioned them toward an empty table.

"Nice to see you back so soon, Miss Gault."

Nancy smiled, and then looked over at Monday."

"Would you ask the waiter to bring two glasses of Armagnac Castarede 1979, and two double espressos."

Nancy moved her hand, and added, "Make mine a cappuccino."

Several minutes later Monday was asking "what we should toast to?"

"How about longevity?"

"Perfect Miss Gault….just perfect."

Nancy motioned to the maître d'.

"Yes Miss Gault?"

"Does that piano get much use, or is it for decoration?"

"A little of both, but light on the first part of your question."

"Do you mind if I put it to use?"

"We'd be honored Miss Gault."

She stood up, shrugged her shoulders at Monday, and then walked to the piano.

After she sat down, she turned toward Monday and smiled, then she started playing "What a Wonderful World."

The room became quiet, as the music transcended the din of voices. The waiters held back, as they too, were caught up in the moment.

As Nancy moved easily from melodies of Chopin, and Broadway show tunes, Monday's thoughts were of earlier that evening.

He turned his head slightly and looked toward the bar. Staring back at him was the Chinese woman. She quickly turned away, finished her drink and signaled for the check. As she walked out, Monday pushed back in his chair, and when she disappeared through the door, he followed.

Moving to a part of the lobby where he could see most of the parking area, and a small section of the paralleling street, Monday waited until the woman came into view. He watched as she walked to a black four door car, entered the driver's side, and slowly drove away. He framed the car in his mind, and then returned to the lounge.

*

Chao Xing Feng circled the house several times before coming to a stop. As she sat motionless, she let her mind free wheel. There was seemingly only one explanation, they didn't come back here after leaving the restaurant, otherwise….and she let the thought fade.

Then Feng wondered why she acted impulsively after seeing them return, and specifically, when she made eye contact with the man. Was it impulse, or rather a need to distance herself from a possible detrimental confrontation?

She started the car and drove it around the block. When she entered the street, Feng backed into the first driveway she came to, shut off the ignition, and waited.

After setting the explosive device, she was okay with learning about the explosion through the local news channels. Now she wanted to witness it herself….to see, and hear the explosion, and verify that one or both of them were terminated.

Parking in the driveway gave Feng several benefits. One, when the detonation occurred, she could exit the area quickly. Secondly, the driveway afforded a partial view of the house, so that she would see the red car when it returned. Additionally the location gave her the anonymity of just another parked car.

For a brief moment, she thought of the repercussions, if she failed to carry out her directive. Feng closed her eyes, shook her head in an attempt to dispel the negativity, and then forced herself to concentrate on the target's house.

*

Each time Nancy looked his way, Monday smiled, but his mind was consumed with thoughts of the Chinese woman, and how he was going to neutralize her. The look in her eyes, even in the dimmed light was revealing. A person's feelings were always expressed through their eyes, whether it was an adversary or a neutral. The eyes revealed what they felt. They couldn't mask it as they sometimes could behind a smile.

His mind chatter was compartmentalized, as he refocused on Nancy Gault, and her music.

The song, "Good Night Irene," was being played in an upscale Latin tempo, then Nancy glided into a jazz arrangement, and then she finally finished the song in a boogie-woogie style.

The applause went on for a number of minutes, with continual calls for, "just one more." Finally Nancy agreed, and motioned everyone down, but the crowd stood on their feet clapping and waiting for the music to begin again.

Nancy's opening notes of the song, "A Kiss to Build a Dream On," was melodic and haunting, and then suddenly, she shifted into a boogie-woogie rendition that brought those few who had taken their seat, back up on their feet.

Monday clapped his hands softly as Nancy approached. "Not bad for someone who hasn't practiced for a while."

"Yep, I thought so too. Not my usual thing, but every once in a while, it's fun to play the standards. They're as enduring as the classics."

Then Nancy turned around, and waved at the still standing crowd. "Thank you....thank you all. It was a real treat for me....thank you," and then she sat down, and reached for her glass of Armagnac.

"Can we talk business for a few minutes?"

"Sure. That's what we're all about, isn't it?"

Monday nodded. "The woman....the Chinese woman....is gone now, but she was sitting at the bar again. We locked eyes. It wasn't one of those casual things that catches one person staring at another. After a few moments, she broke the contact and left. I followed, and saw her get in a black Chrysler, then drive off. It's late for a sightseeing tour of this rich and famous enclave."

Monday paused, studying the woman across from him to determine if she was listening. Then he continued. "I don't think it's a good idea to return to your home tonight. I know you can take care of yourself, but why take any chances....wait until morning. You can get a room here, and then I'll go with you tomorrow. We'll do a check of the house to see if anything else was planted. I don't want to lose you, and I can't...don't want to make a sweep at night. If she's watching the house, and we enter, and nothing happens, she'll know we've disarmed the device. That forces her to act, and I don't want that to happen just yet. I want the chance to terminate her first."

"You're still following me....right?"

Nancy motioned with her head, and Monday picked up where he left off.

"I want her back here, where I can get at her car. I'll use the grenade. Poetic justice in a way."

"Okay, Mr. Monday, let's get that room. I'm tired....mentally, and physically."

Robert Monday was mildly surprised that she agreed without a counter. "Okay, let's get that room."

*

Chao Xing Feng looked down at the luminous dial of her watch. It was a little past midnight, and she shook her head in disgust. She could feel the dull throb at her temples, and the urgency to go to the bathroom. She turned the ignition key, placed the gear shift into drive, and headed toward the hotel.

Seventeen minutes later, Feng circled the hotel's parking lot and saw the red Jaguar parked in a reserved section near the entrance. As she stared at the car, she laughed sarcastically. The effort escalated the pounding at her temples and reminded her of the urgency to urinate.

She parked on a parallel row, then walked toward the revolving doors and entered the lobby. Stopping in front of the reception desk, Chao Xing Feng asked the night clerk if there was a bathroom nearby.

He pointed to his left. "Just down the hallway, second door on the right."

She reversed direction, and disappeared. Moments later she returned, and asked for her room key.

*

Monday stared uncaringly at the TV images, his mind contemplating a host of other things. Shortly before one-thirty a.m. Monday rolled off the bed, picked up a wire hanger, put on his jacket, and then walked out of his hotel room.

He used the stairwell to reach the main floor. At ground level there were two doors marked, lobby and service. Monday pushed the service door open, and was immediately immersed in semi-darkness. The two small wattage bulbs, threw off barely enough light to maneuver through the kitchen, and toward a small doorway.

As Monday turned the knob, and pushed against the door, he anticipated the alarm, and was mildly surprised when nothing happened.

Using several tissues from his pocket, Monday placed them between the back-plate and the door latch. Once he was sure the door would stay open, he let go of the knob, and started walking along the sidewalk toward the parking area. When he reached the main driveway entrance, he paused, and slowly scanned the building's façade for surveillance cameras, and sensor lights. Satisfied, he continued past the entrance, until he reached the end of the parking lot. After looking to his left, and then his right, Monday climbed over the five foot wall, and moved slowly along the lines of cars.

When he saw the black Chrysler, he whispered, "shit." It was parked ten to twelve meters from the hotel's entrance, and close enough to be seen by anyone who might be inside the lobby.

No choice. It's now or….and he let the thought fade.

Monday took out the metal hanger, moved to the driver's door, and then went to his knees. Then Monday straightened the hanger, and wrapped a small piece of duct tape around one end, so that the sticky surface faced outward.

He rose slowly until he was just below window level. Monday peered through the glass, and studied the lobby. As far as he could tell the lobby was empty, except for the night clerk.

He straightened up and inserted the wire hanger between the rubber molding separating the driver's side window from the door frame. Angling the hanger, Monday, after several attempts, was able to attach the duct tape to the recessed door button. He pulled the wire hanger up slowly, until the door release sounded. As he opened the door, he said a quiet, thank you, when the car alarm didn't trigger.

Reaching under the dashboard, Monday pulled the hood release, then shut the driver's door and went to the front of the car.

He lifted the hood just far enough, so he could access the rear part of the engine compartment. For the untrained eye, it appeared that the hood was in its normal alignment.

He secured the M67 grenade between the master cylinder, and the fluid reservoir. Then Monday pulled the grenade's safety pin midway out of its hole, before tying the fishing line as taut as possible to a metal pipe, which was bolted to the firewall in front of where the driver would be sitting. Monday knew that the vibrations from the engine, while driving, would eventually pull the safety pin completely out, releasing the safety lever, and initiate the sequence that would detonate the grenade and kill the woman.

After looking around for anything he might have left on the ground, Monday shut the hood, locked the driver's side door, and returned to his room using the service door.

*

Sleep was evasive. His mind oscillated over the various scenarios that would make "it" happen. When it did, Monday knew they would come for him and the woman. This time, they'd use all the assets at their disposal to prevent a recurrence of the Boka Ami roadblock incident, and this one.

His mind pictured Min Qua Fu at the piano when he triggered the remote. He knew the explosion killed or seriously maimed the ILD Director, but that wasn't what Arias Janco was paying for. The assignment was to kill the target, and that's something he couldn't confirm.

He started thinking about what he could expect after the Chinese woman was terminated. Maybe it was fate or some predetermined thing that brought him to this point. Maybe his Joss, as the Chinese call it….his luck, was used up.

Monday stared at the clock on the night table. Too early to wake her, and too early for the hotel restaurant to open, then Monday remembered the complimentary coffee in the lobby.

He showered, dressed, and was standing in front of the night clerk, thirty minutes later.

"I want to leave a written message for Miss Gault. When do you get off duty?"

"At eight a.m. Mr. Monday."

"That'll work. You know her?"

"Of course, Mr. Monday. Miss Gault is one of Greenwich, Connecticut's most famous personalities."

Monday shook his head and moved the pen and pad closer.

He folded the paper and handed it back to the night clerk.

"Don't call her….just make sure she gets it when she comes down," and then Monday handed the clerk ten dollars.

"This isn't necessary, Mr. Monday."

"Sure it is, and by the way, there's some complimentary coffee around here, isn't there?"

"I've got some coffee brewing in the back. It'll just take a moment. How do you like it?"

"Strong and black."

"Coming right up."

Monday watched the clerk disappear around a partition, and then instinctively glanced toward the parking lot. He pictured the M67 and the moment of shock….that nano-second when the woman would realize that she had become the victim.

The clerk's voice brought him back to the moment, as his mind focused on the words.

"….not hot enough, I can place it in the microwave for thirty seconds."

“I’m sure it’ll be fine. I’ll be over there,” and Monday pointed to a brown leather chair next to the floor to ceiling window.

It was still too early to see anything through the plate glass window, but Monday still turned the chair that way. He crossed his legs, sipped the coffee, and forced his mind to go blank.

Chapter 19

Chao Xing Feng rubbed her eyes with the back of her hand. She knew what time it was....only seconds later than the last time she looked.

Her thoughts returned to the woman....the pianist. She would leave in the morning not too early and maybe he'd accompany her. She wanted to be close by. If the explosion didn't kill, but only wounded one or both of them, she wanted to be there to finish it.

Despite herself, she looked at her watch again, then decided to begin her day, and walked in the direction of the bathroom.

After she was dressed, Feng studied herself in the mirror. What she saw staring back at her was not the person she knew. Have I changed that much?

And then she thought, what difference does it make? This business ages a person, both on the inside, and the outside. It's the way it is.

She picked up her purse and car keys from the bureau. When she reached the lobby, she turned left, toward the door leading to the parking lot.

As she walked, Feng glanced right, and noticed someone sitting in a chair. She thought it odd at this hour, but before she could crystallize her thoughts, she heard the voice of the registration clerk.

"Good morning, Miss Yun."

She nodded and continued walking through the doors into the parking lot area.

Monday heard the name. He let several minutes tick by, then he stood up and went in the direction of the restaurant.

"It's not open yet, Mr…."

The clerk never got to finish the sentence.

*

Chao Xing Feng pressed the keyless remote when she was several yards away from the vehicle, and then stopped for some inexplicable reason.

She had the urge to turn around, and look back toward the hotel entrance, but she suppressed the urge, and continued walking toward the car. She opened the door slowly and then entered the vehicle.

Nerves. I'm letting this situation control me, instead of the other way around.

She leaned forward, turned the ignition key and let the engine idle as she pressed back into the seat. After several deep breaths, Feng shifted to reverse, and backed the car out of the space. As she drove toward the exit, her mind focused on an image, the driveway where she had parked the night before. Not a good place during the day….park on the street, a discreet distance away but close enough for a visual.

Feng hardly noticed when the car's front end dipped at a slight angle as she reached the end of the parking area and turned left onto Steamboat Road.

The vibrations forced the M67 grenade forward. As the grenade shifted, the fishing line, knotted around the safety pin, pulled the pin away from the grenade's housing, and triggered the explosive sequence. When the spring-loaded striker impacted against the percussion cap, it created a spark, igniting the explosive material – five ounces of composition B.

For that brief nano-second, Chao Xing Feng was acutely aware, as the vehicle's firewall and dashboard disintegrated. Hundreds of pieces of razor sharp metal fragments, crisscrossed her body, but she was spared from the excruciating pain, as her mind shut down, and her body functions ceased.

*

The explosion shattered the glass in many of the hotel windows facing Steamboat Road, and tore away small pieces of concrete on the street side of the hotel exterior.

The fire in the Chrysler's engine compartment sent plumes of black-gray smoke spiraling skyward.

Seconds after the detonation Monday instinctively dropped to a prone position, and crawled toward the reception desk. As he braced himself against the wooden front panels, his mind formed a picture of the burning car. Anticipating a secondary explosion, as the flames reached the vehicle's gas tank, Monday stayed in place. He realized that any shards of flying glass, or other debris would kill or maim anything in its path.

It was about sixty seconds after the gas tank exploded that Monday became aware of the voices, all indiscernible. He blotted out everything occurring around him and directed his thoughts to Gault. He took out his cell phone and dialed.

Nancy picked up on the second ring and said, "I know it's you Monday…what the Hell is happening?"

"An explosion near the hotel."

"Is it safe to use the elevators?"

"I'd imagine so. The explosion occurred outside the hotel. Don't think the elevators were damaged in any way, but to be on the safe side I'd recommend using the stairs."

"I'll be down in a few minutes. Where are you?"

"Near the reception desk."

*

The milling groups of people, most looking disheveled from a chaotic awakening to a new day, were served complimentary coffee and tea by the hotel staff, who were doing all they could to reassure those who would listen, that everything was now okay.

Nancy Gault and Robert Monday stood outside on the promenade, watching the disarray inside through the plate glass window.

"And that's it....that's the story. I didn't think it would happen as quickly as it did. I thought that she'd be a mile, or so away from the hotel, before the grenade exploded."

Monday moved his shoulders up in a 'whatever motion.' "Well, there's nothing that can be done about that now. Once the police and fire types leave, we can get back to your house and search for secondary devices. First, I need to get a few things from my room. Do you need to get anything?"

Nancy shook her head no, rethinking the words Monday used – secondary devices.

"You can wait here, or in the parking lot. I'll be back in a few minutes."

Nancy nodded, "I'll be in the parking lot....in the car."

She waited until Monday disappeared into the crowd, and then she made her way along the promenade, and toward the parking area.

*

Nancy was still seething over the inordinate amount of time it took for the police and firemen to leave the premises so she could exit the parking lot. That coupled with damage to her Jag, although minor, added to her dour mood.

After she pulled into her driveway, she sat motionless, both hands on the steering wheel, and staring straight ahead toward the garage.

Monday waited several additional seconds, and then decided to exit the vehicle. Glancing back at the woman, he shook his head, moved to the front of the vehicle, and began waving his arms.

When he saw Gault finally make eye contact, he pointed back toward the garage, and then toward the front door.

Nancy Gault's focus remained on the man until her mind was able to discern who he was. As she came out of her trance-like state, Nancy reached toward the door handle and opened her door.

"Come on, Nancy....for shit's sake, get yourself in gear and let's get moving. We're going to catch a plane back to a tropical paradise, and we have a few things to go over. Move....damn it....move."

Nancy slammed the car door shut and walked closer to where Monday was standing.

"Who do you think you're talking to....some unsophisticated tart, as you English call women? Do you think I'm going to take whatever it is that you think you can say to me, with impunity? Do you think, because you wear pants, that gives you some special privilege to talk to me in any way that pleases you at the moment? Well, let me tell you something, Monday.....you can take a fucking plane back to that paradise shit hole yourself. You're the one who screwed up the mission....not me. As far as I'm concerned, you're history. Now get the Hell away from me....get away from my house, and don't ever come back."

Monday stared after the woman as she disappeared around the side of the house. He was tempted to go after her....to try and explain, and then he thought that leaving it as it was, at least for the moment, was the prudent thing to do.

He went back to the car, and removed his bag. Then he turned, wondering if she was looking, and started walking away.

*

She kept repeating the word, "damn," over and over again, until she realized what she was doing. How could she have lost it? He was right. She wasn't staying relevant....she wasn't staying focused....every little thing was bothering her in a way that never happened before, and that was becoming a problem for both of them. She knew she was prone to mood swings, more so now than ever. In this business that was fatal. She was a professional, experiencing at times, as much, or more pressure than this mission entailed.

Yet for some inexplicable reason, she couldn't overcome whatever it was that was dominating her psyche about this one.

Nancy opened the front door, stared at the retreating figure in the distance and walked to her car.

As she pulled alongside, she lowered the window, and asked, "Can I give you a lift somewhere?"

Monday stopped walking, and looked back at the woman. His mind filled with things he'd like to say – all of them biting, and useless under the present circumstances. If he was to assuage her hurt feelings, he needed diplomacy, or it would all end in this street.

"What did you have in mind?"

"Breakfast, and some talk."

Monday stood motionless, and their eyes remained locked. Then he nodded his head.

"Good idea."

*

The small luncheonette at the bottom of Greenwich Avenue seemed like a relic from bygone days. Monday wondered how it survived among the pricey, high fashioned stores with the high rents, and then he became aware of the woman's voice.

".....and I concur that I might not react or do everything a man can in an operational situation, but the reverse is also true. While I may have some limitations, those can and usually are, compartmentalized. Once in a great while a mood swing takes place. Maybe I try to analyze too much, or maybe not enough. When I try to decide which it is, I don't reach a satisfactory conclusion. On this mission, I broke down in Boka Ami, and for some unknown reason today. I can assure you it won't happen again, and that brings me to the next issue, you."

Gault paused as the waitress approached. She looked first at the woman, who motioned to Monday.

"Scrambled eggs, home fries, dry toast with jelly, and coffee."

Gault nodded. "Make that two of the same."

Nancy stared after the waitress for several seconds, and then looked back at Monday.

"No one, not you, Janco, or any living human talks to me in a demeaning, and sarcastic way. It doesn't go with the territory....my territory....my persona. It has nothing to do with being a woman, but it has everything to do with civility. I know who I am. I don't need negative phraseology to motivate me. You will never talk to me like that again. If I'm in some distant place, and I may well be, I'll come out of it, and if you need to coax me out of wherever I am, there are numerous ways to do that without resorting to shock and awe through disparaging words. I don't know if I'm getting through to you, Robert Monday, but if I haven't, we can call this over, and you can ask Janco, if he'll talk with you, or someone else. I have no intention of placing my life in the hands of someone who doesn't see me as an equal. Going back to that place, requires trust, mutual respect, and focus, as equals, or the mission is doomed."

There were a number of responses that reverberated across his mind screen none of which seemed satisfactory.

"Okay Nancy, I understand. There was no malice intended when I said what I did in the driveway. I was concerned....I didn't understand where you were, and why you were there. I know that this mission seems like a real mess but situations can be rectified. I wanted to get you back to the place where you belonged, here in the present....to clear your house of any additional devices and then discuss Boka Ami and Min Qua Fu."

Monday paused, waiting to see if she would say anything. When Nancy Gault remained silent, he continued. "I don't think of myself as anything special. I know both my capabilities, and my limitations. I try to keep both in balance. I've never encountered a mission like this one, where I didn't succeed. It's troubling and you are correct, it's my fault."

Monday waited until the waitress placed the plates down, filled both coffee cups and then turned away before continuing.

"I've never thought of you as anything but an equal. Sure I was apprehensive when we first met and listened to that little talk from Janco, but I came to realize that we wouldn't be paired unless he thought we were equals, and could accomplish the mission together, far more expeditiously than either of us could alone. Sometimes I forget you're a woman, and my language comes across in a way that I would address a male associate in the same situation. I know, with you, it was the wrong thing to do. I'm sorry Nancy Gault....can we get past this somehow?"

Nancy's eyes didn't break contact with his, as she remained silent, weighing what he said. Her inner self thought, You don't need him or Janco. You are an accomplished pianist. Your lifestyle will not change, if you leave it all here – right now.

For a moment she felt her body relax, the decision was right to leave it all here and now. Tell Janco it's over. Then an alternative voice spoke inside her head. They're coming for you whether you leave or not, and they'll get you.

Nancy broke eye contact, and looked down, lost in thought as the words pounded across her mind – They're coming for you whether you leave it all behind or not. They're coming for you whether....

She breathed deeply and let the air out slowly as she looked up at Monday. "I don't really have a choice, do I?"

Monday was surprised by her response. He expected something different, and wasn't entirely sure what she meant.

"We all have choices, Nancy. That's what life is about, choices. You can accept my apology and we can continue as a team, or you can end it."

"But that's just it, I can't end it. I would like to, but I can't. They'd still come for us. Even after Min Qua Fu's demise, they'll still come after us."

"That's true regarding every mission. It goes with what we do. There's always one more out there somewhere bent on retaliation. So what? It only makes life more interesting."

"Yours or mine?"

"We can't help what we are....what we've become. If this lifestyle didn't benefit us in some very important way, we wouldn't do it. For me it's the means to secure another persona outside the mundane confines of teaching spoiled kids from affluent homes. Kids who feel their pursuits should be the advance of socialism, instead of capitalism... the latter of which enabled their parents to indulge their pampering."

Nancy picked up her fork, and then looked over at Monday. "I'll give you my answer when I finish."

Chapter 20

The omnipresent heat was as they both remembered it. This time there were no reporters, television crews, or dignitaries to welcome them.

As they walked slowly along the tarmac, toward the custom's area, Nancy Gault and Robert Monday were lost in their personal recollections, until the voice of the Military Policeman refocused their attention.

"This way please....have your passports and travel documents ready."

*

The taxi ride to the hotel was uneventful, except for the visible damage to the theater, and surrounding area that brought back individual memories.

Very little seemed to have been restored or cleaned up. Monday thought, Maybe purposely, as a reminder of sorts to the people.

He could think of several very real reasons why the provisional government would want things to remain 'as is,' for a while, as it consolidated power. Certainly, the partially destroyed theater, and battle scarred surrounding area, acted as a constant reminder to the people of what could happen at any time. It emphasized the need for tranquility through compliance, fear of a recurrence, and the need for a stronger rule to suppress the radical elements operating within the country. Then Monday smiled as he assessed the hopelessness of it all....dictators were all alike as they obtained power, or increased it, regardless of what language they spoke or what uniform they wore.

They were both greeted warmly by the hotel's reception staff. After they were handed their room keys, Monday and Nancy walked to the elevator bank.

"I'm hungry. I'll just drop off the bag and then meet you in the garden area….okay?"

Nancy shook her head yes.

As she unlocked her door and stepped inside, the flashback was all too real. It didn't happen at departure in Miami, or when they arrived, as she anticipated it would, but now, suddenly, she felt the anxiety. She took a deep breath, and let the air out slowly, repeating the process several more times until her body and mind normalized.

She thought for an instant that she was going to lose it, but she wasn't going to let that part of her psyche dominate her again.

Although mildly apprehensive she was resolute. She knew she was the consummate professional, just as she was the consummate classical pianist, both of which required more than the average person could give. Nothing, and she uttered a silent oath, was ever going to interfere with either the mission, or how she would handle that mission, ever again.

Nancy walked to the bathroom, looked toward, the mirror, and smiled at the face staring back. Reflections of past successes in Amsterdam, Tangiers, and back alleys of forgotten places, carried out by the woman she was, and would always be....hard and unwavering. As she locked eyes with the face in the mirror, she whispered, "And I mean it....never again."

*

Chen Bao nodded as he walked past the guards stationed along the hospital corridor. When he reached the room, he hesitated, as he again thought about what he would say. After a soft knock, he waited until the door opened.

The guard saluted, and then stepped aside as Bao entered.

Bao stopped a respectful distance from the back of the standing figure. He decided to remain quiet until Fu turned around.

As he stood watching Fu's back, Boa considered his options. Telling it like it was or hedge to the extent he could and buy more time. Either way, it seemed that his longevity was questionable.

When Min Qua Fu turned, what Bao saw was beyond anything he could have imagined. The entire left side of the Director's face was waxy and white. Part of his nose and chin were gone. Facial tissue was charred dark brown, raised and leathery. His left arm, the area that was uncovered duplicated his face.

Bao hoped that the shock he felt wasn't detected by the Director.

Trying not to break eye contact, Bao spoke the words as naturally as he could.

"I will take only a few minutes of your time Director. The matter of the woman and the man," and then he paused as his mind searched for words that would minimize the sting. When he couldn't think of any, Bao simply said, "They have returned to Boka Ami."

*

"Nice to see you again," and the waiter bowed slightly. "Will there be another concert?"

The waiter looked hopefully at Nancy Gault and then added, "The last one was so good....I watched on television with several other families."

Nancy smiled as she replied, "We're trying to arrange one, but I can't be sure."

"I hope it works out," and then the waiter bowed again. "Can I get you a drink?"

"White wine for me," and then she looked at Monday.

"Vodka, with a twist, ice."

“The waiter nodded, and was about to turn away when Nancy asked, “I’m sorry, but I don’t remember your name.”

“I’m Rodney P, and I’ll be back in a moment.”

They watched the waiter enter the restaurant, and then Nancy turned her head toward Monday. “Word will spread that we’ve returned.”

Monday nodded. “It already has. Your Embassy, and the Chinese both know.”

Nancy turned her lips inward, and bit down slightly, then she relaxed. “The sooner we get this over with, the better.”

“Haste makes waste. You’ve heard of that expression?”

“Yes, and those who wait for tomorrow, forget today.”

“I haven’t heard that one before. Is it Confucius?”

“No, it’s Nancy Gault.”

Monday thought for a moment, and then chuckled. “That’s a good one. I’ll have to remember it.”

The waiter returned, placed down the drinks, then moved a step away and waited.

Nancy looked back at the waiter, and then asked, "Is something wrong, Rodney?"

"I was wondering, Miss, if I could have your autograph."

"Sure....If you get some paper and a pen, I'll be happy to give you an autograph."

"I have them here," and the waiter reached into his apron pocket.

"When she handed the paper back, the waiter read the note, and then bowed deeply.

"I shall treasure this Miss Gault....always. My daughter plays or I should say, tries to play the old piano at the missionary school. Perhaps, some day, she will play as well as you."

As the waiter started to leave, Nancy called his name. When he turned back, she motioned him closer.

He held the smile as he asked, "Yes, Miss, you need something more?"

Nancy toyed with the long way around what she was about to ask, but decided on the direct approach.

"Rodney, perhaps you can assist me. I want to make contact with Ronnie Dajan."

The waiter's smile disappeared, and a look of panic replaced it.

"I know nothing of such a person. I know the name, but nothing more. I am a loyal citizen of Boka Ami."

"Of course, you are Rodney. I just thought that if I could contact Ronnie Dajan, there might be something I could do to bring both sides together. I am a neutral person. He knows I was here to give a concert....nothing more. By meeting with him, although unusual for someone like me, I think because of that fact....the fact of who I am, I could perhaps help in some way to stabilize tensions. I am willing to try. I don't have authorization from my Embassy, or anyone else. It's just something I'd like to do....to try. Is there any way you can help me?"

The frightened look never left the waiter's face. Before Nancy spoke the last syllable, Rodney P was backing away, and in seconds disappeared inside the restaurant.

"I've got to admit, Miss Nancy Gault, you are a very direct person. From what transpired, it seems you....how does one say it in American speak....ah yes, have struck out."

After they finished their drink, Monday looked around for their waiter. When he didn't see him, he motioned over another.

"Yes Sir."

"Would you tell our waiter, Rodney P, that we'd like another round."

"I'm sorry Sir, Rodney became sick, and had to leave. If you'll tell me what you are drinking, I'll be happy to serve you."

*

Monday leaned forward on his elbows, and tilted his head toward the woman sitting opposite him.

"Any thoughts?"

"Yep. The food wasn't as good as I remember it."

"Maybe you were hungry last time. Everything tastes better when you're hungry."

"Yep again. Maybe you're right. How long have we been sitting here?"

"I don't know. When I'm with you I don't think about time."

Nancy locked eyes with Robert Monday and smiled. "My, my Mr. Monday, how romantic. We're in a tropical paradise with a hostile Embassy, no friends, some wonton types bent on killing us, and my partner is going high-school on me." Then Nancy laughed.

Monday just sat quietly watching the woman laugh. Each time they made eye contact, her laughter increased.

After a few minutes Nancy stopped laughing. "That was very nice of you to say."

"If what I said was so nice, why the laughter?"

Before Nancy could answer, she saw a young girl standing several meters away. Monday noticed her as well, but remained still.

The girl took several tentative steps forward, and then stopped.

Nancy motioned her closer. "Do you speak English?"

The girl nodded her head, yes.

"Do you want something?"

As the girl shook her head, no, she extended her hand.

"For you."

As soon as Nancy took the envelope, the girl turned and ran, disappearing in a clump of vegetation at the right side of the garden.

There was no addressee, the envelope was blank except for the hotel name imprinted at the top left corner. She tore open the flap with her thumb nail, and then read what was written. She placed the note on the table and pushed it gently toward Monday.

As he picked up the note, his eyes moved slowly along the one written line. "Meet at 1D North Delong, tomorrow at 6 a.m." The note was unsigned.

*

Roland Evers waited until the Ambassador's eyes made contact with his before he spoke.

"As you can see by the customs manifest, they arrived today, and they're booked in at the Tori Hotel."

"I thought you shut down the woman's request for a second concert."

"Not in so many words….however, my message was clear, or it should have been."

"Then why are they here?"

"Maybe they like the excitement of this tropical paradise."

"For shit's sake, Roland, can't you be serious?"

"I am serious Ambassador. I haven't a clue why they've returned, but whatever the reason or reasons, it's not good."

"So what are you going to do about it?"

"I've left a message with the hotel to call me. I'm still waiting."

"When did you leave it….the message?"

"Shortly before noon."

The Ambassador looked at his watch, then back at Evers. “It’s almost 6 p.m.”

“They’ll call. I don’t want to seem too anxious.”

Ambassador MacMahon stared at Evers for several seconds, and then looked down at the papers on his desk. “Anything else?”

“Nope.”

“Keep me updated.”

Chapter 21

The first rays of dawn were appearing in the east, when the taxi stopped in front of a dilapidated wooden hut devoid of windows or doors. The driver pointed but remained silent.

Nancy looked at Monday, then turned quickly back and stared at the structure, wondering how it remained erect.

Monday opened his door and then stopped half-way out. “Stay here for a moment,” then he walked to the front of the taxi and jotted down the license number before walking to the driver’s side.

“Do you understand what I just did?”

The driver nodded.

Monday handed him several dollars and said, “Wait here.”

The driver shook his head no, and then pointed to an open area on the opposite side of the street, about forty meters away.

“Okay.”

“If you’re ready Nancy, it’s showtime.”

Nancy waited until Monday was beside her and then started walking toward the small, open portal.

When she was a few steps away, she stopped and called out, “hello.”

After several seconds passed, she called out again.

The voice that answered was just above a whisper and unintelligible. Nancy moved closer to the opening and called out for a third time.

She thought she heard the word, come, or something similar, so she walked through the opening. Once inside, she stopped, letting her eyes adjust to the semi-dark interior.

The candles in the corners of the room, threw geometrical patterns across the earth floor, and off the interior walls. Near one corner of the room was a makeshift shrine, containing statues in various sizes, adorned with beads, and colorful pieces of cloth. Ten or so candles were burning at the center.

In front of the shrine was a woman seated on a small stool and wrapped in an orange shawl. Her hair was tied in a bun, on top of her head. To the woman's left, on a red and yellow cloth, sat a child, which Nancy estimated was about 13 years old. From where she stood, she couldn't tell if the child was male or female.

The movement off to Nancy's right caught her by surprise. Her body tensed as the figure moved out of the shadows.

"Hello, Miss Gault."

"Rodney P....."

Nancy stopped after she mentioned his name, letting her mind quickly connect the dots.

"What you're thinking is correct Miss Gault. I wrote the letter, and my daughter, seated over there," and the waiter pointed in the direction of the seated child, "delivered it to you."

Nancy turned her head, and looked at Monday. He nodded back in a way that conveyed he was taking it all in.

"Please come closer Miss, but not too close. I will translate for you. The woman seated before you is Princess Obia Tombo. She is a holy person and spiritual leader in our religion called, "Lascano." The Princess possesses the secrets to connect with the spirits who dwell in the dark world. She is revered by many in Boka Ami including Commander Ronnie Dajan."

Nancy took a moment to process what was said, then answered. "Please tell the Princess that it is an honor for me, and my associate to meet her. We are humbled. Please tell her my background and please mention my request."

Rodney P began to translate, but after several seconds, the woman raised her hand, and then with her head bowed, said something in a slow, almost silent voice.

Rodney P bowed slightly and turned to face Nancy. "Princess Obia said she knows who you are, and what you want. She asks specifically why a meeting with Commander Dajan would be beneficial since you are not a diplomat….you are a pianist?"

Nancy was mildly surprised that the woman knew who she was, but with all the exposure she'd received during her initial arrival in Boka Ami, even someone like this, could know. As far as a meeting with Dajan, Nancy speculated that Rodney P must have told her about the request when he made contact, and the rest of what was happening now was for show and to impress.

"I am a pianist, an undertaking not unlike the Princess. I too have to reach the inner part of a person, and I do that through music. I interpret my music so that when I play, the people can understand the complexities that it entails. A face to face conversation is no different for me. I'm skilled at transcending what is difficult. I know that if I can meet with the Commander a mutual understanding will develop."

Rodney P turned and saw the hand raised again. He bowed slightly and waited. Obia Tombo pointed at Nancy and then back, before motioning both of them closer.

This time when the woman spoke, her voice was modulated. The unintelligible language was guttural and seemed to project something ominous.

Nancy tried to maintain her composure as Rodney P translated. "….and your companion is thinking that he too connects with spirits, but those spirits are contained in a bottle. Would you, or your companion, be kind enough to explain what that means?"

Nancy turned her head around and looked at Monday. "I'm not sure I understand, Robert, do you?"

Gault watched as a thin smile formed at the corners of Monday's mouth. He shook his head slightly, looked at Nancy, and then back at the seated woman.

"You are correct in part Princess Obia. I do connect with the spirits occasionally, but those spirits are entirely different then the ones you are in contact with," and then Monday stopped speaking.

The seated woman spoke briefly.

Facing toward Monday, Rodney P said, "The Princess wants you to continue. She still doesn't understand what spirits you speak with."

"Some of us from the West refer to the whiskey we drink as spirits."

Rodney P translated and waited as the women locked eyes with Monday. She held the gaze for an inordinate amount of time, then finally broke eye contact, and looked back at the waiter. After another brief exchange, Rodney P translated.

"The Princess will consider your request. You are to leave now."

As Nancy walked past Monday she tugged at his sleeve. He followed her out through the portal, and into the rising heat that hung heavy in the morning air. They walked toward the parked car in silence. When they reached the vehicle, Monday saw the sleeping driver, and banged his hand against the rear quarter panel. The driver shifted his body as his mind remained partially asleep. As his faculties cleared, he saw them standing at the rear of the car. Apologizing profusely, the driver started to exit the vehicle, when Monday placed his hand against the door.

"Stay where you are. We're leaving."

*

The subdued light only escalated Bao's feeling of dread, a feeling of utter hopelessness. Chen Bao forced himself to concentrate on each of the Director's words searching for clues to his fate. There were moments when he caught himself drifting as he stared at the scarred face of Min Qua Fu.

Then he heard the reprieve, the words that could mean that the failure wasn't his to shoulder alone. "….she was careless. That was her mistake. Taking something for granted, and not understanding or realizing that the longer she failed to act decisively, the greater chance that the hunted, would become the hunter. That is what happened to Chao Xing Feng. She let them take the initiative, and the result was predictable. One must always have a backup plan, and she didn't."

Bao breathed a sigh of relief, but still remained attuned to anything that the Director intimated through speech or motion. He knew the system. He was a willing part of it, and what he ordered for others, could, and would be duplicated for him.

"That makes two failures Comrade Bao."

The Director leaned forward. The close proximity to Boa made him shiver, as he stared into the disfigured face. The word, 'failure' resonated across his mind.

He was unnerved further when the Director asked facetiously, "Are you cold, Comrade Bao?"

"No Comrade Director. I am distraught over the turn of events both here at the roadblock, and now in America. Whatever you see from me in the form of a facial expression, or body motion, is because the words you speak are as piercing as arrows. I realize the failures. I take full responsibility, and will assure the Director, on my life, that the matter will be handled expeditiously, and satisfactorily, on my life."

As Bao waited for a reaction, he believed that by taking responsibility, and offering up his life if another failure occurred, he bought time for himself. A good move, he thought. Nothing to lose, and everything to gain. He smiled inwardly, somewhat surprised at his words, but pleased nonetheless, if they resulted in the desired effect….life for a little longer.

*

As Monday and Nancy Gault walked into the hotel lobby, Monday whispered, "I've heard from Roland Evers....he left a message shortly after we arrived. I didn't want to return the call, something like a little payback for not returning mine."

"Somewhat childish isn't that Mr. Monday?"

"Depends on the perspective."

"I don't understand what that means"

"I'm not sure I do either. It's just something that came out. What I mean is that what's the hurry? You're not playing a concert here again, and his only interest in us is to find out why we've returned. For him our being here is a major concern, and he and the Ambassador want to find out why. Let's go to the garden....get some coffee, and I'll call him back from there. I don't want to use the hotel phone for obvious reasons."

Nancy shook her head, and followed Monday through the restaurant doors, and into the garden. As they passed several waiters, Monday said, "A pot of coffee, and some rolls or croissants....butter and marmalade."

As they waited, Nancy looked around the area, and then back at Monday. "How did she know?"

"Know what?"

"What you were thinking."

"About the spirits.....good deductive reasoning. Most westerners think about alcohol ....whiskey when someone mentions spirits. It's a logical guess to reinforce our belief that she has some mystical powers. It's like all the hocus-pocus with so-called mediums, who claim they can communicate with the dead, know the future, and all of the hooey. Junk nonsense....nothing more."

"Are you so sure?"

"Of course I am. Don't get caught up in all this superstition. It's entirely built on the weaknesses of individuals who want to believe that someone, who claims supernatural powers can reunite, or contact with someone who has passed. They are nothing more than charlatans who use the laws of probability to get you to confirm something about the deceased individual, and then reinforce your belief system so that they seem to be the genuine article. Nothing could be further from the truth. By buying into their schemes and dreams, they will eventually separate the individual from something he has, and they want. We play along with the Princess to get what we want, and that's a meeting with Commander Dajan."

"And by the way Monday, I have the feeling that the Princess speaks and understands English. Also, for the record, I'm not into the occult....just wanted to hear your take. My world consists of a piano, and tradecraft, where I have to please only me in the former, and Janco in the latter.

Monday nodded. “Understood, let me call Evers. If he wants to meet, we’ll meet. Let’s see what the company man wants from us.”

*

“They will leave Boka Ami in body bags….the sooner the better.”

As Min Qua Fu enunciated each word, his face contorted, highlighting the brown leathery and whitish skin that covered the left side of his face. The effect was chilling, forcing Chen Bao to overcome his desire to look away.

“It shall be, Director.”

“Of course it will, Comrade Bao. After all, you have substituted your life for theirs, should you fail. Isn’t that understanding correct?”

Bao couldn’t say the confirming words. He stood up bowed and watched the Director for any sign that something more was required from him. When nothing was said, Bao bowed again and began to turn away, when Fu’s voice forced him to turn back.

“Is that understanding correct, Comrade?”

This time Bao had no alternative and replied, yes.

*

After Monday pushed the end button, he looked over at Nancy Gault. “You heard the exchange. He’ll drill us regarding why we’ve returned, and we’ll state that he gave us no choice, by the lack of civility in not returning my calls. He won’t buy it, but that’s his problem. If you want to give yourself a quick once over, back in your room, I’ll take care of this,” and Monday pointed to the coffee and croissants, “….and wait for you in the lobby.”

“Sounds good. I’ll be down in a few minutes.”

*

As soon as Nancy stepped out of the elevator, she saw her sitting just to the right of the door, knees up against her chest, arms wrapped around her legs, and her head resting sideways on her knees.

Only her eyes moved as she approached. When Nancy reached the point where she was several meters away, the girl lifted her head up, and extended her right arm. Nancy took the folded envelope, and after staring at the girl for longer than necessary, opened it and read the enclosed note.

“Walk north on Mulaffi Road.”

The girl sensing that her job was done stood up and ran toward the stairwell. Before Nancy could say anything she was gone.

Nancy opened the room door with her key card and went directly to the bathroom. She splashed water on her face, dried off with a hand towel, and then looked at the mirror. Instinctively she brushed her hair with her fingers, and then with a brush. She thought, I've looked better, then smiled.

She placed a "Do Not Disturb" sign on the door handle and walked to the elevator bank.

*

Nancy saw Monday standing near the main entrance. When she was alongside, she handed him the envelope. "I think we have to table our visit with Evers for the moment."

"I think you're right. Wait a moment while I find out where Mulaffi and North are."

She watched as he walked to the reception desk. After a few minutes of conversation, he turned, and walked back.

"We go out the front, turn left. We walk a couple of blocks, then turn left again on Mulaffi….left is heading north, or so he says."

"You lead, Mr. Monday. I'll trail slightly behind. If their plan is to take us out, we increase our odds a bit, by being staggered."

"And if the wontons, as you call them, or whomever come at us, what are you going to defend yourself with?"

"Nothing.....but that's going to be remedied soon."

Monday decided to leave the dialogue as is. He wasn't sure what she meant, and at this particular moment, he didn't really care.

*

Director Fu leaned back in his chair. Although Bao could still smell the medicinal odor emanating from Fu's body, the additional physical separation was welcomed.

Bao stood in a position of relaxed attention, unsure whether the meeting was over. His inclination told him to stand fast....wait until some further assurance came from the Director.

As he became aware of the silence that engulfed the room, Bao thought that it was prolonged longer than necessary, but his only alternative was to stand patiently, and wait for the Director to speak.

When Min Qua Fu finally spoke, Bao couldn't help but focus on the Director's mouth. As he watched Fu struggle to pronounce each word, Bao noticed that only the right portion of the Director's lips moved. The left side, discolored and swollen, projected something surreal....an image of something inherently evil.

As the words formed into sentences, Bao thought, thankfully, anticipating that this meeting would end in the next few minutes.

He was wrong.

"Please sit-down Comrade Bao and share your plans with me regarding how you intend to rectify this matter."

Bao's initial thought was to say something to the effect that he hadn't had time to consider all options, then quickly realizing that by taking that direction, he was digging a hole….a six by six hole. Without letting any more precious seconds drift by, Bao said, "I have a man….mobile, watching the hotel. They will be dispatched at the first opportunity."

Min Qua Fu stared at Bao, as he tried to detect something that wasn't there.

Bao sensing an impasse, added, "He is one of my best men, Comrade Director. You know him from the Tibet affair."

The Director continued staring, forcing Bao to state, "Chai Song An."

Min Qua Fu nodded once. "I want to be kept informed. If feasible, I want to be there to ensure that you do not, zaici ta ma de zhe jian shi." (Fuck this up again.)

The words were piercing, and Bao wondered whether the phraseology used was a prelude to a fate that was inevitable, one that he might not be able to alter. He realized unequivocally, that this was his last chance. It was success or failure….the ying or yang, and the outcome would seal his fate.

Chapter 22

With each passing car Monday anticipated, but nothing materialized. He stopped and looked back at the woman who was following a short distance behind.

"Are you thinking what I'm thinking?"

"Yes, it's getting hot."

"I'm not thinking about the heat."

"I am, and I'm wondering if we're being set up. We're exposed like ducks in a shooting gallery walking along some rut filled sidewalk, and supposedly waiting for someone we don't know. It doesn't make a whole lot of sense to me. The image of those wontons at the roadblock, and that seems like a long time ago, keeps crossing my mind. They know we're in country and we're giving them an opportunity only an amateur could dream up."

"Wasn't my idea to visit some Voodoo Princess."

"Now, now, Mr. Monday….let's not get tacky. You knew what I wanted to do when I asked Rodney P the question. The meeting is a result of that question, and here we are. All I'm saying, or trying to say, is that I don't like the exposure."

"Okay, okay….agree. On the left….up a little further, is a petrol station. That's where we stop, and wait. We give it about five or ten minutes, then go back to the hotel, or visit Evers at the Embassy. You can make the call."

They reached the filling station just as a Toyota Tundra truck stopped next to one of the pumps.

As the driver left the vehicle, Monday glanced briefly in his direction and then said, "I wonder if they sell bottled water?"

"I'll ask inside….I want to use the bathroom, assuming they have one."

Monday nodded, and watched as Nancy walked toward the concrete and wood structure.

As Monday turned back, he saw the truck driver walking in the same direction. Probably paying for the petrol first, then Monday's mind formulated another image, one totally different from his initial thought.

He moved quickly, reaching the door just after the driver had gone inside.

When he entered, the musty smell commingled with the odor of lubricants and gasoline hit him head on. Lifting his hand up, and partially covering his nose, Monday scanned the interior. When he didn't see her, he moved toward the make-shift counter, where the driver was standing.

"A woman came in here, where is she?"

The blank look on the boy's face behind the counter, told him that he might as well be speaking Greek.

The driver took a sidestep, then faced Monday. He pointed to the rear of the room, then toward his truck.

Monday watched the money exchange between the driver and the boy, and then watched as the driver walked away.

*

Chai Song An, and Chen Bao watched from their parked car which was sandwiched between a mound of debris and a concrete wall.

Once the truck left the petrol station, Chai Song An started the car, and pulled into the congested roadway. The interval he maintained behind the truck was more than probably necessary, but he reasoned that the distance would tilt the advantage his way. He couldn't afford to give the driver any reason to suspect he was being tailed.

For the first time in a long while, An felt vulnerable. He didn't like situations that weren't of his own making and over which he seemed to have little control. His professional instinct told him that there had been a royal screw up, and the assistant director was caught in the web. He was determined not to become part of the spider's lunch....to take the fall for someone else's fuck up. There were ways to insure that it didn't....wouldn't happen and it was paramount that he maintain awareness to each and every facet of what was happening. It meant survival and that was the only consideration for someone like him.

As he drove, An wondered why they continued to follow the two targets, when there were ample opportunities to take them out. Why didn't Bao give the command before….at the petrol station, or while they were walking, exposed and vulnerable?

After more seconds passed, Chai Song An decided to break protocol and make a suggestion to elicit a response that would hopefully clarify Bao's thinking.

"Comrade, I can pass the truck, and then stop up ahead somewhere.…an area where I can take them out as they pass."

An kept looking through the windshield, but he could feel Bao's eyes staring at him.

"And you will know what area that will be by some special instinct? Will you know whether the truck goes left or right, or reverses direction, or stops and the targets change their mode of transportation before they get to that so-called area where you will take them out? And can you tell me who they're planning to meet and where?"

As he continued to lock onto the truck thirty meters or so to his front, An's mind considered several replies. Then, just as quickly, he wondered whether he said too much.

Chai Song An's dilemma was clarified when Bao said, "Don't say another word. Just continue what you're doing."

Bao's tone was borderline angry.

An, realizing his comments moved him beyond the confines of his station, chastised himself silently for the mistake, then rationalized that it wasn't a mistake at all. Then in a conciliatory gesture, An mumbled, "I'm sorry….so sorry Comrade Bao."

An braced himself as Bao began speaking. "You're right in one respect. We need to take them out. My delay in doing just that was to secure additional information that would be helpful in determining who these two really are, and who employs them. My concern now is, does the latter outweigh the former? It doesn't. We'll do as you suggested."

Inwardly relieved, Chai Song An pressed gently on the accelerator as he negotiated the congested roadway. In a matter of minutes, he was passing the Toyota truck.

Increasing his speed as the traffic thinned, An watched the truck grow smaller in the rear view mirror. He simultaneously looked for an area to pull off and get positioned.

A right-hand curve provided the opportunity An was hoping for. He pointed and then increased his speed until he was approximately fifty meters into the curve. Then An slowed, stopping part way on a makeshift shoulder with the car's front end protruding into the roadway.

"We have to move quickly Comrade Bao, please get out. I will open the hood, and you will stand in front of the car looking into the engine compartment Please place your weapon on the engine block, you will provide the automatic fire. I will stand in the roadway and flag them down. It will appear as if we're stranded. Once they exit their vehicle, we eliminate them. If they do not stop, I will fire my pistol at the driver and you will spray the truck with automatic fire."

*

Monday and Nancy Gault tried to engage the truck driver in conversation, but to no avail. The driver indicated that he didn't understand English through a combination of hand motions and his unintelligible language.

Monday had his doubts but kept his opinion to himself. As he stared out the window, he watched the driver peripherally and saw the constant glances in the rear-view mirror.

As a car passed on the left, the driver was forced because of the narrowness of the roadway, to edge closer to the shoulder. The truck bounced in and out of several deep potholes, causing the driver to let loose with what Monday imagined was a string of expletives. He jammed on the brakes and then pulled completely off the roadway.

After the truck came to a complete stop, the driver rubbed his eyes with the palms of his hands and then turned toward Monday before looking at the woman, seated in the rear compartment.

"That vehicle has followed us since we left the petrol station."

Monday smiled at the driver as he confirmed what he suspected all along.

"Why didn't you tell us you know the language when we asked? Why the charade?"

"My instructions were clear. I was to make a determination about you, partly based on what you might say, or indicate in some other way. If you believed I couldn't understand your language, well, you know the rest. And if I determined you were other than you projected, the meeting would be canceled."

"And what did our silence indicate?"

"Nothing, but now the situation has been changed by circumstances. Those circumstances are this. That vehicle that just passed us has been tailing us since we left the petrol station. I have watched them maintain the same speed, and relative distance, whether I increased or decreased my speed. Up ahead is a sharp curve, and a perfect ambush site. We still have about forty kilometers to go….there is no alternative route unless we go through the jungle, and that is not to my liking. My plan is we continue along this route. Once I get to the curve, I intend to accelerate, and continue to maintain that speed as I negotiate the curve. If what I think happens, it will happen quickly. I want you, and the lady, one looking left, and the other right, to use the weapons I will give you to neutralize the threat. I will not stop."

Before Monday could say anything, the driver opened his door, and moved to the rear of the truck. He opened the lid of a silver long box attached to the truck's bay which obscured Monday's view as he stared at the side view mirror.

When the driver was again inside the cab, he handed Monday an AK-47, and passed a .45 caliber pistol to Nancy.

The driver smiled. "I think you are better able to handle the pistol Miss Gault, and you the rifle, Mr. Monday." The driver held the smile as he said, "I am Captain Sigmundo Montonka….a soldier in the Army of Commander Dajan."

"What makes you think, Captain, that either one of us knows how to use these weapons?"

"Let's say it's my intuition. Now if the lady takes the left side, and you, the right, I'll concentrate on the driving."

As Montonka pressed down on the accelerator, Monday moved the selected level on the AK to full automatic. He lowered his window then looked over at Nancy and motioned her to do the same.

*

Chen Bao stared at the type-79 submachine gun resting on the engine block but his mind was consumed with a picture that resembled the image of comedy and tragedy, an image which appears on the marquees of many theatrical productions – the face of "Tragicomedy." Unfortunately it didn't adequately depict the horrific face of the Director but it was as close as his mind could formulate. As negative thoughts peppered his brain, he knew with abject certainty, that if this failed his life would be forfeited.

Bao placed his left hand on the submachine gun and listened to the sound of an approaching vehicle.

*

Captain Montonka placed his pistol under his left thigh as his foot pressed steadily down on the accelerator.

As they were at the apex of the curve, Monday saw the car and then the man standing in the roadway waving his arm. At the same moment the Captain shouted, "I'll take out the man….you concentrate on anyone else near the car."

Montonka increased his speed as he came out of the curve which made the truck fishtail. He fought for control as he turned into the spin. Once Montonka regained control, he pressed the accelerator to the floorboard and held both hands tightly on the steering wheel as he bore down on the man.

Nancy turned her head just as the 7.62 rounds from the Type-79 submachine gun impacted the truck. The sequence of events that followed flashed across her mind screen in slow motion. First the shattering glass, then the blood splattering her face, and then the body of Robert Monday as it impacted against her own.

Suppressing her instinct to scream, Nancy pried the AK-47 from Monday's hands, and fired at the car and semi-visible individual until the 30-round magazine was empty.

She let the assault rifle fall to the floorboard as she struggled in the confined space to assist her wounded partner. She was trying to stem the blood flow, just as the truck smashed into the other man, vaulting him onto the hood and over the roof of the truck.

*

Sigmundo Montonka looked at the rear view mirror, then moved his eyes to the right. He couldn't see or hear Monday or the woman and assumed the worst.

Nothing was visible as he slowed and passed the stationary car. Montonka speculated that whoever it was positioned behind the car, was probably wounded or dead. Then for an instant Montonka considered stopping to find out but the burst of gunfire told him what he needed to know.

As the bullets tore through the metal skin, the truck vibrated erratically as if it had a life of its own.

Montonka pressed the accelerator to the floorboard, trying desperately to get out of range. Fighting to stabilize the truck while he still maintained pressure on the accelerator, the Captain cursed as he struggled to keep the vehicle from overturning.

Once he was able to stabilize the truck, Montonka looked for a place to pull over.

As he drove his mind replayed the scene at the curve. Then he shook it off and concentrated on where he could stop.

Once out of the vehicle, Montonka opened the rear crew door and saw the crumpled bodies of Monday and the woman.

Deferring Monday to assist the woman first, Montonka placed his left arm around the woman's chest while pushing Monday away with the other. The Captain finally was able to pull the woman free. Through it all she remained unconscious and oblivious to whatever pain emanated from her wounds. Montonka wasn't sure whose blood it was but the woman's pale features indicated she was going into shock.

He cradled the woman and carried her a few meters away from the truck. Stopping near a clump of pygmy date palms the Captain placed her down and then went back to the truck

A quick examination of the man revealed several rounds lodged in his left shoulder and chest. His face was cut by numerous glass shreds, and it appeared he had some sort of head trauma.

Montonka pulled out the first aid kit from the glove compartment and spread the affected area with anti-bacterial cream. Then he covered the area with gauze, paper taping the ends as secure as possible. He lifted the inert body onto the rear crew cab seat, used the safety belts to secure him and then closed the door.

He carried the first aid kit to where he left the woman, opened the tube of smelling salts and placed it under her nostrils. Once Nancy's inhalation reflexes began, the smelling salts acted to cause the muscles that control breathing to work faster. In moments Nancy's eyes fluttered, then opened as her system jolted her awake.

"Tell me where it hurts."

She moved her head slightly and then said haltingly, "Are you trying to be funny?"

"Not intentionally. Just tell me where you're wounded."

"I'm not sure I am. The last thing I remember is Monday falling and me trying to help him, then everything went black."

"Okay....I want you to stand up. Grab hold of my hand and I'll pull you up slowly. We've gotta get out of here....people are starting to congregate."

Before Nancy was fully standing, Montonka jerked his head toward the sound of an on-coming car. In seconds he saw the vehicle which slowed as it came abreast of the truck. He pushed Nancy back down, dropped to one knee and then leveled his pistol at the driver. He continued to squeeze the trigger as 7.62 mm rounds from a Type-79 sub-machine impacted the area around him.

For a moment, it seemed that the car would spin out of control, but somehow the driver managed to correct the radial movement. Once corrected the car accelerated and disappeared.

Captain Montonka looked at the people scattered along the now crowded roadway, and then down at the woman. He saw the crimson spot just above her right breast, and muttered, "Godver," (Damn in Dutch).

He placed the empty pistol at his waist, picked up the woman, and carried her back to the truck. After strapping her in the front seat Montonka got back behind the wheel, started the truck and maneuvered back onto the roadway. In minutes, the Captain had distanced himself from the milling crowd and those injured or dead from the exchange of gunfire.

Chapter 23

Chen Bao watched, with surprising detachment as the truck slammed into his associate. He remained transfixed, as the body of Chai Song An rolled across the hood and onto the roof of the cab, before falling into the truck's bay.

A moment of clarity enabled Bao to get off several short bursts from his sub machine gun as the truck sped away.

As Bao moved into the driver's seat of the car, his mind again pictured the scarred face of Min Qua Fu. Unable to let go of the image, his reasoning mode concluded that what just took place, was another classic fuck up, and his life was as good as over. Now he was living on borrowed time and then he thought, Maybe, just maybe, some of the rounds wounded or killed one or both of them. It was possible but he needed to confirm.

Bao turned the ignition key to the right and was mildly surprised when the engine started.

Ignoring the people milling near and on the roadway, he turned the wheel hard left and pressed on the accelerator. As the tire gained some traction, Bao pressed the pedal down until it was even with the floorboard. The car shot forward hitting several people.

Blotting out the screams and shouts, Bao drove on with abandonment.

Despite a number of bullet holes, and the shattered glass, the car was operational.

As he drove, Bao kept repeating, "nothing to lose, it's over. Get them even if they get you too."

When he saw the truck off to the right, Bao turned the steering wheel so the car would come abreast of the truck. The sudden movement caused the car to careen precariously to the right. As it sideswiped the truck Bao raised his sub machine gun just as rounds began hitting the car. Bao pulled back on the trigger, blowing away his passenger side window.

Firing short bursts, Boa traversed the weapon, so that the bullets impacted the area where the man was kneeling.

Once the weapon was empty, Bao slammed his foot against the accelerator as his mind tried to assess what just happened. There were two of them....the one on the ground and the one kneeling. There was no way to ascertain who the kneeling figure was, but he assumed it was the target. Then his mind questioned the whereabouts of the driver....the third person....maybe behind the truck or dead inside.

Out of ammunition, Bao felt a wave of hopelessness. He still hadn't neutralized the targets, and was seemingly without options. He sped away ignoring the screams, and indifferent to anything but distancing himself from where he was.

Bao slowed when he saw what appeared to be an opening in a cluster of bramble off to the left side of the roadway. As he backed the car into the area, his mind began formulating a plan, a plan where he would use the car as a battering ram to disable the truck if it passed.

The idea, while fraught with uncertainties, seemed to be the only....the last possibility he had. If he could disable the truck, maybe turn it on its side, he could kill the occupants and salvage the operation, thus prolonging his longevity. Yes, he would make it work.

*

"Are you okay?"

Her face contorted as she struggled with the words.

"I'm far from okay."

Montonka shook his head in a way conveying that he understood. "Looks like there's a bullet in your chest....above your right breast. Do you understand?"

The Captain watched as the woman nodded yes.

The reference to her wound, obvious to her because of the pain, was asked by Montonka to determine if she could handle her circumstances without falling to pieces.

"I can handle the pain if that's what you're asking....don't have an alternative, do I?"

Montonka smiled, and shook his head no.

"I'm going to help you up....then get you in the truck, and then try to get where we need to be. We have a doctor, several in fact that work with us because they are sympathetic to our cause. We'll get you and your friend mended," and then the Captain smiled a half smile as he extended his hand. "Ready?"

They walked gingerly toward the truck, despite what Montonka felt was an urgency to distance themselves as quickly as possible. The danger was not only from those who were trying to kill them, but now from the onlookers as well. The growing crowd of onlookers glared and murmured with increased hostility. There were several prostrate bodies scattered around the area which the Captain knew would be the catalyst to attack them momentarily. The only thing holding them at bay, for the moment, was the empty weapon the Captain held in his hand.

Montonka opened the passenger side door, and started to help Nancy inside, when she pulled back.

"Wait, I need to get something."

Captain Montonka let his hands drop away and watched as the woman managed to open the rear door by herself.

Nancy leaned in and retrieved the .45 caliber pistol from the floorboard. After a quick glance at Monday lying across the rear cab seat, she shut the door and let Montonka help her into the front passenger seat.

As Montonka slid into the driver's seat, Nancy held up the pistol. The Captain looked away and started the engine without saying anything. In moments, the truck was back on the roadway.

*

Was it the tropical heat, his nerves, or a combination of both that made him sweat so profusely?

Bao looked down at the empty type-79 submachine gun resting on the passenger's seat. Useless, he thought. Why didn't that stupid shit have extra magazines?

As Bao watched the slow-moving traffic pass, his mind replayed the sequence of events since first meeting with Min Qua Fu in the hospital room. The more he thought about what transpired, the more he couldn't believe he was still alive.

He should have been sent to his ancestors after the Chao Xing Feng screwed up. How could it have happened? She was one of my best, and then Bao laughed.

Chai Song An....dead, and for what? And they're still alive, and....his thoughts quickly dissipated as he reacted to the sound of a fast-approaching vehicle. Bao turned on the ignition and with one foot on the brake, pressed down on the accelerator.

The droplets of perspiration streaked Bao's face and ran into his eyes as he struggled to keep the car from moving. He was tempted to remove one of his hands from the steering wheel and rub his eyes, but fought off the urge.

As the sound seemed to reach its zenith, Bao lifted his foot away from the brake and the car shot forward. The car's front end slammed into the rear quarter panel of the truck, forcing it to spin right.

Bao turned the steering wheel hard left so that the front end of the car continued to make contact with the truck. When the truck began toppling onto its right side, Bao eased up on the gas pedal and jammed his foot against the brake.

*

Montonka's hands tightened around the steering wheel when he saw the car peripherally on his left. Before he was able to say anything, the force of the impact against the rear quarter panel spun the truck right.

The Captain instinctively turned the steering wheel hard right in an attempt to come out of the spin, but couldn't correct it as the car's front end continued to push the truck toward the shoulder. Seconds later, Montonka felt the truck losing its equilibrium and tipping over.

Nancy Gault let out a string of expletives, as she reached up with her right hand, and grabbed the 'oh-shit' handle above the passenger side door. Moments later the truck was on its right side.

*

Chen Bao pulled the empty sub machine gun across his lap with one hand while he used the other to push open the car door. As he walked to the overturned vehicle, he motioned the onlookers back with a wave of the weapon.

Standing next to the exposed undercarriage, Bao looked up at the driver's door and pictured what he hoped was inside, crumpled bodies – unconscious or preferably dead. If any were still alive he'd use the sub machine gun to beat them to death.

Using the front bumper as a ladder, Bao climbed up on the truck fender and then crawled to the driver's door. The weight of the door, because of the truck's position, proved difficult to open. Bao was forced to stand and use both hands. Once he had the door open, he waited until a number of seconds passed. Then he tried angling his head in a way which he hoped would enable him to see inside, while preventing those in the cab from viewing him.

*

Montonka was conscious, and cognizant of what happened, aware that his body was pressing against the woman. He heard the outside movement and speculated what was occurring and what was about to occur. He moved slightly left, as he tried to take the pressure off the woman, and then saw the .45 caliber automatic in her hand.

Prying the weapon loose, Captain Montonka turned on his side, partially covering the woman with his body and looked up waiting for what he knew would come. When the driver's side door was pulled open, Montonka aimed toward the opening.

*

It wasn't working. Bao couldn't see inside the cab but felt he couldn't chance moving his head any further than he had in case one or more were alive and armed.

He was suddenly distracted by the murmur to his rear. A quick glance back told him he was running out of time. The accident acted as a magnet, drawing the locals to the unfolding scene as it always did. Bao looked back toward the dark interior and then moved his head over the opening.

Montonka squeezed the trigger and watched as the rounds tore through Bao's neck and forehead. The third bullet propelled Bao back and away from the door.

Ignoring the unconscious woman, the Captain angled his way off the floorboard, grabbed the steering wheel and using the dashboard as leverage, made his way through the open door.

The crowd stopped moving and backed away when Montonka appeared. As he climbed down from the overturned vehicle he cocked the weapon and pointed back toward the truck, as if saying, 'it's all yours.'

Several people took tentative steps toward the truck and then stopped, waiting to see what the man would do. When Montonka moved away, the crowd rushed the truck.

Once inside the idling car Montonka shifted into reverse. After several meters he placed the gear shift into drive and maneuvered through the crowd until he was on the roadway again. The damaged vehicle was difficult to steer but he had no choice, the sirens at his rear were all the motivation he needed.

*

The sequence of events related to Police Lieutenant Meno Rengada, were similar to those taken by his associates at two other sites. The overturned truck conformed to earlier descriptions, and alerts for the car were issued basis information by those interviewed.

Nancy Gault and Robert Monday, minus some of their personal belongings which were stolen by scavengers at the crash scene, were taken by police van to the General Sabroka Military Hospital. Both were quickly identified, and their respective Embassies alerted.

Once informed, the American Ambassador, Joseph P. MacMahon contacted the hospital, but was advised only that both were in surgery.

*

Montonka slowed as the smoke increased from the car's firewall. Several seconds later he jammed his foot on the brake and tumbled out the door as the engine compartment belched black-gray smoke, and then burst into flames.

After several seconds Captain Montonka started walking, oblivious to the commotion around him. After a hundred or so meters, he had blended into the crowd of people moving aimlessly in both directions.

He continued his slow gate walk until he felt reasonably safe. Then after moving into the shadows under a cluster of tall trees, Montonka took out his cell phone and dialed.

"This is Captain M. I'm walking, repeat walking north on Makiska roadway. Estimate six kilometers from the city. Need a pick up and this is priority. Acknowledge."

"Understood. Estimate an ETA of minimum forty minutes, possibly longer. Confirm."

"Confirmed…out."

*

Roland Evers stopped briefly at the security desk on the first floor of the General Sabroka Military Hospital. After showing his identification card indicating he was a Consular Officer in the United

States Foreign Service, he was directed to the woman's room.

As Evers got off the elevator, he became immediately aware of the heavy military and police presence. As he approached the hospital room, he was blocked by several armed military policemen.

After a few minutes of unintelligible dialogue, one of the military policemen motioned Evers to remain in place, while he entered the room. After what seemed like an excessive amount of time, the door opened and the military policeman reappeared, together with a man in civilian attire.

"Why are you here?"

The question was asked in heavily accented English.

"Official Consular duties....American Embassy. The woman, Miss Nancy Gault, is an American citizen."

"She can't be disturbed. She is recovering from an operation....from surgery."

"Obviously she is okay."

"What....what are you saying? Didn't you hear me?"

"She is obviously okay, or you wouldn't be in her room. Are you questioning her? If you are, you are ignoring her rights....rights to be represented by her Embassy during any questioning period."

Evers knew she had no rights, or better put, very few. This was foreign soil and here they did what, and as they damn well pleased.

Evers kept pushing, figuring he had nothing to lose. “Are you denying me access to her? If you are, I can assure you that this will not sit well with my Ambassador. I don’t think either of our governments wants a diplomatic impasse over this, especially in light of my country’s economic aid to Boka Ami.”

The man stared at Evers and then finally said, “She is under arrest.”

“Why?”

“She was involved in a shooting.”

Evers let the words bounce around in his head and then pointed to the door. “I’ll only take a few minutes and then I’m gone. If you don’t let me see her, I’ll file a formal complaint with your government as soon as I return to my Embassy.”

The man held his gaze and then looked back at the door. “I will give you five minutes, then you will leave.”

Roland Evers shook his head in agreement and then opened the hospital room door. As he moved into the room the man followed.

“Not you. I want to be alone with the woman.”

After a few moments, the man turned and left.

Evers continued to stare at the closed door, then redirected his attention to the woman. Her sallow complexion told him all he needed to know about her condition, and her eyes revealed her mental state.

"From the look of you Miss Gault, I don't think you're ready to give that second concert."

She tried to smile but couldn't pull it off. Haltingly, she said, "Not at the moment, Mr. Evers."

"We don't have much time….five minutes, maybe four now," and Roland Evers made a thumb movement toward the door. "Tell me what I need to know….not what you think I want to hear. If I'm going to help you, I need something to work with. Find the strength you need….go."

"The Chinese…..I guess Min Qua Fu, who I assume is still alive, blames me and my manager for what happened at the concert hall. They sent an agent to the states….to where I live….and…."

"Go on Miss Gault, time is of the essence."

"A woman operative tried to kill me, but something happened to her while she was driving and the threat was ended. Robert and I decided to return here….try to sort things out."

"And how were you going to sort things out?"

"By contacting you to see if you and the Ambassador could help. I am or was….no I still am a concert pianist. I don't know how or what happened at the concert hall. Neither Robert nor I can continue living, if that's what you can call it, under a misconception that we had anything to do with what happened here."

"Someone tried to kill you?"

"Yes."

The knock on the door startled Evers. He opened the door partially and said, "I need a few more minutes."

"We agreed to five minutes and they're up."

"Okay, let me say goodbye....it'll take another twenty seconds."

The man shook his head in the affirmative and Evers closed the door.

Evers wanted to know the circumstances that necessitated a police presence, but decided to hold off. He knew he didn't have sufficient time.

"Anything you need?"

"Yes....some make-up, perfume, eye drops, and get word to Monday that I'm okay."

Evers nodded. "I'll be back as soon as I can. Rest easy Miss Gault. You're still alive and on the mend," then he smiled and left the room.

Chapter 24

Nancy stared at the ceiling and watched the dancing fingers move across the piano keyboard. The slow-motion sequence enabled her to follow along, easily recognizing the notes to "What a Wonderful World."

The image was shattered by a knock.

The door opened slowly and in the dim light she saw a woman. As the woman approached the bed, she recognized her from the American Embassy, the place where she stayed after the theater attack.

"You're the last person I expected here."

"And you Miss Gault, are the last person I expected to see here."

The play on words brought smiles to their respective faces.

"Mr. Evers said you need some girlie stuff, so here it is….lipstick, some perfume, eye shadow and, oh yes, a bottle of eye drops, some sugar packets, and a few other feminine things. I'll stop by in the morning and if there's anything else you need, I'll bring them."

"Thank you. It's very much appreciated." After a brief pause, Nancy asked, "Could you do me a favor….are my clothes in the closet."

After checking, she shook her head slightly. "I don't think you would want to wear them again…pretty soiled, and stained."

Nancy moved her head, acknowledging what the woman said. "In that case can you bring me some undies, some jeans, maybe a cotton sweater or blouse?"

"Sure. Consider it done. It'll be delivered depending on who is back here first, Roland or me."

"Thanks again, Alice. This is the second time you've helped me, and I won't forget it."

"No thanks necessary. We're one and the same. We take care of our own," then the woman smiled, and walked toward the door. After she knocked once, she opened the door and then closed it behind her.

Nancy kept her eyes on the door as she listened to the muted conversation in the hallway.

Then everything became quiet again. She felt both depression and exhilaration. Time would tell which would dominate.

*

"How is Mr. Monday doctor?"

"We have him sedated. His wounds are considerably more serious than yours. Time and his will to survive, will determine what happens."

"You're scaring me doctor."

"That wasn't my intention. You asked me how he was, and I answered you as truthfully as I could."

Nancy, sitting in a chair, let her head slump slightly.

"Cheer up Miss Gault. Your situation is improving nicely. I would think that there's an excellent possibility that you could be leaving us next week, that's six days from now. You'll soon again be bringing joy to many through your music."

Nancy moved her head slightly, then smiled weakly.

As the doctor started turning away, Nancy chanced something that she had compartmentalized, but now felt she needed to know.

"Is Min Qua Fu, a friend of mine from the Chinese delegation, injured in the theater incident, still recovering?"

As the Doctor thought about what the woman stated, he inadvertently asked out loud, "He's a friend of yours?"

The doctor turned back and before Nancy could reply, he answered, "Yes, considerable improvement. In fact, he is nine rooms from you, room 472. You make a right turn at the end of this hallway."

"It might be uplifting for him if he sees a friendly face," and then he paused over his choice of words as he pictured Fu's face.

"He was seriously injured. Perhaps when you feel up to it, in a day or two, I can arrange a visit."

*

Slightly past nine-thirty p.m., Captain Sigmundo Montonka, together with another man stopped by the main desk at the General Sabroka Military Hospital, flashed their credentials and inquired about Gault and Monday.

Once they reached the fourth floor they paused at the nurse's desk to confirm what they had been told moments before.

As they approached room 463, Montonka saw a police guard nudge his sleeping partner. As the man stood up, he assumed a blocking position in front of the door.

Before either could speak, Montonka lashed out at their dereliction of duty, stating he would report their lax attention to their superiors for disciplinary action. Then Montonka removed his black leather wallet-like case containing the badge and identification card that indicated he was an agent from State Security.

Now that he controlled the situation, Montonka moved his hand in a sideward motion. Both police guards moved to their left, and the Captain and his associate entered the room.

*

Nancy was startled from her restless sleep by the voices outside her room. When the door opened, she saw two men enter. As they came closer, she recognized Montonka.

"It's nice to see you again Miss Gault."

Then he paused and pointed to the other man. This is Ono Urbano, personal assistant to the Commander. We are here to take you to our long delayed meeting. Are you ready to go Miss Gault?"

"I can't go yet. I have something that needs to be taken care of. Besides, I was told I'll be leaving here in several more days."

"Miss….you may be leaving the hospital in a few days, but once you are given that okay, you will be taken to Rockhanah Prison. In case you are unaware, you and your friend, have been charged with the murder of a member of the Chinese Embassy and the death of several civilians. As they say in colloquial English, "Your goose is seemingly cooked, Miss Gault."

Nancy stared wide eyed at the man. "Are you joking…arrested for some killing…we had nothing…."

The Captain held his hand up. "It doesn't matter Miss Gault whether the charges are true. What does matter is that you and your associate are being charged with murder. Prison here is not a desirable place to spend time, but that's exactly where you will be going after a show trial. The trial will give the Chinese, who by the way are very friendly to Boka Ami and their respective power elite, their due."

Captain Sigmundo Montonka let the silence build and then said, "We are leaving, all of us together. Just let what we have planned play out."

Nancy nodded, and watched Montonka pass a silent command to his associate. Urbano turned, and walked several steps to the door. He opened it and then closed it behind him.

The two police stood at relaxed attention as Urbano said he was getting a nurse for some minor problem.

"Make sure no one comes in or out until I return."

Once they confirmed that they understood his command, Ono Urbano walked toward the nurse's desk.

"Excuse me….I need one of you to come with me and check the woman. While my superior was questioning her she asked for water…there is none in the room and she keeps pointing to her throat…will you help me?"

When the nurses didn't move, Urbano asked pleadingly, "Please…we're wasting time. Seems she's dehydrated and we need to finish the questioning. It will only take a minute or two and then if that's not the problem, you can call the doctor."

One of the nurses stood up slowly, went to a closet, took out a small plastic pitcher, and several paper cups. After filling the pitcher with water she followed Ono Urbano back to room 463.

Before he opened the door, Ono Urbano motioned with his head toward the door. "No one is to enter here until we're finished. Is that understood?"

Both policemen nodded and looked away as Urbano turned the knob. After nudging the door so it was partially open, Urbano took the pitcher and cups from the nurse and then motioned with his head again for her to proceed him.

Urbano used his foot to close the door as Captain Montonka stepped from behind it. Montonka quickly covered the nurse's mouth with the chloroform rag as he gripped her tightly with the other arm. After approximately fifteen seconds, he lowered the inert body to the floor.

"Quickly, Miss Gault....change into her uniform. We don't have much time."

Nancy ignored the stares from both men as she changed into the nurse's uniform. Once the changeover was complete, Montonka and Urbano dressed the nurse in the hospital gown and placed her in the bed.

"Let's go."

"I need to do something first. There's a man in room 472, and I need to take care of a small problem. This uniform gives me that opportunity."

Nancy waited for the reply which came first in the form of a head shake followed by a "no….no time."

"We'll make time or I'm not going."

Urbano looked over at Montonka and moved his shoulders up in a way conveying, "Let's not waste any more time. Let her do it."

"Can't walk in her shoes. I need mine from the closet over there."

After she slipped into her shoes she asked Urbano for one of the paper cups and the water pitcher. She walked over to the small table next to her bed, picked up the bottle of eye drops and poured the contents into one of the paper cups. Then Nancy tore open one of the sugar packets with her teeth, and emptied the white crystals into the cup. She stirred the substance with her finger until the liquid became clear again.

"Okay, I'm ready, but neither of you can come with me. I need to do this alone. Wait in here or in the corridor for about three or four minutes, then walk toward room 472. I'll wait further down the hall for you. If there's trouble and you're in here, you'll know it. Then I'll need some help but I hope it won't come to that."

"Do you mind telling us what this is all about? We're wasting precious time and we have little enough of that. Both of us, Urbano and me, are taking a considerable risk and you're not cooperating, Miss Gault."

"I'm all yours in about five plus minutes. Now open the door please."

Once Nancy was in the corridor she walked toward the end, then turned right and made her way toward room 472, carrying the water pitcher and cup.

When the three guards blocked her way, Nancy made a drinking motion with her hand and mouth and then extended her arm toward the door.

She moved her head up once and smiled weakly. One of the guards finally opened the door and Nancy entered the darkened room. It took a few seconds for her eyes to adjust, and then she saw the seated figure and several silhouetted outlines standing nearby.

As she approached the seated man, one of the outlines moved out from the shadows and took up a position by the left side of the seated man. Nancy could see the pistol in his hand but forced herself to concentrate on the seated figure.

As his hideous face registered, a wave of shock and revulsion overcame her. She fought to normalize herself and prayed that her demeanor hadn't revealed her shock.

"Please drink this sugar water, Director Fu. The more liquids you take the faster the healing process. We can't let you become dehydrated, can we?"

The words were spoken in a normal tone. Nancy was surprised that she was able to regain control so quickly. "Please drink this now Director. The doctor says that I must confirm that you consumed this."

Fu eyed the nurse for longer than what Nancy thought necessary but as the man stared, she kept resolute. When he finally reached for the cup, Nancy felt a moment of relief.

"Excellent Director Fu. I'll place the pitcher on the table. Please continue to drink the water until the pitcher is empty."

She held the smile as she turned, and walked toward the door. She turned the knob, then moved to her left once she was in the hallway. She was aware of the footsteps as she continued walking toward the stairwell. When she reached the door, she pushed and then braced her back against the landing wall.

Moments later she saw the door opening. Expecting Montonka and Urbano, the shock of seeing two of the Chinese guards sent panic reverberating through her body.

As one of them grabbed her by her throat, her brain sensors immediately registered the increasing pain and contraction of oxygen to her lungs. The blackness was closing in and she knew her body functions were shutting down. Then, just as suddenly, the pressure on her throat dissipated and she became aware of a struggle.

Despite her best effort, she was unable to keep her body erect. As she began falling, someone grabbed her.

When she was able to focus, she saw Montonka's face several inches away.

"Are you okay?"

"Yes, I'm okay. What happened….why did they come after me."

Montonka ignored the question. "Move, Miss Gault….move."

*

Min Qua Fu's eyes glared at the nurse standing in front of him. He took hold of the paper cup and slowly sipped the water, but didn't swallow, keeping his mouth as natural as he could. As soon as the woman left the room, he lowered his head and spit out the liquid.

Fu lifted himself up, awkwardly, from the chair and reached for the pitcher. He washed out his mouth and again spit out the water.

Then Fu turned to the guard standing at his left. His face contorted, and his voice raspy, shouted, "The shoes….GET the woman….KILL HER."

The guard nodded and left the room. Grabbing one of the three guards stationed outside the door by the shoulder, he shoved him forward. "Get the woman."

They both ran to the stairwell and found the woman braced against the inside wall. As one of the men began strangling the woman, the other turned to confront Montonka and Urbano.

Montonka using a .357 magnum pistol with a silencer attached, shot the closest guard several times, then placed two rounds into the man choking Nancy Gault.

As Montonka held onto the woman, Urbano placed two more rounds into the cerebral cortex (Cerebrum – brain) of each man.

Chapter 25

"Unnecessary.....completely un-fucking necessary."

Nancy, sitting in the rear seat, knew full well who Montonka's anger was directed at. She kept her head turned, purposely and stared through the car window.

"I must have been crazy to let you waste time with that nurse's bit. What were you trying to accomplish, except maybe to get us all killed?"

Nancy toyed with the idea of leveling with the Captain about Min Qua Fu, then decided to answer his query simplistically.

"I needed to know if he was still alive, and before you ask me who, the man's name is Min Qua Fu. He's with the Chinese Embassy."

"What importance is he to you, alive or dead?"

"He was playing the piano at the concert hall when your soldiers attacked. There was an explosion near the stage. I assumed he was killed and only found out yesterday from one of the doctors, that he was only injured and was recovering at this hospital....several rooms down from mine. I needed to confirm."

Montonka turned in the passenger's seat and looked back at the woman.

"You must take me for a fool, Miss Gault. Do you think I'm a fool?"

"From what I've observed, Captain Montonka, you are anything but a fool."

"Then why do you talk to me like one? I asked you a simple question. What importance is this man to you? That question requires only a simple answer."

"I was trying to gauge the amount of trust I could place in you."

"After what we've been through, Miss Gault, I think I've earned a certain amount of your trust....wouldn't you agree?"

Nancy shook her head yes, and then let her eyes drop.

"Now that we clarified that Miss Gault, please tell me what you were trying to accomplish by going to the Chinese man's room? Who and what is he, and how that relates to you, and why do you care whether he's alive or dead?"

Nancy thought, What the Hell, and then answered, "I wanted to kill him. I wanted to make sure he was dead," then she paused. "An explosion at the theater during the recital, by coincidence, went off at the same time your attack began. The explosion which was set to detonate after Min Qua Fu began playing the piano obviously didn't kill him. My associate and I returned to Boka Ami to correct that. The nurse's uniform gave me an opportunity to spike the water. I did this with a bottle of eye drops. Once the mix was swallowed by Fu, it would induce a rapid heartbeat, nausea, blurred vision, convulsions, and then death. I watched him swallow the contents....he's dead, or soon will be."

Montonka continued to stare at Gault, then he shook his head no. "No Miss Gault, the Chinese man isn't dead."

Nancy's eyes widened reflecting the unconscionable.

"Oh no....he's far from dead. Those men were sent by him to kill you. Obviously, something about your appearance....your facial features....whatever. Whether he recognized you, or his suspicions were aroused, is immaterial. He didn't swallow what you handed him despite appearances. The Chinese man is still very much alive."

The look on Nancy's face revealed her shock and disbelief. Before she could speak, Montonka asked, "Why is this Chinese man a threat to you?"

"He's only a threat, Captain, because we failed to terminate him. Min Qua Fu is head of the ILD....the International Liaison Department which is a Chicom covert operational group."

"I still don't understand. Why is this man, despite what he does, a threat to a concert pianist?"

"Perhaps, Captain Montonka, people are not always what they appear to be."

*

As the doorknob turned slowly, Robert Monday reached out, and pulled the IV pole toward the side of his bed. Then he removed the needle embedded in his arm, and held it clenched in his right hand.

When the man reached down, Monday grabbed his hair, and twisted sideways, simultaneously plunging the needle into his neck. Ignoring the pain reverberating throughout his body, Monday stroked the needle back and forth as the man struggled to break free.

As Monday's strength waned, the man was able to extricate himself. He staggered backwards as his hands moved toward his neck.

With each breath, blood spurted from the open carotid artery and over the man's hands. In one final attempt to kill Monday, the man staggered forward.

Monday still on his side, gripped the IV pole with both hands. Just before the man reached the bed, Monday swung the pole striking the man's shoulder and stopping him momentarily. Using what little reserve was left, Monday brought the IV pole back and swung it at the semi-erect man. The contact drove the man sideways where he remained teetering for several seconds before falling to the floor.

*

"This is as far as we go."

Nancy Gault stared at the dense brush through her side window and then she turned and looked at Montonka. She held the contact for several seconds, then glanced through the front windshield and saw the same seemingly impenetrable underbrush.

"In anticipation of your question Miss Gault, we walk from here.…walk to where we'll meet Commander Dajan. It's not as bad as it seems and you'll do just fine." Then Montonka said sarcastically, "Although that borrowed white nurse's dress may get a little dirty, you'll still have your own shoes to walk in."

As her brain conjured up several stinging retorts, the words that overrode her momentary anger were, "You still have your own shoes to walk in."

Her mind replayed the words several more times and then she understood...understood why it happened. The shoes.…my shoes.…dark leather flats instead of the usual nurse's laced-up whites. Damn, damn, damn, and damn again. Montonka's right. Min Qua Fu is still alive. That cunning Chinese bastard has more lives than a cat, and then she smiled.

"Something that you could share with me, Miss Gault?"

Nancy moved her head down and then up. "You're right, Min Qua Fu is still alive, and my shoes were the give-away. Maybe he also recognized me in the semi-darkness. I should have known better but life is a continuing learning process, isn't it Captain Montonka?"

"For some, yes, they learn quickly and survive. But for most, they find that their lives are shortened dramatically because of their inattention to detail."

As the words resonated, Nancy's mind replayed the salient events leading to this moment. The concert hall, Min Qua Fu at the piano, the detonation, trying to survive the Maroon attack, and the roadblock en route to the airport where the attempted assassination took place. Then the hand grenade in her Greenwich, Connecticut home, the link-up with Montonka leading to a firefight with the Chinese assassin, her subsequent hospitalization, and now here to meet Ronnie Dajan.

"Yeah, Captain Sigmundo Montonka, you are absolutely correct....for some they learn quickly and survive. I've been lucky, but I do learn and oh yes, I will survive."

*

His mind urged him to move....his body told him something else.

Can't stay here, and then Monday was caught in a time warp and transported back in time, back to a

place whose memories he couldn't erase…
memories of his service in Afghanistan.

The animal carcass was intact, lying in the middle of the road. The desolate terrain in Helmand Province was anything but. He knew eyes were watching his every move and those of his fellow British soldiers deployed in defensive positions a hundred or so meters behind.

As he knelt down in front of the stomach cavity, he wondered whether his ABS, Advance Bomb Suit – a full body ensemble that protects the explosive ordnance soldier against blasts, heat, and flame, would once again protect him. He always wondered….always.

Noting both the animal's entrails hanging out from a hole in the stomach wall, and the seven inch incision hastily sewn, Monday then scanned the carcass for wires, first left to right and then in reverse. Satisfied, he moved on his knees to the head of the animal, pried open the mouth and examined the inside. After checking the animal's ears and nose, he moved back to the stomach cavity and carefully examined the entrails.

After determining that there were no wires or caps hidden in the hanging pieces of intestine and sinew, Monday, starting at the incision, slit the skin up the belly until he reached the animal's chin. He carefully peeled away the skin with his fingers until the diaphragm was exposed. And there it was….a block of C-4, armed with an electro-magnetic blasting cap.

Monday separated the blasting cap from the C-4, and then removed the plastic explosive from the body cavity. He methodically rechecked the cavity to ensure that he didn't overlook a secondary explosive device. After letting his body normalize for a few seconds, Monday stood up, lifted the visor of his helmet and then held up his right hand as he spoke via radio to the embedded unit commander. Once the all clear signal was given, Monday watched as the troops remounted their respective vehicles and started moving forward.

He was wiping away the sweat with the back of his hand when the explosion occurred. He stared hypnotically as the lead Humvee was lifted off the ground, and then turned on its side as it contacted the road surface approximately seventy meters to his front.

After successfully neutralizing the IED (Improvised Explosive Device), Monday's relief was replaced with a sense of dejection. Did they miss it during their initial sweep, and then he tried to reconcile it all, thinking, it wasn't my responsibility….I just render them safe. If I knew about it….and then he let the thought melt away as he walked toward the wreckage.

After several meters, the red-orange cloud obliterated the roadway to his front and the blast wave propelled him backward and off his feet. Monday struggled to get back up. He turned onto his side and saw the outline through a misty haze. As the haze slowly cleared from his mind, the images from that forsaken place faded away, and he realized that he was now lying next to the man he just killed.

But how was that possible? His last recollection, moments after the attack was being in bed staring at the inert body on the floor. Now he was lying next to it.

Monday became aware of both the pulsating pain, and the need to distance himself from his present circumstances. Moving his fingers toward one of the pain areas, Monday felt the warm stickiness which he knew was blood. Although he needed no further confirmation, he still brought his fingers up and saw the red stained tips. He had reopened his wounds, and while that was bad, it paled in comparison to what would be in store for him, unless he extricated himself from where he was and quickly.

After moments of excruciating pain, Monday was standing. Swaying precariously on rubber legs, he fought to gain equilibrium.

Once he felt reasonably confident, Monday took baby steps toward a small closet, where he found his clothing. He dressed as quickly as he could, ignoring the constant pain that ravaged his body.

As Monday was about to turn the door handle, he hesitated, picturing the police guards on the other side. Figuring he had no choice, he turned the handle and opened the door just wide enough to see part of the hallway. One guard was slumped in a chair and the other, crumpled next to it. Figures, he thought, he couldn't have gotten in here otherwise.

He opened the door wide enough to get out and then leaned down toward the guard in the chair. He placed his index and middle fingers against his neck and felt for a pulse that wasn't there. Then moving as fast as his legs would allow, Monday entered the stairwell several meters from his room and disappeared.

Chapter 26

As he made his way down the stairwell, the sudden piercing screams stopped Monday in place.

His mind quickly depicted various scenarios. He blotted out everything but the one thing he needed to concentrate on – distancing himself from this place.

He knew he was leaving a blood trail with every step he took, and his dirt encrusted clothing was beginning to stain crimson, but none of that could be helped. Forcing himself to take the next step and the step after that, Monday finally reached the bottom landing. Using his shoulder to push open the door, he found himself at the rear of the hospital where the emergency entrance was located.

After closing the door, Monday braced his back against the wall, as much to steady himself as to assess his options.

Letting the shadows envelope him, Monday watched as a military type ambulance stopped by the emergency entrance. The driver went to the rear of the ambulance and opened the two bay doors. Then he assisted two white uniformed attendants wheel someone inside.

Monday's brain shouted the word, 'move,' across his mind screen. He willed himself to take the first painful step, then another, until he was standing adjacent to the cab.

The pain Monday experienced as he reached up and opened the driver's door was as excruciating as walking but dulled in comparison to the pain that reverberated up and down his body as he climbed into the driver's seat. Trying not to call out, Monday bit down on his tongue and tasted the blood.

Every movement caused his pain sensors to escalate. Unwilling to scream, Monday let loose a torrent of tears as a relief valve. Wiping his eyes as best he could, he twisted the key in the ignition and started the engine. After placing the gear shift in reverse, Monday toe-tapped the accelerator until he was able to turn the ambulance toward the roadway.

He tried to calculate what time it was. The moon, what there was of it, didn't help. It was night time and despite the pain, Monday laughed. Yep, no sun…only a moon. I guess that makes it night, and he laughed again oblivious to the pain.

As the lights from the hospital dimmed in the rearview mirror, Monday wondered where he was and how could he possibly find his way to the Embassy….the one on Lindonstraat.

*

"I'll go find her….can't imagine what's taking her so long."

The nurse edged her way out from behind the desk partition, passed another seated nurse and then began walking toward room 463.

As she came within several meters of the guards stationed outside the room, she asked, “Have you seen Marlay?”

One guard’s quizzical look forced her to add, “the nurse….Marlay, the nurse. She was carrying a pitcher of water.”

“Yes, she left a while ago.”

“Where did she go?”

“Down the hall….that way,” and the policeman pointed toward the end of the corridor. “She turned at the corner. Haven’t seen her since.”

The nurse pushed between the two police officers and entered the room. As she approached the bed, the shock of what she saw dulled her senses. When the momentary shock passed, she started screaming.

*

The throbbing that resonated throughout his body made Robert Monday painfully aware of his deteriorating condition. The incessant pain combined with the blood loss and inhospitable darkness of the night, made steering the ambulance increasingly difficult.

Monday estimated he was fifteen minutes away from the hospital and still no pursuit. Lucky, he thought. Maybe they’re confused and trying to piece it together, but why hadn’t they noticed the missing ambulance….maybe they did and…..

Before Monday could finish the thought, he was already into the turn.

A nano-second later, the front end of the ambulance smashed into a grass embankment. The impact drove Monday rearward, and then forward again. As his upper chest struck the steering wheel, he screamed and continued screaming, until only the guttural sounds reminiscent of some dying animal were choked out.

Monday remained conscious and aware of what happened. Without hesitation he pressed down on the handle, and used his left foot and shoulder to push the door open, wide enough to maneuver out. Ignoring the pain, Monday kept repeating the word move, over and over again until he was hobbling away from the wreckage.

He suddenly stopped. Unsure why, he let his mind free-wheel, as his head turned back toward the ambulance.

He stared into the darkness beyond the ambulance, and after a few seconds, he saw it….off in the distance – the theater, still a partially burned out shell.

Then he turned his head too quickly and the pain resonated across his brain. He wanted to scream, but somehow suppressed the urge. As he tried to refocus, Monday remembered a park….a park that ran parallel to Lindonstraat, the street where the American Embassy was located.

Staring into the darkness, Monday reasoned this was the same park. As he continued to stare into the blackness, he thought, Not much choice....can't stay here. I'm hurt....hurt badly, and don't have the luxury of time on my side. So you've got to move mate....you got to move through it....you can't walk around it.

*

With each step Nancy wondered how many more. The low hung branches and waist high elephant grass, nipped at her exposed arms, and legs, and tore her uniform in numerous places.

Then when she thought she wouldn't be able to take another step, her reserve drained beyond what she considered possible, she heard Montonka call her name.

"We're almost there Miss Gault....just a little further....over the knoll, and then we're home."

The word home continued to resonate as she followed the Captain.

When she reached the crest, Montonka was waiting. He pointed down, "There."

"Where?"

Nancy looked at a heavy covering of thick tropical foliage. Nothing was visible.

Montonka smiled, and then motioned with his hand. The descent was easier than the assent, and despite the sheer tiredness that enveloped her body and senses, Nancy somehow managed to reach the jungle floor.

The camp consisted of wooden structures, many with brown corrugated roofs, and camouflaged nets, that provided added concealment from low-flying aircraft.

Light was at a minimum, blocked by the natural growth from trees that surrounded the area. The shafts of light that did manage to penetrate the thick natural canopy, made the moment all the more surreal.

There were armed men everywhere. A few acknowledged Montonka, but for the most part kept busy with their respective tasks.

"The Commander knows we've arrived. I need a moment with him alone. Wait here….I'll be back in five or so minutes."

"I can't wait here. I need to take care of some personal hygiene."

Montonka stared at her for a moment as the words registered and an image materialized.

"Yes, of course you do. Just a moment."

Montonka called out to the nearest soldier, and moments later a woman dressed in a colorful sarong appeared. After a brief conversation with Montonka, she took hold of Nancy's hand and pointed toward an indistinguishable hut.

After several steps, Nancy looked back at Montonka.

"I know where to find you," and then he started walking toward the center of the compound.

*

With each step Monday groaned. At times, animal-like sounds escaped from his clamped lips. He was getting weaker with each step, and with each step, he envisioned the Angel of Death coming closer. Is this what it's like....is this how it ends?

The park seemed enormous, without end. He didn't know whether he was walking a straight line, or circling back on himself. He knew if he didn't somehow get out of this maze, which had ensnared him, he was finished.

Unable, or unwilling, to take the next step, Monday raised his eyes upward. Although he was far from a religious man, he felt compelled to now ask for help, knowing there was no one else to turn to. Momentarily perplexed, he wondered how? What can I say? After a few moments, Monday intoned slightly above a whisper, "Just help me. I'm not one of your best, but I'm not one of your worst either. Don't let it end like this," and then he added, "Please."

His bravado had long since disappeared. He was humbled at just being alive but wondered for how much longer. His wounds had reopened, and he was losing blood at a steady rate, since he left the hospital. Maybe it was over, and he shouldn't fight it - just sit down and let it happen....make it easier on himself.

As he stood on shaking limbs, his chin now resting on his chest, his mind screen depicted an image....an image of him, again, lying on that roadway in Afghanistan. The orange fireball rose upward from the secondary explosion and obliterated everything to his front. Then he became aware of the gun fire, the shouting, and screams, as the firefight escalated in intensity.

His hand instinctively reached to his side. Then anticipating the inevitable, Monday aimed the Glock-17 pistol toward the black-gray smoke that now hung like a curtain to his front.

The two figures seemed to move in slow motion as they broke through the smoke screen and ran with abandonment toward where he was lying.

Monday squeezed off several rounds from the 17 round magazine and watched the lead figure stagger several steps before falling. As he aimed at the second figure, Monday saw the dirt puffs impact the dirt road surface to his front, but somehow couldn't hear the automatic fire coming from the AK-47.

He squeezed off five or six rounds before the figure stopped in place and fell forward.

Moving the pistol left to right, Monday waited for the next onslaught which didn't materialize. Then, as the adrenaline rush normalized, he became attuned to the intermittent gun fire and then the silence.

It was when Monday was lifting himself into a standing position that he realized he'd been wounded. Trying to compartmentalize the pain, Monday moved in the direction of the dissipating smoke. When he was through the cloud like curtain, he stopped as his mind tried to comprehend the carnage he saw.

Bodies and body parts were everywhere, black clad Taliban and British soldiers alike. Monday transversed the area searching for anyone still alive, but the eerie silence that prevailed over the battle zone told him there were no survivors.

All of the Humvees were destroyed or critically damaged. As the sole survivor, Monday realized that the only means of distancing himself from a place that would soon be crawling with Taliban, was under his own power. Was this how the Almighty was answering his plea for help….telling him that everyone needs to make an attempt to help themselves initially, and then, at some later time, He would do the rest?

Monday began walking, and as he saw himself taking each successive step away from the death behind him, he became cognizant that he was, actually walking in real time-a slow, tenuous gate, but he was moving….moving through the park.

He moved as if he was already dead but he continued to move. After what seemed like an eternity, his feet touched a concrete sidewalk. Monday hesitated only momentarily, thankful that the Almighty guided him to this point, but apprehensive that it might be too late.

Peering into the night, Monday saw the outline, an outline of what appeared to be a compound – the American Embassy compound. So I made it….made it miraculously to Lindonstraat, but not home yet….keep moving, Monday….keep moving.

As he passed several Boka Ami soldiers, he waved feebly, and then pointed at the compound entrance.

His blood stained clothing and disheveled appearance prompted one of the assembled men to move forward. His path was blocked by another soldier who whispered something, and then moved his head in Monday's direction.

The man nodded and took several steps back, as he and the others watched Monday hobble past and make his way to the Marine guard post situated just inside the main gate.

*

Min Qua Fu listened with surprising calmness as the man rendered his report.

When he finished, he stood motionless, waiting for the seated man to say something. After a prolonged period of silence he bowed, and then resumed his post outside the hospital room door.

The silence was dramatically shattered by the sound of breaking glass.

Unwilling to enter the room alone, the man ran toward the group of people clustered around the nurse's desk. Speaking Mandarin, which he knew they didn't understand, he pointed frantically back in the direction of Fu's room.

Several Police Officers and State Security personnel who were interviewing various members of the hospital staff regarding earlier incidents, turned in the direction the man pointed and began running.

One of the State Security officers pointed at one of the doctors and at a nurse, and motioned with his hand.

When the group reached Fu's room, the guard moved sideways, allowing the uniformed police officers, and security personnel access to the room.

After Min Qua Fu was restrained, the doctor and nurse were ushered in. The lone interior Chinese guard stood quietly at one corner of the room, watching as the doctor and nurse administered to the Director.

"I'm going to give you a sedative. It is imperative Director, that you follow our protocol regarding what you can and cannot do...." and then he motioned toward the broken glass on the floor. "This is a hospital and we mend the injured here, not the other way around. Whatever it is, that is agitating you, let it go. Only by adhering to our instructions will your body heal. You were only days away from leaving us, but now…."

"I don't need a sedative, and I am still days away from leaving here, Doctor. Shall we say Monday, that's five days from now."

*

The Marine Guard's eyes widened as his mind processed the individual outside the gate. Before he could say anything, Monday spoke.

"I need to see Mr. Roland Evers. Just tell him Monday, Robert Monday is here to see him, and it's a matter of life and death....mine."

The Marine Corporal reached for a phone and moments later a Marine Sergeant appeared.

"This man, Staff Sergeant, wants to see Mr. Evers. Says, it's a matter of life and death."

The Staff Sergeant moved closer to the gate. "Were you in an accident?"

Monday shook his head no. "Please....just tell Evers I'm here."

"You speak with a British accent. Aren't you at the wrong Embassy?"

Monday tried to laugh, but couldn't pull it off.

Then he said in a painfully slow cadence, slurring most of his words, "Heard that before. If Evers was at the British Embassy I'd be there, but he's here. Now if you don't want to get me Evers, then tell Ambassador Joseph P. MacMahon that I'm here and need help. As much as I'd like to continue this chat, I'm in a bit of an awkward way."

The effort drained Monday's reserve and he fought to remain upright.

"Someone's head is going to roll....I guarantee it Sergeant."

The Staff Sergeant picked up the phone, pressed several numerals, and waited.

"Sir, this is Staff Sergeant Raines at the main gate. I'm sorry to bother you at this late hour, but I have an injured man who identifies himself as Robert Monday, asking to see you."

*

When Nancy Gault left the hut, Captain Montonka was waiting. He was tempted to inquire whether her needs were taken care of, but decided it wasn't any of his business. He asked instead, if she was ready to meet Commander Dajan.

After she nodded yes, Nancy moved her hand up to her hair and brushed it back.

Montonka thought, Why do all women do that, and always at that precise moment when meeting someone? A woman's thing, I imagine.

It was a short walk to a wooden hut, approximately the same size as the one Nancy left. This one, however, was ringed with sandbags, firing steps, and armed guards.

As they walked through the single entranceway, the guards came to attention. Montonka acknowledged them with a nod. They continued walking until they reached the rear of the hut, where several wooden tables and chairs were positioned in an open area. The canopy of trees and surrounding dense vegetation were a constant reminder of where she was.

As they approached one of the tables, the men seated around it stopped talking.

When Nancy and Montonka were several meters away, the Captain extended his arm and Nancy stopped in place.

She followed Montonka with her eyes as he resumed walking toward the table. He saluted and then bent forward. After several moments of whispered conversation, all but that one man departed.

Montonka then motioned the woman forward and pointed toward the seated man.

"Nancy Gault, meet Commander Ronnie Dajan. Commander Dajan speaks several languages, English included. He was educated in the Netherlands, and in the jungles of Boki Ami."

The mention of the latter brought a smile to the Commander's face.

Before Nancy could say anything, Dajan spoke.

"Please sit down Miss Gault....there across from me. Education, in any form, whether it's the jungle, or from a university, or a music school, can be a building block toward one's destiny....wouldn't you agree Miss Gault?"

"I'm not sure I understand Commander. If you're referring to one's profession, of course, both formal and informal education is important to reach a level of competence."

"And when one reaches that level of competence, do they do it for self-gratification, Miss Gault?"

After a few seconds, Nancy answered, "Perhaps initially Commander, but after reaching that elevated level of success, the individual usually does it for other reasons. My music for example, Commander, I struggled to master complex compositions....hours of practice, and still more hours to perfect my technique. After my initial successes, what I do now and in the future, is to benefit others."

"Well stated Miss Gault and does that include your other profession as well?"

"I'm not sure I understand, Commander?"

"You were doing so well Miss Gault. Of course you understand. We are both involved in a profession that is equal to, or surpasses our chosen endeavor. I was trained as an Attorney, the law is what I practiced until circumstances changed all that. And you, Miss Gault, how did you choose the other profession….the one you practice along with your classic music career?"

Nancy wondered how he knew, or was it pure speculation to draw something out of her that he wasn't sure of. Then her mind screen flashed vivid images of Roland Evers and Min Qua Fu.

For an instant, Gault toyed with the idea of denial, but that would impede her credibility if she couldn't pull it off. Based on the questions that were asked so far and her answers, a certain understanding had been established between her and the Commander. Was she willing to place that understanding in jeopardy and risk all that she had gone through to get to this point?

Locking eyes with Ronnie Dajan, Nancy replied, "I never chose the Profession….it chose me."

Chapter 27

Monday remembered the brief conversation with Evers at the gate and the slow, agonizing walk with the aid of a Marine guard to the Embassy dispensary. He remembered the cursory examination and being asked his blood type.

He remembered the doctor shaking his head, "Only six percent of the world's population has O-negative blood, and probably a lower percentage among our Embassy personnel."

He remembered Evers saying, "I have O-negative blood."

Then came the transfusion and re-stitching of his wounds.

Everything, from the moment that Evers appeared to this moment, was remembered with abject clarity.

Monday felt better than he should have and was mildly surprised, considering what he'd been through. Maybe I'm more resilient than I thought. He smiled and then, as he waited for Evers to speak, said to himself, Naw, I've always been tough, Afghanistan, what I do, and how I live….not surprising that I'm more or less in one piece.

After what Monday thought was a prolonged unnecessary silence, Evers spoke.

"You keep showing up, Mr. Monday, like a bad penny. Right now you look like a train-wreck. We keep fixing you up and you keep tearing yourself down. Maybe you should try your own Embassy for a change."

"My fellow subjects of the Queen wouldn't be as hospitable as you Colonials are."

Evers was forced to smile despite his rancor.

"Where's your partner? I figured you two were joined at the hip."

Monday took the connotation for how it was clearly meant and responded, "Only in a business sense. Right now she's handling other business."

"What other business?"

"For the moment, I'll defer my answer to another time."

"There's not going to be another time. I want to know what's going on in detail and I want to know now. What I don't want is your British accent bullshit talk, because I'm not buying what you're trying to sell Monday. Level with me or we end it here, and you'll be gone. Think Monday and decide, and do it quickly. I don't have any more time for you unless you make it worth my while."

*

Min Qua Fu was wheeled out of the General Sabroka Military Hospital to a waiting limousine flying the flag of the People's Republic of China on its right front fender.

One side of the Director's face was covered with a loosely taped gauze bandage. A specially woven jacket that allowed the air to penetrate, was draped over the brown, parchment-like scar tissue which covered his torso and arm.

The ride to the Chinese compound was made deliberately slow, so that any discomfort that Min Qua Fu experienced was held to a minimum.

Once situated in his quarters, Fu waved back the medical orderly and motioned forward a man, whose mongoloid features seemed to duplicate and to some extent, exaggerate his own.

The man had prominent cheekbones, epicanthic folds about his eyes, long black hair, and his complexion resembled the hue of Fu's scarred face.

Those features, plus his powerfully built body, radiated caution.

"Si Shen, I appreciate your quick response to my request. How was your trip?"

Fu addressed the man by his "Nom de Guerra," which in Chinese translated to the "The Grim Reaper."

"Tedious and uneventful."

Fu moved his head ever so slightly but said nothing.

After several minutes of silence, the man spoke. "I am at your disposal, Director. How may I be of assistance?"

"Please take a seat."

"If it's all the same to you, Comrade Director, I'll stand for awhile."

Min Qua Fu turned his head and looked first at the medical orderly, and then at the guard. "Please wait outside, I'll let you know when I'm finished." Then Fu locked eyes with the guard. "Under no circumstances is anyone to enter this room until I advise you. Is that understood?"

"Completely Director Fu."

"Good, now leave."

Fu waited until the door closed before looking back at the man.

"We have a dilemma Si Shen, part of it…." and then the man interrupted.

"Comrade Director, I'm fully aware of how some refer to me and I am not in the least bit offended. In fact, I'm somewhat amused by the comparison, but at certain times I prefer to be addressed by my formal name, and this is one of those times."

Min Qua Fu bristled at the breach in protocol, but contained his urge to redress the man.

After a few seconds, Fu spoke without acknowledging anything the man stated.

"The salient points of this dilemma are as follows. An assassination attempt, ingenious I might add, took place during a concert recital here several weeks ago. The results are what you see." Fu pointed to his face and moved his jacket to his right, revealing his charred skin. "The perpetrator was the concert pianist, one Nancy Gault, an American. Her Manager, a British citizen, at least by birth, goes by the name of Monday, Robert Monday, and was.... I'm speculating here, her principal control. We have reason to believe that the American and possibly the British Embassies are involved as a command center, or at least as a part time operational base."

Fu paused as he studied the man, trying to discern if he was absorbing what was stated. Their eye contact remained steady and his facial features neutral, rendering an opinion either way, questionable at best.

"Their motive is immaterial. The danger to me is inherent with the position I hold. That's understood. With that said, these two cannot continue to live and toward that end, the lives of several agents have been lost. They were some of my best, and ....."

Min Qua Fu stopped in mid-sentence as a smile appeared at one corner of the man's mouth. Again, Fu repressed the urge to lash out verbally and instead intoned in a softly modulated voice, "You find something I've said amusing Zhang?"

The man moved his head up ever so slightly, conveying an acknowledgement to Fu's question.

"Yes, I was thinking if these agents were your best and failed, what would be categorized as your worst?"

Fu let the words bounce around his head. As he continued to stare at Zhang, his mind formed images of Chen Boa and the woman, Chao Xing Feng.

Then, enunciating every syllable slowly, Min Qua Fu replied, "Indeed they were some of my best. The problem is and continues to be, that they, the woman and the man Monday have proven themselves better....more resilient and more capable of taking a negative and turning it into a positive."

Fu waited. When the man remained silent he continued. "After the attack at the theater, the two avoided an attempt by our people to neutralize them in Boka Ami and managed to escape to the United States. A female agent was dispatched there and failed. Surprisingly, Gault and Monday returned to Boka Ami a short time ago and another attempt to neutralize them was made, and again failed, but this time they were both wounded."

Fu paused and shook his head, more agitated by the frustration of relating these failures, then the discomfort he was feeling from his injuries.

"At the hospital I was advised that they were there, both of them, recovering from those injuries."

Almost at the same time that Min Qua Fu finished the last word, he slammed his fist into the wall and then slowly brought his hand back to his lap as he re-established eye contact with Zhang.

Somehow managing to keep his voice modulated, Fu continued. “I sent one of my men to kill him, but as unimaginable as it is to me, the attempt failed and the man, Monday escaped. His whereabouts presently are unknown.

“Then to add further to the inexplicable, that bastard woman dressed as a nurse tried to poison me. Luckily, I noticed her nursing attire didn't make sense, and her face, though obscured due to the minimal light in here, seemed familiar. That's why I’m still here. We tried to kill her before she could escape from the hospital grounds but “FAILED.” The last word was spoken at a shrill octave causing Zhang to inadvertently move his eyes away from contact with the Director.

Unexpectedly, the room door was flung open and the guard rushed in.

“I heard screaming, Comrade Director, are you alright?”

“NO…..NO…..Zhang…..STOP.”

The guard turned his weapon toward where the Director was looking, and saw the squat man holding a pistol pointed in his direction.

“Both of you, lower your weapons….Now!”

"Let me kill him, Director. He disobeyed your orders….orders not to enter the room until you advised him."

"While that is true, Zhang, the circumstances under which that directive was given changed. Something I said was obviously interpreted as a distress call, necessitating a response and a change in the guard's orders. The guard used personal initiative to determine that I was not in harm's way. That's what I expect from those who work with me." Fu purposely used the word, with, instead of the word, for, which is really how he felt about all people.

The Si Shen holstered his pistol as the guard lowered his weapon, turned away and walked out of the room.

Minutes passed as Zhang stood quietly in place letting his body normalize. He watched as the Director's eyes studied him. That's okay, he thought, he's wondering whether I would have killed the man.

"Yes, Director, I would have killed him." Then Zhang paused before he spoke again. "There's no need Director to continue. I completely understand."

"Do you, Zhang….do you? They're all dead, six, maybe seven….dead and those two are still alive."

"Not for much longer, Director….not for much longer."

*

"From time to time, Commander, I am called upon to become a person other than what I am perceived to be. That other person has many personas. What persona I assume depends on the task I have been assigned. As a professional, I am able to transcend between personas, bringing them into play as circumstances dictate."

"And who are you now, Miss Gault?"

"I am Nancy Gault, a concert pianist of some renown, and an operative for an organization that will remain unnamed."

"What does your organization want with Boka Ami?"

"Nothing with Boka Ami, but with a person who resides here presently."

Dajan lifted his chin up slightly and held it in that position. The movement was understood by Nancy. "Fu, Min Qua Fu, the Director of Chinese ILD. The initials stand for International Liaison Department, an organization involved in a range of covert activities by the Chinese Communist Government against western interests. My organization wants Fu eliminated."

"Obviously, you have encountered…." and Ronnie Dajan paused as he searched for the appropriate word. When he spoke again, it was at the break point, "….some difficulty. You seem injured. The nurse's uniform you wear seems out of place and you are here in this jungle fortress to accomplish exactly what?"

"To answer your question, Commander, I need to provide you with some background. During a recital, a piano recital, several weeks ago, an explosive device was detonated which should have killed Min Qua Fu. Instead it wounded him, wounded him severely. Despite his grave injuries, he's still alive and functioning. That means we failed. In order to rectify that, we returned to Boka Ami. Since I'm in country, several attempts have been made both to kill me, as well as the Director. The attempts failed....both of us are still alive...me to the degree you see."

"Do you want to be examined by one of our doctors Miss Gault?"

"No thank you Commander. I'm okay and mending."

"What about your partner, Monday, where is he?"

"Don't know for sure....I can only speculate. As Captain Montonka can confirm, we were both injured while traveling here. I was taken to General Sabroka Hospital for treatment and assumed Monday as well, or he's dead."

"Go on, Miss Gault."

"While at the hospital, I made an attempt to kill Fu as soon as I found out he was still there. It failed and if not for Captain Montonka and one of his men, I would be six feet under. The nurse's uniform was taken from a resident nurse and used by me as cover when I tried to poison Min Qua Fu, but the slant eyed bastard seems to have more lives than a cat."

Nancy watched the smile form on the Commander's face and then she started laughing. After many seconds, the laughter was replaced by several tears. As she wiped them away with the back of her hand, she said, "It's frustrating....and that's why I'm here Commander. Maybe we can help each other."

"How so?"

"You want to replace the government here. I want Fu. I have some contacts at the American Embassy in Paramarmico who would like to see this country tilt away from alliances with the Chinese and North Koreans. I think I could persuade them to remain neutral if you should contemplate another attack."

Chapter 28

"The bullet holes I'm wearing are compliments of the Mainland Chinese. What you're thinking is correct. They want me and my female friend gone….gone in a permanent way. They think we had something to do with the explosion that wounded the ILD Director, Min Qua Fu."

Evers moved his head in a way that conveyed a question, a question which Monday interpreted as asking whether he was involved.

"I owe you Evers," and Monday pointed to his bandages, "so I'm going to level with you to the extent I can. Min Qua Fu represents an obstacle to certain interests, not the least of which is your country. Geo-political games are played every day and everywhere. Countries, business interests, and the politically powerful are in constant flux to maintain, or shift the pendulum of advantage in their favor. I work for an organization not unlike your own and which will remain unnamed....an organization that handles wet work (assassinations) when necessary on behalf of those interests. That's it."

Monday thought about what he said as he waited for a response from Roland Evers. As he replayed the words in his mind he decided to add something more.

"Boka Ami is not US territory. There are many interests here using diplomatic cover to achieve certain objectives for their respective countries. Additionally, there are private interests who work here on behalf of some of the same Embassies, as well as for a specific business or political entity which cannot or will not undertake what has to be done to accomplish whatever it is that they want accomplished. That is why organizations like mine exist. You're aware, of course, that these organizations exist. They have always existed and they will continue to exist and function, as long as the power struggle continues to dominate every facet of daily life on this planet."

Evers maintained eye contact with Robert Monday for several seconds before he spoke.

"Okay Monday, you've confirmed what I suspected."

Monday remained silent as Evers went into a quiet mode again. As he waited he tried to speculate about what Evers was thinking, and whether there was something more he should add, or did he already say too much?

"Tell me why Min Qua Fu was a target."

"I don't know. It's never my place to know. I'm given an assignment and either I accept, or reject it. Why, never enters into it. I would imagine it's much like what you do for the company."

Monday waited for a reaction.

When none came, he kept silent.

"From what I see, Monday, you're not in any shape to do much to anyone. I imagine the woman,

Gault, is a duplication of what you look like, so the same applies to her. Since you both failed more times than "Carter has Liver Pills"….that's an American saying you probably don't understand, but I'm sure you get the drift. I would guess that the Chinese know you're the ones who orchestrated the attempt on Fu. Seems to me your days are numbered. What bothers me about this situation Monday, is the linkage here….with us. We're not interested in fostering a diplomatic incident that can have serious repercussions for my country, and a blow-back for me and the Ambassador. You're trouble Monday….the worst kind of trouble. You failed to execute, and you're reaping the rewards of those failures."

Monday's eyes stayed riveted on Evers as he continued.

"This is the last time we're going to see each other. Don't come here under any circumstances. Personally I don't give a flying shit about you or Gault. Once the Doc says you're good to go, you go. Understood?"

Monday made a yes movement with his head.

"Good. I'm glad we've reached an under-standing."

Evers kept eye contact for several seconds, then turned and left.

*

The Commander used the index finger and thumb of his right hand to rub his eyelids.

She watched the movement, typical of someone trying to gain time as he considered what was stated. Dropping his hand away, he looked back at Nancy Gault.

"I'm not sure that you can assist us in any meaningful way, Miss Gault. I think the belief that you can, is misguided and motivated by your desire to kill this Chinese person."

Nancy was about to interrupt when Dajan moved his hand back and forth.

"The Americans, the Chinese, and other foreign powers, can't alter what we intend to accomplish here. Our only concern is removing the corrupt government....that political elite class that rules Boka Ami for their own personal gain. They care nothing of us....the people. Their concern is maintaining the status quo so that they can continue to enrich themselves while we suffer. I have chosen to rectify this injustice and that is why I now fight them in the only way they can understand. Do you think they respect the rule of law that I once swore to protect? Of course not. They are a law unto themselves."

Gault was surprised how articulate this man was. Although what he said made complete sense, Nancy felt that she needed to clarify several misconstrued assumptions.

"There is always an interest, Commander, on the part of the United States to keep a country tilted toward the west. There is, and continues to be, a struggle of good versus evil. The good defines America as it sees itself. The evil is represented by those who adhere to the failed doctrine of Communism and Socialism. The countries who embrace the latter are numerous. Additionally, there is another element to add to the equation – Islam, whose radical jihadists think they have the answer to everything. Boka Ami is rich in minerals and strategically situated geographically. Certainly the United States would like the Government of this country to sit in the western camp of nations. Countries like Communist China, North Korea, and others would like just the opposite. As such, I believe I can persuade my Embassy here to remain neutral during any future coup attempt."

Dajan started to interrupt when Nancy duplicated his previous hand motion.

"The man, Min Qua Fu, is not the once confident man he was. He has been injured....severely injured, both mentally and physically. Physically, part of his face and body are badly scarred. This plays on his psyche, and his mind is now consumed with total hate. That hatred, in its entirety, is directed toward revenge. After a number of failures to kill us, he will come out into the open, away from his Embassy confines to personally make sure that we are both terminated. Once Min Qua Fu is eliminated, some of the Chinese influence with the present government and various factions within that government, will be impaired. Since Boka Ami has received a considerable amount of military and economic aid from the Mainland, after this high ranking official is assassinated, a cooling in the relationship between your two countries will take place....at least for a time, until the matter is clarified to Cicom's satisfaction. That will give you time to consolidate relations with the United States once you assume control. I can start that process before you effect a change, so that when that change occurs, the United States will recognize it quickly."

She stopped and continued to look at Dajan who sat quietly, almost rigid, as he waited for her to continue.

"I was caught in the midst of your attack a few weeks ago....a battle between your forces and Boka Ami soldiers. I survived and I'm here, a testimony that I'm a survivor and just like you Commander Dajan, I have a propensity to live. Perhaps the forces of circumstance have brought us together."

"For your clarification Miss Gault, the attack in Paramarmico was a test....a test to determine how effectively the Boka Ami forces would react to an assault against their capital. And despite Chinese and North Korean advisors, the military didn't perform all that well. They will fail in repelling any major attack by my forces. In fact Miss Gault, many units will switch sides as the tide of battle shifts to reflect our military superiority."

The Commander pushed back in his chair and then moved forward placing his elbows on the table, and his chin in the palms of his hands. "Now Miss Gault, what do you want of me?"

*

Robert Monday dressed in borrowed khaki pants, a polo shirt, and wearing flip-flops, compliments of Roland Evers, walked slowly into the lobby of the Tori Hotel. When he reached the registration counter, the clerk, anticipating the question, stated that his personal belongings and those of the woman had been packed in their respective suitcases, and were now in the storage closet.

Monday nodded and looked away briefly as he tried to spot anything out of the ordinary. When he moved his head back, he saw the clerk's eyes scanning him.

"Automobile accident. Just released from the hospital."

"I'm sorry to hear that Sir. Your room is still available if you want it back?"

"Keep it that way. I'll let you know shortly."

Monday started to walk away, then reversed direction. "I want to speak with Rodney P. Is he in the restaurant?"

"Let me check Mr. Monday."

The clerk lifted up a clipboard and scanned the top sheet.

"Not yet Mr. Monday, but he's due to come on duty at 3 p.m. and then looking at his watch the clerk added, "That's twenty minutes from now."

"Thank you....I'll wait in the restaurant."

Monday was about to leave when the clerk asked, "Will the lady be joining you?"

"Possibly, but I'm not sure when. If you see her please tell her I'm in the restaurant."

Turning away from the reception desk, Monday placed both hands in his side pockets and felt his left hand touch something. When he withdrew his hand, he was holding crumpled US currency. As he smoothed out the bills, Monday counted a hundred and thirty dollars in ten and twenty dollar denominations, and thought, Evers, sometimes unpredictable and this was one of those times.

He turned back and handed the clerk a twenty dollar bill. "Thanks for looking after my personal belongings and the lady's too."

"My pleasure Mr. Monday," and then the clerk pointed to the money. "Thank you very much."

Monday nodded and then made his way to the restaurant. He took a seat in a booth where he could see both the door connecting the restaurant with the lobby, as well as the one leading to the garden.

He ordered coffee and then sat back letting his mind free wheel. Various options were considered and then dismissed. Management still had his credit card on file, so getting the room back wasn't a problem even though he no longer had the physical card. The problem was that his adversaries might expect him to do just that, or at the least that would be their starting point in hunting him down.

Monday pushed the still untouched coffee cup away, and looked up as the voice called out, "Hello again Mr. Monday."

"Hello, Rodney P."

"Are you alright, Mr. Monday....I mean...."

"I experienced some minor difficulty while enroute to see the Commander....me and the lady, but I'm on the mend."

Rodney P forced a smile.

"Do you happen to know anything about Miss Gault?"

"I was informed by Princess Obia that she is....at least she was, yesterday, with the Commander."

"So she's okay?"

"Yes, as far as I know."

"That's good news, Rodney. Is there a way I can contact her....get a message to her?"

"Yes, but I'm not sure how quickly I can make that happen."

"Okay....maybe first things first. I can't stay here. I'm being tracked....hunted, and this is probably the first place they're going to look. I've taken a chance coming here, but you're here, and I need your help. I need a place to stay….will you help me?"

"Sure Mr. Monday, give me a minute."

Monday watched as the waiter disappeared inside the kitchen. When he returned, he handed Monday a folded piece of paper. "Give this to the taxi driver. He'll drive you to Princess Obia. You'll wait there for me."

As Monday stood up he placed a twenty dollar bill next to the coffee cup. "Take out for the coffee and keep the change. If you're able, please tell Miss Gault where I'll be. Thanks. I have a long memory for those who do me favors."

"Me too Mr. Monday, and for those who do the opposite."

Monday smiled, and then slowly walked toward the restaurant door.

*

Min Qua Fu watched from the parked car as Si Shen entered the Tori Hotel. He cursed silently and then out loud. Why did Fu-Xing (Chinese God of Good Fortune) allow this to happen to him? Hadn't he always been respectful of his ancestors and the Gods? Was he careless, or was it fate?

He leaned his head back against the leather headrest and closed his eyes. He remembered how he once looked and how that had been changed forever. Fu felt the rage slowly build until he experienced the acrid taste of matter from his bile duct. Then he cursed until he was spent.

As his body slowly returned to normal, he vowed not to let his emotions dictate his mood. He would be measured and resolute, with a single purpose in mind and his entire being dedicated to achieving that purpose before moving on. He was confident of his abilities to lead and lead he would, using Zhang as his instrument to extract revenge.

*

Nancy let the Commander's last words replay themselves and then she answered. "What I want from you, Commander, is help. In return, I will help you with the Embassy so that they maintain neutrality once your coup begins and recognize you as the legitimate government of Boka Ami after you've taken control."

After a brief pause Nancy continued. "The help I need right now is in the form of weapons....I need several pistols and spare ammunition for myself and Monday. I need those weapons for protection while I....we, try to formulate a plan to kill Fu. Presently, I'm the hunted and defenseless. I may need additional help from you later, but right now I just need those pistols. I can't get them from my Embassy and my organization can't....won't help. Monday and I are still alive because we've been lucky, but no one's luck can continue indefinitely."

Nancy kept staring at Ronnie Dajan until he finally answered her.

"If you can't get weapons from your Military Attaché or from the CIA at your Embassy, I doubt, seriously, Miss Gault that you could influence them regarding me or my cause. Additionally, you work for an organization that won't help you. That makes no sense to me but raises concerns about you, your friend Monday, and the organization that you claim to represent."

"I agree, Commander, it's confusing but it's the way my organization works, despite the illogic of it. Monday and I failed to assassinate Fu. My organization doesn't look favorably on failures. We're on our own until the matter with Fu has been satisfactorily resolved....then we're back in the organization's good graces, or so I hope."

Dajan shook his head as if he was trying to understand what was said, but somehow couldn't manage.

Nancy picked up on the head movement and said, "It's just the way it is Commander. We're supported to the extent possible and when we screw up, the organization sets us adrift to rectify the matter on our own. I personally don't like it, but that's the way it is. I fully understand that unnecessary exposure, especially negative exposure, is the one thing the organization can't afford. Its ability to act in a shadow world, without consequences for either their clients or themselves, is why the organization is sought out by many to handle sensitive matters which require the utmost discretion. Their hallmark is to insure that no blow-back will occur to the paying interests, to themselves, or their assets."

"Secondly, it's one thing for my Embassy to understand that a change of Government in Boka Ami can be beneficial for the United States. It's another thing for the Embassy to openly support a coup that will bring about that change. Working clandestinely toward that end, is something else, but there is always an element of risk and that risk extends to me. They're not going to give me weapons, but they do understand that both Monday and I are a little more than we seem to be. We have an okay, although somewhat strained relationship with a CIA operative there, as well as access to the Ambassador."

"What I'm asking for, Commander Dajan, isn't much....just two pistols and your trust for a short while."

Chapter 29

Zhang stood off to one side of the hotel entrance, at a place that gave him an unobstructed view of the reception desk. Satisfied, he entered the Tori Hotel and scanned the lobby as he slowly walked toward the reception desk. When he was several meters away, the clerk looked up and smiled.

"Can I be of assistance?"

The Si Shen replied in broken English. "I from Embassy. Need talk with woman player of piano who stay here."

The reception clerk forced his face to remain placid despite the urge to laugh at the bastardized English coming from this short man with long black hair and Mongolian folds around his slanted eyes.

When he replied, it was in the same pigeon English that Zhang used.

"The player of piano no here."

"Where go?"

"No sure. Long time go."

"What about man with player of piano?"

"No here....go too."

"When back?"

The clerk moved his shoulders conveying he didn't know.

"I wait."

"Player of piano no here for days. Maybe no come back. You wait but no sure if hours or more days."

"Man too?"

"Yes, same with man too."

"Okay....I go now....come back."

The clerk continued to stare at the man until he disappeared into the parking area. After several more seconds, he looked away, lifted the phone and dialed the number for the restaurant.

Zhang, again positioned where he could see the reception desk, watched as the clerk lifted the receiver to his ear.

*

The Commander motioned to Sigmundo Montonka and spoke rapidly in a language that Nancy Gault assumed was a local dialect. Montonka nodded once, saluted and then walked away.

"I want you to have the weapons you requested, Miss Gault. Not because of what you can do for me. I still have reservations about that, but I like your," and then Dajan stopped. After a few seconds he said, “As you Americans say, grit….I like your grit.”

Nancy remained quiet knowing the Commander hadn’t finished.

“If possible, I will arrange to alert you to when the coup will begin. Once we commence operations it will be a fight where one side will be completely devastated, and the other victorious. There will be no quarter given by either side and the brutalities of war will have its effect on everyone and everything. Once you receive my alert you are free to do, or not to do, what you’ve indicated to me. I hold you under no obligation. The pistols are my gift to you, someone who shares my professional aspirations in a less overt way,” and then the Commander smiled.

He held the smile until Montonka reappeared.

“Hand the pistols and spare magazines to Miss Gault, Captain.”

Montonka handed Nancy a small cloth bag containing several loaded magazines, two 9mm automatic pistols and silencers.

Nancy looked at the pistols and then back at Dajan. “These are ghost pistols aren’t they?”

Dajan moved his head slightly.

Nancy’s mind pictured the ghost pistols manufactured in a secure area of this jungle compound without serial numbers or manufacturer’s identification. Smart, avoids the difficulty of acquiring them from outside sources. Then she returned to the moment and locked eyes with Dajan.

"Thank you, Commander....thank you."

"I think our business is concluded, wouldn't you agree Miss Gault?"

Before Nancy could reply, Dajan added, "The Captain will take you back to Paramarmico. Until we meet again in better times, good luck," and the Commander extended his hand.

Nancy gripped it firmly, locked eyes with Dajan and said, "Never stop believing Commander, never."

*

Monday heard his name and walked back to where Rodney P pointed. He lifted the receiver, listened and then said, "Thank you."

He motioned Rodney P over and then motioned toward the phone. "That was the front desk, someone, a Chinese man, was asking about me and Miss Gault."

The waiter nodded. "Follow me to the kitchen."

Several pairs of eyes watched as Rodney P took a white uniform and apron from a wall hook and handed it to Monday. "Get dressed and sit over there....at the sink with your back toward the door. You can't leave now....just keep your back toward the door no matter who comes in." Then Rodney P walked over and engaged several of the kitchen help in conversation. Before he turned, he reached into his pocket and handed each of them several folded bills.

*

Zhang entered the lobby and went directly to the reception desk.

The clerk eyed him with trepidation and hoped that what he felt inside wasn't evident from his facial features.

"Need speak you."

"Okay."

"Very important," and the man took a step back as he opened his suit jacket just enough to reveal the butt of a pistol.

"No lie….understand?"

The clerk shook his head yes.

"You use phone….call man."

"I use phone to answer questions many times from many people when I here. No understand what you say."

"If you no tell me true, I kill you here….now."

The clerk's mind reeled as he tried to weigh the Chinese man's words. Would he actually do what he indicated….kill me here in the hotel lobby?

"One time more. You talk man?"

The clerk nodded yes.

"Man in hotel now….yes?"

The clerk again nodded yes.

"Where?"

The Chinese man's eyes moved where the clerk pointed and then he started walking in the direction of the restaurant.

*

As they were swallowed up by the jungle, Nancy's mind replayed the images of what she experienced getting to the camp. Wondering if the return trip would be a duplication of that, she felt a mild tremor of trepidation. Shaking it off by reasoning that she was at a better place mentally than she had been and physically her wounds were on the mend, and her strength had returned to near normal.

At their first break while Nancy was sitting with her back against a large tree trunk, Montonka walked over and sat down beside her.

"I forgot to give you these before we left the camp….compliments of the Commander."

Montonka handed Nancy two cell phones.

"In case you're wondering, they're from the United States. They're stolen, with the original data erased....or erased to the extent possible. Use them, you and your friend, while you're in Boka Ami, and then I suggest you discard them at some time of your choosing."

"Stolen....how surprising," then Nancy chuckled.

"Indeed so, Miss Gault. There's rather a large underground market throughout South America and other places for these phones. Like drugs, weapons and human cargo....everything is available for a price."

"I was wondering about something, Captain. While at the camp, I occasionally heard sounds....sounds like pigs make. At first, I thought my mind was playing games, then I was sure I heard them."

"What you heard were indeed pigs....hungry pigs. The Commander uses everything to further the cause for which we fight. The pigs are used as well."

Nancy let Montonka's words replay and then she made a motion with her shoulders that conveyed she understood. Although she wasn't sure what Montonka was saying, the last thing she wanted now was to prolong a conversation about pigs.

*

The Si Shen walked into the restaurant and slowly let his eyes canvass the interior. The man wasn't there. Then Zhang's attention was diverted as a waiter carrying a tray of dishes walked past and entered the saloon doors to the kitchen.

Zhang's mind calculated the possibility quickly and after several seconds he followed the waiter into the kitchen.

Three of the four people staggered around the kitchen continued doing whatever it was they were occupied with, except for a man in a tall white chef's hat and soiled apron. He looked at the Chinese man and asked, first in Dutch, and then English, what he wanted.

The Chinese man smiled and held the smile as he looked around. Then he started walking toward one of the men who was leaning over a sink.

Before Zhang's third step the man in the tall chef's hat blocked his way.

"Out, now….OUT," and then he slowly raised his right hand until the seven inch meat cleaver was visible.

The Si Shen moved several steps away as he kept eye contact with each of them, except for the man at the sink who didn't turn around.

Holding a smile, Zhang walked out through the doors until he was several meters away. Then he turned and walked back through the restaurant and into the lobby. He continued past the reception desk, noting that the clerk kept his head and eyes down.

Once in the parking lot he paused briefly, then continued to the parked car. He opened the driver's side door and got in. Without looking at Fu, Zhang said in rapid Mandarin, "He's there….in the kitchen. I didn't take him out Director….too many people….it wasn't opportune, but he will be dead by nightfall. I'll cover the back. Chances are that he won't come out the front but you can, Director, continue to watch the main entrance from the car. I'll let you know by cell if he uses the back door, and you can do the same for me for the front."

The Si Shen waited several seconds and when nothing was said, he opened the door, nodded once, and then walked toward the parking lot entrance and disappeared around the side of the building.

*

As they made their way out of the tree line and into the thinning brush, Nancy saw Ono Urbano waiting beside the partially hidden car. He waved as they approached, and then opened the passenger side front, and rear doors.

When they were situated inside the vehicle, Urbano turned toward Montonka and asked, "Where to?"

Montonka looked over at Nancy who replied, "Tori Hotel."

"Is that a good idea Miss Gault? If the Chinese are looking for you, as I assume they are, the hotel would be one of the places they would keep under surveillance."

"You're probably right, in fact I know you are. I'm walking on the edge by going there but I have a feeling that it's the place where Monday would go first, assuming he's still in one piece. And if he's alive, I need to hook up with him. Thanks to the Commander, I have a means to shift the odds in my favor a bit," and then she touched the bag on her lap which held the ghost pistols.

*

Rodney P held the saloon doors open with both hands and said, "He's gone."

Monday straightened up slowly, turned around, and then walked to where Rodney P was standing. "He's still here....not in the building but he's where he can maintain a visual.....probably has one or more people with him."

"I don't have the luxury of time to think this out the way it should be. So I'm improvising. I need some women's clothing....big size....something that will confuse whoever is out there for a few moments....a sarong, or whatever and some kind of cloth headpiece. And I need a taxi....a waiting taxi."

Monday stopped when he saw the confused look on Rodney P's face.

"Look, I'm not going to get out of here in one piece unless I do it quickly and with my appearance altered to the fullest extent possible. I need the advantage it might give me for a few precious seconds....the few seconds it will take me to get from the main lobby door into the waiting taxi."

Monday reached into his pocket and peeled off three twenty dollar bills and handed it to the waiter. "Get me what I need. Do it now and do it quickly, or I'm cooked meat and you might be as well. Come back here, and please hurry."

*

Rodney P returned with some multi-colored cloth draped over his arm. "Best I could do. Not many tall women in Boka Ami."

As Monday took hold of the material and shook it, a smaller piece of cloth floated to the floor. Monday reached down and picked it up while continuing to stare at the waiter.

"That was an effort....now help me get this on."

Monday bent over as Rodney P passed the sarong's opening over his head and helped him as he struggled to get his arms through the small openings.

"Too tight, and too short, but nothing we can do about that, can we? Don't want to bend over again....please roll up my pants so they're under the sarong."

Rodney P moved his shoulders up once and then, after a moment went down on one knee.

"This," Monday held out the cloth, "is for the head – right?"

Rodney P nodded yes.

"Please wrap it the way a woman would wear it."

Again the waiter nodded.

"More or less okay Rodney?"

When he didn't answer, Monday started to move toward the saloon doors.

"The taxi is waiting and I have a wheelchair in the lobby which will help disguise your height."

Monday turned and smiled. "Very imaginative Rodney....very clever. Let's go."

*

As Min Qua Fu stared through the windshield from the driver's seat, he scrutinized each of the people entering and leaving the hotel. The combination of boredom and frustration were weighing heavy on his psyche. Additionally, his urge to urinate was growing stronger with each passing minute. When that urge reached its maximum, Fu opened the car door, and got out. Using the open door to shield what he was about to do, Fu felt reasonably sure he could pull it off.

He unzipped and began urinating, when he noticed a woman in a wheelchair being pushed toward a waiting taxi. The woman dressed in traditional multi-colored clothing and headdress stood up for a brief moment, and then entered the taxi.

Fu's mind began racing, dissecting what he saw, and separating the plausible from the implausible as he had been trained to do over many years.

Tall....maybe too tall for a local....sarong looked too short and the visible parts of her legs seemed masculine. The facial features were indiscernible as to whether it was a man or woman, but Fu felt that something didn't jell the way it was supposed to and that was enough for him.

Contracting his muscles so that he stopped urinating mid-way, Fu pushed his penis back into his pants, and cursed as some of the urine dripped down his leg. He got back into the driver's seat and started the ignition, just as the taxi was pulling away.

Depressing the accelerator too quickly, Fu forced the car to jolt forward, impacting the front quarter panel of an adjacent car. Blotting out the car's alarm, Fu backed up and maneuvered around the vehicle. He ignored the shouts from the hotel doorman as he drove toward the parking lot exit, and in moments, he was on the street with the taxi in sight.

Chapter 30

Several minutes after Min Qua Fu's car left the area, the vehicle carrying Nancy, Montonka and Urbano pulled in front of the Tori Hotel entrance. The chaotic scene made Nancy shake her head. "Seems we go from fire to fire. I wonder what this is all about."

"Whatever it is doesn't concern us. Let's get inside and get you settled or whatever."

Nancy opened the door and waited until Montonka was standing beside her. After instructing Urbano to park the car, he and Nancy entered the lobby and approached the reception desk.

"Hello Miss Gault. We've been expecting you."

Nancy looked quizzically at the clerk who followed up quickly with, "Mr. Monday said you might be arriving here today."

Feeling the relief of knowing he was still alive, Nancy asked, "Is he in his room?"

"No....he was in the restaurant waiting for Rodney P to come on duty, but I think he's gone....I mean he's not in the hotel."

The clerk looked around the lobby before he again locked eyes with the woman.

"I need to tell you something Miss Gault. A Chinese man....very sinister looking was here asking about you and Mr. Monday. I did what I could to avoid revealing anything. But he showed me a gun and I knew he wouldn't hesitate to use it if I didn't answer his questions. I'm really sorry….I like both you and Mr. Monday and wouldn't do anything to hurt either of you."

After glancing at Montonka, Nancy looked back at the clerk. "It's okay. You did what you had to do. Is the Chinese man still here?"

"I don't think so Miss Gault, but I can't be sure."

"Are my clothes still in my room?"

"No Miss Gault. Since you were away for a number of days, the management had your clothing and Mr. Monday's packed. The suitcases are in the storage closet."

Nancy nodded her head. "Is Rodney P on duty?"

The clerk shook his head once.

"Thank you," and then she turned and started walking toward the restaurant, with Montonka trailing several steps behind.

She walked through the restaurant's open door and waited until Montonka caught up. Before Nancy saw him, Rodney P was moving in her direction.

"Hello Miss Gault."

"Hello Rodney. This is a friend of mine, Mr. Montonka."

"I know the Captain Miss Gault."

Nancy drew air through her nostrils until her lungs were full and then slowly let it out, thinking, of course you do Rodney P....you're something more than what you appear to be, aren't you?

"Is there a place we can talk?"

Rodney P pointed to the saloon doors. "In there."

The three made their way into the kitchen and huddled near one of the room corners. The kitchen attendants, after glancing once in their direction, ignored them as they continued whatever it was they were doing.

"Mr. Monday is on his way to see Princess Obia. He is being hunted by a Chinese man," then Rodney P stopped to gauge their reaction.

Before he could begin again, Nancy said sarcastically, "Get on with it," and then she offered an apology.

"We dressed Mr. Monday as a woman with a sarong and headpiece, and we used a wheelchair to get him to a waiting taxi. He thought someone was watching the main entrance, maybe the Chinese man and others helping him. After Mr. Monday got into the taxi and the taxi started moving away, there was an accident between two other cars. The car that caused the accident didn't stop....it left the parking area in the same direction that the taxi was going."

Nancy reached out and patted Rodney P's shoulder. "Did you notice what type of car was following the taxi?"

Rodney P wiped the sweat beading on his forehead with the back of his hand. "It was a four door Mercedes….something an Embassy would use."

Nancy nodded slightly and then looked at Montonka and then back at Rodney P. "Please describe to Captain Montonka where Princess Obia resides….her home….her home address."

"The Captain knows where the Princess lives Miss Gault."

And for the second time, Nancy knew she messed up, giving both of them reason to question her ability to grasp….understand quickly.

"Yes, of course….my mistake by not thinking the way I should."

Then turning to Montonka, Nancy asked, "Do you happen to have any money you can loan me Captain?"

*

Min Qua Fu held onto the cell phone with his left hand as he gripped the steering wheel with the other. Trying to follow the taxi through the congested roadway and talk at the same time, while his pain sensors tormented his body, was becoming intolerable.

Giving into the rage, Fu screamed into the phone, "Zhang, Bi Zui….Ting Wo Shuo." (Zhang shut up….listen to me)

The Si Shen moved his hand away from his ear, stared at the phone and then cursed silently before bringing the cell back up.

As the voice of the Director escalated, he bristled over this half human's tone, his choice of words and the manner in which he spoke. Sure, he was part of the Chinese culture that had ingrained itself over centuries. A culture that mandated a respect for his elders, for those in authority and for his ancestors. But he had traveled and seen a different world and his ways now, were not of that time. He considered himself a craftsman at the trade he plied….he was the Si Shen….the Grim Reaper, and those who failed to remember that, did so at their own peril, regardless of their status.

The Director lowered his voice and then modulated his tone.

"Zhang, I'm following a taxi that I believe has the man we're looking for. I had no time to stop for you. Go to the main entrance, go now….see if the woman is there. I'll call you as soon as I know where this taxi is going and if I'm right about the passenger inside. If the woman is back at the hotel….Kill her Zhang….KILL HER."

*

The taxi driver slowed the car but didn't stop, as he scanned each of the wooden structures that lined both sides of the street. Then he stopped suddenly and pointed.

The bleak, wooden form, with one small open portal at the front left side seemed vaguely familiar. Although Monday wasn't confident that this was the place, he had no choice but to trust the driver.

Suddenly, Monday began experiencing trepidations about being here. Reasoning it was a place that was known and visited by a host of locals seeking advice and contact from, and with, the spirit world. Monday calculated that too many people meant too many eyes. The more visuals, the more prone he was to being outed.

He leaned over the driver's backrest and said two words in slow, modulated English. "Wait, Stay," and then he pointed at the driver and then downward, hoping that what he was trying to convey was being understood.

To reinforce what he wanted the driver to do, Monday took out two US ten dollar bills and held them up. "One now, and one when I'm back in the taxi....understand?"

The semi-quizzical look in the man's eyes and his lack of a response, telegraphed to Monday that he was fighting a losing battle.

Monday quickly removed the woman's clothing and placed them on the seat. Then as he opened the rear door, he waived the ten dollar bill and pointed to the driver.

"Wait here," and then, again, he pointed to the driver, then back at himself and finally toward the ground.

As Monday approached the open portal, the engine sound forced him to turn back. He watched as the taxi moved away, disappearing into the congested sea of humanity, animals, trucks and cars that were traveling in both directions.

"Dumb shit," and then as he stood there, Monday wasn't sure whether he was referring to the taxi driver or to himself.

He shrugged and then began walking toward the wooden structure. When he stopped at the portal, he stood motionless for several seconds as he listened for anything that would indicate danger. Satisfied, he knocked several times and then entered through the portal.

*

Facing the clerk at the reception desk, Nancy Gault moved her hand across the counter and handed him fifty dollars in Boka Ami currency from the money that Montonka had given her.

"Thank you again for what you've done....and at considerable danger to yourself."

The clerk smiled weakly as images of the long haired Chinese, and what he threatened to do, flashed vividly across his mind.

"Would you arrange for someone to bring Mr. Monday's suitcase and mine to the main entrance."

As the clerk nodded, Nancy extended her hand again.

*

Zhang placed the cell back in his pocket as he began walking away from the rear area, and toward the main entrance.

Moving slowly along the walkway, the Si Shen pictured the Director as his mind formulated several thoughts. What would he know about killing? It's a word to him. He gives orders for something he might not be able to do himself, and then the Si Shen smiled. But then again, he's not quite the man he was, or is he more of a danger because of what happened to him? I need to be careful. Enemies exist everywhere, among those in power, and those seeking to obtain power.... no one can be trusted.

Then his mind focused on something he remembered from a western book he once read. One who lives by the sword, dies by the sword. Admonishing himself, Zhang intoned softly, "Careful, Si Shen, or that sword may well strike you."

The words of the Director continued to replay until Zhang stopped and shook his head. After a moment, his mind was clear and resolute.

As he neared the driveway entrance to the hotel, Zhang slowed his approach. With the right side of his face pressed against the edge of the building, he moved his head until he was able to see part of the driveway in front of the main entrance.

He watched as two men loaded several bags into the trunk and then shook hands with someone dressed as a waiter. Seconds later a woman appeared, shook hands with the same waiter and then entered the rear compartment of the vehicle.

Zhang moved quickly across the driveway and entered the first taxi in line.

The driver looked back at his passenger with his long dark hair and Mongolian eye folds and wondered, Why me....why my taxi? But before he could offer up an excuse, why he couldn't accommodate him, the Si Shem took out his pistol and pointed it at the driver's head.

"You start car....you go when I say go."

The driver nodded realizing that whatever fate had in store for him, that day of reckoning was today and maybe this very moment.

As the four door Toyota Crown exited the driveway, Zhang said menacingly, "GO....now go. Follow and if lose car, I kill."

*

It took Monday a few moments to adjust to the darkened interior. The candle light added to the surreal sensations he felt as their geometric patterns played off the interior walls. He let his eyes wander, as much to reorient himself as to determine if there was any visible danger. The statues were still there, more it seemed, adorned with colorful beads in doll-like forms and grotesque misshapen images.

He turned toward the voice but couldn't see a form. As the voice spoke it seemed to change direction, from his front, to his side and finally at his rear.

Monday stayed rigid after moving his head once. He continued to face his front as the voice moved around him.

"All roads lead back to where one seeks sanctuary. That sanctuary takes many forms, as do those who reside in this and other worlds. A homing instinct that one uses to reach a zone of comfort, is as strong as the emotion of love, hate and revenge. It is those emotions that dictate the choices one makes during his or her lifetime, and those choices sum up the worth of the individual."

Monday didn't understand what she was talking about, but reasoned that wherever she was going, she would take her time getting there.

"You are in danger Monday man….grave danger. Those who seek to rectify a perceived wrong are coming. They will extract revenge from you and the other one, if you are not vigilant."

The voice stopped and the silence that replaced it hung heavy in the musty air.

Monday closed his eyes to dispel the feeling of hopelessness that had suddenly occupied his mind.

When she began again, the voice spoke from his left.

"They are coming, and I see them here. What will you do Monday man? Can you survive? Will you survive?"

Again the voice stopped.

Monday waited, but as the minutes passed the voice remained silent.

After what he thought was a reasonable time, Monday started moving in the direction of the portal when the voice called out, "Stop."

"Going to where Monday man? Without a plan, you will find what inevitably is coming for you sooner than is necessary. Sit and think. The other one will be here shortly," and then a semi-circle of light seemed to appear around a small bench.

Chapter 31

Min Qua Fu slowed the car and began edging his way off the roadway while at the same time, spewing curses at the people who felt no urgency to move out of his way. Unable to position the vehicle where he wanted it, Fu stopped.

Refocusing on the passenger exiting the taxi, Fu smiled as his suspicions were confirmed. He watched as the man and driver engaged each other. Then the taxi drove off and the man entered a dilapidated wooden structure.

As Fu began dialing the Si Shen his cell rang.

"Yes."

"I'm following the woman....a gray, four door Toyota Crown. As soon as we get to wherever it is, I'll call back."

The Director was about to say something, then lost the thought. "Okay. I'm watching the man. I'll wait for your call," then Fu pressed on the end button.

As he sat motionless the thought returned. Why didn't you kill her....why are you following her? Then he felt the rage begin and dissipate just as quickly, as he forced his mind to focus on what he couldn't see – the man inside the structure.

*

Monday toyed with the idea of leaving....trying Evers again despite his ultimatum not to return. But what was his bargaining chip? He'd worn out his welcome and he doubted if he was going to be able to talk his way past the Marine sentry again.

As he sat contemplating his limited options, he watched as a girl of fourteen or fifteen entered the room. She ignored him as she went to one of the shrines, and began some unintelligible ritual that she had obviously done many times before.

The magnetic draw that kept him fixated on the girl wasn't about what she was doing, but how she was dressed. She wore a short skirt which seemed to barely reach her thighs and a loose white blouse that revealed too much.

Monday forced himself to look away. Then he let his eyes move around the semi-darkness as he tried to discern other eyes that couldn't be seen, but were surely watching. Was this some type of test to determine something that was momentarily beyond his understanding?

Unable to see anything definitive, he forced his eyes to drift toward the floor as he continued debating with himself whether to stay or go.

*

The four door gray Toyota stopped in front of the wooden structure, and three pairs of eyes turned toward it.

"We're here," and then Montonka asked, "did you see the black Mercedes sedan parked at an angle about thirty meters back that way," and he moved his thumb over his shoulder.

Urbano nodded but said nothing. Nancy remained silent.

"That's an official car….the flag holders on the fenders confirm it."

Then Nancy spoke up. "I saw it, and I'm guessing it's Chinese….those Chinese."

"Could be."

Montonka looked at Urbano. "Stay here. Watch, and let me know if the car begins to move, or when any of the occupants get out."

Urbano nodded again.

"Okay Miss Gault, let's get you settled."

"Not just yet Captain. I'd like to check in with the Princess and find out about Monday before I commit to staying here."

Montonka was about to reply, but decided to hold off and said only, “Your call. Let’s see the Princess.”

*

As Montonka and Nancy Gault entered the portal, a taxi slowed and parked behind the Mercedes Benz.

Zhang leaned over the back of the driver’s seat and moved his head forward until it was inches away from the driver’s face. “You wait….no wait I kill,” and he used his thumb and index finger of his right hand to form the image of a gun.

When the driver didn’t acknowledge, Zhang grabbed his hair and pulled his head back until it rested on the back edge of his seat. The driver gurgled and brought his hands up toward his throat as he tried to breathe in air. Zhang repeated what he said the first time and then loosened his grip. Once the driver’s head was free from Zhang’s grip, the driver moved it up and down slowly.

Zhang got out of the car and walked to the Benz. He opened the passenger side door and got in.

*

Montonka and Gault took several steps inside before stopping to let their eyes adjust to the semi-darkness. Several moments after they entered, Monday turned and stood up.

“Welcome to my humble abode.”

Nancy saw who it was and rushed forward. She hugged Monday and whispered, "I'm happy you're in one piece Monday."

He hugged her back as he replied, "Well not exactly in one piece, but on the mend."

Montonka came over and was about to say something when Urbano called out. "We've got company. A taxi drove up after you both entered here, and the single occupant is now in the front seat of the black Mercedes."

"Were you able to see who he was?"

"Mongolian or Chinese….long black hair, and powerfully built."

As Montonka was about to speak, Princess Obia entered the room and said, "Welcome. Now that you're all here, what is it you want?"

Nancy thought about Obia's sudden ability to speak English, and her so-called psychic powers. She should have known why they were there. Maybe she did, but wanted reconfirmation. Taking an added second or two, Nancy decided it was easier to answer as if the Princess was unaware of why they had come.

"We were in contact with Rodney P and we thought….no he thought, that this might be a place we could stay for a short while."

Obia stayed in the shadows as she spoke so only her outline was visible, and then only at certain times depending on how the candle light flickered.

"You cannot stay here. You know what has to be done….don't you Monday man?"

"Yes Princess, I think I do. Two of our adversaries are within our reach. They need to be dealt with. My only concern….my dilemma is just how."

"Think Monday man….one uses all the tools that are available. What tools are available to you Monday man?"

Before Monday could respond, Nancy opened the small bag, took out one of the two ghost pistols and handed it to Monday along with one of the silencers, and a cell phone.

Monday checked the magazine, and then looked back toward where he last saw the Princess. He could no longer see the outline, but spoke anyway.

"I have the means Princess," and he held up the weapon…."but I need one thing more. There was a young girl in here just moments ago. I have a plan that needs her participation. There is an element of danger but without her I don't think we can accomplish what I have in mind. Do you want to know what I have in mind?"

"I already know and you are placing her at a considerable risk."

"I don't see it that way Princess. There is always a possibility of something going wrong. I understand that, but she'll be exposed for only a minute or so."

After a prolonged period of silence, Obia finally replied. "I have summoned her. Her name is Kinetta. Tell her what you want and she will comply."

*

Zhang looked at Min Qua Fu and then turned his head so he was looking at the windshield. He spoke without turning back.

"We should burn the place."

"With what?"

When Shi Shen didn't answer, Fu spoke. "We wait….let them get comfortable and then we go in and kill them….kill them all….everyone."

Zhang nodded.

*

Monday smiled at the girl. "You understand, don't you?"

Nancy Gault had just finished explaining what Monday expected from the girl with the help of Montonka. Anticipating an outright no, Nancy was surprised when the girl agreed immediately.

"Give us a few minutes to get into position, and then you go."

The girl smiled and moved her head up and down more times than was necessary.

Monday turned toward Montonka, then looked over at Urbano. "You follow us out. We'll try to take them alive, but…." and then Monday stopped. More words were unnecessary.

He motioned with his head, and then Nancy moved toward a curtain that hung over a portion of a back wall. Once past the curtain, a small door led to a rear alleyway. They ran until Monday said, "Far enough."

They edged between two dilapidated wooden structures then reversed direction once they reached the roadway. Keeping low and hugging the front facades of various wooden buildings that lined the street, they moved slowly toward the rear of the black Mercedes.

The girl carrying several books was already approaching the car from the opposite direction.

Moving his head slightly, Monday whispered, "Hold up. I'll tell you when, and then we rush the car. You take the driver….I'll take the passenger."

The girl, now several meters away from the car, suddenly stumbled. As she bent over to pick up her books, her short skirt lifted up revealing her minimal under-garment.

"Now."

Monday was a step ahead when they reached the rear of the Mercedes.

*

Zhang couldn't help himself, he stared. He knew the Director was fixated on the young girl as well. When the passenger door was yanked open, their momentary lapse proved fatal.

As Zhang's head turned right, his hand, which held a pistol, moved but not in tandem. The nano-seconds lost was sufficient for Monday to fire off several 9mm bullets into Shi Shen's chest.

As Zhang slumped forward, Monday pointed the ghost pistol at the Director who sat motionless with his hands gripping the steering wheel.

Nancy opened the driver's door with her left hand while she pressed against the rear quarter panel, her pistol aimed at the back of Min Qua Fu's head.

"Tell this one in Chinese, Monday, to sit quietly and don't move, otherwise he'll meet his ancestors."

Monday called out the Director's name and when their eyes were locked said, "Jing jing de zuozhe bu dong."

Fu's eyes widened as he stared at the man speaking in perfect Mandarin.

"Is the other one dead Monday?"

"Probably, or soon will be."

Seconds later Montonka and Urbano were standing next to Monday.

"We'll take this one to the Princess. Urbano will handle the other one and the car.

"Get out."

When Fu didn't respond, Montonka moved quickly to the driver's side, motioned Nancy away, and then with the butt of his pistol began pounding Fu's hands until he released his grip on the steering wheel.

Montonka pulled Fu out and then shoved him in the direction of Obia's home.

Urbano slid into the driver's seat, leaned over, grabbed the hair of the inert Si Shen, and pushed him forward so that he was wedged below the firewall.

Montonka was prodding the reluctant Min Qua Fu forward as the Mercedes passed them.

Nancy, trailing slightly behind, suddenly realized Monday wasn't alongside. She stopped, turned back and watched as Monday did a three-sixty. After calling his name several times, Monday answered with, "She's gone."

Nancy looked around quickly and then answered back, “Yeah....probably back with the Princess.”

When Monday caught up, Montonka and Fu had disappeared.

“We’d better hurry, or we’re going to miss the fun and games.”

Nancy’s face contracted and she looked at Monday quizzically.

Monday half-smiled. “Okay, we’re not playing fun and games. I was just trying to make light of a situation that seems to have no end.”

“You don’t have to explain anything on my account Robert. I’m okay with everything that’s happening and those happenings seem to be turning in our favor. We’ll get through this as we have with everything else, but now we’re going to have an ending. That man with Montonka.....”

Monday moved his hand back and forth. “I know....that man, Fu, is going to meet his ancestors shortly.”

*

Urbano drove the Mercedes several hundred meters away from Obia’s place, before he pulled over onto the shoulder. He removed the Si Shen’s weapon from his death grip, left the keys in the ignition, and started walking back.

As Urbano walked he thought, It won't be long before the car and the body are stripped clean....a lot easier than setting it on fire, and drawing local authorities sooner than necessary.

*

Princess Obia walked slowly around the bound and gagged man as she chanted in an unintelligible language.

Fu, lying on the floor in front of one of the many shrines that adorned the room, became part of the surreal scene as candle light danced across his scarred face and exposed arm. The geometric patterns cascading off him made him seem like one of the many unearthly caricatures, positioned on and in front of the numerous shrines.

When Obia finally stopped, it was in front of Monday.

"Monday man, the object of your obsession is here thanks to the little one....Kinetta. How predictable men are, their fascination with certain parts of one's anatomy is beyond the bounds of normalcy. Empires, men of wealth and power have all succumbed to it. Look what we have here Monday man....an example of which I speak."

The Princess turned slowly and walked to where Montonka was standing. "He's a gift to the Commander. Before he satisfies the appetite of those who hunger, Monday man may be able to extract something of value."

Interrupting the Princess, Nancy said, “That one is our property.”

The Princess spun around, took several steps until she reached Nancy Gault and then slapped her across the face.

The blow was stunning as well as humiliating.

Monday started moving forward when Obia’s arm shot out, blocking his way.

“Stay back, Monday man, or I won’t be responsible for the consequences.”

Monday ignored the command and moved between the Princess and Gault. Without turning back to look at his partner he asked, “Are you alright?”

“I’m far from alright,” then Nancy shoved Monday away as she moved close to Obia. “If you ever do that again, or touch me in any way, I will filet you like a fish and make a coat out of your skin,” then she slapped the Princess hard across the face.

*

The eerie silence, and electrified tension that prevailed among the four occupants of the car, forced each of them to re-think what transpired with the Princess and then to anticipate what the consequences would eventually be.

It was Nancy Gault who finally spoke up.

"What happened back there is over. Fu is ours…. bound, gagged, and locked up in the trunk. The other one is dead, or soon will be and we're alive. Once we get to the Embassy, Monday and I will do what was promised the Commander."

Nancy paused to think about where she wanted to go, then she continued.

"The incident with the Princess, while unfortunate, was necessary to establish an understanding. I know how you feel about her….how you think, perhaps know, what she is capable of. If she is bent on satisfying some misguided hurt, then she'll do what she has to and that will be directed at Monday and myself. You Captain, and you Lieutenant, are not parties to what happened. You both are, shall we say, observers to an unfortunate happening. Whatever the problem, that problem is between me and the Princess and Monday….not you two. And for the record, do you really think that I was going to let anyone slap me with impunity?"

Nancy laughed sarcastically then added, "Not in this lifetime."

The silence continued until the car pulled up to the gate of the American Embassy on Lindonstraat.

Monday opened his door and got out. Nancy held back and leaned forward toward Montonka who was sitting in the front passenger seat.

"There's something much larger and more important than dwelling on Obia and what happened back there. It's my problem, and I'll deal with it. That's all I'll say about it, and I'd like you both to table whatever it is you feel about me until a later time. Right now Monday and I need to follow through on something I've promised the Commander. We won't be long. I expect you, and the car to be here when we return.'

Nancy opened the door and joined Monday as he walked toward the Marine guard.

*

Nancy whispered, "Let me do the talking Monday," then she took several long strides and moved in front.

Stopping when she reached the guard post, Nancy asked to see Roland Evers.

The Duty Corporal asked their names, and the nature of her business, then eyed Monday as he waited for a reply.

"I'm an associate of Mr. Evers. My name is Gault, Nancy Gault, and he's Robert Monday. Please advise him we're here, and it's urgent that I speak with him."

The Corporal stared for several moments before moving away. When he returned, he looked first at Monday and then at the woman. "He'll be here in a few moments." The Corporal opened the gate and motioned with his hand. Once they were inside, he pointed to a place a meter or so away. "Please wait there."

Nancy looked over at Monday who broke eye contact and looked toward his left. Nancy moved her head in the same direction and both watched Roland Evers approach.

Evers stopped several meters away and motioned them over. "This is going to be short and sweet, and it better be worth my time."

Then before Nancy could speak, Evers looked at Monday. "Didn't I tell you that you were never to come back here....like in persona non grata. Do you have trouble hearing....understanding, or is it just your Limey attitude that makes you a continual fuck-up, so that you bring your troubles to my door step?"

Nancy shot a glance at Monday and then spoke. "We're on our way to see Dajan. There's going to be a coup....don't know when, but that's what I'll find out shortly. Once I know, you'll know. I've already met with the Commander....what's about to take place was discussed with me only in generalities. I'm not going to try to con you....I'm....we're not going to be privy to his operational plans and before you ask, I'm not going to be able to tell you anything more than the date."

Again Nancy stopped. Seconds later she started again. "My professional assessment is that the chances of success, based on what little we've been told, are high. One element that tilts the operation in Dajan's favor, is that a number of Boka Ami troops will switch sides once the coup begins. Dajan will launch simultaneous attacks to secure the communications centers, the airport, the parliament, and the Blue House, where the interim President should be."

Nancy stopped once more as she tried to gauge Evers.

"I know what you're thinking, but maybe you're concluding that it's a lot of surface talk and not much substance. But that depends on how you filter what I said. There's enough there for you and Ambassador MacMahon to make a reasonable calculation of where the United States should be after the coup….standing with Dajan and his new government, or nursing at a cow's udder and siding with the disposed, former government of Boka Ami. It's your call."

Evers had to smile at her use of the euphemism. "You mean like sucking hind tit, Miss Gault?"

Nancy smiled back, "Yeah, something like that," and they started laughing.

"Okay, I understand. Do you have a phone?"

Nancy nodded.

"I'm going to give you a number….a very private number that you'll use to call me once you know when. I'll let you know at that time what the Ambassador decides."

"Not good enough. I want to tell the Commander definitively, before the coup, that the United States will recognize him as the legitimate government of Boka Ami once he assumes power."

"And what about this one," pointing at Monday, will the Brits fall in line?"

"Not an issue now Mr. Evers. Dajan is only concerned with the United States….and yeah, Britain will fall in line along with other countries once Dajan secures control. What choice do they have, whether it's Britain, North Korea or the Chinese."

"Ah, the Chinese. They're never far from my mind and how is your problem with the Director?"

"Shall I say, tied up nicely so that he and several of his associates are no longer troublesome."

"Okay Miss Gault, we'll leave it at that. You do have a way with words," then Evers smiled. "Call me at this number." Evers took out a piece of paper and pen, jotted down a series of numbers, and then handed the paper to Nancy. "Take a minute to memorize the numbers and then hand the paper back."

Chapter 32

"Can't figure out the Limey. I have my ideas, but one can't judge a book by its cover....at least not in our trade. Gault has a way about her.....easy, and yet there's something lying underneath the surface that shouts caution. I rate her as credible....the coup will take place. How she managed to meet with Dajan at this point, is unimportant. What is important is that she has his trust. We can use her to further our interests once Dajan takes control."

"The unknown, Roland, is always an element of consideration. For example, what if the Boka Ami forces don't switch sides, or the Commander doesn't neutralize the nation's communication apparatus, etc?"

"Sure, unknowns always exist in every situation Joseph. The French have an expression to describe a mode of adaptation to changing circumstances.....a race with destiny called, "Fuite en avant." The attack on the theater was a warm up to determine Boka Ami's military response. Seems to me that Dajan and his Maroons got the upper hand. It's your call Joseph, but for the record, I want to be on the winner's side no matter who, and right now I assess the winner is going to be Dajan. If we calculate incorrectly we're behind the eight ball, but isn't that where we were with Muguanasi's government and the interim one now. We're stuck in the mud behind the Chinese, the North Koreans and other adversaries. I don't know who exactly Gault and the Limey work for, but they're in parallel work, and that makes them knowledgeable about what constitutes a "probable." I'm willing to bet positive on her assessment that Dajan will come out on top."

Ambassador Joseph P. MacMahon pushed back in his chair and studied Evers.

"If this doesn't go down the way you see it Roland, it's going to be a career fuck-up for both of us. I don't need the Ambassadorship. I got it through politics anyway. It just was something I thought would look good in my obituary, but you....that's a different story. You'll go down with me and I don't know how many jobs are available for Chiefs of Station who call a loser of this magnitude."

"Don't worry about me Joseph. I'm a big boy," and Evers smiled thinly. "I have a sworn duty and if what I do can enhance my country's power and prestige where it was limited before, well....that's what it's about. I neutralize my country's enemies by any and all means available, and Joseph, that means using everything at my disposal. If we ride this horse to the winner's circle, we benefit....we come out on top ....we can call many of the shots with Dajan, and his government. Instead of a career ending situation, we have a career enhancement situation. Think about it Joseph, and let me know ASAP. I can't be sure how soon that call will come and I want to give Gault the right answer."

*

Monday and Gault walked in silence to the waiting car. Moments later they were driving along a familiar road that would lead them to the place where they would again proceed by foot through jungle terrain, and back to Dajan's camp.

Nancy envisioned the trek, recalling vividly how difficult the first one was. She blotted out those images, becoming resolute, that this time it would be different. She was healing and Monday was moving, more or less normally, without indicating that anything bothered him. The body has a way of healing itself and despite the rigors they were exerting on it, it was healing.

The silence that prevailed let a tiredness that was just below the surface take hold. The last thing Nancy remembered was the heaviness behind her eyes. The soft touch brought her back to the moment.

"We're here, Miss Gault."

It was Captain Montonka who was leaning over the back of his seat. The others, Urbano and Monday were already standing outside the car.

"We walk from here Miss Gault. It shouldn't take too long. You remember don't you?"

Nancy rubbed her eyes and then tried to smile. "If the first trip didn't kill me, I guess I can handle another."

"I'm sure you can. Shall we?"

Nancy opened the door, waved at Urbano who was standing by the vehicle, and then joined Monday, Montonka, and a number of heavily armed Maroons as they made their way into the jungle.

*

"I'm to telephone the Embassy when you plan to begin."

Nancy purposely avoided using the word "coup," or any other that had the same connotation. It wasn't semantics, just a need to avoid the obvious while conveying what she needed.

"You haven't stated Miss Gault, whether your Embassy will recognize the new government."

"I'll know that when the call is made."

Dajan leaned back in his chair, placed his hands behind his neck and interlocked the fingers.

"You expect me to tell you one of the most crucial elements of my plans, and trust that your government will not act in a way that will be detrimental to me. For example, to curry favor with the present regime and reveal when the attack will commence."

"I didn't get that impression from the individual I spoke with."

"And what impression did you get?"

Dajan asked the question while staring at Robert Monday. He held the gaze until he heard Gault respond.

"My evaluation....my assessment was that the individual believed what I told him. In our tradecraft it's referred to as, "credible"....he believed I was credible. There is one person above him and that person will make the final decision."

"Why didn't you go directly to that person Miss Gault?"

"There is a chain of command, just like your organization Commander. We don't breach protocol for the sake of expediency. That proves disastrous most of the time. Besides, the individual I spoke with would have been consulted before any decision was reached. His input was required and necessary. If I ignored the chain of command, I would have caused an unnecessary conflict....ruffled a few feathers that didn't need ruffling."

The Commander unlocked his fingers from behind his neck, and placed his elbows near the center of the table as he leaned toward Nancy Gault.

"At two-thirty a.m. two days from today. Now make your call."

*

Due to the heavy jungle canopy, Nancy was escorted to a small clearing at a higher elevation where the GPS connection could be made.

Evers picked up on the second ring….waited for several seconds to pass and then answered, "Yes."

"I have the bang and burn."

Nancy used intelligence terminology that referred to demolition and sabotage but knew that Evers would understand.

"Noted….go ahead."

"I'll need your confirmation first."

"That's not the way it's going to happen."

Nancy let the words play back in her mind as she thought of a response, one that wouldn't bring the call to a negative ending. Concluding that she had no choice, she stated, "Thursday this week."

"Time."

"Zero two-thirty."

"Copy….we will recognize," then before Nancy could respond the connection was severed.

*

Nancy was again seated across from the Commander. His body language and the look in his eyes, made her wonder whether she or Monday would leave this camp alive if what she was about to indicate was in the negative. She doubted it. But then again, would she have stated it. Truthfulness has its place, and so does self-preservation.

“The American Embassy will recognize the Government of Commander Ronnie Dajan.”

The slight nod of his head sent relief waves though her body.

“I have to meet with my Officers shortly, but before I do, we’ve arranged a little entertainment for you.”

The perplexed look that crossed Gault’s face prompted Dajan to continue. “It involves your nemesis, the Chinese man.”

Nancy looked at Robert Monday and then back at the Commander. “I’m not sure I understand.”

“It will become perfectly clear in a few minutes. Now if you and Mr. Monday will follow me.”

Dajan nodded to Montonka, and then together with several heavily armed Maroons, started walking toward a clearing enclosed by a wooden fence.

The intermittent sounds of “Huuughhh,” “Huunkk,” and Scrruuu” grew louder as the group neared the enclosure. The waist high, rough cut fencing, secured a filthy compound where a number of pigs were kept.

Dajan turned his head slightly as he said, “I think the little devils are hungry,” and then he chuckled.

Peripherally, Nancy saw a figure being pushed forward. As the scarred face became visible, Nancy made a sucking sound with her mouth. Several pairs of eyes turned in her direction as she tried to ward off what they were thinking by smiling weakly.

Would she ever stop having these moments? Despite what she purported to be, she felt that the femine side of her always seemed to dominate, and it seemed at the most inappropriate times. Resolute, dear Nancy Gault....one must remain ever resolute, and then she smiled broadly feeling what she believed she was.

Min Qua Fu was prodded until he was several meters away from the Commander. Dajan turned to face Nancy and then pointed to Fu.

"He doesn't look so powerful at the moment, does he Miss Gault?" When Nancy didn't answer the Commander answered his own question. "No, he doesn't look so powerful."

As Nancy locked eyes with Fu, she could see, in fact feel, the loathing that was there....no fear, only a deep seeded hatred for her and the desire for her death, which would go unfulfilled.

"Is there anything you'd like to say before we proceed Miss Gault?"

Nancy moved her head up and down several times. "Yes....yes, I do." Nancy inched closer to the Director. "Because of you, I have learned things about myself. Some of these things were better secreted away, but they surfaced, and I had no choice but to address them. In time they will become minor issues while others will benefit me as

I go forward. You understand Fu, that we are both professionals, you by choice and me, because they found me, not the other way around. It is unfortunate that you were injured instead of killed, but sometimes we are not able to control the outcome of all situations no matter how carefully they are planned and executed."

Nancy smiled as she thought of the last word she used.

Fu remained composed but the look in his eyes seemed to grow more hostile.

"What my partner and I do is something we undertake with indifference. It's a job like playing the piano. Both can be equally satisfying depending on the outcome, and I believe that outcome is going to be decidedly in our favor."

Monday motioned with his hand. "Let me translate. I want to make sure he gets all of what you said."

Then in fluent Mandarin, Monday translated. When he was finished, Dajan said, "Take him to his reward."

Several Maroons lifted the bound man and carried him to the enclosure. Seconds later they tossed Min Qua Fu into the pigpen.

The ravenous animals milled around the screaming Fu for several seconds and then a pig tentatively nudged the squirming body. Moments later the others moved in quickly. Starved for days, the pigs tore, ripped and shredded the screaming man in a diabolical feeding frenzy.

Nancy, repulsed by what she was witnessing, turned away as she fought the bile that was rising to her throat. She kept her eyes closed until the screaming sounds were a painful memory. She then walked away oblivious to the laughter and cheering.

When she reached the wooden table, she sat with her back to the fenced enclosure. Moments later, Monday joined her and without looking at her, said in a subdued voice, "It's over....it's their way Nancy and as unpleasant and morbid as it might seem, it was for you and it ended a chapter in our lives that needed closure."

"Oh no Mr. Monday, what they did was for themselves."

Monday brought his hand up and rubbed his eyes. "Yeah, you're right. It's entertainment for them and it's obvious they use the enclosure as an execution ground."

"That wasn't an execution Monday. That was barbarism, straight from the depths of Hell. Wouldn't a bullet have sufficed?"

Monday replied in a compassionate voice, "Nancy....it's not their way....let it go....it's over."

Behind them, they heard the chuckles and laughter and then silence until Dajan called out, "You both missed the endings....quite a sight," and then he laughed again.

Once the Commander and Montonka were seated, Dajan leaned forward. “Don’t feel pity for the likes of that Chinaman. He deserved what happened to him. It’s the way things are done here Miss Gault. This camp is not a cemetery. If we buried everyone we executed, or who died naturally, the animals would dig up the corpses, and eat whatever was left of them. We just handle the details a bit more expediently,” and then the Commander laughed as Montonka and several soldiers joined in.

“Your problem is now solved Miss Gault. Captain Montonka will escort you both back to civilization and I look forward to seeing you again in several days. Thank you for your successful efforts with your Embassy. Until we meet again,” and then Dajan extended his hand.

Nancy hesitated for only a moment, and then shook the Commander’s hand.

“Thank you Commander for….” and then she let the words trail off.

As she stood up Nancy regained her composure. “I’ll see you in Paramarmico.”

Chapter 33

Montonka, Urbano, Monday, and Nancy Gault stood in front of the main entrance of the Tori Hotel. Nancy extended her hand, first to Montonka, and then to Urbano.

"Thank you Captain and thank you Lieutenant Urbano. Both Robert and I are appreciative of all you did and the 'entertainment' surpassed anything we could have imagined." Nancy emphasized the word, "entertainment," and then she forced a smile.

"I know Miss Gault, that we perceive things differently, but isn't it the end result that counts?"

Nancy thought about the Captain's words for several seconds and then replied, "Yes, we differ only in the methodology used."

"Sometimes circumstances dictate the unpleasant, but in our situation rules are made for the majority, not the minority. We will see each other again shortly, and I would suggest that after you get settled in, you secure yourself in your respective Embassies as soon as possible."

"Thank you again Captain. We hope your mission meets with success, and I haven't forgotten about the money you loaned me."

"Consider it a payment of sorts for assisting us."

Monday and Nancy watched the car until it disappeared, then picked up their bags and entered the hotel.

*

"Did you get the same feeling I did?"

Nancy shook her head in the affirmative. "Yeah....something tells me Dajan didn't level with us. I'm thinking the attack will begin before the date and time he indicated. Guess he just couldn't trust us a hundred percent, and Montonka more or less confirmed it by giving us the heads up re the hotel....it isn't a safe haven for us."

"You're right. Get settled and I'll meet you in the lobby in twenty minutes. Does that give you enough time?"

"See you in twenty."

*

Nancy and Monday stood just inside the gate of the American Embassy on Lindonstraat Street. They watched the Marine guard replace the phone and then motion them toward the main entrance.

As they walked Nancy whispered, "Let me open. Once I'm finished and depending on what he says, you can chime in."

Monday nodded.

When they reached the door, they knocked once and then entered. Seconds later they were seated in front of Roland Evers.

"And what do I owe this visit to? I was under the impression that everything either one of us had to know, was known. Why are you and the Brit here?"

Monday bristled at the slang reference to his nationality but kept quiet.

"We have our suspicions that the coup will begin before the time indicated. I....we, can't be sure, but I would anticipate an earlier attack. My suggestion Mr. Evers, is that whatever you have to do in preparation be done as quickly as possible. If what I....we, believe will happen, doesn't, you're still on full alert for the attack as originally projected."

Evers stared at the woman and then at Monday trying to determine if what was just related had validity, and then concluded quickly that he had nothing to lose, and possibly something to gain.

"Please stay here. I have something that needs addressing. I'll be back shortly."

Evers closed his office door and then picked up the phone on his secretary's desk. After a brief conversation with the Ambassador, he dialed the Commander of the Embassy's Marine contingent. He alerted the head of the Consular section, the Military Attaché, and then his fellow CIA officers.

As Evers opened the door to his office, the first wave of Maroons began their attack against the Communication Centers and International Airport.

*

During the previous twenty-four hours, teams of Dajan's Maroons infiltrated into the Boka Ami's capital city of Paramarmico. Organized in groups of four or five men called firing teams, they smuggled in light weapons including the Ina-45 machine gun, considered ideal for urban warfare, Molotov cocktails, mortars, and limited amounts of ammunition.

Firing teams would be in place to assault military installations and police barracks as a means of securing additional ammunition, explosives, and military hardware.

Teams would mine principal roads to and from the airport. Kill teams would be in place at strategic points along major highways and principal secondary roads, to engage police or military personnel that refused to join the insurrection, and remained loyal to the present regime.

The attacks against the police and military installation, the International Airport, all communication facilities, such as the TV and radio broadcasting stations, and various government buildings would be undertaken simultaneously.

Dajan banked on the surprise of the attack to create pandemonium within the civilian population and create havoc among government personnel, and the military, still loyal to the regime.

Through the element of surprise and coordinated attacks from both the main north/south accesses into the city, Dajan believed that he and his troops, together with those troops and officers who would switch sides, would result in securing control in a minimum amount of time

At fourteen hundred hours on Tuesday, the fifth of May, thirty-three hours before the date indicated to Nancy Gault, the attack began.

*

Princess Obia stood before the ornate shrine twisting a prayer wheel in ever smaller circles. She then carefully placed the wheel at the feet of the statue, reached into a clay jar, and threw a handful of dirt into the statue's face.

"That you see through the fog of earth and hear what I have instructed you to do, Maxilla Mero, Queen of Distress. For all that I have done for you, you are obligated to bring that unearthly creature to me. She must pay for her blaspheme....she shall not go unpunished. Bring her to me, Maxilla Mero, or the fires of damnation will consume us both."

*

Battles raged across the length and breadth of the capital city of Paramarmico, resulting in considerable collateral damage.

One critical military group that Dajan had counted on to switch sides - the Air Force contingent, remained loyal to the interim government, and only through the concerted actions by Maroon and Bush Commandos were the scales tipped in favor of the attackers.

During the battle to secure the airport facility, Dajan's commandos destroyed or disabled, seven Chinese manufactured Shenyang J-16 fighter jets, and twelve Z-5 turbo-shaft helicopters, neutralizing any opportunity for these aircraft to be used to repel the rebel forces.

With the Boka Ami Air Force rendered non-operational, Dajan, together with the 1st armored unit who had joined with the Maroons, attacked the two main government buildings, and the Presidential residence. The military guard contingents at all three locations, reinforced by several loyal police battalions, were bombarded at close range by 105mm guns, and laser guided missiles from ZTQ-105 light tanks. The tanks developed and manufactured by the Chinese military for jungle and river terrain, typical of Boka Ami typography, were given to the Muguanasi government through military aid grants.

Attempts to surrender were ignored as Dajan unleashed one devastating barrage after another, until the Presidential residence and government structures were reduced to rubble.

With sporadic gunfire continuing to come from the destroyed buildings, Dajan ordered the 1st armored unit's Commander to fire a sustained combination of laser guided missiles, and 105mm projectiles at the defenders. As intermittent gun-fire continued, the Maroons, and Bush Commandos attacked and slaughtered what remained of the opposing forces.

Six hours and fourteen minutes after the initial foray by Dajan's forces, announcements were made over the captured TV and Radio networks that fighting had ceased, and that Paramarmico was a free and open city with certain interim restrictions. Among which was the establishment of martial law effective from eight p.m. through six a.m. each day, as the new government of Boka Ami assumed control of the country.

Food and medical facilities were established throughout the capital city. Looters were shot on sight. Demonstrations and acts deemed hostile against the new government, were viewed as treason and those participating, both individually or collectively, were tried by a military tribunal and executed.

*

"Both of you get away from the window. I want you both to leave now….go to one of the secure rooms in the basement."

"Come on Roland…..don't pull rank. We're four stories up and sure a stray bullet or some errant RPG might take us out, but what's the big deal? We'll be out of your hair, and you'll have a free hand with Dajan."

Nancy watched both men as she waited for Evers' reply to Monday's soliloquy.

"Ya know Mr. Monday, you have a very irritating way about you. Perhaps with a little luck, what you indicated might happen, might just become a reality."

"Ya think so, do you?"

"Why is it that you Brits always answer everything with a question?"

Just as Monday was about to reply, a series of explosions rattled the windows.

"Closer than I imagined....probably the Parliament building, or maybe they're attacking the President's residence....who knows, and who cares."

Monday kept his eyes locked on Roland Evers as he waited to see if he'd continue. When he didn't, he answered.

"I care, and so does she," pointing at Nancy. "We've got a vested interest in the outcome and so do you. While our initial reason for being in country was directed elsewhere, Dajan's success or failure now has considerably more implications for us and for you."

"There's nothing we can do. It's his show. I told you that if he succeeds, we'll recognize his government. If he fails, we're no worse off than we were before all the shit hit the fan, and that shit includes you Monday and her."

Evers tone was hostile as he tried to convey that the subject had now ended.

"Stay at the windows and watch the show. I'm needed elsewhere." The sarcasm was blistering, and both Monday and Gault felt the sting. "When I get back, if you're both still in one piece, we'll commiserate. If not, we'll patch together what we can, or if we're not able to do that, we'll send your pieces back home."

Evers lifted his hand up as he turned and walked out of the room. The metallic sound as the door lock engaged caused Monday and Nancy Gault to look at each other, and then at the door.

"Do you think he locked us in?"

Monday took several long strides to the door, turned the handle and pulled, but the door was locked. He looked back at Nancy Gault while still holding onto the doorknob and said, "Guess so."

*

Rodney P stopped at a respectful distance away from the Princess. He closed his eyes and bowed. After several seconds, he righted himself and stood quietly in place watching as Obia moved slowly along a wall of statues, before stopping in front of one he knew as Maxilla Mero, Goddess of Distress.

After a period of prayer, Princess Obia turned. "Bring her to me, the one who plays the piano. She is now in a box....a concrete box but she will leave that box, and return to where you can find her."

Rodney listened carefully to each word, and while her dialogue was riddle-like, he couldn't afford to err in translation, the consequences would be dire.

He immediately knew of whom the Princess spoke. The reference to a box was confusing, but he deduced it was a house, or something similar. Her returning to where he could find her meant the hotel.

Rodney P bowed again, and then straightened. "I know of whom you speak, Princess. As it is stated, it will be done."

Moving backward slowly, Rodney P kept his head down and his eyes focused on the floor so as to avoid any further eye contact with Obia. He turned quickly, then exited through the portal. Once he distanced himself from the structure, he stopped and rubbed his eyes with the palms of both hands.

She has the power to know if I do not comply. The American woman means nothing to me. I have to live.....that takes priority. I will do as she has commanded. Self-preservation is all that matters.

Rodney felt a moment of calm, and then trepidation overcame him, as he mulled over the conclusion he'd reached. I'm already dead, one way or another - dead, and this is the way she will extricate my inner soul from my physical body if I fail to complete what she has commanded of me. She will send my soul to the caverns of the most evil, where I will suffer damnation forever.

As Rodney P began walking again, incoming mortar rounds impacted the area to his rear, the area where the Princess resided. He looked back transfixed as plumes of black/orange smoke spiraled upward. Small fires grew into large ones, engulfing the various wooden structures and turning them into raging infernos. The screams of those entrapped and injured were unrelenting.

Suddenly, a feeling of escalation returned to Rodney P as he pictured Obia trapped inside her hut with no way out. He smiled as he visualized the flames devouring the statues as the Princess pleaded for mercy. Then his mind screen depicted, in graphic detail, images of her burning to death.

I have been vindicated. Whom do I thank…there are so many Gods, and then Rodney P looked up and said, "Thank you all….I thank you all."

Chapter 34

Captain Sigmundo Montonka, Lieutenant Ono Urbano, and several Maroon soldiers waited patiently outside the gate of the American Embassy compound. Minutes went by before a Marine Lieutenant approached.

"Open the gate Corporal. Let the two officers enter "

Montonka spoke rapidly to the soldiers who acknowledged they understood and would remain in place.

When the gate was opened, Montonka and Urbano followed the Marine Lieutenant across the compound expanse and into the Embassy building. When they reached the fourth floor, Roland Evers was waiting just outside one of the doors.

He turned the key, pushed open the door, and then motioned with his hand that Montonka and Urbano enter first. Evers looked quickly at the Lieutenant conveying some silent command, and then entered the room closing the door behind him.

Nancy Gault and Robert Monday were already facing the door when the three men entered. After several moments, Nancy moved toward Montonka.

"It's nice to see you again Captain. We were watching some of the action from the windows as Mr. Evers was kind enough to assure us we'd have a continuing view by locking us inside."

Montonka's eyes darted to Evers and then back at the woman. He was trying to make sense of what she just said, and then recalled that the man called Evers opened the door with a key.

After another moment Montonka said, "Maybe that was his way of making sure you'd remember how we, and you through your efforts, lifted the chains from the people of Boka Ami, and gave them something they never experienced before – freedom."

Evers' smile wasn't lost on any of them. Montonka has defused the situation and brought everyone back to the moment.

Before anyone could speak, Montonka followed by saying, "Despite the imposition of martial law, which should be lifted in a matter of days, the City of Paramarmico and the country of Boka Ami is now free and open."

Four pairs of eyes were locked on the Captain. When the silence prevailed, Montonka continued.

"Commander Dajan will be addressing the nation at one p.m. today. His message will be carried simultaneously by television and radio. He requests that the Ambassador join him and use this opportunity to confirm that the United States of America recognizes his government. A more formal diplomatic declaration can be made later. I am here to escort the Ambassador and his personnel to meet the Commander."

Evers kept his eyes on Montonka as he replied, "I will inform the Ambassador accordingly."

Montonka nodded once.

Evers looked at Nancy Gault and then at Monday before he turned back to the Captain.

"Will they be there?"

"Perhaps, why?"

"It may be better if they're not. I'm suggesting….not ordering. The initial meeting between my Ambassador and Commander Dajan should be limited to those who need to know, and neither of these two need to know or for that matter, be there."

Montonka again nodded, but the movement didn't convey either agreement or disagreement with Evers' statement.

"Please contact your Ambassador. I'll wait here with Miss Gault and Mr. Monday until you return. Then we'll proceed to the Commander….and time, Mr. Evers, is of extreme importance," and then Montonka paused, "….of mutual importance for your Ambassador and Commander Dajan to meet as soon as possible."

*

Rodney P, exhausted and somewhat lightheaded from his ordeal with Princess Obia and the harrowing experience of navigating back through a city at war, waved to the reception clerk as he made his way through the lobby, and into a room reserved for male hotel personnel.

Nodding at several men as he entered, Rodney walked hurriedly to his locker. He twisted the combination lock, opened the door and immediately experienced a paralyzing effect that transcended his entire body. On a narrow shelf at the top of his locker, was a small wooden statue of the Goddess of Distress, Maxilla Mero.

He stood transfixed as his mind struggled to comprehend what he was seeing. Was the statue placed there before the meeting with Obia? Then recalling the explosions that obliterated Obia's home along with other structures, Rodney wondered if by some incomprehensible circumstance she survived. Did she use her powers of the occult to place the statue there, a reminder of what he was commanded to do?

His mind flooded with questions. One that kept flashing across his mind was, how could she have possibly survived? Then instantaneously he reasoned, Obia could not have survived the explosions....they were devastating....the wooden structures were reduced to mere charred pieces of timber.

Rodney felt a moment of calm as his reasoning mechanism deduced that what he saw was what actually happened. No one could have survived that bombardment. Obia was dead, and the command she gave him along with her. Rodney smiled a tortured smile as he stared at the statue.

Then he began breathing erratically as his mind replayed the scene with Princess Obia and the command. Should he err or the side of caution and bring the woman to Obia? But where would he bring her?

As his mind sorted through various answers, he finally concluded that there was no more shrine, no more statues of the Gods and Goddesses, and no more Obia. Then he thought, I will await a sign. If the Princess is alive she will let me know. Until then I have only an obligation to survive.

*

Monday and Nancy Gault watched from the windows of Evers' office as the two black Chevrolet Suburban SUVs followed Montonka's Toyota truck. This time the door to the office was left unlocked and partially open.

"Let's go back to the hotel Monday….get cleaned up, and get something to eat. I can't remember when I ate last."

Monday rubbed his left eye with the palm of his left hand and stared at the woman with the other eye.

"Are you going bonkers on me Monday?"

Monday let his hand drop away and looked quizzically at Gault.

"Bonkers Monday....Bonkers....it means tilting toward crazy....out of control. What's the one eye bit supposed to convey?"

"Didn't realize I was actually trying to convey anything or as you put it, "bonkers." Just trying to rub away some of the tiredness."

"Sorry Monday....didn't mean to come at you that way. Guess I'm slightly pissed and relieved that we didn't....that we were left out of that little party."

"My feathers are still intact, old girl, none of them ruffled. I've been thinking that we've done what we came back here to do. We should be planning our departure.... going home and settling up with Janco. Min Qua Fu is dead, Dajan has taken over Boka Ami, and the US Ambassador, if he plays his cards right, should be sitting in what you Colonials call, "The Catbird Seat." That's all extras that we initiated and should be of benefit to Evers and your American Ambassador if they play it right. We're not going to get anything....no credit that is, but circumstances did work in our favor, didn't it Miss Gault?"

Nancy moved her head slightly. "Haven't thought about that....about Min Qua Fu being terminated and that's what we were supposed to do, wasn't it? The rest was how fate played with us....Dajan, Evers, and the rest. Yeah Monday, let's go home."

*

Monday and Nancy Gault walked toward the Hotel Tori restaurant when Monday stopped. "Go on ahead and get a table. I need to visit the little boy's room."

Nancy nodded as she continued walking. Once inside, she paused, looked around the room and then settled on a table near the main door.

Lost in thought, Nancy didn't realize the waiter was standing in front of her until he spoke.

"Nice to see you back again, Miss Gault."

Nancy looked up and stared at the waiter for several seconds before saying, "Sorry Rodney, I didn't see you."

Rodney P smiled as the command from Princess Obia replayed across his brain.

"Will you be dining alone?"

"No Rodney, Mr. Monday will be joining me shortly."

"Would you care for something to drink while you wait?"

"Yes Rodney, please bring me a glass of Sauvignon Blanc."

Nancy watched the back of the waiter until he disappeared. And then her mind conjured up images of the last time she saw Rodney P. They were together at the home of Obia. Then she saw herself being slapped and then her retaliatory blow against the cheek of the Princess. She remembered the last words Obia spoke and then the thoughts evaporated as Rodney P placed the glass of wine in front of her.

"Would you like to see the menu or wait Miss Gault?"

"I'll wait Rodney."

The waiter moved his head up once to acknowledge, and then started turning away when Nancy called out softly, "Wait."

When the waiter was facing her again Nancy asked, "What about the Princess….I mean that episode before Mr. Monday and I left with Captain Montonka? Is there anything I should know about Rodney, and I'm asking that as a friend."

Rodney P rapidly sorted through the responses he could give and then quickly settled on one.

"The Princess, Miss Gault, I believe was killed during the attack. A few minutes after I left her, the structure was hit, along with numerous others, by artillery shells or mortars or both. There was nothing left of the structure except charred pieces of wood and concrete. I don't think she survived." After a momentary pause, Rodney continued. "But she is a Princess of the Occult and has powers we mortals cannot understand. Perhaps she did survive the bombing. I just don't know Miss Gault."

*

Nancy Gault lifted her glass and moved it toward Robert Monday. "We're going home Robert, we're going home."

Monday touched her glass with his just as the wheels of the Airbus A300 lifted off the tarmac of Paramarmico's International Airport. "Yes Miss Gault, we're going home. Nice of Evers to give us a ride. I guess we scored some points with him, or better put, he scored some points with his Ambassador regarding Dajan and his successful coup."

"I'm so glad to be away from there. I must confess Monday, I've felt some trepidation after that incident with the whack-job Obia. Did you see the look on her face when I slapped her back? A look that could kill."

She took a sip of her drink and then added, "I guess Rodney P was right. She died in Dajan's attack and that solves any potential problem, so why am I continuing to think about it Monday? What could she do to me anyway? What she professes to be all about is as real as a cat having nine lives."

"Beats the Hell out of me why you're wasting any time thinking about it. As you termed it, she's some whack-job, and that occult crapola is just that....crapola. Look Nancy, we've had a nice vacation....an extended one in a tropical paradise. We've been shot at, injured, lived through a coup, and threatened by a host of people including a Voodoo Princess....so what's not to be concerned about?" Then Monday started to laugh. In seconds Nancy was caught up in the laughter as they both struggled to bring themselves under control.

"Just so you're clued in, I left those Ghost pistols, the 9mm's, the ammo and some other items in a locked bag, and arranged for the bag to be placed in the storage locker at the hotel. In time, a long time from now, someone will come across them and wonder. Now….relax, old gal, we need to conserve our strength and wits, until we meet Janco in Philadelphia. May I suggest another libation as we wing our way home," and before Nancy could answer, Monday held up his glass and made a "two" sign with his fingers at the stewardess.

Chapter 35

Nancy and Monday sat facing Janco in the library of the three story townhouse on Pine Street in Philadelphia, Pennsylvania. As she watched Janco, she thought back to when it all began, and that time seemed so very long ago.

"Go over the last part for me again, regarding your last meeting with Dajan."

Nancy nodded and then looked over at Robert Monday. Monday moved his head in a way to convey, you start and I'll fill in where necessary.

"Dajan was grateful….genuinely grateful for what we did with MacMahon and the quick recognition from the United States. Things happen….sometimes negatively and at other times, positively. This was one of those latter times. Good for us, and good for MacMahon and Evers too. They'll get the recognition for putting the pieces together and coming out on top with the new Boka Ami government."

Nancy paused for several seconds and when Janco remained quiet, she continued.

"We accomplished what we set out to do, no thanks to you Arias. Leaving us naked (operating without cover or a back-up) doesn't bode well with me and Monday. Instead of remaining objective and doing what you could do to assist us during our second foray to terminate Min Qua Fu, you assumed a position of nothingness that impeded our efforts. I'm messed up physically, and to a certain degree mentally. I haven't touched a piano for….I don't know how long. I'm not sure I can regain what I had before you set us adrift. Yeah, I know you asked only for the tail end of what happened, but you've got to know the rest, and the rest is that I'm pissed off with you….you and the organization. You owe Monday and me some very hard earned money, and after that deposit is confirmed, you and the organization can go fornicate with each other. And one more thing, Dajan requested that I come back to Boka Ami to play at his inaugural and you know what, Arias….I'm going to be there."

Janco stared at the woman, and then clapped his hands softly. "Very nice Miss Gault. You articulated that very well…. fitting of a Tony award for outstanding actress in a broadway production."

Then Janco paused before beginning again.

"I personally don't give two shits whether your prissy feelings are hurt, or you feel in any way slighted. Failure has its own rewards. We have limited assets available. We are engaged, so to speak, in various activities at various times, and these assets are deployed accordingly. You were given assistance initially. You do remember a man named Hayek, don't you? I decide how and when assets are deployed, not you. Min Qua Fu should have been terminated during the first go. You and that one," looking over at Monday, "failed. ….do you both understand….FAILED?"

"We have experienced repercussions because of that failure. Do you think this is a church where some Pastor forgives all without consequence? You could have pulled the plug with the organization after your first failure, and told me then, as you so eloquently stated now, that I should go fuck myself. You didn't have to go back….that choice was yours. While it was the correct thing to do, you didn't have to do it. We make choices and then we live by them. Once you decided to go back, you knew the ground rules. You couldn't expect help from me or the organization. You were flying solo, and to whatever ends you would find yourselves, it would be of your own making."

Monday started to speak when he was cut off with a wave of Janco's hand. Then Janco turned slightly and said, "You will have time to speak in a few moments. Right now I have center stage."

Janco let his voice assume a more normal octave. "You accomplished the mission and then some. Excellent work. You've proved something to yourselves, to me, and the organization. You are to be congratulated. Your compensation, plus a substantial bonus, has been deposited in your respective accounts. After a brief rest and your inaugural concert Miss Gault, we presume you and Mr. Monday will be ready for another assignment."

Monday moved forward in his chair as he started speaking. "You presume incorrectly Arias. Neither Miss Gault nor I are interested in anything you or the organization wants. It's over," then Monday looked toward Nancy who shook her head to confirm.

"What we do and what you both do has become, whether you realize it or not, part of your physical and mental being. In addition, the remuneration for your work provides a very adequate lifestyle for both of you. I will consider your remarks to be made in haste, where emotions dictates to the brain instead of the other way around. You both are an integral part of what we are. You are valued as proven assets in a very complicated world. Shall we say we need each other."

"I don't need you Arias. I am a concert pianist. I didn't choose the profession, it chose me. Now if there's nothing more, I'll be going home to Greenwich."

"And you Mr. Monday?"

"I'm returning to merry old England."

Arias Janco let the smile form on his face and held it as he said, "Until we meet again."

*

Nancy stared down at the piano and then let the fingers on her right hand ripple over the white keys. After she placed her left hand on the lower part of the keyboard, she tentatively began playing. As her confidence built, Nancy played with more enthusiasm until she was lost in the music.

Robert Monday, sitting in a soft, brown leather chair, closed his eyes as the music resonated in his mind. Then the words slowly formed across his mind screen and he began singing softly at first, and then louder.

"I see trees of green….red roses too. I see the blooms for me and you, and I think to myself, what a wonderful world."

Nancy joined in …."I see skies of blue, and clouds of white. The bright blessed day, and the dark sacred night, and I think to myself, what a wonderful world...."

Nancy stopped, looked over at Monday and began to laugh. She shook her head and smiled. "It is a wonderful world, isn't it Monday?"

"Considering the alternative….absolutely."

"Will you join me Robert? I want you to accompany me back there. The concert is a kind of closing for me, and maybe you feel the same way. There were times I didn't think we'd make it back here….really Robert…..but somehow we did."

"You can never doubt yourself Nancy. Look….that song….wow….just like I remember you playing it all those months ago. After a little practice you'll be back to where you were, and yes, I'm going back with you."

"I was hoping you'd say that Monday," and Nancy moved away from the piano and into an embrace, followed by a lingering kiss that made her head swirl.

*

"I'm both apprehensive and relieved....an unusual combination of sensitivities, wouldn't you say Robert?"

"But this time you're returning on our own terms and doing something you want to do, so why the apprehension?"

"The memories Monday, the memories, and I have plenty....a lifetime's worth."

"The memories go with the territory. We take on an assignment, experience events that are unimaginable for the average person, and then we return to a world we know and compartmentalize those experiences so they don't play mind games with us at will."

"Some of us do....some of us don't, and not ever completely."

"Look, Nancy we're a million kilometers from where we were when we first came to Boka Ami. Min Qua Fu is gone....a fitting meal for some hungry swine and along the way we took out several of his agents. Dajan capped it off with a coup, and the United States, compliments of one Nancy Gault, one Roland Evers, and an Ambassador named MacMahon, moved your Uncle Sam into a very enviable position with the new government. I think you should be rather proud of your achievements. Evidently Janco is, based on the handsome remuneration we received and then some."

Nancy thought for several moments and then nodded.

When the “Buckle Seat Belts” sign came on, Nancy was smiling at Monday. “I’m really looking forward to this.”

“I know you are, and so am I.”

“One question Monday. Did you bring along the pillows?”

Monday’s face took on a serious look and then as it registered. He shook his head from side to side and chuckled.

“I don’t think you’ll need them for this concert.”

*

“A bit hectic back there….at the airport. It seems there were so many more people, more reporters, and camera crews, than I remember the first time.”

“It’s due in part Miss Gault, to the articles that ran in the newspapers, and the background stories on TV about you and Mr. Monday, and how you both helped the Commander during his cause to restore democracy to Boka Ami.”

“Whatever we did Captain, was for mutual benefit.”

“The Commander doesn’t see it that way and by the way Miss Gault, it’s Major now….I’ve been promoted.”

"Congratulations Major….a well-deserved promotion and both Mr. Monday and I are grateful for everything you did for us….you know what I mean, don't you Cap….err, Major."

Montonka smiled and then nodded his head. "Whatever I did was for mutual benefit," and then he smiled as he watched both Nancy and Monday smile back.

"I'll wait in the lobby…..take your time getting settled and then we'll go to the theater. I think you'll be surprised at what we've managed to accomplish during your absence."

"I'm looking forward to it, Major Montonka. We'll be a few minutes, meaning twenty at most."

Nancy and Monday walked to the reception desk of the Tori Hotel and exchanged greetings with the reception clerk.

"I've taken the liberty Miss Gault, of arranging adjoining rooms for you and Mr. Monday."

"Thank you….that'll be perfect."

The reception clerk handed them each a key card and asked if there was any further way he could be of assistance.

Nancy said, "No," followed by another, "Thank you."

Monday interjected with a, "Yes, there is one thing….a bag I left in the storage locker. It's a black canvas bag," and then Monday handed the clerk a check stub. "Please send the bag to my room as soon as possible."

As they started turning away the clerk called out, "Please wait....I've just remembered....there's a package for you Miss Gault."

Nancy stared at the beautifully wrapped box and then looked back at the clerk. "I don't see a card attached."

"Oh, Miss Gault, I'm so sorry again. The man who delivered the gift said you'd know who it was from once you opened it."

*

Monday opened the door on the third knock and stared at the ashen face of Nancy Gault.

"What happened.....what's wrong....Are you sick?"

"Come with me Monday....come now."

Monday followed the woman into her room and stopped when she did. He watched as she pointed toward the bed.

At one corner of the bed were the torn pieces of wrapping paper, and the opened gift box.

"Go ahead Monday....look inside."
Monday walked to the bed, stopping when his knees came in contact with the edge. He took hold

of the box and moved it closer before looking inside.

He stared at the contents for several seconds, and then whistled softly.

"Holy shit," and then he turned to face Gault.

"It's Rodney P, or should I say it's his head wrapped nicely in cellophane. I wonder what his open eyes and smile is supposed to convey? Looks like someone is trying to tell us something. Are you thinking what I'm thinking?"

Almost in unison they each said, "Princess Obia."

*

Major Montonka looked into the box for several seconds and then turned toward the woman.

"Do you have any idea who did this and why?"

In the first few moments after hearing Montonka's question, Nancy thought simply to answer no, but instead answered, "remember, we….that is I, had an altercation with the Princess during our last meeting. He was there. Obia slapped me and I slapped her back. Since he was the one who made the initial introductions, the Princess probably held him responsible for what happened between us. She probably gave him an ultimatum regarding us, and when he failed, or couldn't do what she wanted, she extracted retribution."

Nancy paused waiting for Montonka to say something. When he didn't she looked over at Monday.

"That's the way it happened Major."

"No good can come of this. She has powers I can't explain."

"She has no powers, Major beyond what we have. It's all superstition and wishful thinking to the believers."

Montonka looked back at the box, then at Monday and Gault. "If you're alright Miss Gault, we should proceed to the theater. You have a recital in," then Montonka looked at his watch, "….in less than two hours. I'll take the box with me."

*

"Surprisingly Monday, I'm pretty calm. Amazing what you can do when you compartmentalize the mundane, and concentrate on the relevant. I'm relaxed and confident. Did that arrogant bitch think she could shake me after all we've been through? It's had the opposite effect, I'm charged. I can't wait to begin, and look forward to the reception afterwards."

Robert Monday smiled broadly.

"Wouldn't have expected anything else. I'll be sitting in the second row center, in the area reserved for Dajan and his guests."

Chapter 36

Robert Monday's eyes remained transfixed on the left side of the woman's face. She had made it a point to greet him curtly as she, and her military escort took their seats. As he stared he wondered, what affect her presence would have on the evening.

He forced his eyes away as Nancy approached the piano from the right side of the stage. Pausing when she was several steps away from the piano, she waited as several young girls, in colorful sarongs and carrying bouquets of multicolored flowers, approached from the opposite side of the stage.

The applause was thundering as Nancy bent down and kissed each of the girls on their cheek. Cradling the bouquets of flowers against her left arm, Nancy watched as the girls left the stage. Then she descended the stairs, stopping in front of where Ronnie Dajan and his party were sitting, and handed several bouquets to the female sitting next to him.

She then walked to where the woman was sitting. Leaning into the woman's space and speaking in a voice only slightly above a whisper, said, "These flowers will look lovely on your grave Princess Obia," and then Nancy smiled.

Straightening up Nancy glanced at Monday, nodded once and then broke into a radiant smile.

The audience, unsure what was happening, broke into applause as Commander Dajan and members of his party stood up.

Nancy walked back on stage and looked toward the Commander and bowed slightly. Taking hold of the microphone Nancy began speaking.

"I am honored to be back here in Boka Ami. I look forward to performing for your new President Ronnie Dajan, his distinguished guests, the United States Ambassador, Joseph P. MacMahon, Mr. Roland Evers, also of the Embassy, and so many citizens of this great country."

The applause and shouts forced Nancy to raise her hand and motion for quiet. After several minutes she was able to continue. "You have come to hear me play, not to speak, so let's get on with it."

The polite applause continued until she was seated at the piano. Taking the microphone again in her hand, "My first song is dedicated to President Dajan. It is Chopin's Heroic Polonaise, opus 53."

Fighting the momentary desire to look at Obia, Nancy obliterated everything from her mind except the music she was about to play.

She was soon caught up in the haunting melody of what many consider Chopin's finest composition. At the conclusion, the audience stood up and applauded until Nancy motioned them to be seated again. After a little more than two hours of Chopin, tunes from Broadway musicals, and American songs from the thirties and forties, Nancy, with microphone in hand, stood up and moved toward the edge of the stage.

"I am going to play one last song for you....a favorite of mine and a perfect way, I think, to end this very joyous occasion. This song is dedicated to my manager, my friend and my confidant, Mr. Robert Monday," then Nancy pointed toward Monday and coaxed him to stand.

As she watched Monday rise, she noticed Obia was no longer sitting in her seat.

After a moment of hesitation as she thought of the Princess, Nancy started to play, "What a Wonderful World."

*

"Wow, a few seconds alone. I've never shaken so many hands in my life. I think I need to trade these in for a set of bear paws."

Robert Monday smiled as another male guest grabbed Nancy's hand and pumped it several times. As he watched, he was forced to turn away as he tried to suppress the laughter.

When the man finally departed Nancy shook her head. "That wasn't funny Monday. This is killing me," and then she started laughing. "I might need some rest and recuperation in some far away tropical paradise," then they both started laughing.

Commander Dajan, along with his female escort, and Major Montonka walked toward the laughing couple.

"We couldn't help noticing the laughter and thought we would come over and join you."

"A very real pleasure Mr. President. Nancy and I were laughing about how many hands she has shaken this evening. Nancy said something about needing to trade in her hands for a set of bear paws."

"Now that is amusing. I would imagine Miss Gault, that after several hours at the piano, and the strain of performing the concert, the last thing you need to do is shake a few hundred sweaty and food stained hands."

Nancy looked at the President, letting a smile form and then she burst into laughter. They all joined in as heads turned in their direction.

After a few more minutes, Dajan and his companion excused themselves, while Major Montonka remained.

After motioning them toward a corner of the room, Montonka looked around. "I think you are both in grave danger."

The unexpected words sent chills through Nancy's body. Monday remained riveted, his eyes locked with the Major's.

"My suggestion to you both is to leave Boka Ami as quickly as you can. There is nothing I can do to help you. There are forces beyond what I'm capable of dealing with."

Nancy and Monday watched as Montonka walked away, and then disappeared in the mingling crowd of people that occupied the reception room. Before either of them was able to articulate their thoughts, Roland Evers walked over.

"Very nice performance Miss Gault, absolutely captivating, especially your opening selection of Chopin's Heroic Polonaise. I think it's one of the most beautiful pieces of music ever composed, beautiful, simply beautiful. Now I need you to pay particular attention to what I'm saying. You both are in a considerable amount of danger."

The wide eyed look from Nancy gave Evers reason to pause.

"I don't say things lightly and certainly not those things. We have our sources....let's leave it at that. I've arranged for a car to take you to your hotel. Please expedite your departure. On behalf of the Ambassador and myself, thank you both for," and then Evers motioned toward where Dajan was standing. "We had our issues which are now in the past. Please make Boka Ami part of your past as well and quickly."

*

Roland Evers walked to where Nancy Gault was standing, then interrupted the conversation taking place among the small group.

"Please excuse the intrusion, Ladies and Gentlemen, but Miss Gault and Mr. Monday have a pressing engagement which they are already late for."

Evers moved back slightly and waited as Nancy and Monday said their goodbyes.

When Nancy glanced at Evers, he pointed to his watch. Nancy motioned negatively with her head and then edged herself away from the group and toward where Commander Dajan and some uniformed officers were huddled.

Nancy, with Monday standing directly behind her, waited until Dajan turned toward her before speaking.

"It's time for me to leave. It's been a wonderful reception and a pleasure to play for you this evening, Mr. President. I hope our friendship will endure and perhaps I can return on the first anniversary of your inauguration and play for you again."

"I hope you won't wait that long to return Miss Gault. If there is any way I can be of service to you in the future, please don't hesitate to call on me."

Nancy smiled as she said, "Thank you."

"When will you be leaving?"

"Possibly tomorrow, or the next day."

"Have a good trip and until we meet again, please accept this token of my appreciation."

Dajan looked over at one of the military officers who then removed a small black, velvet box from a table, and handed it to the President.

Dajan opened the box which contained a diamond encrusted pin in the shape of the country of Boka Ami, and then handed it to Nancy.

"It's beautiful, Mr. President. I shall treasure it always. Thank you." and then Nancy dabbed her eyes with the back of her hand. "I'm overcome Mr. President, please excuse me."

"Nothing to excuse....good luck Miss Gault," and then Commander Dajan extended his hand.

*

Roland Evers held the car door open until Nancy was seated. Then he smiled and shut the door.

Nancy rolled down the window and smiled back. "Thank you Mr. Evers."

"Martino," and then Evers moved his head in the direction of the driver, "works with me. I urge both of you to take what I've said seriously. Please do whatever is necessary to expedite your departure from our lovely, tropical paradise."

As the car pulled away, Monday brushed his hand against Nancy's leg. When she looked in his direction he motioned toward the floorboard. In each hand, Monday held a ghost pistol.

He lifted his left hand and placed it on her lap. Nancy gripped the weapon without diverting her eyes.

Using a minimum amount of words, Monday said, "The black bag…storage room."

Passing the initial moment of shock, Nancy moved her head slightly and said, yes, and then fell into an uncomfortable silence as the vehicle picked up speed.

Fifteen or so minutes into the ride, the vehicle passed a road closed sign. Monday wondered why the driver ignored the sign when a blinding glare from the high-beams of an oncoming car enveloped the vehicle. Momentarily blinded, and unable to focus, the driver lost control.

The car crashed through something unexplainable, careening hard right over a rutted shoulder, and finally coming to a stop after smashing into an immense, tropical hardwood tree.

The force of the contact snapped the driver's seatbelt and propelled him through the cracked front windshield. Nancy and Monday were thrown against each other and then in the opposite direction.

As Monday regained focus, he became aware of the sound of movement. Leaning left Monday whispered, "Are you okay?"

"I think so."

"We have company…."

Before Monday could finish, a face appeared at the driver's side window.

He fired several rounds and the face disappeared.

Then a hail of bullets impacted and ricocheted off the metal skin of the vehicle's front and rear quarter-panels.

Returning the gunfire, and shooting blindly into the night, Nancy emptied her magazine.

"I'm out....give me another clip."

"Don't have any….get down, and stay down."

The minutes ticked by without incident, then Monday peripherally saw a silhouette move out from the thick pocket of trees and stop. When it began moving again, Monday fired through the glassless windshield until the silhouette fell away.

"Don't move….stay put….can't be sure if there's more, or if any of what we shot at are still functional. Give it a few minutes…. and then we'll move."

After what Monday estimated was more than sufficient time, he whispered a soft "okay." Then he placed his forearm against her shoulder and said, "Stay put. If someone is playing possum, he gets only me. Take my weapon. If I counted correctly, there are two rounds remaining."

Monday pressed down on the door handle and slowly pushed the door open with the sole of his shoe. He hunched over and moved out of the car listening for anything that would alert him to possible danger. Then he dropped to a prone position and began crawling away from the vehicle and toward the first body.

After checking for a pulse, Monday removed the pistol from the man's death grip, and then crawled toward the front of the car. He saw the outline of a prostrate figure several meters away. When he reached the lower part of the body, Monday tapped one of the man's shoes with the barrel of the weapon and watched for any movement. He repeated the exercise several more times and then shifted into a kneeling position.

Staring into the night, Monday listened for the sounds of something....anything that would confirm his feeling that more people were lurking in the darkness. Still feeling apprehensive, Monday lifted himself into a standing position and moved to the upper part of the body.

Using the heel of his right foot, Monday turned the body over so it was lying on its back. He bent over and picked up what appeared to be a small wooden statue. Then after straightening up, he looked at the man's face for the first time. As he continued to stare, he swallowed several mouthfuls of air and began coughing.

Dropping to his knees again Monday placed several fingers against the man's carotid artery. He held them there longer than he should have and then lifted his hand away.

Turning his head toward the car, Monday called out, "clear."

Moments later, Nancy was standing beside him and staring down at the dead man.

"Is it really who I think it is?"

"Yes."

"Urbano....Ono Urbano....but why?"

"Maybe this explains it in part," and Monday handed her the wooden statue.

There was a sharp intake of breath and then the words, "Maxilla Mero."

"Obviously an adherent."

"Yeah, okay....an adherent but why us? Isn't he an Officer with...." And Nancy let the words trail off.

"Speculation. Maybe he's a converted follower and this has nothing to do with Dajan or Montonka, and then maybe again, Urbano and Evers and

Montonka have everything to do with…." and then Monday stopped.

"Take his pistol and see if he's carrying any extra magazines. I want to check something."

"What?"

"What it was that we crashed through. It wasn't another car, but certainly seemed like one."

*

As Monday walked toward the road he saw the reflection of light from what appeared to be pieces of a mirror. Bending down, he confirmed his suspicions were correct.

Turning quickly and still looking down at the several pieces of mirror in his hand, Monday inadvertently bumped into the woman.

"Sorry Nancy, you gave me a scare for a moment….guess I'm losing my edge."

"I think we all are Robert."

"Look at this….fragments from a mirror and scattered back there are pieces of wood. Urbano, and the other one, placed a mirror across the road, and kept it in place with some type of wooden support. When our headlights hit the mirror, the reflection appeared to be the headlights from an on-coming car. Damn clever, and it worked. They knew that the driver would take some type of evasive action so that it resulted in one, or both of us being killed or injured. Whoever was still alive, they could deal with it quickly. They didn't anticipate we'd be armed."

"I thought we were past all of this.....excuse me, shit, but it keeps piling up higher and deeper."

Monday laughed despite himself. "I couldn't have expressed it better myself."

"Okay Mr. Monday, now what?"

"We do as Evers and the Major suggested. We leave this tropical paradise ASAP."

"Do we go back to the hotel?"

"Why not?"

"That's a rhetorical answer but doesn't answer what I need to know."

"There are no aircraft taking off at this time of night. The hotel is a good layover point....people friendly," and then Monday chuckled, ".... several restaurants, bars and a place to crash....to get some rest and plan. Could there be someone waiting for us there, for the specific purpose to make sure we don't leave in one piece? Of course, but at the moment, it's the only place I can think of that gives us a wee bit of sanctuary."

"Why not my Embassy?"

"You're forgetting that Evers provided the driver and car."

"But the driver is dead. He couldn't have wanted that, or anticipated that….could he?"

"Everything is possible. At this stage we trust no one. There's no way to be sure about Evers, Montonka, or even Dajan. If we were eliminated it might be beneficial to certain interests who would like to keep our involvement in the Coup d'etat squirreled away in some dark place. The fewer number of people who know what happened, and the way it happened, might be perceived in certain quarters as prudent. So yes, we're exposed if we go back to the hotel and yes we're exposed if we go to the Embassy, which isn't exactly neutral territory at the moment. I think it's better to take our chances at the hotel until morning, and then home to the states. Give it a minute or so, and let me have your answer."

"That's nice of you Monday….a minute or so."

"Take several more," and then Monday smiled the smile of a Cheshire cat.

Nancy laughed softly. "You're insane Monday."

"Answer please."

Nancy moved her head up once and then down. "Okay….the hotel, how do we get there?"

"You're not thinking, old girl. They had transportation. Search the other body for the keys….I'll check Urbano."

*

"Nothing on this one."

"Ditto re Urbano. Look for the vehicle.....maybe it's still in the ignition."

Monday went through Urbano's pockets again as Nancy walked into the darkness.

After a few moments, she called out, "Over here....keys still in the ignition, and it's idling."

Monday walked toward the sound of her voice and then saw both outlines.

"Get in, and let's get out of here."

"I just realized Monday, that no traffic has come in either direction."

"Didn't you see the road closed and detour signs back there?" Then Monday pointed with his thumb toward the rear.

"Nope."

"The detour sign pointed to the left but Martino ignored it, and kept driving straight. He knew what was coming but he didn't count on hitting a tree at that speed, or his seat belt snapping."

"What time is it?"

Looking down at his watch Monday replied, "Almost one-thirty a.m."

*

Monday drove the Toyota flatbed onto the road and then slowed as he came to another road closed sign. “There’s the reason Nancy….the reason for the traffic stoppage. What little there is at this time of night….err morning, followed the detour. To anyone driving, the road was perceived to be closed in both directions. Clever….it gave them time to do what they did, unencumbered. ”

Monday continued driving in the direction he thought the hotel was located. After too many minutes, he was hopelessly lost.

“I don’t have a clue where we are.”

“That’s encouraging Monday. What do we do….stay here in the truck for the night?”

“Good idea, since we’re lost.”

“It wasn’t a suggestion, Monday. I was being facetious.”

Chapter 37

Monday opened his eyes as he tuned into the low din of chatter outside the truck. The first rays of light were already bouncing off the windshield. Monday looked to his right, toward the woman whose head rested on his right shoulder and said, "Time to get up Miss Gault."

Nancy lifted her head slowly off his shoulder and then stretched her arms forward.

"I feel like I'm coming out of a sardine can."

"Can't be that bad."

"Oh, but it is, and I need to go to the bathroom and I don't see any."

"You're not looking carefully," and then Monday pointed toward a clump of bushes.

As Nancy pushed open the truck's door, she mumbled, "All the creature comforts of home."

"Spoken like a true outdoors woman," and then he laughed.

"There's nothing funny you Limey son of a bitch."

"My, My, such atrocious language so early in the morning."

Nancy made her way toward the bushes, the middle finger of her left hand raised high.

Monday continued to laugh until she disappeared.

When Nancy was back inside the cab, Monday started the truck and began driving.

"Before you ask, I still don't have any idea where the hotel is located, but anything is better than staying here."

"There, off to the right…an Army truck."

Monday stopped the Toyota behind the military vehicle.

"Wait here."

Once he reached the truck, Monday looked inside and then back at the Toyota. As he walked, he closed his eyes for a moment, shook his head from side to side and then stumbled into a slow moving pedicab.

Unable to right himself, Monday fell backwards. As he was getting up, he saw the driver using his arms in a sequence of hammer motions. With each movement, the driver screamed in some unintelligible language.

Monday took several dollar bills from his pocket and offered them to the out of control man.

The driver hesitated and then grabbed the money from Monday's hand. As he looked away, he started mumbling to himself.

Monday said quietly, "Hotel Tori," then reached into his pocket for more crumpled dollars. He repeated "Hotel Tori," and when the driver turned around, Monday pointed to himself and then at the Toyota truck.

The pedicab driver stared at the truck and then looked blankly back at Monday.

"You don't understand me, do you?"

Monday asked the question knowing that the disheveled man standing in front of him had no idea what he just said. Then he called out Nancy's name, and watched as the passenger's side door opened.

As Nancy waited by the pedicab, Monday walked back to the truck and tossed the ignition key through the open window.

*

The doorman shouted as he moved quickly toward the pedicab. Then he stopped abruptly as he recognized the two faces.

He waited until they left the pedicab, and then approached.

"Sorry Miss and Sir. I thought...." and then he stopped as Monday smiled.

"It's okay....you were just doing what you thought you had to do."

The doorman nodded once and then hurried to open the side door.

*

"Has anyone been inquiring about us?"

"I've just come on duty Sir, but the night clerk didn't say anything."

"Okay. Will you please get our keys and if anyone asks about us, you'll tell us immediately, right?"

The clerk shook his head yes, and then handed Monday and the woman their respective room keys.

Monday palmed the clerk some crumpled bills, and reminded him again what he said moments earlier.

*

As they rode the elevator up, Monday asked, "Do you have any money with you?"

"A few dollars at most, why?"

"I'm out."

"So?"

"What do we do if we need another pedicab?"
It took Nancy a moment for the lunacy of what Monday said to register and when it did, she couldn't help but laugh.

"I guess we walk."

"I guess we do. How long will it take you to get ready?"

" I don't know. What's the rush?"

Monday stared back blankly.

"Okay, I understand and I don't know....maybe twenty....maybe twenty-five minutes."

"Make it fifteen."

"Can't do that Monday. It's always fifteen with you types. I'm a woman. I need time to do what women do."

Monday just stared.

"I'll do my best."

Nancy inserted the key card and pushed on the door.

"Fifteen...right?"

Nancy slammed the door shut without answering. She switched on the light and walked to the bed.

After removing her clothes, she walked to the bathroom, pulled back the shower curtain and stepped in. She adjusted the water with one hand as she pulled the curtain closed with the other.

Seconds later, the curtain was torn away. Princess Obia, knife in hand, stood smiling at the woman.

"Failure is tolerated only up to a certain point and then one must take matters into their own hands. Wouldn't you agree, Miss Gault?"

As Obia pronounced the last syllable, she lunged forward.

Nancy blocked Obia's forearm with her own, and then slammed her fist into Obia's midsection. The force of the blow dislodged the knife from Obia's hand, and drove her backward.

Those several seconds gave Gault an opportunity to step away from the shower stall, and charge her adversary.

When the two came in contact, Nancy's wet body worked to her advantage. As she grabbed a handful of hair and pulled back, the Princess struggled in vain to maintain a grip on some part of Nancy's body.

As they fell, Nancy twisted so that the Princess would take the brunt of the impact with the floor.

When they hit, Nancy grabbed Obia's hair with both hands and started pounding the Princess' head against the tile until a pool of blood appeared.

Still on her knees when she stopped pounding, Nancy moved back against the heels of her feet, and watched as Obia's eyelids began fluttering, and then closed.

Turning her head, Nancy stared through the open bathroom door. Did she hear a door opening or was it her imagination?

Before she could decide, a blow landed solidly against her forehead, and propelled her backward. She became aware of the pain resonating inside her head. Then, as quickly as it began, it ended.

As she tried to refocus, she heard what sounded like a scuffle and then everything became quiet again. The voice she heard in her brain was just above a whisper, and then it grew louder until she recognized it.

Struggling to bring clarity to her tortured mind, she identified the voice as belonging to Monday. She wasn't sure whether she screamed his name or said it in a normal tone, but either way she knew that whatever had just happened to her was over.

Monday dropped to his knees, and cradled Nancy's head in his arms. "Are you okay?"

"Yeah....but I'm not so sure what okay means."

"Take your time. Let the cobwebs evaporate, and then try to sit up. Do you want some water?"

"No.....just give me a few minutes."

After several minutes passed, Nancy got slowly up. Realizing she was naked, she said softly to Monday, who was still on his knees, "Stop staring and turn around. Haven't you ever seen a naked woman before?"

Monday smiled and looked away. “Sorry, I was more concerned with you and didn’t realize I was staring….really sorry.”

“Okay Monday…..out, and drag that out with you.”

Monday reached under both arms of the Princess and pulled her away from the bathroom.

Nancy shut the door and then went to the shower. Once she was under the water, despite herself, she began to cry.

*

“How did you know Obia was in my room?”

“I heard something in the hallway and thought it might be you. I saw her opening your door….the rest you know.”

“Well, she’s still breathing….now what?”

“I’d like to kill her, but don’t think it’s the right move for us.”

Surprising herself, Nancy asked, “Why not? She’ll never stop trying to kill us.”

“You’re absolutely right, but she’s not the only one. Urbano was part of whatever she is. I’m speculating that Montonka is also, and I’m willing to bet even money that Roland Evers is in that camp as well….remember the driver Martino.”

Nancy shook her head.

“And if we kill her, how are we getting the body out of here?”

“You're making sense Monday, no need to continue….I understand. So, we leave her here, and go back home?”

“Yeah….we leave her here and go back home.”

A knock sounded on the door just as the room telephone rang.

“I’ll get the door….you get the phone.”

“Don’t open the door Nancy….wait….let me get the phone first.”

Monday locked eyes with Gault as he picked up the receiver.

“Yes.”

“It’s reception, Mr. Monday. You asked me to call if anyone inquired about you.”

“Okay….yes….go ahead.”

“It was an Army Major. He wanted to know if you and Miss Gault were in your rooms. I told him yes and he walked toward the elevators.”

“Thank you,” and Monday hung up the receiver.

"It's Montonka," and Monday pointed toward the door. He heard the intake of breath as he moved beside her.

"Ask who it is."

"Who is it?"

"The reception clerk, Edger. There is a small issue with your credit cards."

"We'll be down in a moment. Thank you."

"That isn't necessary Miss Gault. This will only take a moment. Is Mr. Monday with you?"

"No, he's in his room."

Monday moved behind the door, and then motioned with his head to open it.

"Okay, one moment."

Nancy unlocked the door and then began to open it when the door was pushed back with such force that it knocked Nancy off her feet.

As Montonka moved into the room, Monday, using both hands, slammed the door back, staggering Montonka. Before he could regain his balance, Monday punched him repeatedly in the face and mid-section, until he dropped to the floor. Then he straddled the prostrate figure and beat him until he was spent.

Chapter 38

"That should hold them."

Nancy stared at Montonka who was bound and gagged, and propped up against the bed's headboard. Her eyes shifted to the woman who was hog-tied, and placed horizontally on her right side across the bottom of the bed.

"They can stare at each other. The Major can use his eyes to feed off the Princess, and Obia can do the same with him. Sort of a fitting tribute for these two kindred spirits, wouldn't you say?"

Then Monday laughed.

"I think we should kill them. You know what happens if we don't."

"Too complicated. I think we've done all we can do here. Are you ready?"

Nancy shrugged her shoulder. "Yeah Monday, let's go, but...."

"Stop Nancy and think…..the bodies…..we've got enough trouble. There's no way of disposing", and then Monday stopped knowing that he made his point.

After Monday closed the door and locked it, he placed the do not disturb sign on the knob.

"Where to?"

"Your American Embassy."

"Why? I thought we were going to the airport."

"I'm not sure we'd make it. Did you figure on Montonka being part of this shit?"

"Sure….after that road incident, it was a natural, but why the Embassy?"

"Didn't you ask that question just a moment ago?"

"Yes Monday, and I didn't get an answer."

"We're going to the Embassy because I need to speak with Evers and MacMahon about getting us out of here, and you don't have a passport."

"Nancy held up the small purse, "I have my passport, and I still have the Ghost pistol."

Monday removed his pistol from his waistband, and ejected the magazine. "Have a few rounds left. You're out, right? Reload with these. Doubt if we'll be able to get more ammunition, so I'm discarding my weapon."

He bent down and tossed the 9mm automatic under the bed.

*

As they walked to the elevator bank, Nancy whispered, "Stop."

"If Evers is part of this too, we're giving up some advantage, aren't we?"

"We don't have much leverage. We're adrift here and right now we need some political clout to get us out. I'm counting on MacMahon being unaware of what's happening."

"And if he's not?"

"Then the water we're in, just got a little bit deeper."

*

"How much money do you have?"

"Give or take twenty or so dollars."

"Let me have ten please."

Nancy handed over the money just as the elevator doors opened.

"Get us a taxi. I'll be out in a minute or so. I need to take care of the clerk."

Nancy nodded, and walked toward the hotel entrance.

As Monday approached the reception desk, the clerk smiled. "Is everything okay Mr. Monday?"

"Yes, thank you so much for the telephone call."

As Monday handed the clerk the money, he said, “I’ve placed the “Do not disturb,” sign on the door handle. Leave it that way until we return, and please inform housekeeping accordingly.”

After the clerk nodded, Monday turned away and walked through the hotel entrance doors and to the waiting taxi.

*

The Marine Sergeant watched Monday and Gault exit the taxi.

“Back so soon?”

“No place like home Sergeant,” and then Nancy smiled.

The Marine Sergeant remained stone faced and then asked how he could be of assistance.

“I….we need to see Ambassador MacMahon.”

A surprised look crossed the Sergeant’s face and then he sarcastically asked, “not Mr. Evers?”

“Not this time, we like to alternate between the two….less boring that way.”

The Sergeant was about to say something when his military discipline took over.

“One moment.”

Nancy and Monday watched as he picked up the telephone and spoke. Thirty seconds later, he motioned them both through the main gate.

*

"My time is short, so let's get to whatever it is you're here for. And by the way, the only reason you're both sitting here is what you did with Dajan."

"We, Monday and I need your help. We need help in getting a booking back to Miami, a safe ride to the airport and that's it."

MacMahon started to rise up from his chair and then sat back down.

"You're wasting my time with what you can do yourselves."

"Mr. Ambassador, for reasons we're unable to clearly explain, not that we don't want to but simply because we can't understand it ourselves, we're being pursued....hunted, and we need to extricate ourselves from this paradise as soon as possible. If we make the booking, we're telegraphing to unknowns what we're planning. If we take any type of local transportation to the airport, we're placing ourselves in considerable danger along the route. We need one of your trusted personnel to accompany us, and one of your vehicles with diplomatic plates to drive us....help us clear customs and make sure we get on the plane. Please Sir....after all we've done, I'm asking you to help us.....please."

Nancy dabbed her eyes, but several tears streaked her cheeks.

MacMahon stared at the woman, then looked over at the man and then back at Gault.

When their eyes locked, the tears were running down her face unabated.

MacMahon reached into a desk drawer, brought out a box of tissues and pushed them toward Nancy.

"Okay Miss Gault. I owe you both. I'll have two tickets booked for you to wherever you want to go and just where is that Miss Gault?"

"Philadelphia, Pennsylvania."

"Okay, Philadelphia and I'll arrange with customs to clear you as part of our diplomatic corps….no luggage or physical screening. I'll also arrange for one of my assistants and a vehicle to accompany you to the airport. Anything else?"

"Will that be Mr. Evers?"

"He's no longer with us….transferred, but I'm not at liberty to reveal where. Okay then, our business is concluded. Please wait in the outer office."

"Thank you, Mr. Ambassador."

"Whatever debt you believed is owed you, is now settled. Is that correct, Miss Gault?"
Nancy nodded, as she got up from her chair.

*

They both faced Arias Janco from across the table in the library of the three story townhouse on Pine Street.

"Out of professional courtesy we've come back here, Arias, to close out this chapter in our respective lives."

Nancy then related the salient details of her recital for Dajan, while leaving out any mention of Obia and the road incident. Then as Monday began speaking, she clutched her purse which rested on her lap.

"I only want to reemphasize Arias that the Ambassador, the United States, and certainly our organization has benefited from the positive outcome from this assignment. From every disadvantage, there is an advantage, if one can find it. In our case several setbacks resulted in a positive, that none of us could have imagined at the outset. I trust Arias, that you understand that, and our differences, whatever those differences are, can now be a thing of the past."

"Not quite yet Mr. Monday. There is a matter that requires closure."

Monday looked quizzically at Janco and then over at Nancy.

Aria Janco called out, "Please join us."
The door opened, and Princess Obia entered the room and walked toward the table.

"You, of course, know the Princess."

Monday and Gault stared at Obia, as she smiled at each of them and then sat down next to Janco, who now held a .45 caliber semi-automatic pistol in his hand.

Nancy never moved her eyes away from Obia's, as she opened the purse and wrapped her hand around the Ghost pistol.

"Please stand up….both of you."

As Nancy made a tentative move to rise, she fired off a round into Janco's stomach, and then several more into the Princess' midsection. Before she could aim again at Janco, he managed to fire several rounds at Monday, who toppled backward.

Just as Janco turned the weapon back, Nancy fired again. She watched as Janco struggled to keep his head erect, and then unable to control his body, he fell forward.

She moved quickly to Monday's side, and cradled his head in her lap. "Don't leave me Monday. Fight it until I can get help. Don't leave me….don't…" and then she saw his head move sideways, and his eyes close.

Nancy was unsure how long she stayed in that position, but finally she moved his head off her lap and gently placed it on the floor.
She stood over Janco and then looked at Obia. They appeared dead, but she wondered.

After a few moments, she aimed the Ghost pistol at Janco's head and squeezed the trigger but the magazine was empty.

She removed the weapon from Janco's hand, fired off two rounds into his head, and then she did the same with Obia.

Nancy wiped the pistols clean with a napkin, and then placed one in each of their hands.

After staring at the prostrate body of Robert Monday for longer than necessary, Nancy Gault finally left the house.

*

Sitting at the piano, and staring at the white and black keys, Nancy wondered if it was possible to regain any semblance of what she once had....her career as a pianist. Was it possible, and then she slowly moved her hands toward the keyboard.

She felt as if her hands were being guided by an alternative force. Her fingers gently caressed the keys and the music began to flow. Almost at once, she and the music were one.

Then suddenly, she became aware of the movement behind her.

She turned just as the weapon fired.

Looking into his eyes, she tried to form the words that wouldn't come. Then her eyes closed.

When a person dies, the first sense to go is sight and the last is hearing. As Nancy fell sideways, the words of the song she was playing resonated across her brain.

"I see skies of blue and clouds of white. The bright blessed days, and the dark sacred night, and I think to myself, "What a Wonderful World."

Roland Evers holstered his pistol, and then checked to confirm that the woman was dead. Satisfied, he walked out of the Greenwich, Connecticut house to the waiting car which would take him to the airport and the flight back to Boka Ami.

***

Acknowledgement: "What a wonderful world," by Bob Thiele/George David Weiss

***

About The Author

Harris L. Kligman

Born and educated in the "City of Brotherly Love," the author left Philadelphia, Pennsylvania in his early twenties. For over thirty-five years, he interacted with various military governments and business entities who dominated the spheres of influence throughout the Far East, Africa, and South America.

A linguist, a devotee to the Martial Arts (holder of a Black Belt in Hapkido, earned while living in South Korea) and a retired United States Army Intelligence Officer who is also cross-trained as an Infantry Officer, the author brings his varied experiences to these writings.

Made in the USA
Las Vegas, NV
08 April 2021

21006650R00266